THE
REPORTER

A JESSE CONOVER ADVENTURE

MARK PAUL SMITH

North Carolina

The Reporter
© 2021 Mark Paul Smith. All rights reserved.

This novel is based on a true story. Some of the names have been changed to protect individual privacy.

Published in the United States by BQB Publishing
(an imprint of Boutique of Quality Books Publishing Company, Inc.)
www.bqbpublishing.com

978-1-952782-10-7 (p)
978-1-952782-11-4 (e)

Library of Congress Control Number: 2021945024

Book design by Robin Krauss, www.bookformatters.com
Cover design by Rebecca Lown, www.rebeccalowndesigns.com
First editor: Caleb Guard
Second editor: Andrea Vande Vorde

SPECIAL THANKS TO:

Editors Caleb Guard, Allison Itterly, and Brenda Fishbaugh; and to Terri Leidich, President and Publisher of BQB Publishing.

OTHER BOOKS
BY MARK PAUL SMITH

Rock and Roll Voodoo
(A Jesse Conover Adventure)

Honey and Leonard

The Hitchhike

CHAPTER ONE

Jesse let the phone jangle three times before lifting the receiver off its rotary dial base. The chord stretched long enough so he could type while he talked.

"This is Jesse," he said, trying to sound busier than he was.

The person on the other end of the line paused for dramatic effect so he could ask who it was. Jesse wasn't playing that game. It was 10:00 p.m., one hour before the reporters at the *Fort Wayne Journal Gazette* finished their shift. The presses began rolling at 11:00 p.m. He was tired and he knew who was calling. He could tell by the breathing.

When the caller finally spoke, his deep voice sounded like a Boris Karloff impersonator narrating *The Monster Mash*. "I've got another cold one for you, Jesse."

Jesse chuckled. "Harold, you and your ghouls at the funeral home are setting a record today. What's this, six in one day? You know it's too late for the morning paper."

Harold mustered his most villainous chortle. "I know all about you and your *dead*lines."

"You've been waiting all night to use that line," Jesse said. "I can't believe I didn't see it coming."

Harold returned to his hushed tone of funeral home formality. "Why, thank you, Jesse. Coming from you, I regard that as high praise. And might I say, as I always do, you are my favorite death editor of all time."

It was April 16, 1973. Jesse Conover was twenty-three years old. He had an athletic build and a handsome smile that couldn't quite hide an inbred contempt for authority. He'd been writing obituaries at the *Journal Gazette* for three months. The work had been exciting and even frightening at first, seeing his copy printed in the paper and hoping he hadn't made mistakes. He wrote careful notes on his pad regarding the name, date of birth, date of death, life accomplishments, survivors, and details of the memorial service. He had to be even more careful as he typed out the obit in proper order and form.

He was a thrill-seeker of the motorcycle riding and water tower climbing variety. Writing obituaries had gotten old in a hurry.

"So, what was the cause of death?" Jesse asked.

There was a pause. "You know I can't talk about that."

Jesse took his hands off the typewriter and placed both elbows on his desk. "You know, this is starting to piss me off. I always have to leave out the most important part of the story. People want to know the cause of death."

"It's the newspaper's policy, not ours."

Jesse's shoulders sagged. "It's stupid."

"I'll tell you how she died if you promise to keep it confidential."

Jesse sat up straight in his chair. "I never reveal my sources unless they want to be revealed."

"Very well, then. I believe you," Harold said. "So here's what happened. Mrs. Donaldson slipped in the ladies' room at the country club and cracked her skull wide open on a toilet."

Jesse paused to let the imagery settle, then asked the probing question, "Was the seat up or down?"

Harold's voice lightened up. "Ah, my boy, you are a natural reporter. You have put your finger on the real mystery. The seat was up. Now, can you tell me why the toilet seat was up in the women's bathroom?"

Just then, the city editor, George Weatherly, yelled from several desks away, "Who the hell you gabbin' at now, Jesse? I need the School Lunches from you ASAP." The venomous command sent Weatherly into a coughing jag so violent he had to light a Camel cigarette to regain his breath.

The newspaper was the heartbeat of the community in Fort Wayne, Indiana. Political candidates issued press releases to announce their agendas. Elected leaders held press conferences to answer questions from the public. Sports fans had to wait for the morning paper to find out if their team won or lost. Mothers read the School Lunches section to see if they needed to pack a lunch for their finicky children.

There were twenty-five reporters and eleven editors working at the morning paper with Jesse. Desks were arranged in rows of four or five in one high-ceiling room the size of a high school gymnasium. There were no windows. The clatter of typing and teletype machines was as loud as the chatter of discussions and arguments among the staff. The air was thick with the smell of cigarettes, coffee, and newsprint.

Most of the desks were piled high with papers, reference materials, empty beverage bottles, and overflowing ashtrays. Jesse's desk was too neat and clean for comfort. Restrooms and a small cafeteria were down a long hall at the other end of the building.

Jesse hung up the phone without saying goodbye and jumped up to report to the city editor's station, which comprised of three desks in a U shape at the center of the room. "That was Harold from Wayne Funeral. He says a lady died when she slipped and bashed her head on a toilet at the country club."

"I don't care *how* she died. All we need to know is that she's dead." Weatherly exhaled a storm cloud of smoke that might as well have been a bucket of cold water on Jesse's excitement.

He was a wiry man and stood at five-seven. He was bald on top with bushy gray hair on the sides. His eyebrows were long and wild, and they stuck out at odd angles when he furrowed his brow. His voice sounded like he was already dying of emphysema.

Jesse was undeterred. "It sounds like a story to me. If people are dying because of unsafe conditions at the fanciest club in town, that's news to me."

Weatherly motioned for Jesse to sit in one of two wooden chairs on the other side of his desk. "What do you know about news? You're still a kid. Everything is news to you. Obits aren't news. They're death notices. Banks and creditors keep track of them. Families want their privacy. We respect that."

Jesse folded his arms over his chest and frowned. "We do stories on car crashes all the time. What's the difference? She died in an accident."

Weatherly took a deep drag of his cigarette. "It'll be news when it's a lawsuit. We don't put the cause of death in an obit. Period. You do obits on people who die in cars all the time, but you never give the details of the crash or the cause of death. Why? Because it's an obit."

"So how about a story on safety conditions at the country club?" Jesse asked.

Weatherly laughed so hard he nearly choked to death. It took a moment for him to regain his voice. "Stephen Longstreet is a member of that club. Does that name ring a bell? He's our publisher. He's a friend of your father and the reason you got hired, and the reason I'm stuck trying to educate you right out of college with no journalism experience."

Jesse was surprised to hear the editor admit his prejudice so openly. He felt like he'd been sucker punched below the belt.

Damn, he thought. *This guy might never give me a chance unless I stand up for myself. It's time for a showdown.* He took a deep breath and spoke slowly. "How can I get experience if you won't send me out on a story?"

Weatherly stared toward the back of the newsroom where the automated teletype machines were clacking away with news from the *Associated Press* and *United Press International* wire services. He returned his gaze to Jesse with a sad look in his eyes. "You know, Jesse, you're a nice kid, but I'm afraid you might be in the wrong business. Even on the obits, your copy is not that clean. And this School Lunch thing . . . I can't seem to get bulletins out of you when I need them."

Jesse realized he was on shaky ground. "I gave you the School Lunches at seven. There they are, buried in your in-basket."

Weatherly sifted through several piles of paper on his desk before shuffling through his overflowing in-box. "Oh, I see. Guess I forgot they were there." He glanced at the copy and looked back at Jesse with only a fleeting apology in his eyes that quickly morphed into stern inquiry. "So, you really want to be a newsman, or is this job just some step on your ladder of success?"

"I want to be a reporter more than anything in the world. Give me a chance. I can do this. I know I can. I'll prove it to you." Jesse had risen to his feet without realizing it. He looked around to see the entire newsroom paying attention.

For the first time, the city editor smiled at Jesse and shook his head in reluctant approval. "All right, I like enthusiasm from my cub reporters. Tell you what. I'll see if I can find a story for you to prove your case. I'm gonna give you one chance and you better not blow it."

Jesse raised his arms to flex his biceps. "Yes. That's all I need. You won't be sorry. Thank you, thank you, thank you."

Weatherly waved him away from the desk. "Don't thank me yet."

CHAPTER TWO

Jesse drove down the highway, beating on the steering wheel like a bongo drum. He was heading to the tiny town of Pierceton, Indiana, to do a story on a fundraising benefit for Henry Coffey, a high school wrestler who had been paralyzed from the neck down in a car crash. This was his first big chance to do a news story on his own. Weatherly had finally sent him out on assignment.

He glanced at his watch. It was six thirty. He had to get the facts and return to write the story and file it by the eleven o'clock deadline. He wondered whether his beat-up 1967 Plymouth Barracuda would make the eighty-mile round trip.

Jesse had written stories in high school and college, but none of them under the time pressure of a deadline. He hoped he wouldn't choke up with some last-minute writer's block. He couldn't think about that right now. He had to focus on the task at hand. First, he had to find the high school gymnasium. Then he had to somehow wrangle an interview with a young athlete who could no longer move his arms and legs.

Jesse didn't have a camera and there was no photographer with him. Weatherly told him to bring home whatever family photos he could borrow for the story. The paper already had the young man's photo from a promotional flyer for the event.

Once he was in town, it wasn't difficult finding the gym. All Jesse had to do was follow the steady stream of cars headed for the benefit. He had to park a football field away from the gym. He grabbed his pen and notepad.

Jesse headed across the large parking lot toward the gym

with the other high school students. He seized the opportunity and stopped to ask a few students why they had come. The kids were eager to talk to a newsman even though the only credential he had was an eight-by-four-inch reporter's notebook and a ballpoint pen.

Jesse was taller than most of the students. He stood at six-three and weighed one hundred and eighty-five pounds. He had curly brown hair, hazel eyes, high cheekbones, and strong eyebrows. His mother always told him he was handsome, but he never felt that good looking. He'd been short until a major growth spurt his senior year of high school.

He was wearing a white shirt with a collar and a tie but no sport coat. He didn't own one. It was a chilly night, but he left his black leather jacket in the Barracuda.

Once inside the building, he took names and notes from well-wishers as he wedged his way into the center of the gym. The place was huge, a basketball court with ten rows of bleacher seating on every side. The ceiling was thirty feet tall with bright lights hanging from every section. A portable stage was set up at one end of the court with a sea of folding chairs in front of it.

The gym was seriously overcrowded when Jesse waded in and began asking questions of crowd members about why they had come and how they knew Henry. People repeated the usual platitudes about what a great guy Henry was and how his tragedy afflicted the entire community. The story was shaping up to be a colossal cliché until Jesse met an athletic young woman with a long blonde ponytail who burst into tears when he asked for her name.

"I'm Karen, Henry's girlfriend. I know I'm not supposed to cry, but I can't help it. He's being so brave, and everyone has been so kind. But I don't think I can do this alone."

Jesse sensed she was talking about much more than attending the fundraiser. He asked questions about how she and Henry had met and what kind of things they liked to do together. *My first interview as a reporter*, he thought, *and the questions are coming naturally. All I've got to do is ask about what I want to know. Or what the reader needs to know.*

She almost stopped crying as she answered his questions. Finally, she stopped talking and grabbed him by the arm. "Come over here. I've got to tell you something in private."

Karen led him to the back of the event stage. Henry was paralyzed from the neck down and propped up on a hospital bed less than twenty feet away. Karen's mascara was running down her cheeks as she leaned in close enough for Jesse to smell the spearmint gum she was chewing.

"I haven't told anybody this. Henry doesn't even know. And you've got to promise you won't put it in the newspaper."

Jesse nodded his head.

"Here's the deal. I'm pregnant. Henry's the father. I want to marry him no matter what. Should I tell him tonight?"

Jesse stopped taking notes after hearing the word *pregnant*. He was speechless. Evidently, she regarded him as some kind of moral authority because he wrote for the newspaper. He wondered what he had done to earn her confidence so quickly until he realized she had never been interviewed by a reporter. Answering his questions had put her in a confessional mode. He resisted the urge to tell her that he'd only written obituaries.

He put the notebook in his hip pocket. "How old are you?"

"I'm sixteen, but Henry's almost eighteen."

Jesse looked at her stomach and couldn't see any sign of pregnancy. "How long have you been sixteen, and how long have you been pregnant?"

Karen rubbed her stomach self-consciously. "I'm two months pregnant and I turned sixteen last week." Her hazel eyes were brimming with tears.

Jesse clenched his jaw. It was clear that she had no idea it was a serious crime to have any kind of sex with a person under sixteen in the state of Indiana. He realized she'd become pregnant at fifteen years old.

Karen looked away and waved at Henry, who was summoning her by raising his head to come up onstage and be by his side.

"I would like to meet Henry. Will you introduce me?" Jesse asked.

Karen wiped the eye makeup off her face with a tissue as she led Jesse onto the platform and introduced him to the guest of honor. "David, this is the man from the *Fort Wayne Journal Gazette*. He drove all this way to do a story on you."

Henry smiled broadly. "Sorry I can't shake hands. All I can do is say thanks for coming."

Jesse nodded. "You've sure got a lot of people on your side. I didn't think wrestlers got this kind of attention, only basketball stars."

Henry tried to smile again, but ended up biting his lip. A tear rolled down his left cheek. Karen wiped it away with her tissue and got mascara on his face. "It's okay to cry, honey. I've been crying all night," she said.

Jesse pulled up a folding chair and sat down next to Henry's hospital bed. "I guess we're lucky to have you with us. There wasn't much left of your car from the photos I saw. Do you remember what happened?"

Henry closed his eyes. "I only know what they told me when I woke up in the hospital. They think I swerved to miss a deer or something and ended up crashing head-on into a big old oak tree. I wasn't drinking or anything. They tell me the tree is fine." He opened his eyes. The people around him laughed a little too loudly, grateful that Henry was attempting to maintain his sense of humor.

Jesse took out his notebook and pen. "So, how long were you in the hospital?"

Henry stretched his neck. "I was in a little over two weeks. I've been in rehab for five weeks. They rolled me out on this bed for the fundraiser."

Jesse had no idea what to say next, so he asked the only question that came to mind. "What are the doctors saying about your future?"

Karen intervened. "It's too soon to tell."

Henry shook his head. "I'm paralyzed for life. My spine is severed. I'll never walk again or do anything again." He fell silent and closed his eyes. Nobody knew what to say. Jesse knew better than to ask any more questions. Karen stroked Henry's hair as the school principal spoke into the microphone to begin the program.

Jesse stayed to hear the glee club and the band and most of the speakers. Finally, the clock in the protective wire cage hanging over the exit told him it was time to go. He said goodbye to Karen. She gave him a long hug and handed him a photo of her and Henry after one of his wrestling matches. They looked so happy and blissfully unaware of what the near future would bring. Henry's muscular, glistening physique shined in the photo like nothing could ever beat him.

All the way back to the newsroom Jesse debated what he should write for his lead sentence. Should he focus on the wrestler or on the event? The girlfriend needed to be included to flesh out the story. The stand-by-your-man angle was a tearjerker for sure. But should it be a sad story about the victim or a hopeful tale of a community coming together?

He had no idea what it would be as he sat down to his new Smith Corona electric typewriter and stared at the blank paper. He wasn't that great a typist, maybe sixty words a minute with a few mistakes. It was ten o'clock, and he was running out of time.

Weatherly walked over to Jesse's desk and noticed the photo of the wrestler with his girlfriend. He picked up the photo. "Nice touch. Work her into the story."

Jesse looked up at his boss and grinned. "She's pregnant with his child and hasn't told him yet. She wants to get married anyway."

Weatherly searched Jesse's eyes to make sure he wasn't kidding. "Don't work her in that deep. Stick to the benefit. This isn't a story about teen pregnancy."

Jesse kicked himself as Weatherly walked away. He never should have divulged the young girl's secret. What if the city editor wanted him to write about it? Would he violate her confidence? Trying to impress his boss could have backfired. He vowed to keep his big mouth shut in the future. But something else was bothering him. Why had the girl told him her secret? What had he done to earn such trust? And what kind of internal censor told him not to write about her pregnancy?

Weatherly was right. It wasn't a story about teen pregnancy. And it wasn't a story about a paralyzed wrestler who would never take his child for a walk in the park. It was the story of a young man, crippled in the prime of his youth, and the humanitarian reaction of his small town. People were coming together to try to help in any way they could.

He tried to collect his thoughts. A lead sentence had to be

written and written fast. He closed his eyes and typed the first thought that came to mind. "The town of Pierceton raised the roof for one of its own last night at a benefit for a paralyzed high school wrestler."

He opened his eyes. The lead sentence read back much better than Jesse thought it would. Lucky thing. He had no time to rewrite it. The second sentence followed naturally and was much easier to write. By the end of the article, Jesse was clacking the keys on his typewriter like the deadline was all he ever needed to kick him into gear. The sense of urgency inspired him. It was a thrill like nothing he had ever experienced. Sentences were writing themselves, paragraphs parading into his mind's eye. He had to remind himself to breathe. The deadline rush felt addictive. It was heart-pounding. His doubts about becoming a reporter vanished as he felt the printers' ink surging through his veins. That's what older reporters loved to say. "They got printers' ink in their blood." Printers were the blue collar boys upstairs who set type and turned giant rolls of newsprint that arrived by railroad car into newspapers.

He worked the girl into the fifth paragraph. "Henry's girlfriend, Karen Wagner, remained at his side throughout the two-hour program of music and speakers. Henry's mother cried when she stepped up to the microphone and spoke about the shock of her only son's horrible accident. At that moment, Karen leaned down and kissed Henry on the forehead. The crowd saw the tender gesture and filled the gymnasium with a thunderous cheer of support."

Jesse typed the story on a continuous roll of copy paper. When he finally ripped it off the typewriter, it was nearly three feet long. He handwrote "-30-" on the page to show the piece was complete.

Weatherly was both impressed and annoyed when Jesse laid

the copy on his desk. "Jesus Christ, I don't have that big a news hole for this piece. The advertisers are taking up all my space." He read the first few paragraphs. His growls and mutterings made Jesse think he might wad the paper up and throw it in the wastebasket.

When he finished reading, he stared at Jesse long and hard. "Who the hell uses *thunderous* in a news story? What are you trying to be? Some kind of Ernest Hemingway?"

Jesse started to defend his copy, but Weatherly waved him off. "All right, all right. I don't want to hear it. You make me nervous. Go on. Get out of here. I'll see what I can do to turn all this overblown bullshit into something people can actually read."

Jesse headed back to his desk, relieved to have the story completed, and surprised and elated at how easily the words had flowed. Still, he wasn't sure if he had passed the Weatherly test.

He stopped by the desk of the police beat reporter, Glen Barnes, a forty-four-year-old newsman who'd bounced around Midwestern newspapers for twenty years. He was bowlegged and walked with a slight limp to favor his right hip. He had a beer belly that made his belt disappear. He wore inexpensive suits, wrinkled as the many days in a row he wore them. Glen was a kind-hearted, old-school journalist who loved to teach young reporters the techniques and ethics of their profession.

"So, you got her done under deadline. Good show," Glen said. "Let's go celebrate at Henry's Bar. Nobody's getting murdered. Our work here is done. We can drink until the paper comes out. You can see your first byline. It's a big moment. You don't want to miss it." He paused. "You are getting your name on this piece, aren't you?"

"I don't know," Jesse said. "Weatherly didn't seem to like the story much. And, by the way, why do they call it a *byline*?"

Glen laughed. "Because it's *by* somebody."

The two men left the newsroom and walked across the street to Henry's. It was nearing midnight, and the paper would come out at 1:30 a.m. Jesse felt flattered that Glen would hang out with him while they waited to see if he got a byline.

Henry's was a downtown neighborhood bar known to be a hangout for reporters and actors and musicians and novelists and politicos and dancers and artists and hustlers of all sexual and professional persuasion. It was a freakishly cosmopolitan crowd for a Main Street tavern in a city surrounded by never-ending corn and soybean farms.

Glen paused with his hand on the doorknob of the side door entrance before opening it. "He didn't tell you to sit down and rewrite it, did he?" Jesse shook his head. Glen smiled. "That means he liked it."

Glen opened the door to a blast of rock and roll on the jukebox and noisy conversation in the air. The bar was long and narrow, fire coded for seventy-five people, but often served more than one hundred tightly packed partiers. The air was thick with cigarette smoke as Glen and Jesse wedged their way in and looked for a place to sit. The booths beneath the round leaded glass exterior windows were occupied, as were the stools facing the ornate mahogany bar. Henry, the bald-headed proprietor, was helping two bartenders mix drinks by the dozen behind the bar.

"Looks like your typical Friday night free-for-all at Henry's," Glen said as he wedged into the bar and held his fingers up like a peace sign to order two draft beers. They were served so quickly the frothy heads were spilling over the glass mugs. Jesse and Glen had to slurp to keep from getting wet.

They drank standing up for a couple beers until a booth opened and they slid in. "How does it feel?" Glen asked.

Jesse drained his beer mug. "Nice to finally get a table."

Glen took a big gulp and smiled as he shook his head. "No, I mean how does it feel to do your first story on assignment?"

"To tell you the truth, Glen, I can't believe it actually happened. I was beginning to think I'd be writing obits the rest of my life." Jesse raised his arm to get the waitress's attention for another round. "And, let me tell you. It felt good, writing on deadline. It felt like getting high, like I've been doing it all my life."

Glen emptied his mug with a satisfied sigh. "That, my fine young friend, is the acid test. If you get a kick out of writing on deadline, you're a reporter. If you don't, you're not. It's as simple as that. I remember my first story. I was scared to death. It was a murder in Des Moines. I got there just as they were loading this poor guy into the ambulance. He got shot in an alley behind a bar over some gambling dispute. I didn't know he was dead until the next day. They didn't identify the body until the day after that."

Jesse raised his eyebrows. "So what did you write?"

Glen set his mug on the table with authority. "That's what had me terrified as I sat down to write the story with the city editor breathing down my neck. Before I really knew what was happening, the story started writing itself. And it was just like you said. It was a rush."

Jesse leaned in closer to Glen. "But what did you write if you didn't even know it was a murder?"

Glen tilted his head back and laughed. "You write that a man was shot and seriously wounded behind Poor John's bar on the city's south side last night at ten thirty. You write the *who, what, when, where, why* and *how* as best you can, and you leave it at that. You don't worry about it. You write the facts and let the chips fall where they may. You don't try to solve the crime. That's what detectives are for. But you do get to know the cops, so they'll tell you what they find."

Jesse exchanged his empty mug with the waitress for a full one. "I gotta say. The police beat scares the crap out of me. I'm afraid I'll miss a big story and get scooped by the afternoon paper."

Glen hoisted his new beer to clink Jesse's mug. "No, no. You don't have to worry about that. You develop your sources. They'll tell you what's going on. Believe me, they want to see their name in the paper as much as you do."

Glen regaled Jesse with tales of how to cover cops. He went on until Chuck Macy, the school beat reporter with eight years in the business, came up to the table with a beer in his right hand and a copy of the freshly printed morning paper under his left arm. It was 1:35 a.m.

Chuck was round faced and slightly pear shaped, but he moved like he might have played shortstop in Little League. "Well, well, well. Look who's here, Mr. Byline Reporter himself. Look at this, front page, city section. 'Pierceton Raises the Roof' by Jesse Conover. You finally did it. Not bad. Not bad at all."

Jesse grabbed the paper. The story was above the fold, upper right. It was the lead local story. His name looked larger and even more impressive than he imagined. It jumped off the page at him like a neon sign. He tried not to act too impressed. "I'll be damned. Weatherly kept my lead." He kept reading. "Damn, he ran the whole story. I can't believe it. He ran the whole goddamned story. Holy shit, he even kept in *thunderous*. He made fun of me for that. Look, there it is, big as life, right where I put it."

Glen took the paper from Jesse and read the article carefully, reciting several paragraphs out loud. When he was finished, he looked over the top of the paper at Jesse. "By Jove, I think you've got it. You might make it in this business after all. Did you come up with that thing about raising the roof?"

Jesse nodded.

Glen reached across the table to shake Jesse's hand. "Welcome to the news business, young man. I hereby anoint you, Jesse Conover, cub reporter and future king slayer."

Jesse took a long sip from his beer and set the mug down carefully. "I get the cub reporter part, but what's this about a king slayer?"

Glen smiled a tight-lipped smirk as he looked Jesse in the eye. "You've got real power now, boy. The pen is mightier than the sword. One story from you could bring down the mayor. Look how they're exposing Nixon. Those two reporters for the *Washington Post*, what are their names?"

"Bob Woodward and Carl Bernstein," Chuck said.

Glen pounded his mug on the table. "See, you know their names. Those guys are going to be national heroes before this Watergate thing is over. Either that or they'll get shot."

"But their sources are anonymous," Jesse said. "Is that even legal?"

Glen half stood up and leaned across the table to get closer to Jesse "People are too scared to talk these days," he whispered, his breathing smelling like stale beer. "You've got to protect your sources. A good reporter will go to jail before he reveals his source. Without anonymity, the bad guys take over. And don't think they won't."

Jesse was surprised by Glen's passion, but he appreciated the lesson. Glen sat back down, winded from the outburst. He lit a cigarette and then told more hair-raising stories from the police beat.

Chuck had his own lessons. "Glen's right about the power of the pen and slaying dragons or whatever. But the main thing is to get the facts right. Never believe any one source. Crosscheck everything. Get as many points of view as you can. Don't take sides. Be fair. Most of all, don't believe what you read in a police report. Get the names of witnesses from the report and talk to them yourself. They'll tell a much better story than the cops."

As Chuck and Glen and Jesse were clinking their mugs in a boisterous toast to the principles of journalism, Henry, the club owner, came over to the table with four shots of tequila on a tray. He was six feet tall and a broad shouldered two hundred pounds. He looked like a man who could have played football for Notre Dame. In fact, one of his three sons did play for Notre Dame. When Henry had too much to drink, he would stand on a chair and sing along with the "Victory March" fight song playing at top volume on the jukebox.

"Did I hear somebody got his first byline tonight?" Henry said.

Jesse held up the paper as his fellow reporters cheered. Henry served the shots and kept one for himself. "We have a little tradition here at Henry's. New reporters get their first byline shot on the house. Consider it your initiation ceremony."

Glen raised his shot glass high. "Here's to Scoop Conover. Long may you report the truth, the whole truth, and nothing but the truth."

As Jesse winced down his shot, he followed Henry's gaze to the front door of the bar. A man in a flowing black cape and broad-brimmed hat was making an entrance like he was on the red carpet at the Oscars. He waved the cape at the booths and tipped his hat to the barstools in flowing, dancelike motions.

He promenaded up to Henry and asked, "And what, may I ask, are we toasting at this fine witching hour?"

Henry bowed to the man in the cape and announced loudly, "Ladies and gentlemen, did you notice that Charles Allen— *the* Charles Allen—has finally decided to grace us with his presence?"

Charles did not return the bow. He performed a curtsy so deep it looked like a yoga move. "Ah, my Henry, my Henry the Eighth, so sorry to be late. I've been unavoidably detained." Charles exaggerated a wink. "So who have we here? I see Glen Barns, my beloved police reporter, and Chuck Macy, my favorite school reporter. But who is this gorgeous young man?"

"This is Jesse Conover," Henry said. "Jesse got his first by-line tonight."

Charles arched his head back and extended his hand for Jesse to kiss his ring. Jesse shook his hand and stood up as best he could in the tight booth.

"No, no, my dear boy. Please remain seated. 'Tis I who must bow in your presence." Charles bowed like a butler. "And please, my good friend Henry, would you be so kind as to allow me to purchase another round of whatever these fine gentlemen are drinking? You know, I'm never above bribing members of the press, or the *fourth estate* as we like to call it."

Jesse scooted over on his bench to make room for Charles to have a seat. Charles slid in and immediately placed his hand on Jesse's knee. Jesse firmly removed the hand before it could slide up his thigh. "So, you're the famous Charles Allen. I've been wanting to meet you."

Charles responded to the flattery like a cat getting stroked. He was a tall, thin man, who would never admit to being sixty years of age. His long, pointed goatee and handlebar mustache made him look like Don Quixote. He grabbed the newspaper and read Jesse's article aloud and with theatric embellishment. He finished with a flourish as the next round of tequila arrived.

"This is good. This is very, very good. I'd love for you to come do a story on my dance studio."

Jesse began to see why people were paying him so much attention. It wasn't about him. It was about the free advertising he could provide. Damn, he'd have to be careful about getting used. It felt good to have something everybody wanted. He felt the power of the pen surging into his consciousness. He realized, right away, he couldn't let that power go to his head.

CHAPTER THREE

Two weeks after his first byline, Jesse got his first chance to cover the police beat. Glen Barns made it happen by calling in sick on a Thursday, twenty minutes after the two o'clock starting time for reporters. His unscheduled absence would leave Weatherly no choice but to throw Jesse into the fray.

Weatherly put both hands on Jesse's desk. Ash from his cigarette fell onto the typewriter. "Jesse, you're all I've got to take the police beat today. Glen's out and everybody else is on assignment. Can you handle it?"

Jesse had jumped up from his chair and tried to sound confident. "No problem, Mr. Weatherly. I'll get on it right away. I know the beat. I'll start at the lockup, then make my way up to the city detective bureau, and head over to the County Sheriff's office at the jail. Glen filled me in on everything." Jesse understood that police reporters had to make the rounds of their sources in order to find out what was happening in the world of cops and robbers.

Weatherly grunted, "Don't go over there acting like you own the place. Some of those cops have been at it for thirty years. They don't need some hippy-dippy kid fresh out of college asking too many questions. Do more listening than talking. You got two ears and only one mouth. You understand what I'm saying?"

Jesse nodded without saying a word.

A smile began to form on Weatherly's face as he nodded in appreciation of Jesse's silence, but he caught himself and reverted to a tight-lipped grimace. "By the way, they found a body in Foster Park. It came across the police scanner about an hour ago."

Jesse tried to act cool as he grabbed a pen and notebook, headed out the newsroom door, and walked three blocks to the nine-story City-County Building. His mind raced. A body found? Oh shit, this is a murder. It's big, front page. Maybe I should call Glen. No, I can do this. This is my chance. I can't freak out.

He entered the building and walked down a long flight of metal stairs. No one answered the call button at the basement lockup window. Prisoners were processed there before being transferred to the jail. It was as good a place as any to start looking for a body. Jesse looked through the bars and the bulletproof glass of the window and saw a confinement officer talking on the telephone with his back to the window. Jesse waited until the officer hung up before buzzing him again. The officer got up slowly and shuffled to the window. He shook his head obviously annoyed by the intrusion.

"Who are you?"

"I'm Jesse Conover from the *Journal Gazette*. The police radio says they found a body. Can you tell me where it is?"

The officer didn't ask for identification. He raised his head slightly at the mention of the newspaper and became reluctantly helpful. "Check the coroner's unit, down the hall to your right. They wheeled her in about an hour ago."

So it's a woman, he thought. Or a girl. He tried to stay calm and remind himself that he was a reporter even if he didn't feel like one yet.

Jesse walked down the hall slowly and paused in front of a double door. It didn't say "coroner" anywhere, but it was the only entrance wide enough to accommodate a gurney.

Jesse listened and heard no one inside. He looked both ways down the hall. He was alone; the area was eerily quiet. He detected the scent of rubbing alcohol and human feces in the air. Hopefully, they hadn't started an autopsy. The only dead body he'd ever seen had been in a casket at a funeral, nice and neat and fully clothed with no blood anywhere. There was no telling what lay behind those doors. He wasn't even sure he would be allowed entry. It could be a crime to walk in on a dead person. He took a deep breath and pushed on the doors. Unlocked. They made a whooshing sound as they opened and closed behind him.

There was no one in the room except for a woman in her early twenties lying on the table with both arms outstretched as if she was about to hug somebody. Jesse thought she was alive at first until he approached the table and realized her arms were frozen in rigor mortis. Her left eye was half open but there was clearly nobody home. Jesse imagined the corpse springing to life and trying to strangle him. He wanted to run out of the room, but he knew he couldn't.

The woman was fully clothed except for bare feet. Her mouth was closed with a hint of faded lipstick on her lips. She was pretty, or at least she used to be. Her frozen face was expressionless. It had been wiped clean. There was dirt and dried grass in her blonde hair. Jesse was looking for signs of trauma when a man in medical scrubs walked through a back door and yelped loudly in surprise at seeing a live person in the room.

"What are you doing in here?"

Jesse jumped at the sudden intrusion. He recovered quickly and tried to act nonchalant. "I'm a reporter for the *Journal Gazette*. I heard you had her in here, and I was wondering how she died."

"Well, good," the man said. "You scared the crap out of me. You're not supposed to be in here, you know." The man paused and looked at the corpse. He looked back at Jesse with lips pursed and eyebrows raised like he was thinking about answering the cause of death question. Jesse saw his chance and came at him with a slightly different angle of questioning.

"Are you the coroner?" Jesse asked.

"No, I'm a pathologist assisting the coroner on this case."

Jesse nodded as the doctor invited him to the other side of the table. *Never underestimate the power of asking the right questions*, he thought.

The doctor puffed his cheeks as he let out a deep breath and nodded his head. "All right. I'll tell you. People have a right to know, I guess. But you can't tell anyone we had this conversation."

"Off the record, doctor. Strictly off the record."

Without saying another word, the doctor used both hands to turn the woman's head to her right. The back of her head had been blown off and what was left of her brains began oozing out onto the table. The doctor rotated her head back as Jesse doubled over and barely kept himself from puking into a container that was already half filled with blood and human tissue.

"First time, eh?" the doctor said. "Surprised you didn't blow lunch. I think we can safely say she put a gun in her mouth and pulled the trigger."

The room was spinning as Jesse straightened up. "What was her name?"

"You'll have to ask the detective about that. And you know they won't release the name until the next of kin have been notified. So, get out of here for now and remember what you saw so next time you won't go nosing around a medical facility without permission."

Jesse's knees were shaking as he stumbled out the doors, down the hall, and up the stairs to the fresh air of the afternoon. It crossed his mind that he might not have the stomach for the job. He had never considered how much blood and guts would be involved in the daily upheavals of a modern city.

Before he had time to dwell on the wrenching sloppiness of violent death, his curiosity saved him from despair as questions popped into his mind. Who was that poor woman, and what happened that would make her kill herself? Maybe someone put the gun in her mouth to make it look like suicide. What would her mother think?

Jesse went back in the building and up to the fourth floor to the detective bureau and knocked on the open-door frame. There was only one person in the room, a broad-shouldered man with a bald head bent down within inches of the desktop. He was filling in a form and took his time before looking up to acknowledge the interruption. Jesse introduced himself and asked about the dead woman.

The detective shook his head. "Sorry, pal. It's not front-page news, just another suicide. She left a note. Bunch of bullshit about how depressed she was. And, no, I can't tell you her name until we notify her people."

Jesse wasn't about to be summarily dismissed. "Can I see the note?"

The detective hung his head in exasperation. "No, you can't see the note. It's evidence in an ongoing investigation. And if I showed you the note, you'd know who she is, wouldn't you?"

Jesse left the detective bureau and walked down the hall in a dejected frame of mind. The story wasn't even an obit yet. The cop was right. Kill yourself, no story. Kill somebody else, front page news.

Just then, the door flew open and slammed against the wall. The detective he'd been talking to came running out, strapping on the shoulder holster for his 9 mm handgun as he ran. "Robbery in progress, First Bank, downtown, shots fired!" he shouted at Jesse.

Jesse kept up with the cop as he ran for three blocks to the bank. Squad cars surrounded the crime scene with screaming sirens and flashing lights. Two masked robbers had fled on foot. A manhunt was underway as Jesse followed the detective into the bank. People were standing around, frozen in place, still in shock. A middle-aged female teller staggered from behind the counters with blood gushing from her right upper arm. She had been shot. A male customer was lying slumped in a pool of his own blood on the floor in front of the main counter.

The wounded female teller lurched around the counter and headed straight for Jesse with outstretched arms. He wondered what he had done to attract her attention. He had never seen the woman before, but he was the first person in her path. She stumbled as she got within reach and fell into his arms, smearing blood all over his shirt.

Jesse laid her down as gently as he could and put his hand over the gunshot wound to apply pressure. He switched hands on the wound and wiped his brow. Her blood dribbled down his face. It tasted like sweaty wine. She was gasping for breath as she looked into his eyes. "I told him he couldn't have the money. I told him no. This is all my fault. I should have just given him the money. He wouldn't have started shooting if I had just given him the money."

The woman strained her neck to look at the man lying on the floor. He was motionless but still clutching a wallet in his right hand. "Is he dead? Can you see? Is he gone? Oh, please, God. Tell me he's not dead."

"He's going to be fine," Jesse said, not knowing if it was true. "What did the guy who shot you look like?"

"He was wearing a mask over his nose and mouth. I could see his eyes. They were evil. It looked like he came from hell. He was a young white guy and he was high on something. He was jumpy and angry, and then he started shooting when I wouldn't give him the money." She closed her eyes and sobbed. "I saw the fire come out of his gun. Am I going to die? My whole left side is going numb. Why didn't I just give him the money?"

Jesse kept one hand over the gunshot wound and stroked her head with the other. "You're going to make it. Look, here comes help."

Paramedics rushed into the bank and raced over to Jesse and the woman. They told him to lie down on the floor, thinking he was a gunshot victim, while they took over treating the woman.

"I'm fine, I'm fine," he said, and scooted away. Blood covered his shirt and hands.

The woman moaned incoherently before passing out. Jesse watched to make sure she was still breathing as they loaded her onto a stretcher and hauled her out to an ambulance in front of the glass doors of the bank. The wounded customer looked like he might regain consciousness as medics were treating him. Jesse thought he saw him move the hand that still clutched his wallet. The robbers must have been in too much of a panic to grab it.

A female medic turned her attention to Jesse. It took some talking, but Jesse convinced her he was a newspaper reporter, and that the blood all over his shirt was not his own. As he stood up to demonstrate he wasn't injured, he saw Chuck Macy, the school reporter, running toward him. He arrived out of breath and looked like he might pass out from looking at the blood all over Jesse and puddling on the floor.

"Weatherly figured you'd be on the scene. He sent me over to help with the story. Looks like you could use a little."

Jesse held his arms out to his sides. "I'm fine. The teller who got shot bled all over me, that's all. She said the robber was a white male, in his twenties, high as a kite. He started shooting when she wouldn't hand over the money."

Chuck looked around the bank, taking stock of the situation. "Okay, here's what we do. I'll interview the cops and see if they catch the robbers; you go talk to the tellers. Try to get their names and numbers so we can follow up later. See if you can get a quote from the manager. Find out what the robbers stole. Looks like the whole thing blew up before they got any cash. Find out how many of them there were. Ask about cameras. Tell them we'll run photos to help catch the creeps."

Chuck turned to leave and then looked back at Jesse. "Sure you're okay?" Jesse nodded. "You got this?" Jesse nodded again. "You take the tellers and I take the cops?" Jesse nodded a third time, amazed that Chuck could be so organized in such a chaotic situation.

Jesse began interviewing tellers and filled up his notebook with names and numbers and quotes. Bank employees were eager to talk until the manager came to his senses and corralled them into his office for a meeting. A camera crew from each of the three television stations arrived too late to talk to the bank staff. Two radio station reporters tried to interview Jesse until they realized he was a newspaper reporter who wasn't about to share his story.

When Jesse got back to the office, Weatherly stood up and dropped papers on the floor when he saw him covered in blood.

"What the hell happened to you?" Weatherly asked.

Jesse explained what had happened. "The teller who got shot is blaming herself for the whole thing because she refused to hand over the money. They took her and the other victim to St. Joseph Hospital."

Weatherly sat down and put his hands on his head. "You interviewed her as she was bleeding all over you?" Jesse nodded. "That's good work, kid. That's what I call keeping your head in the game. Not bad at all for your first day covering cops. Now get cleaned up and get yourself over to the hospital. Call me if you can get a photographer in for a shot. That gal's a hero."

CHAPTER FOUR

After going home to shower and change, Jesse arrived at the hospital and walked past the security desk like he knew what he was doing. A nurse took him to the bank teller's private room. She was surrounded by her husband and her three school-aged children. Her arm was bandaged and in a sling.

"Hey there," Jesse said. "Remember me?"

The woman's eyes lit up, and she held out her one good arm for Jesse to come in for a hug. As they were nearly cheek-to-cheek, she told her husband, "Honey, this is the man I was telling you about. This is the man who saved me."

Jesse backed out of the hug. "No, I didn't save you. I just happened to be there. But do you remember what you told me before you passed out?"

She closed her eyes. "I think I said something like the whole thing was all my fault."

Her children moaned their disapproval. Her husband said, "Honey, I think we all know it wasn't your fault. You did what you thought was right."

"He's correct, Sheila," Jesse said. She gave him a puzzled look. "I know your name because I'm a reporter for the *Journal Gazette* and your coworkers told me your name. They're all very proud of you. I'm here to follow up on what a hero you are." He turned to the husband, who nodded consent. Jesse kept talking. "Now, would all you beautiful people mind if I got a family photo?"

"I don't know," Sheila said. "I don't have my makeup on." Her children told her she looked fine. They were excited to get their picture taken for the newspaper. Jesse used the phone in the room to call for a photo. He chatted with Sheila and asked the kids if their mother had always been a hero or if she had simply risen to the occasion. "She's always been our hero," the youngest daughter squealed in delight.

The photographer, John Musser, arrived. He was a seasoned newspaper veteran. He dressed crisp and casual and looked like he might be on the professional golf circuit as he carried three bags of camera gear over his shoulder. He wasted no time getting the shot.

Jesse said goodbye to Sheila and her family, then he and John raced back to the office, John to develop the film, Jesse to write the story.

The newsroom was buzzing with excitement about the robbery as Jesse sat down to his typewriter. His first attempt at a lead sentence did not feel right. "Bank teller Sheila Winters felt guilty when a robber shot her at close range because she refused to hand over the money."

"No, no, no," Weatherly screamed across the newsroom when he read the copy. "You went out and got a great story. Don't blow it by making her the guilty one. Write me a lead with a goddamn hero in it."

Jesse could feel the eyes of reporters and copy editors on him as he worked on his second lead. He knew he could do it, but he wasn't sure how. Once again, he wrote the first thing that came to mind. "A heroic bank teller foiled a robbery attempt yesterday when she refused to hand over the money."

He nervously took the new copy to Weatherly's desk. The whole newsroom held its collective breath as he read the sentence.

Weatherly stood up and shouted, "Foiled! The kid actually used the word *foiled* in a lead. I haven't seen that word since it was a subtitle in a silent movie. I love it." He read the entire sentence at full volume.

The other reporters murmured approval and relief. Jesse, the cub reporter, was surviving his test under fire. Chuck jumped out of his chair to hold Jesse's arm up like a victorious prizefighter. Everyone laughed, even the reporters who were secretly hoping the new kid in town would fall flat on his face.

As Jesse was getting ready to leave for the night, Weatherly called him over. "Hey, what about the body they found earlier in the day?"

Jesse spun around and plopped down at his typewriter. He had completely forgotten the ghastly experience with the corpse. "How much you want?"

"Three paragraphs, max," Weatherly said. "That's all the room I've got."

Jesse rolled up his sleeves. "Can I say it was a suicide?"

Weatherly got out of his swivel chair and walked slowly over to Jesse's desk. "What did the coroner say?"

"He said she stuck a gun in her mouth and blew her brains out the back of her skull. And the detective said they found a suicide note about how depressed she was."

Weatherly leaned so far over the desk that Jesse could smell his smoker's breath. "Did they say these things on the record?"

Jesse turned back to his electric typewriter. "They said don't quote me."

Weatherly came around the desk and sat in a chair to look Jesse in the eye. "Then you can't use it. If you quote these guys on something they say is off the record, they'll never talk to you again."

Jesse brightened up like a light bulb. "Maybe I could cite anonymous sources like Woodward and Bernstein."

Weatherly shook his head. "They're not anonymous if everybody knows who they are."

"Oh, right," Jesse said, feeling incredibly stupid. "So what do I say?"

"Fort Wayne Police found the body of a young woman yesterday morning in Foster Park." Weatherly rattled it off like it was coming off the news wire. "Throw in some stuff about the investigation continuing and the identity of the victim won't be released until next of kin are notified."

Jesse banged out the copy and took it to Weatherly's desk for review. "So, why isn't suicide a news story?"

Weatherly lit up a cigarette. He thought about the question for a long drag and a slow, billowing exhale. "Don't think every death is a story. People die all the time, mostly for no good reason. Everybody knows it, so what's the point? It's not news. In fact, once this girl's identity is released, you won't even be able to call it a suicide in the obituary. Why? Think about her family. They're not going to want it out that their little girl killed herself because she was unhappy. It makes them look like bad parents. It makes her look like a bad person. How people die is their own business. We don't make it news unless it's out of the ordinary, like a murder or a car crash. Let me put it this way. We don't have enough space to turn every death into a news story. The advertisements have cut our news space down to nothing as it is."

"What about when a famous person kills herself?"

Weatherly took another long drag on his cigarette. "Famous people are different. They've got no right to privacy, and too many people care about everything they do, including what they had for breakfast. Now get out of here. You ask too many questions. You sound like a rookie."

The party was raging at Henry's. Chuck was at a table in the back with Charles Allen, the dance instructor, as well as Larry Borne, director of the local college theater, and Jayne Milson, co-owner of the city's only French restaurant. They cheered as Jesse walked in the door and invited him to squeeze in at their table. He was flattered to be included in such creative company.

Jayne was in her mid-fifties and glamorously shapely with her hair pulled back in a platinum bun. She stood up and planted his nose in her deep cleavage as she hugged him. "Oh, you're such a big new deal. And so young and tall and handsome. Is it true you've been out chasing bank robbers all day?"

Charles pulled Jayne off. "Let the boy breathe, Jayne. You're suffocating him with your fabulous new ta-tas."

Larry remained smug. He was of fragile build, with dyed blond hair that tried to compensate for his receding hairline. He looked like he was wearing an ascot even when he wasn't, and he gestured with the sleight of hand of a magician as he spoke. "Why don't we see how well he can tell a story?"

Jesse didn't know what to say once the table settled down and looked at him. He was intimidated at first by their collective intelligence and experience. Chuck came to his rescue. "I arrived at the bank to find Jesse covered in blood. The teller who got shot collapsed in his arms and bled all over him until he stopped the bleeding."

As Jesse noticed people at nearby tables beginning to listen, he rose to the occasion and told the story for all it was worth.

"She came running right at me, blood spurting out of her arm from a gunshot wound. Her eyes were wild in panic and pain. She'd been shot at point-blank range by one of the robbers. She said she saw the fire come out of his gun."

He paused to let the image sink in. Nobody said a word. Even the jukebox was quiet.

"I tried to put my hand over the wound, but the blood made it slippery. Some of it got on my face. I could taste her blood. It was hot and salty."

He paused again to see if anybody thought he was overdoing it. Nobody so much as took a breath or a sip from their drink. "She was gasping for air as she told me it was all her fault, and that the shooting would never have occurred had she simply turned over the money."

Larry slapped the table for emphasis. "I think I've got a spot for you in my next play." Everybody laughed.

Charles was excited. "I've got a spot for you on my casting couch," he added. People groaned and urged Jesse to continue.

He was standing by the time he finished the story. "With any luck at all, we'll see it on the front page in about an hour."

Chuck ordered a round of tequila for the table as the bystanders slowly returned to their tables and barstools. He offered his own praise for Jesse. "His first day covering cops and he gets the lead story on the front page. That is some kind of record. He covers himself with blood and glory. I never saw anything like it. But you know he got lucky. The story literally fell into his lap."

The table roared in laughter. Jayne tilted her head back in a haughty gesture as she took center stage once things settled. "Here's to luck. I'd rather get lucky than be good any day."

Larry folded his arms across his chest. "And we know he's lucky because he's sitting at the table with us."

The clever repartee continued unabated until Chuck went to retrieve the morning paper at 1:30 a.m. He threw it on the table for all to see. Even in the dim light of the bar, it was obvious that the photo of the teller and her family was front page, top right. The banner headline was big: "Heroic Bank Teller Shot During Robbery Attempt." Beneath the headline was Jesse's byline, looming large. The story recounted how the bank hadn't lost a single dollar thanks to the teller who wouldn't turn over the money. It ended with the teller's daughter saying, "She's always been our hero."

Charles read the entire story out loud for everyone. When finished, he couldn't resist making an editorial comment. "The headline should have said, 'She Took a Bullet for the Bank.'"

CHAPTER FIVE

Jesse saved enough money in his first six months at the newspaper to afford his own apartment. He found a one-bed-room for $95 a month in the West Central historic neighborhood near the newspaper and the city center. It was within his budget. He was making $130 a week, plus overtime for covering cops on weekends, not terrible for his age and experience.

The first time Jesse walked in the front door of 1114 West Wayne Street was like meeting a stranger he knew would become a good friend. The two-story brick Italianate building had five units in the main house and two in the carriage house. It had a communal feel. Doors were left open. He heard rock music and smelled the faint aroma of marijuana from the apartment at the top of the stairs.

Jesse paid his first month's rent and a security deposit and moved in the same day. He had a single mattress with no bed-frame for the tiny bedroom and a table with four chairs for the spacious, high ceiling living room. His mother and two younger sisters came over with dishes, silverware, pots and pans, and an old sofa from the family dining room. Amy was seventeen and thought the apartment was the coolest, most grown-up thing she had ever seen. Laura was fourteen and sad to see her brother moving out of the house.

Jesse had everything he needed to set up housekeeping. Best of all, he wouldn't be waking up his mother and father when he came home at 5:00 a.m. after partying all night. His father was an attorney who understood quite well how much trouble happened after midnight.

He put his suitcase full of clothes in the narrow kitchen and sat down on a chair in the main room to play guitar and sing. The room had resonating acoustics. He only knew a few chords on the guitar, but he loved to play. He felt compelled to play.

This was his first time living on his own. It felt lonely at first, but Jesse quickly fell into a routine of playing guitar and singing to keep himself company. The practice paid off. He could feel himself getting better. It was always difficult to stop playing before 2 p.m. and be on time to the newsroom.

Meanwhile, Jesse was making some progress in his relationship with City Editor Weatherly. Getting covered in blood for the bank robbery story helped, but Weatherly continually taunted him at full volume across the newsroom. "Just because you got lucky on a couple of stories doesn't make you a newsman."

Jesse was starting to enjoy getting to know Weatherly. In fact, the editor was slowly opening up to him. He shared stories of his younger days as a reporter. "Back in the 1940s, we had a world war going on and nobody knew who was going to win. I was writing stories about rationing sugar and mothers who lost sons in places they never heard of before. I tried to enlist in the Army, but they wouldn't have me because of my feet. I hated it at the time, but, looking back, flat feet probably saved my life."

Jesse nodded his appreciation for the perspective. "Don't look now, but we've still got a war going on. It's called Vietnam, and we still don't know who's going to win. We've got a lot of boys coming back in body bags."

Weatherly surprised Jesse with his response. "It's just the same old McCarthyism and anti-communist bullshit as far as I can see. It's not good for the country."

And so, the cub reporter and the seasoned city editor

found common ground in their opposition to the war. That shared opinion became a toehold in the long climb to mutual understanding. Jesse had avoided military service by getting a high number (213 for March 8) in the birthday-draft lottery on December 1, 1969. One month earlier he had marched against the war in Washington, D.C.

Although he was anti-war, Weatherly despised the anti-war *movement*. He was politically liberal but quite conservative socially. "If you think all this free love and smoking dope and Woodstock bullshit is going to work, you've got another thing coming. It's not a political party, it's just a party. And by the way, didn't I tell you to get a haircut?"

"Oh, come on," Jesse said. "It's not the fifties anymore."

The haircut debate was never ending. Weatherly did his best to make sure all his male reporters kept their hair short and their faces clean shaven. It was a constant battle in the newsroom. One that Weatherly was destined to lose as long hair became the norm. Chuck summed up Weatherly's aversion to long hair one night at Henry's. "He's just jealous because he's bald."

The time for Jesse to convince Weatherly of his reportorial skills happened one day when a local radio station broke a story about a young German woman looking to marry an American so she could gain citizenship. The man who had promised to marry her backed out of the deal when he became acquainted with the legal consequences of fraudulent marriage. Jesse knew right away what he had to do.

Jesse called the radio station, and they gave him the phone number for Micki Topper, the German woman. He called her without getting Weatherly's permission. It was time for Jesse to show his editor he could go out and get a story on his own. It was time for him to throw himself into a story and come out with a first-person account. Jesse had been inspired by what was being called Gonzo Journalism ever since he read "Hells Angels" by Hunter S. Thompson in 1966.

"Hello, Micki, this is Jesse Conover from the *Journal Gazette* here in town."

Micki sounded sad and defeated. "I already talk to reporter from other paper, the *News-Sentinel,* I think. He say nothing we can do. To marry for passport is no legal."

Jesse realized he could scoop the rival newspaper. The morning and afternoon papers in Fort Wayne were both housed in the same grey brick building on Main Street, but the editorial competition was stiff and getting the story first was the main goal of every reporter in the building. "Micki, listen to me carefully. Are you listening?"

"Yes, I listen."

He paused for emphasis, then said, "Micki Topper, will you marry me?"

There was a long silence on the line. Micki finally spoke in a dejected tone. "You don't mean it, I know."

"Okay, okay," Jesse said. "You got me. I am looking for a story, but you sound sad and lonely and I'll bet you could use a little company."

Micki took a couple of breaths and then spoke with a note of cautious optimism in her voice. "You want story. Okay. I like you. We meet. Come see me now. I would like to talk."

Jesse got her address, hung up the phone, and marched up to Weatherly's desk. "You know that German girl who wants to get married to stay in the country?"

Weatherly looked up quickly. "She's not your type. It's illegal, and we can't get her address."

Jesse held up the piece of paper with the address. "Not only do I have her address, but I have her phone number. We just had a lovely conversation. She's invited me over to her place right now. I'm pretty sure we're getting married."

Weatherly leaned back in his chair and laughed. "What kind of con man have you turned out to be? I love it. Go get the story. Readers will love this." Jesse turned to leave as Weatherly raised his voice so the entire newsroom could hear. "Do not marry that woman under any circumstance."

Jesse kept walking.

By the time Micki let Jesse in the aluminum door of her studio apartment, she was taking a call from a radio DJ in Los Angeles. Jesse realized the story was beginning to get national attention as he stood there awkwardly waiting for her to finish. The only furniture in the room was a couple folding chairs and a mattress on the floor. Jesse could see she was living out of a small suitcase lying on the floor with clothes piled high on top.

Micki was nearly six feet tall with short black hair, striking eyes, and the build of a runway model. She stood out in the messy apartment like a pearl in an oyster.

Finally, she hung up the phone and shook Jesse's hand carefully as she searched his eyes for kindness or any kind of understanding. "The story is already too big. I have calls from all over. But one is bad. It is from Immigration who say it is crime to marry this way."

Jesse presented her with a bottle of Mateus rosé wine. "I brought this over as a peace offering so you would know I am a gentleman." He hoped it would break the ice and loosen her up for the interview.

Micki smiled and breathed a sigh of relief as Jesse sat down at a small table and opened the bottle with the corkscrew on his Swiss Army knife. She got two large paper cups from the cupboard. "This is what I need after what a crazy day," she said.

They drank half the bottle, and each smoked several cigarettes as they got acquainted. Jesse told her about life as a reporter and how readers would be interested in her story. She seemed relieved that the interview was not going to be strictly business and began opening up about her trip from Germany and how she ended up in Fort Wayne. "I come to see friend, but she is no here. Maybe she move. So, I stay and put ad in paper for husband for my visa to not be bad."

Jesse reached out and took her by both hands. He tried not to chuckle at the absurdity of her situation, but when she looked in his eyes, they both started to giggle. Then they laughed hard enough to end up sighing together in smiles. Jesse decided to address the topic at hand. "Why not go back to Germany and then return to the United States on a new visa?"

Micki drained her cup and set it back on the table for another pour. "I see you want to help. Why no Germany? I tell you what I tell nobody. I need help. I have big trouble in Germany. Please, you not write this?" Jesse nodded. "I was in radical group. We blow up building. They look for me. Both police and my people. My old friends are afraid. I—how you say it—become rat on them."

Jesse stopped pouring the wine and set the bottle down on the table. "Whoa, let's get right down to true confessions. Did you actually blow something up?"

Micki stood up and walked over to peek out the window through the curtains. "I never do dangerous, but my boyfriend lost arm in explosion. They arrest him at hospital. He might get out of jail never." She lowered her head and her shoulders shook. He knew she was crying before he heard the soft sobbing echoing off the window glass.

Jesse waited to speak until she collected herself, dried her eyes with a Kleenex, and sat back down. "You know the police in this country might already be looking for you? Are we talking East Germany or West Germany?"

Micki smiled weakly. "West Germany. Is better but not really."

As they finished drinking the wine, Jesse got up and stared out the window. The view was nothing but a parking lot. "You know you can't stay here. All this publicity will bring the police to your door. Do you have any money? I'm pretty sure it's time for you to hit the road."

Micki agreed. "I have car and some money. I leave tonight. I go to California. Maybe I find commune to, how you say, no one can see?"

Jesse gave her a long hug. She responded like she needed one. "*Disappear* is the word you're looking for," he said.

She looked at him with gratitude in her eyes. At last, somebody was trying to help her. They talked for another hour about how to "get lost" in America. Jesse warned her to obey all traffic laws and to pay cash for everything. "If I were you, I'd head for Colorado. Don't go to a tourist town like Aspen. Find a little town and ask around. There are lots of communes in the mountains."

Once they finished the bottle of wine, Micki suggested they start in on a bottle of cognac she had in the cupboard. He wanted to stay, but there was no way. One more minute with her and he'd end up spending the night. Micki kissed him hard as he was trying to leave. She tasted like fine French wine. He kissed her back softly and walked out the door.

Once he was back at the office, Jesse sat down at his typewriter with a heavy heart, knowing he couldn't tell the whole story. As he began to type, he realized that censorship began in the mind of the reporter. Choosing what to write involved making moral decisions. Sources had to be protected. Much of what was said was usually off the record. People were telling him things that could land them in jail.

His lead was, "Yesterday was a day Micki Topper would rather forget." Jesse told the story about a broken-hearted German girl who would have to return home because she couldn't find a man to marry her. He left out her involvement in a terrorist organization. Part of him felt like a fool for not reporting the more explosive story, but most of him was unwilling and even unable to violate her confidence.

Too bad for the news, he thought. *This could be front page around the world if I wrote the real story about Micki. So what if she wouldn't talk to me in the future? She'd be in jail anyway. But no. I promised to keep her confession off the record so that's where it's going to stay.*

He almost called her back to read her the story but thought better of it. Her kiss had been tempting, but the last thing he needed was to get emotionally involved with a wanted terrorist. Jesse feared for Micki and anybody close to her if the FBI ever caught up with her.

Weatherly loved Jesse's story about Micki, especially since his morning paper scooped the rival afternoon paper, the *News-Sentinel*. He was impressed that Jesse could get the interview when no one else could.

As usual, he delivered his assessment of Jesse's efforts at full volume so the entire newsroom would hear. "Nice to see you're not going to marry that German girl. Good job on the story. I'm beginning to see what you are. What you are is a con man."

He meant it as a compliment.

CHAPTER SIX

In late September 1973, less than a month after the Micki story, Jesse got his first real promotion at the newspaper. No more writing obituaries except when he had to fill in or train the new kid fresh out of journalism school.

Jesse was promoted to the position of social services reporter. He could hardly believe it. He was no longer the low man on the totem pole. It looked like he might have a future in journalism after all. Weatherly had been ready to fire him not so long ago. Now, Jesse had to live up to new expectations.

Sylvia Johnson was assigned to teach him the social beat. She had been promoted to school beat reporter, and Chuck moved up a rung on the ladder to county government. The previous county reporter had moved on to a bigger news market.

Sylvia was stocky and plain and not pleased to see Jesse rising so quickly in the ranks. He was now her competition. She was driving Jesse around town to meet some of her sources as she explained his new job. "Social services are basically any United Way agency along with churches and other volunteer groups like the Lions' Club or the Rotary Club."

Jesse hated to reveal his ignorance, but he had to ask the dumb question. "What do you mean, United Way?"

Sylvia rolled her eyes. "United Way is the fundraising organization for agencies like the Red Cross, Big Brothers, Big Sisters, the Salvation Army and a bunch of others. We'll visit the office. I'll introduce you to the director. He'll get you a pamphlet."

She softened her tone when she saw the look of bewilderment in Jesse's eyes. "I know it seems like a lot but it's really not. They all send out press releases and you decide what you want to cover. I'll help you pick. You'll get the hang of it in no time."

Jesse smiled broadly. An idea had come to him. "What about doing feature stories on the agencies?"

Sylvia tried to explain the facts of life. "Features are another thing. You can't just start writing features. The paper is organized into beats and there is a hierarchy. You know this already. You start at cops then go to social, schools, county government, area, courts, city council and state government. On top of all that are feature storywriters. They get to write whatever they want. But I don't know, I guess you could do feature stories on social agencies. I never did, but why not? You'll have to clear it with Mr. Weatherly."

Sylvia got off on the next exit, and they remained silent for a while. Jesse knew she was trying to lure him into the trap of overstepping his new assignment. He looked at the city skyline. There were church spires everywhere he turned, shining gloriously in the sunny, blue Autumn sky. The moment was inspirational. He didn't care about Sylvia's game playing. He knew what he would do. He would investigate social agencies around town and see what kind of a job they were doing.

Jesse played the press release game for a while, writing stories about fundraising, reporting who was giving how much and what plans they had for spending the money. Stories that scratched the surface but didn't dig into what was really going on.

Readers are curious, he thought. *And they probably want to know about the same things that make me want to ask questions. And I always wanted to know, even as a little boy, what goes on inside the State School, the facility for the severely mentally handicapped.*

People always said they chained the wards to the walls and treated them cruelly. Let's go see what's really happening.

So Jesse decided to do a story on the State School. Not only do a story, but go in undercover to work as an attendant. That meant Jesse had to convince Weatherly the story had merit, and he had to convince the State School to let him come to work.

Jesse argued his case to Weatherly. "Mental health is a big deal these days. They've got thousands of patients out there and nobody knows what's really going on."

Weatherly leaned forward in his chair and pretended to whisper. "Maybe that's because nobody cares."

Jesse pressed his case. "Every single patient has family members who care deeply about how their loved one is treated. Look around this newsroom. I'll bet there's several people here with somebody in a mental hospital."

Weatherly looked around the theater-sized room and smiled broadly. "There are several people in this room who belong in a facility themselves."

Jesse laughed politely as he realized the city editor had not said no and was reluctantly agreeing to let him do the story. Now all he had to do was convince the State School super-intendent to let him work in the facility as an undercover mental health aide. To Jesse's surprise, the superintendent was immediately enthusiastic about the idea, hoping the publicity would generate additional funding. Arrangements were made for Jesse to come to work the last Friday in October.

Jesse didn't get nervous about the story until he arrived for work at the appointed hour. The State School was a campus of five two-story buildings that looked like a university setting. It had been built five years earlier to replace an ancient, stone Gothic mansion that every child in town was convinced had to be haunted.

Horror stories from mental asylums flooded into Jesse's mind as he walked in the front door. What if some deranged soul tries to slit my throat with a fork he stole from the cafeteria? He looked around nervously. The reception area was clean enough, but it had that nursing home smell of air-freshened human waste.

He heard screams of horror and anguish reverberating through the halls. It sounded like people were being tortured. The receptionist noticed his wide eyes and tried to reassure him. "Some of our patients cannot control their vocal responses. Don't worry, nobody's hurting them."

Jesse didn't have time to worry about the creepiness of his circumstance. Less than an hour after entering the State School, he was in a brown jumpsuit trying to bathe thirty naked residents in a stinky shower room.

Jesse turned to Ed, the other aide. "What do you do when they start pissing on each other?"

Ed was muscular and towered over everyone. He was soaping down residents with a bucket and an oversized sponge. "Use your hose. That's what it's for."

The hose was hooked up to a cold-water spigot. Jesse sprayed down a few residents. They recoiled in anger. One resident came at Jesse and grabbed the hose in an effort to wrestle it from him. Jesse was able to hold him off, but he realized a change needed to be made.

"Can't we hook this up to some hot water?"

Ed was getting soaking wet holding a resident under the shower. "Use the cold. It backs them off."

Jesse did not like that idea. It seemed cruel. He looked around but couldn't find another spigot. Once he left the shower to look for a hot water hook up in the adjoining room with the sinks, the residents began ganging up on Ed. Jesse heard the growling commotion, came back into the shower room, dropped the hose, and began peeling naked bodies off his fellow worker. Excited residents became physical, kicking and swinging. Jesse slipped on the wet floor and almost went down as he got punched accidentally in the back of the head.

"What do we do now, Ed?"

Ed was beginning to emerge from the pile. "Keep cool. Don't agitate them. Get them back under the water one at a time. Don't worry, they're just having fun." He started humming "Singin' in the Rain."

Jesse began to see the humor in the situation. Instead of struggling against the residents, he danced them into the shower, one at a time. Of course, he was showering with them. Ed came over and took his turn dancing with Jesse. Once they started laughing, what had been a riot about to happen became a happy event.

"What do we do about hard-ons?" Jesse asked Ed as several residents began touching each other.

Ed laughed in a high-pitched giggle at Jesse's baptism by fire. "If you can't bring yourself to use the hose, just let it go. Nobody's getting hurt. But right now, turn off the showers and let's get the towels going. We need to dry them off and get them dressed."

Jesse looked down at his soapy, wet jumpsuit. "What about us?"

Ed giggled again. Jesse looked like a man who got puddle-slimed by a passing truck. "We've got plenty of suits in our locker room. Some days I go through three or four changes. This place gets messy. Wait until we try to feed them."

The residents understood the drying-and-dressing routine.

They cooperated at the level of cows being herded toward the barn for feeding. Jesse was helping a tall middle-aged man into his jumpsuit.

"Where is my mother?" the man said.

Jesse shook his head. This man had emotions and fears like people with normal intelligence. The man was a human being. Only the luck of the genetic draw had given Jesse a higher IQ. The humanity and inhumanity of mental incapacity suddenly weighed heavily on him. Jesse realized how prejudiced and even frightened he had been of people with below average intelligence who couldn't function in society.

"Where is my mother?" the man repeated.

Jesse looked him in the eye and lied. "She'll be joining us for lunch in just a few minutes. Now, come on, let's get you suited up, so you'll look nice when you see her."

Ed overheard the comment and took Jesse aside. "Don't give them expectations like that. They do remember, and they do suffer like you and I when they get disappointed."

"So what am I supposed to say?" Jesse said.

"Promise them only what you can deliver," Ed said. "And, right now, all you got is lunch. But don't worry. Lunch works every time."

Jesse was shocked that he had unwittingly opened up Pandora's mental health box. Centuries of chaining mental patients to damp walls in forgotten dungeons were burbling up from the underground rivers of depravity to the sewer-flooded streets of social conscience. Once he stopped to think about it, Jesse realized he'd been reading exposes about mental health since Ken Kesey wrote *One Flew Over the Cuckoo's Nest* in 1962. Jesse hadn't gone after the story looking for the horrors of shock treatments or frontal lobotomies. He just wanted to see what was going on inside the State School. Jesse had not intended to uncover the beating hearts of the mentally handicapped. The story was supposed to expose how society sweeps handicapped people under the institutional rug. Now, he had a much better understanding of not only the facility but the people within it. He knew he would begin the story with the man asking for his mother.

During the course of an eight-hour shift, Jesse developed a profound respect for Ed. The man had been working at State School for nearly ten years. He didn't make much money, but he loved helping the residents. He was good at it, gentle and kind but firm. In talking with Ed, Jesse realized the man was revealing way too much of his personal history, particularly the part about being a convicted sexual offender in another state.

A warning bell in the back of Jesse's mind sounded off. A pattern was beginning to emerge. He was starting to feel like a priest in a confessional. People he interviewed seemed compelled to tell him their deepest secrets. The pregnant girl at the benefit for the paralyzed wrestler, the wounded bank teller, the German girl, and now the mental health aide.

Throughout his life, Jesse had been mostly a talker, the class clown, the life of the party. But being a reporter forced him to become more of a listener, more of a question asker. He was discovering that looking people in the eye and asking them personal questions had a hypnotic effect that made them want to talk.

Asking questions wasn't entirely new to Jesse. His mother had taught him how to be nice and how to care about other people. "If you're at a party and you don't know what to say to a girl, just ask her about herself. You know, where do you live, how many brothers and sisters do you have, who's your favorite teacher? Remember, everybody's favorite topic is themself. Don't be shy, and don't talk too much about yourself. Ask questions."

Jesse wrote the State School story from the point of view of the residents and from a first-person point of view about working with the kind-hearted people who did the dirty work of tending to the needy under nearly impossible circumstance.

Weatherly was not impressed. "What's all this about *I* did this, and *I* did that? Journalists don't write from their personal point of view. We're supposed to be objective, not subjective. Where did you get your training? Oh, that's right, you didn't get any training."

Jesse had learned to stand his ground with Weatherly. "I got my training from you, thank you very much."

Weatherly rolled his head back and looked at the ceiling before he could respond. "What are you trying to be? Some kind of, what do you call it, gonzo journalist, like that guy, what's his name?"

Chuck stepped up to Weatherly's desk. "Hunter Thompson is the gonzo journalist. It's first-person journalism. The reporter takes the reader with him into the story. It's becoming popular at papers around the country. Readers love it."

Weatherly was unmoved. "Well, I'm a reader and I don't like it one bit."

Chuck didn't let up. "I read Jesse's story. So did you. And you have to admit, it takes the reader inside places no one has dared to go. It's exciting to be in the shower with all the morons."

"We can't call them that anymore," Jesse said.

Weatherly threw his hands in the air and erupted into

laughter. "So now the gonzo journalist has to be careful what he says. That's rich." He let his arms fall to his side in resignation. "All right, all right. I'll go with the story, just this once, and we'll see what happens."

What happened was far from what Jesse imagined. The story generated surprising community response. Letters to the editor came in about inhumane conditions at the State School and how it was time to stop warehousing the mentally handicapped. Other letters criticized Jesse for sensationalizing the story. The State School superintendent accused Jesse of exaggerating the overcrowded conditions and underpaid staffing. The controversy and debate attracted participants from the Board of Health Commissioner to the mayor. Nobody could agree on anything.

The story and the surprising community reaction were Jesse's first exposure to the fact that reporters judge success by the number of letters to the editor. The more community response, the more impact the story had.

Melissa Franken, the head feature writer, had a fit about the story once she saw all the letters. Jesse was infringing on her territory. Melissa had just turned fifty, but she was sexy, especially when she wore the occasional tight sweater with her over-the-knee skirts, black eyeglasses, and pixie bob hairstyle. She had never married and had what she liked to call a "twenty-year love affair" with the newspaper.

She stomped up to Jesse's desk. "Congratulations, Jesse. You've made yourself the most important part of the story. That might seem smart and cute to you, but the story suffers when it becomes all about you. Journalists aren't supposed to take sides. There's his side and her side, but there's never your side. Our job is to be objective, to tell both sides of any story. I don't know what's wrong with you kids today. And since when do social services reporters write feature stories? That's my job and if you think you're going to take it away, you got another thing coming."

She left in a huff before Jesse could respond. Glen Barnes, the police reporter, heard the commotion and came over to talk to Jesse. "You must be doing something right if you pissed Melissa off that much. Don't worry. I'm old school too, and I thought the story was pretty darn good. I read the whole thing. Look how many letters to the editor you got. That's why she's mad. You're getting too popular."

Jesse was wary when the publisher of the newspaper, Stephen Longstreet, invited him into the office for a personal chat. He thought he might be in for a lecture on the evils of first-person journalism, or maybe even getting fired.

Longstreet remained standing behind his desk as he motioned for Jesse to have a chair. The older man let his reporter sweat a bit until he sat down himself and let a smile creep across his businesslike face. "Your story on the State School was exceptional. I want to see more of it. Your father and I had a good chat about it this morning. This paper needs to start sweeping out some cobwebs in this town."

Jesse couldn't believe his ears. "Thank you, sir."

Longstreet put his hands behind his head. "My phone hasn't stopped ringing. Some people loved it; others hated it. It doesn't matter. They're reading the paper. More importantly, they're buying advertising in the paper."

Jesse said nothing as the publisher continued. "Times are changing in the newspaper business. Hell, we got Woodward and Bernstein running Richard Nixon out of office. I can say, as a lifelong Democrat, I'm proud of those boys. And I'm proud of you. In fact, you're getting a fifty-dollar-a-week raise as of today. Keep up the good work." He put his hands back on the desk.

"You know, Jesse, what I like about you is your enthusiasm. That's a God-given gift. You can't teach it. So, get out there and show me what's really going on in this town."

Jesse stood up, shook the publisher's hand, and walked out of the office in a pleasant daze. Weatherly caught Jesse on his way back into the newsroom. "So what did he say?"

Jesse walked to his desk, sat down and looked up at his city editor. "He said he's proud of us."

Weatherly smiled slightly. "Proud of *us*? What did I have to do with it?"

"You're the one who authorized the story." Jesse knew he had to be careful. Talking to the publisher could easily be seen as going over the city editor's head.

Weatherly's sly grin turned into a full smile. "What are *we* going to do next? Give blood at the Red Cross?"

Jesse was ready with his next story idea. "No, I think I'll get myself locked up in the old jail. I hear the place is cruel and unusual."

Weatherly nodded thoughtfully. "You won't have any trouble getting in. I hear the sheriff wants a new jail."

CHAPTER SEVEN

The Wayne Newton Fan Club was born on a slow news day. Sherman Goldstein, the area news reporter, discovered a secret place in the newspaper building to smoke marijuana after work or even during working hours. After deadline on a Friday night, he invited Jesse, Chuck, and Glen up onto a metal platform at the top of four flights of stairs.

It was a small room of sorts. Two sides were metal railings, a third side was a wall covered with pipes, and the fourth side was a wall with one window overlooking the vast machinery of the paper's printing press.

Sherman was twenty-two with a spring in his step and an impish grin that made you want to laugh at anything he said. Jesse met him when he moved into the top floor of the carriage house at 1114 West Wayne Street. The young man had a degree in journalism from Indiana University and had just returned from a combat-support stint in Israel during the Yom Kippur War. Even so, he couldn't get a job at the paper until Jesse lobbied hard for him with Weatherly.

"This is some good Columbian, boys," Sherman said as he fired up a joint before anyone had time to think about potential consequences. "You're going to love it. And what about this hangout? Nobody can even smell us all the way up here."

Glen took a hit and looked through the window at the massive mechanics of the printing press. "I can't believe it. I've been in the news business for twenty years and I've never seen a printing press from this angle. It's a bird's-eye view. It looks even bigger than I thought it was. It's an ink monster."

Chuck took the joint, then took a hit. He burst into a coughing fit. "I'm not sure I like this place. There is literally nowhere to run. What do we do if somebody comes up the stairs?"

Sherman had thought the whole thing through. "In the unlikely event that somebody dares to enter our holy sanctuary, we simply eat the pot, light up cigarettes, and head down the stairs."

Jesse took the joint from Chuck. "It's nice to know you're thinking ahead, Sherman."

Glen couldn't stop looking at the printing press, even as he took another hit. "This is the coolest thing I ever saw. And listen to the rumble. It sounds like a train coming down the tracks. Who cares if anybody catches us? We'll just tell them we're watching our stories being printed and coming to life."

Chuck recovered from choking. "Oh, great plan, Glen. That's so believable. Four grown men, smoking pot, pretending to be innocent bystanders in the tower of Babel."

"It's not going to be the cops, anyway," Sherman said. "It'll be some maintenance man who won't give a shit." He took a long draw. "But I love the reference to Babel."

Jesse clapped his hands in agreement. "Yeah, we'll definitely be doing some babbling up here. Anybody who comes up will probably just want in on the action. We'll invite him up for a hit."

Glen was caught up in the marijuana moment. "Man, can you feel the whole building shaking? Listen, it feels like an earthquake down there."

"I think we've lost Glen," Chuck said.

All this time Jesse was getting an incredible buzz from the smoke. "I think I'm getting a little lost myself. So, I know hot air rises, but does marijuana smoke rise or fall?"

"It doesn't go anywhere," Chuck said. "Look at this room.

It's filled with smoke. The more we smoke, the thicker it gets. It's got no place to go."

The joint went around a couple more times until Sherman took the last hit and ate the roach. "There, the evidence is destroyed."

Chuck hung his head with dizziness. "I think we're all destroyed."

Sherman's eyes were red. "Hey, did you guys see Sylvia's stories on the school board's plans for adding new junior highs? Did it seem like she was quoting the school superintendent too much?"

Chuck, who had turned the school beat over to Sylvia, pounced on the topic like a panther on a monkey. "I warned her about becoming a public relations lackey for the school administration. They spoon-feed the press releases so it's easy to get lazy and only report one side of the story."

"What's the other side?" Jesse asked.

"The other side is the teachers' union," Chuck said. "They're fighting for better pay while the administration is spending too much money on bricks and mortar."

Sherman smirked. "Something tells me Sylvia is not a big fan of organized labor."

"She doesn't need to be a fan of either side," Chuck said. "What she needs to do is tell both sides of the story as fairly and factually as she can. You know, like Weatherly loves to say, 'Every story is like a pancake. It has two sides and you can't eat one without the other.'"

Everybody laughed at Weatherly's famous saying, but Chuck's lecture on journalism 101 created a thoughtful pause in the conversation. Glen had not been listening. He was spellbound by the giant rolls of paper streaming through the printing process.

Jesse looked down on the presses through the little window with Glen. "This is a cool hangout. It's kind of like a tree house. We built one when I was a kid. It was our clubhouse. Hey, that's what we need. We need to start a club and we need a cool name. Look, here we are, high above the presses, starting our own thing. How cool is this? Let's build a fort."

"We could call ourselves the Outlaws," Sherman suggested.

Chuck shook his head. "No, no, too much like a motorcycle gang."

Jesse rubbed his chin and then moved his hand to tug on his ear. "How about the Newsroom?"

Chuck and Sherman had to think about that one for a minute, as if they weren't sure if it was a terrible or wonderful idea. Glen did not join the discussion. He seemed mesmerized by his window view until he blurted out, "How about the Wayne Newton Fan Club?"

Glen turned from the window and stared at them. Nobody said a word as the total absurdity sunk in.

Sherman nodded. "Wayne Newton. Far out. Is he still alive?"

Glen laughed. "Is he alive? He's younger than me. He's Mr. Las Vegas. He's Mr. Entertainment."

Sherman winced in confusion. "Is he the guy with all the jewelry and capes?"

"That's Liberace," Glen said.

Jesse was warming up to the idea. "Wayne Newton is about as un-rock and roll as you can get. It's crazy. I love it. It's so bad it's good. The Wayne Newton Fan Club. It has a ring to it."

Chuck raised both fists in the air. "Then it is agreed. So adjudged and so adjourned. The Wayne Newton Fan Club will now take its first meeting down from the smoking chamber and across the street to Henry's. I, for one, could use an ice-cold beer to wash down all this smoke."

The four of them floated into Henry's where the usual crowd was assembled and drinking heavily. Charles Allen, the dance instructor, stood up to gracefully and dramatically offer them a place at the table. "Look what the wind blew in. You boys look stoned to the gills."

Jayne Milson, the restaurateur, motioned for Jesse to sit next to her. "Loved, loved, loved your story on the State School. Everybody's talking about how awful it is out there. But I must say, you can give me a shower any time you want."

Jesse gave her a hug and remained amazed at how embarrassingly forward she could be. Even so, she smelled tempting and her lips on his cheek were luscious. She loved leaving lipstick marks on him.

Once the four reporters found seats and crowded around the table, Sherman made an announcement in hushed tones. "I'd like to let everybody in on a little something special. There's a new secret organization in town."

"It won't be a secret if you tell everybody," Glen said.

"Only the intelligentsia will be informed," Sherman said. "And it looks like everybody at this table qualifies."

"I love the sound of that," Larry said with a wave of his hand that looked like a question mark. "Intelligentsia: it sounds so Russian Revolution."

"It's a revolution, all right," Sherman said. "It's a marijuana smoking club known as the Wayne Newton Fan Club."

Larry and Charles squealed in delight. "That's so gay," Larry said. "I love it more than intelligentsia."

Sherman looked wide-eyed at Larry. "What do you mean 'gay'?"

Charles patted Sherman on the arm. "Dear boy, don't you know, Wayne Newton is gay as nine guys."

"What's that supposed to mean?" Sherman asked.

"It means you're in a gay smoking society." Larry folded his hands under his chin and grinned like the Cheshire Cat. "Oh, we'll have to design special smoking jackets. I vote for red velvet with black leather trim."

Jesse looked at Glen. "Did you know Wayne Newton was gay?"

Glen sighed deeply and looked around the table. "Yes, I did. And, if you must know, now that we're all in the same secret smoking society, so am I."

Charles, Larry, and Jayne cheered wildly as Sherman, Jesse, and Chuck stared at Glen like he'd announced he was from another planet. Glen looked more macho than any of them. His suits were wrinkled, and he always had a five o'clock shadow on his square-cut jaw. He smoked like a truck driver and cursed like a frame carpenter. He wrote like a cross between Ernest Hemingway and Truman Capote, which should have been a dead giveaway.

Jesse pursed his lips and tried not to ask, but it came out anyway. "You're gay?"

Charles intervened. "Don't sound so disappointed. Of course he's gay. Everybody's gay. Some people just don't want to admit it. And don't forget, it's against the law. I did five years in prison for being gay back in the 1950s."

Jesse lowered his head and raised his eyebrows to Charles, not wanting to ask questions that could lead to way too much information. He returned his attention to Glen. "No, no, I'm totally cool with it. It's just that you never mentioned it."

Glen chuckled and drained his beer glass for emphasis. "Well, now that you know, I hope we can still be friends. Don't worry, I won't hit on you."

"Leave that to us," Larry said as he, Jayne, and Charles looked like three cats that swallowed three canaries.

"Okay," Sherman said. "So you're gay. Good to know. Doesn't change a thing."

Jesse thought back on the late-night conversations with his colleagues at the bar, and a thought occurred to him. It was funny how everything with reporters was always a huge secret and simultaneously the story of the century.

CHAPTER EIGHT

Jesse was working long hours and sometimes seven days a week through the winter of 1973-74 to establish himself as a reporter. He did stories on blood drives and fundraising campaigns and new mental health facilities. Heads of social service agencies clamored for his attention. This was flattering at first, but Jesse had learned they were only after the free publicity of news coverage to increase donations to their organizations.

He was playing guitar almost every day at noon with Butch, who moved into the apartment next door on the second floor of 1114. Butch came home for lunch from his job as an insurance salesman. His sport coat and tie with dress slacks looked a little out of place with his shoulder-length blondish hair. Butch was a couple years younger and five inches shorter than Jesse, but he was three times the guitar player. He taught Jesse lots of new chords and scales and lead runs. They sang well as a duo and quickly discovered they could write songs together.

The biggest national story of February was the kidnapping of Patty Hearst, granddaughter of the American publishing magnate, William Randolph Hearst. The bold abduction was pulled off by a left-wing, anti-capitalist group known as the Symbionese Liberation Army. They called themselves *urban guerillas*, and a couple of them came from Indiana.

Jesse wished he could get involved with that story. Reporters covering the kidnapping were becoming celebrities in their own right. The more news stories Jesse wrote, the less he doubted his own abilities. And the less he doubted himself, the more ambitious he became.

But just as he was beginning to feel comfortable in the wide world of journalism, a story broke locally that shook his confidence. A train derailed west of the city and three fuel tankers were leaking so dangerously that hundreds of nearby residents were being evacuated. Jesse was covering cops that day. He was one of the first reporters on the scene.

People were running away as Jesse approached to get a closer look. The massive tankers were off the track and upside down with their wheels in the air, looking like dogs begging for a belly rub. Jesse smelled the gasoline and saw a smoky mist rising from each of the tankers. He heard a steamy sizzle as he stopped walking toward the wreckage and realized he could be emulsified in a fireball at any moment. He looked around for someone with a camera. He had to get a shot of this bizarre scene.

As he took another step toward the train wreck, a sheriff's deputy grabbed him by the arm and began dragging him away from the danger. "Where do you think you're going? That's gas you smell. It's going to blow."

Jesse freed his arm and kept walking away with the deputy. "I'm with the newspaper. I've got to find a camera."

The deputy grabbed Jesse's arm again and picked up the pace. "You're not going to be with anybody if we don't get the hell out of here."

Jesse jogged back to his car and drove to the nearest gas station to call Weatherly from a pay phone. "What should I do? The police won't let me anywhere near the scene. We need a camera out here."

"You stay out of harm's way," Weatherly said. "Focus on the people being evacuated. Ask them where they're going and how it feels to be kicked out of their homes. The feds are taking over the investigation. I've got our state reporter, Karl Stone, doing the main story. He should be on the scene by now. I'm on the line to the governor's office."

As he spoke, a monstrous explosion rocked the phone booth. Jesse looked toward the train and saw an angry orange glare growing on the horizon.

"What the hell was that?" Weatherly shouted.

Jesse held the phone out of the booth and yelled over the continuing roar of the blast. "One of the train cars exploded, or maybe all three of them. I've got to get out of here. State cops and fire trucks are all over the place. They're evacuating the area. I'll call you from another phone."

Jesse hated to admit it, even to himself, but he was glad a more experienced reporter was taking over the story. Karl Stone was an award-winning reporter and had more than ten years' experience at several mid-sized newspapers. He worked a few desks down from Jesse but had never really spoken to him. Jesse felt a combination of relief and jealousy over losing the story to Stone as he watched the fireball turn into a column of black smoke that became a mushroom cloud. It looked like somebody had dropped a nuclear bomb.

This was fast becoming a regional disaster. Jesse tried to talk himself out of it, but deep down, the story scared him. He felt like a rookie again. He wouldn't know where to start on a story like this. He was lucky he hadn't already gotten himself blown up. And he had never even thought of talking to the governor's office.

He drove his car away from the explosion zone and told himself to focus on his angle, the evacuation. His hands were shaking on the steering wheel. His courage in approaching the scene had been foolhardy. Yes, he had proven himself. Proven he was quite capable of crossing the fine line between courage and stupidity.

Cars were jammed up at intersections. Pickup trucks were plowing through fields to escape the smoke, billowing westward and away from the city of Fort Wayne. Emergency vehicles were picking up people from the side of the road. A general panic had taken over by the time Jesse began interviewing runaway stragglers in the parking lot of a shopping center about half a mile from the blast.

"Where are you going to stay if you can't go back home tonight?" Jesse asked one woman with three small children in the back seat of her car.

The woman was in a wide-eyed state of shock. "I have no idea. Are people dead? Is this some kind of bombing attack? What is going on?"

As Jesse tried to explain the situation, a second woman came running up to the car. "Jennifer, get those kids out of here. They're evacuating the entire county. We've got to get down to the high school. They're setting up a shelter there."

Jesse tried to reassure the two women. "Now, now, everything's going to be fine. It's a gasoline explosion from a tanker car on a derailed train. The federal clean-up crews are on their way. They'll get the situation under control in no time."

The two women paused to listen, then gave one another an urgent look that showed they didn't believe a word he said. The woman he was interviewing gunned her car out of the parking lot, leaving Jesse in her dust, as her friend ran back to her pickup truck.

Despite the panic of evacuees, crowds of curious onlookers began to form at the police road blockades. They were mostly high school students who had been let out early because of the explosion. Photographer Dean Sorenson arrived and started taking pictures of the chaotic scene. Dean was a chubby guy on the short side, but he could still move quickly when necessary.

He got a great shot of a pickup truck with nine children in the back holding each other and looking frightened as they passed through the roadblock.

A command truck from the fire department paused at the police-car barricade just long enough for Jesse to talk his way into a ride back to the action for himself and Dean. "We're from the newspaper. We need to get some shots of your guys fighting the fire."

The driver nodded and motioned to the back of the truck. "Climb in."

"I hope you know what you're doing," Dean said to Jesse as they opened the door and climbed into the truck.

Three firefighters all geared up moved over so they could have a seat. One of the men raised his mask. "Who said you guys could come onboard?"

Dean flashed his press pass. "We're going to put you guys on the front page."

Jesse followed up with a question. "Anybody know how the train derailed?"

The firefighter with his mask up fidgeted with his helmet. "Yeah, some erosion under the track at the curve had been washing out for a long time. Today was the day it finally caved in and flipped the tankers. Funny thing is, they had it scheduled for repair for over a month."

Jesse was about to ask the firefighter how he knew so much about the cause of the accident when the truck jolted to a halt. The firemen exited the vehicle. Jesse and Dean followed them out and found themselves way too close to a forty-foot wall of flames. Dean got great photos of the upside-down tankers as the flames shifted to reveal the charred remains. The firemen sprayed chemicals in an attempt to contain the blaze, but all they could do was watch it burn.

Dean got his shots as he and Jesse retreated quickly from the fire. "It's too damned hot here. My film's going to melt. I've got all I'm going to get. Let's get out of here."

Jesse needed no further encouragement to follow Dean out of the heat. He wiped his face with the back of his hand. "My face feels like it's on fire."

Dean looked him over after they were outside the burn zone. "You still got your eyebrows. How about me?" Jesse gave him an okay sign.

They made their way to the barricade, where television and radio reporters were on the scene. Karl Stone was there looking cool and professional. He stood over six feet with excellent posture. Karl was all business. His tie was perfect, and his shirt was crisply buttoned down at the collar.

"You guys look like you got a little close to the campfire. How did you even get back in there? Dean, did you get some good shots?"

Dean nodded. "I hope so. Never can tell until we work it out in the darkroom. The heat might have ruined the film. I don't know." Karl turned to Jesse. "Any idea why this train derailed?"

Jesse was pleased to see the more experienced reporter take out his notepad. "One of the firemen told me the railroad hadn't properly maintained the track. The ground under the railroad ties eroded at a curve in the track and the rail collapsed under the weight of the train. The scene had been scheduled for repair for a month."

"Any confirmation on that from the railroad?" Karl asked. Jesse shook his head. "The problem area was scheduled for repair for more than a month and they let it go? How do you know that?"

Jesse shrugged. "One of the firemen said it as we drove into the fire. He jumped out of the truck before I could ask any questions."

Karl patted Dean on the back. "Hope you got some great shots."

Jesse started to describe the upside-down tankers, but Karl spotted a fire chief nearby and ran off to interview him. Jesse felt inadequate as he watched Karl chasing down the story.

What little Jesse knew about Karl made him wonder why the man had ever become a reporter. His father owned a chain of funeral homes in Kentucky. He could have made a fortune in the family business instead of working for the modest salary paid to even an experienced reporter. No doubt, the man loved the thrill of chasing down a story. Jesse was beginning to understand how addicting that adrenaline rush could be.

The next morning, Jesse read Karl Stone's front-page story with interest. The lead wasn't bad: "Southwest Allen County was rocked by a massive gasoline explosion yesterday at 2:30 p.m. when a Norfolk and Western tanker train derailed one mile west of I-69 at U.S. 24."

It was the second sentence that galled Jesse. "Sources at the scene said the soil erosion that caused the derailment had been scheduled for repair for more than a month."

That son of a gun, Jesse thought. *He only knew that because I told him. He didn't get any more confirmation from the railroad than I did. Karl was a seasoned reporter, and he should have gotten a reliable, confirmed source.*

In a huff, Jesse sat down to talk to Chuck at his desk and air his grievance. "The guy treated me like a second-class citizen at the scene and then used me as his star witness for the story. He quoted me verbatim. He asked if I had railroad confirmation. Of course, I didn't. And look at this story. Neither does he. Now, watch him act like Mr. Big Shot today when I was the one who got Dean in for the photos, and I found out how the damn train wreck happened in the first place."

Chuck read the entire article and set the paper down. "The railroad's not going to admit fault right off the bat even though it's obviously a case of bad track maintenance. Trains don't derail on their own. What you're really mad about is Karl taking over the story and getting all the glory."

Jesse frowned and thought about what Chuck had said. "What I'm really mad about is being afraid of the story. Now that I see how Karl did it, I know I could have done it myself, maybe even better."

Chuck stood up to go get a cup of coffee. "Big stories are just like little stories. The witnesses might be more important but it's still the same questions about the *who, what, where, when* and *why*, the five *w's*. Oh, and don't forget the *how*."

Jesse watched Chuck walk away. He looked at the front page of the paper. The fire photos were fantastic and took up the whole page except for the headlines. Jesse was patting himself on the back for making the photos possible when Weatherly called out, "Jesse, get over here!"

He got up and walked over to the editor's desk, then slumped down in the chair. Weatherly sized him up with a knowing chuckle.

"I liked your story about the evacuation. Great bit about the old man grabbing his grandsons off the swing and throwing them in the truck. And I heard how you got Dean up close for the photos. Crazy, but good work. So, let me guess why you look like someone just stole your lunch."

Jesse sat up in the chair.

"You're mad that Karl got the story, and you think you could have done it better."

Jesse sat up straight and lowered his voice. "How could you possibly know? Have I turned green?"

Weatherly's booming laugh filled up the newsroom. "No, I know it because the same thing happened to me when I was your age. It was a flood story. A bad flood. I was just a cub reporter, so I got taken off the assignment. Then I had to read what I already knew in the paper the next day. It was awful. But you know what happened to me that day? I lost my fear. I became a reporter that day."

"I wasn't afraid of that story yesterday," Jesse said.

Weatherly leaned back in his chair. "Yes, you were. We all are. But you won't be in the future. You've got to see somebody else do it so you know you can do it yourself. So you want to do it yourself."

Jesse shifted back and forth in his chair. "You do know I was the source at the scene who told Karl about the bad maintenance causing the derailment." Weatherly nodded. Jesse stood up. "And I'm the one who told him it had been scheduled for repair for more than a month. He asked me for confirmation on that like I should have a full confession from the railroad. And then he writes a story that shows he never confirmed it himself."

Weatherly motioned for Jesse to sit down. "You're as good a source as any. Be thankful he didn't name you. Let the railroad try to prove it isn't true. That'll be a better story than the derailment."

Later that day, Karl Stone came over to Jesse's desk and sat down at a chair across from the typewriter. Jesse gave him full attention. Karl had never befriended him in the newsroom. Jesse figured he was going to ask some follow-up questions.

Karl held up the front page of the paper and pointed to the main photo. "See that photo? That's all you. I saw what you did out there yesterday. It was good reporting. We didn't get a chance to talk at the scene, so I just wanted you to know I was paying attention."

Jesse maintained a straight face and tried to hide his surprise at what amounted to a "welcome to the club" moment. "Was I the source at the scene you quoted?"

A smile crept across Karl's face. "You were my first source. The fire chief confirmed it later, but he would only do it off the record. He didn't want to be seen as pointing a finger at the railroad. Actually, the derailment did a pretty good job of that on its own." He continued without missing a beat. "The point is, you got it right and that's what it's all about. But the photos really blew my mind. How did you and Dean get past the cops? They wouldn't let me anywhere near the scene."

"I think the driver saw Dean's camera and thought we looked pretty official," Jesse explained. "Once we got inside, Dean flashed his press pass and the guys in all the gear made room for us to sit down."

Karl slapped himself on the forehead. "That's my problem. I didn't have a camera. I'm going to start carrying one even if I never use it." Then he looked at Jesse and got serious. "I'm kidding. It's not just the camera. You've got something about you that makes people want to let you in places. I'm here to tell you that's a priceless gift in this business."

Jesse was surprised by the compliment.

"Anyway, I just wanted to say good work yesterday. I'll look forward to working with you in the future."

"Thanks, Karl. Me too."

Karl got up and went to his desk, leaving Jesse to ponder how he could have so completely misjudged a fellow reporter.

CHAPTER NINE

Despite working long hours at the paper, Jesse's personal life at 1114 West Wayne Street was becoming communal. Cheri lived downstairs in apartment number one. She was a Montessori teacher whose door was always open. Michael lived downstairs in number two. He was an abstract painter who loved to talk philosophy and Eastern religions. Upstairs, between Butch and Jesse, was Kay, a shy secretary who managed to hold her own when the house started rockin'.

Sweet Lucy lived in the bottom apartment of the carriage house out back. She was a single flower child who took care of the garden and worked at the downtown health food co-op. Sherman from the newspaper lived in the top unit, number seven. The two of them gathered with the others for regular front porch parties that attracted musicians and writers and artists. Everyone at 1114 felt part of the magical energy that made it the creative center for the neighborhood.

So it was no surprise that when all seven residents of the house decided to welcome spring of 1974 with a block party, the event became a happening of the highest order.

It would also be Butch and Jesse's first public performance as a singing duo.

Nobody thought to get a permit for street closure. There was no security, no food, and no portable toilets. Just kegs of beer, live music, and bring your own drugs. Traffic barricades were unnecessary. The crowd of more than five hundred people forced drivers to detour.

The weather was sunny and hot for the middle of May.

People drank the free beer like it was the last liquid on earth. By the end of the second musical group, Jesse had to call out over the sound system for donations to make a beer run. "We've gone through four kegs of beer, people." Everybody cheered. "I'll be coming through the crowd, collecting money. We'll get as many kegs as we can."

Enough money was collected to purchase five more kegs.

Cheri, from apartment one downstairs, opened up her bathroom to the public and was immediately sorry. Toilet paper quickly became a concern. Kay came to the rescue with seven rolls, but she did not open her own bathroom. "No, no, no drunks in my bathroom," she said. "Drunks in the bathroom is always a problem."

Butch and Jesse opened up their upstairs apartments for women to use their bathrooms. Most of the men didn't need bathrooms. They used backyards and alleys.

The crowd became increasingly unruly as it grew larger throughout the afternoon. Butch and Jesse became more nervous about playing in public for the first time. They were the last of four bands on the schedule.

By the time Jesse and Butch started playing, the crowd was cheering hysterically for much more than the music. The party had become a genuine celebration of life. West Wayne Street was jumping. Woodstock nation had finally arrived in the Midwest.

Jesse smiled at Butch. "Told you we could pull this off."

Butch leaned into Jesse's ear. "I can't believe nobody called the cops to shut us down."

The event was Jesse's first performance as a musician. It felt like destiny calling. It was more fun than he could remember having. All those hours playing with Butch had finally paid off. Jesse had become a decent rhythm guitar player. His singing wasn't bad, and he was a natural showman on the microphone.

They played as well as they could and sounded dangerously close to professional. The wild cheers of a drunken crowd thrilled something in Jesse that needed to be thrilled. It felt as good as getting his story and byline on the front page of the paper.

Butch hugged him as the applause continued after their last song. "Looks like we got ourselves a band." They took a bow together.

It was 7:30 p.m. Jesse was announcing the party was over when he caught sight of a gorgeous, light-skinned African American woman staring up at him from the crowd. He stepped down from the porch to the sidewalk and greeted her. "My dear woman, I can't help but notice you are unaccompanied this evening."

"Not anymore," she said, extending her hand and captivating Jesse with her exciting and intelligent brown eyes. She was nearly six feet tall with a tangled afro that made her look even taller. "My name is Cora. Friends call me Kelly, but I dance under the name Brown Sugar."

Jesse tried not to stare at her short shorts and long legs. "What? You're a stripper?"

Kelly gave him a tight-lipped smile and a wrinkle of her nose. "I prefer the term *exotic dancer.* But I am so much more than that. One day you'll see my name in lights."

Jesse finally stopped shaking her hand. "I think I've already seen your name in lights. You're dancing down on Pearl Street at Poor John's, aren't you?"

"That's me," Kelly said. "And aren't you the newspaper guy? I didn't know you could play guitar. You guys sounded pretty good up there. I sing, too, you know."

Jesse was flattered and intrigued by this exotic creature of a woman. He was also hungry. "Hey, I know what let's do. Let's go get a bite to eat at Henry's. We can walk from here. Half the party's probably going there anyway."

They sang a few songs on the walk to the bar. Kelly was not a singer, and she didn't have the ear to know it. That was fine with Jesse. She didn't need to be a singer. She was enchanting as a walk into the magical forest.

Jesse and Kelly got to know each other quite well over the next two months. They took long walks in the park, swung on the swings, and seesawed on the teeter totter. The romance was so sudden and sexually charged that it took them back to a childlike state of wonderment and discovery. Flowers and trees became one with the birds and the bees.

They talked for hours, watching sunsets like movies. Jesse learned early on that Kelly had a six-year-old daughter named Berta who lived with her grandmother. Kelly lived with a girlfriend in an apartment on Main Street, although she spent more and more nights at Jesse's apartment. One late morning over coffee, Jesse asked her, "So, how did you get into dancing?"

She was still waking up as she responded dreamily, "You know, when I was a little girl, I always wanted to be in theater. I was the star of the school plays and everybody always told me how beautiful and talented I was. Then, I got pregnant at the age of sixteen—don't ask me about the good-for-nothing father—and all my dreams got sidetracked. I wasn't ready to be a mother, so my mother stepped in. I dropped out of school and started making good money dancing at clubs. I had to lie about my age, but it was the closest thing to showbusiness I could find."

Jesse didn't pry any further with the hundreds of questions

that sprang to mind. Kelly looked at him with an expression that asked, "So, what do you think about all that?"

"It all makes sense to me," he said. "I don't know what you're gonna to do with all that talent, but I have a feeling it's gonna be big."

By July 4, 1974, Kelly had moved in with Jesse. Her girlfriend was leaving town and Jesse thought it would be okay if she lived with him while she looked for an apartment of her own. He had never lived with a woman before.

Meanwhile, Butch, his guitar partner, had been feeling left out. He grabbed Jesse in the hall one day as Jesse was buttoning his shirt on the way to work. "Are you two okay in there? I haven't seen you in days."

"Oh man, I'm sorry," Jesse said. "Are you jealous?"

Butch smiled and shook his head. "No. But I am wondering when we're going to play guitar again."

All at once, Jesse realized how totally preoccupied he had been in the weeks since Kelly swirled in and took over. "You are right. It's been too long. Don't worry. I'm ready to rock. How about tomorrow at noon?"

"That's cool," Butch said. "Don't stand me up now."

Kelly didn't have many possessions, but Jesse was worried about her six-year-old daughter and how the child would inevitably affect their relationship. The little girl was living with Kelly's mother, Alberta, a well-respected public-school teacher and community leader.

Alberta was a fabulous cook. Kelly and Jesse spent most Sundays at her house. Alberta's friends from teaching and others from the neighborhood often dropped by, bringing dishes and plates of food that turned mealtime into potluck dinners. Jesse learned to love soul food almost as much as watching Kelly spend time with little Berta. The child was bright and beautiful and loved being the center of attention.

Kelly was good with her daughter. They loved to climb the Buckeye tree in Alberta's fenced-in back yard. Kelly lifted Berta onto the lowest branch, then swung herself up. She let Berta climb as high as she could, but the mother in her followed close behind, waiting to catch her baby if she fell.

Jesse tried to join in the fun one afternoon, but Kelly shook her head to show she needed the alone time with her little girl. Jesse took the hint and realized he would never be fully invited into their mother-daughter club. He smiled to himself as he heard them giggling together when a Robin flew in to take a seat on an upper branch.

One afternoon after dinner at Alberta's, Jesse noticed a baby photo of a cheeky, curly-haired Berta that was framed and prominently displayed on top of the cupboard in the dining room. Jesse reached up and pulled it down for closer inspection. "This kid should have been on the Gerber baby food jar."

Alberta responded sarcastically, "The day they put a Black baby on the Gerber jar will be the day white folks stop buying Gerber."

Kelly lowered her head. She was embarrassed by her mother's comment. Race had never been an issue or even a topic of conversation between her and Jesse.

Jesse decided not to be intimidated. "Look at this child," he pointed at Berta. "She'll be on the cover of a lot more than a baby jar before she's through."

"You got that right," Alberta said, pleased to see Jesse standing up for her granddaughter.

Jesse saw the matriarchal look in Alberta's eyes and his mind traveled back to a scene he had almost forgotten. Before Kelly moved in, Cheri, the Montessori teacher downstairs at

1114 West Wayne St., had taken him aside and tried to talk some sense into him. "Kelly's great, Jesse, and we all love her. But if she moves in, you're going to become a proud papa whether you want to be or not."

"No, the child lives with her grandmother," Jesse said.

Cheri pointed her finger at him. "What do you think that grandmother's gonna do once her daughter has a home with a man who can help pay the bills?" Jesse looked at her blankly. "She's going to send that little girl back to living with her mother, that's what she'll do."

Jesse shifted uncomfortably in his chair. Cheri put both hands on his shoulders and got in his face. "Oh, and let's not forget one more little thing. Are you and Kelly prepared to be an interracial couple in the middle of the Bible Belt?"

Jesse thought about the warning for several days, but he never mentioned it to Kelly. They were having too much fun just being a couple, young and in love.

He drove Kelly up to his parents' secluded cottage on Lake Michigan for a rare weekend when no one else would be there. It was perfect weather for late July, sunny and in the eighties. They ended up sunbathing nude on the beach and swimming far out into the deep-water waves.

When they got back to the cottage, they drank wine and smoked pot and never bothered to get dressed. All was right with the world. The sun was shining. The waves were rolling in sensually. Their bodies were beautiful and tender to the touch.

As they were floating along on their pink cloud of sexual freedom, three friends of Jesse's mother decided to make an unannounced visit. Jesse and Kelly heard them coming as they shut the car doors and chatted their way around the deck to the lakeside of the cottage. Kelly reached frantically for a towel, but Jesse remained reclined on a lounge chair as he spoke in a stoned, calm voice, "Don't panic. Act natural. They won't even notice."

The women made it around the corner of the cottage and almost to the center of the deck before they realized what they were interrupting. The woman in front covered her eyes as she led her companions in an abrupt about-face. The uninvited guests gasped and clucked and disappeared without saying a word.

Jesse and Kelly convulsed in laughter as the car doors slammed. Tires kicked up gravel as the intruders fled.

"Do you think it would have helped if I had thrown on a towel?" Jesse teased.

Kelly tilted back her head and drained half a glass of Lancers Rosé. "Nothing we could have done would have helped. But did you see the look on those faces? Oh my God. It looked like they stumbled onto a murder scene. They'll be talking about you and your naked Black girlfriend for the rest of their lives. And you have not heard the last of this. Your mother's going to have a fit."

CHAPTER TEN

Even as Jesse's romantic life became more complicated, the world of journalism kept coming down the tracks like a freight train without an engineer. One Thursday night, the county sheriff called to say he could book Jesse into the jail Saturday morning.

"Is this really Sheriff John Meeks?" Jesse asked.

The sheriff sighed. "I know it's late, but I can't call from the jail. This whole thing has got to be undercover. You could get hurt. And, yes, this is Sheriff Meeks."

Jesse recognized the voice. "Saturday's kind of short notice. What's the rush? I mean, I can do it, but we've been talking about this for months. And what are you saying about I can get hurt?"

The sheriff whispered, "Our jail is not a safe place, as you know. It's overcrowded and understaffed. If some of those prisoners find out you're not one of them, they might try to make an example of you. Not that I think that's going to happen. That's why only you and I know about it. The county commissioners would never approve. So, I've decided to go ahead on my own. People need to know how bad it is in our old jail."

Jesse was so excited he stood up at his desk. "I'm all in. Just tell me what to do and when to do it."

The sheriff chuckled. "I wish all my prisoners were as eager as you. Here's what you do. Walk into the Calhoun Street entrance to the jail at eight on Saturday morning. They'll cuff you and book you in. I'll make it look like you've got a warrant.

And remember, the only person you can tell is your editor. Tell your girlfriend you're going out of town. Tell everybody you're off on a confidential assignment. Only your editor can know you're in jail, so he won't miss you at work."

"What's my charge?" Jesse asked.

"You're a cocaine dealer."

Jesse thought for a moment. "Won't they all think I'm a snitch?"

The sheriff laughed. "Not if you're in jail, they won't."

Jesse ran his fingers through his hair. "What should I tell them about my case?"

The sheriff's voice became stern. "Don't talk to anybody about your case. If anybody keeps asking, tell him your lawyer told you to remain silent. That way they'll know you're a real criminal. The less you say the better."

The sheriff hung up before Jesse could ask any more questions. He held the phone in his hand for at least a minute before he managed to hang it up. Now that he was finally going to jail, the thought began to unnerve him. He'd written stories about prisoners being beaten to death in that jail. And about mentally ill people being stuck behind bars for no good reason. Not to mention the guard who got carted out on a stretcher last month after being stabbed in the back by a prisoner with a blade.

His mind raced. Good Lord, what have I gotten myself into now?

"Jesse Conover. What the hell is going on over there? You look like you just got some bad news," Weatherly called out, breaking Jesse from his thoughts.

Jesse slowly walked over and sat down across from Weatherly. "The sheriff says they're ready for me to check in to jail on Saturday morning."

Weatherly's eyes widened. He took out a pack of Camel cigarettes from the breast pocket of his white shirt, snapped up a single, lit it with his chrome Zippo lighter, and took a long thoughtful drag. Before exhaling, he gave Jesse a raised eyebrow look that communicated for him to continue.

"They're booking me in as a cocaine dealer. The sheriff says he'll let me out after three days. You're the only person I'm allowed to tell. Come to think of it, if I'm not out in three days, I expect you to get me out."

Weatherly exhaled smoke over Jesse's head. "You are some kind of con man. I must admit I didn't think you had it in you. But now I'm beginning to think maybe you do. We've been trying to get a reporter in that goddamn jail for years. The sheriff must be getting desperate for a new facility. So, I guess you won't be working this weekend. I'll find somebody to cover for you. Have you ever been in jail?"

Jesse smiled. "Once, for a night, when we got caught drinking beer in a farmer's field."

Weatherly pounded his desk once with a closed fist. "Oh man, you are one dangerous criminal." He laughed with Jesse and then got serious. "Now listen, this isn't a game. You're heading into real danger. Keep your mouth shut and your eyes and ears open."

Jesse reported to jail at the appointed time. He didn't bring any extra underwear or even a toothbrush. All he took was a deep breath as he opened the tall oak door and walked into the one-hundred-year-old Victorian building. The place smelled like a leaky tar roof and a bad sewer.

An annoyed attendant came out from behind his glass window, handcuffed Jesse behind his back, frisked him for weapons, and took his belt. Then he led him into the jail. As the door banged shut behind them, Jesse realized why they call it the *slammer*. The thunderous clang, along with the handcuffs, jolted him into the disheartening power of the police state. He was no longer a free man. He was at the mercy of people who hated everything but quitting time.

The attendant removed the cuffs as he steered Jesse into a cell with four men on bunk beds and a fifth inmate lying on a floor mat. At one end of the cell was a metal toilet with no seat. Jesse instantly realized that every defecation would be a public performance. He took a seat near the bars that separated the cell from the narrow hallway.

The man on the floor mat spoke first. "You missed breakfast." The others laughed as though calling it breakfast was a ridiculous glorification.

"How was it?" Jesse asked.

"You mean what was it," a skinny Black man on one of the top bunks said. "I couldn't tell you. Some gruel slop that tasted like somebody already ate it and puked it back up."

As he spoke, a fat white guy in his early forties groaned out of the bottom bunk and stumbled toward the toilet. "You're just in time to get a good whiff of whatever it was."

Everybody groaned. The skinny man pulled a blanket over his head. "Flush as you go, man, flush as you go. Last time you stunk this place up the whole day."

The fat man slid down his pants and sat down in one motion. He immediately exploded what sounded like half his intestines into the toilet and groaned like he was having sex with a buffalo. The grunting noises lasted for twenty extra-long seconds and reverberated in the tiny cell.

The man was without shame. Before the echoes of his bowel

movement faded, a nauseous stench began to fill the room like mustard gas in a World War I trench.

Jesse buried his head into his knees with his arms a little too late to avoid seeing and hearing and smelling the horrific phenomenon. The man wasn't embarrassed, he was showing off. His wild-eyed grin was missing a few teeth, and even several hairy layers of belly fat couldn't hide his shrunken penis.

Jesse learned his lesson quickly. By the time the next guy took a crap, Jesse used both hands to cover his nose, ears and eyes.

One of the men in Jesse's cell was a stout white man in his forties who everybody called "the Preacher." He read Bible verses out loud and followed up each passage with a mini sermon. Nobody tried to shut him up. There was no other source of entertainment. The Preacher's comments always led to his thoughts about the second coming and the rapture. "The Lord will appear and remove the believers from this hell hole called Earth. The rest of you will be left behind. But do not despair. There is still time to be saved. You there, Mr. New Guy. Do you accept Jesus Christ as your personal savior?"

Jesse tried to avoid the question. He got up from the floor and went to the toilet to take a piss. On the way back to his corner of the cell, the Preacher became more agitated. "I asked you if Jesus Christ is your personal savior."

Jesse looked the Preacher in the face. "He's my savior if you're talking about love thy neighbor. He's not my savior if you say he'll send me to hell for not believing exactly what you believe."

A low murmur of disapproval came from his cellmates. They did not want to get the Preacher agitated. The skinny man threw his legs over the side of his upper bunk mattress.

"Now, now. Don't go sending the Preacher into a tailspin. And Preacher man, nobody wants to hear you go off on a rant. You heard him say Jesus is fine with him, so let's just leave it at that."

The Preacher talked loudly about how there was only one way to get into heaven until the huge man in the bunk below began kicking the mattress above him so hard it almost bounced the Preacher off the low ceiling. "Don't even start, Preacher. I'm in here for murder, so it don't matter to anybody if I kill one more asshole who won't shut up."

The Preacher turned down his volume and addressed his next comment to Jesse. "We'll discuss this matter once we can talk in private in the day room."

At 10:00 a.m., the prisoners were let out of their cells and into a common area with three metal tables and attached metal chairs. There were decks of cards and the inmates eventually settled into poker games. Jesse wandered around the room until one of his cellmates invited him to a game of five-card stud. The players gambled with tiny bits of paper for money.

The men told tales from their past. There was little talk of current events. There was no newspaper in this jail, and no television or radio. Jesse tried not to talk. He started winning early, getting lucky on the deals. About a half hour into his lucky streak, Jesse's full house beat the three aces of the short, middle-aged man across the table.

Without warning, the man jumped up and punched Jesse in the face. Jesse saw the punch coming and lowered his head to take the blow on the top of his forehead. The man hurt his hand, cradling it in his other hand.

Jesse laughed at him. "Is that all you got?"

Every inmate in the room focused on the confrontation. Jesse was obviously not backing down, and the short man didn't seem to know what to do. He yelled over his shoulder as he left the room, "I'm gonna cut that smirk off your honkey mouth."

Everybody stared at Jesse, including two big guys who looked like they might side with the short man. Jesse didn't flinch or even get up from his chair. His mind was sprinting, and his heart was beating hard to keep up. He was certain the man was going to retrieve a weapon. He didn't want to get in trouble for fighting, but he was more than ready to defend himself. His head was starting to hurt from the punch.

The short man returned, waving his instrument of destruction in the air. It was a number-two lead pencil, sharpened down to about six inches long.

Jesse pointed to the pencil. "What you gonna do with that little thing? Take a note on my ass?"

The inmates broke out laughing, which only served to further infuriate the man with the pencil. He came at Jesse and waved the pencil in his face. "I'm gonna poke out your eyes. That's what I'm gonna do."

That was enough to spur Jesse into an adrenaline-spiked fight mode. The next time the pencil came close to his face, Jesse grabbed the man by the wrist, dragged him to the ground, and almost broke his arm behind his back. He pressed his knee between the man's shoulder blades and was screaming obscenities when several prisoners intervened and restrained him.

No one was more surprised than Jesse by the intensity of his violent reaction. He'd been in a few fights, but never anything that felt like life and death. His rage blew up so fast that he might not have been able to stop if others hadn't grabbed him. He took repeated deep breaths and gradually relaxed enough for the inmates to let him go.

The man with the pencil got up slowly and did not need to be restrained. He put the pencil in his pocket as the inmates let Jesse go. Jesse tried to smile and offered to shake hands. "It's just a card game, man. I didn't try to steal your woman."

One of the big men who restrained Jesse shouted, "Come on, Sam. Shake the man's hand. We don't need no more trouble in here."

Sam, the man with the pencil, shook Jesse's hand reluctantly and the room settled down to playing poker. No guards were anywhere in sight throughout the entire event. Jesse could see he would be on his own no matter what happened and realized it would be a good idea to make alliances with other prisoners as quickly as possible.

The guards made a cameo appearance when lunch was served, one tray at a time, through a narrow slot in the wall just above the floor. Jesse was so hungry that even a slice of baloney on white bread tasted good.

The Preacher tried to sidle up to Jesse as he ate. "You need to repent."

The comment caught Jesse off guard. He thought the Preacher was talking about the fight. "Repent for what?"

The Preacher pulled out his Bible. "Repent for your sins. You brought the devil with you into this jail."

Jesse was in no mood to suffer fools gladly. He glared at the man and moved so close to him their foreheads were almost touching. "You take that preachy bullshit somewhere else, or I'm gonna take out *all* my sins on your sorry ass."

The Preacher stood up without saying a word, flashed a peace sign, and walked away. Jesse felt sorry for being mean, but he was beginning to feel like an animal backed into a corner.

Time dragged by slowly the rest of the first day and all of the second. There were no clocks in the jail, and no windows to gauge time by the sun. Only the serving of mystery meat and something squashed beyond recognition let the prisoners know if it was breakfast, lunch, or dinner. Jesse apologized to the Preacher after lunch on the second day. The Preacher accepted the apology as if suffering from delusions of adequacy. "Thank you, my son."

Once Jesse passed his trial by combat, most of the prisoners, even Pencil Man Sam, were willing to talk to him. He tried not to sound like he was conducting interviews. It didn't matter. The prisoners were ready to talk to anybody who would listen. Every man was growing more insane from the sensory deprivation of nearly medieval confinement.

Many prisoners were in jail for not paying child support or for petty offenses like possession of marijuana or public intoxication. They railed against the total lack of fairness in the legal system and all the rules they didn't understand. In the end, each had no choice but to accept the absurdity of his incarceration. There was no telephone for calling lawyers or family. A sickening sense of hopelessness pervaded the cold cruelty.

Near the end of his second day, Jesse finally got a floor mat and a black-and-white prison jumpsuit. It took one night of sleeping on a concrete floor to make the mat feel like a luxury. The only way to get a bed would be to fight for it, and even that might not work. The inmates had a strong sense of first come, first serve.

Nobody in the jail admitted to guilt. They were all framed or set up, or the victims of civil rights violations and police brutality. Except for Jonas, an Amish kid who freely admitted to killing his father. "The sinner was making my sisters have sex with him. He deserved to die. I blasted him in the chest with his own shotgun. Everybody in my family knows what happened and they're all fine with it, even my mother. What the hay, especially my mother. But none of that seemed to matter when they hauled me away. Now, I've got no bond for six months while some public defender, pretend lawyer, tries to figure out what to do with me."

Every soul in the jail had a heart-wrenching tale. To Jesse's way of thinking, only a few of them actually belonged behind bars. Most of the guys he talked to would have done reasonably well on probation. The sheriff needed more than a new and bigger jail. He needed better laws to lock up fewer people.

As Jesse listened to prisoners pouring their hearts out to him, he realized how much people need to tell their stories. The more he sharpened his listening and question-asking skills, the more they testified. No doubt, much of the testimony was untrue. Jesse had already learned that people loved to lie and boast as much as they needed to talk.

I've got to remember, he thought, *these guys are telling only one side of their stories. The victims of their crimes would certainly offer different perspectives.*

The smell of the jail became less offensive as Jesse began his third day without a shower. He became part of the stench. But what concerned him most as the day wound on beyond lunch was when he was getting out. He was only supposed to be in for three days. What if the sheriff forgot about him? What if Weatherly couldn't get in touch with the sheriff? He could be in jail for days, or worse. No exact time had been agreed upon for his release. Did three days mean three nights as well? It became impossible not to obsess about it.

Mercifully, shortly after dinner, a guard called Jesse's name and escorted him out to freedom. Nothing ever felt as sweet as walking down Calhoun Street with a big bruise on his forehead. The sun was still shining. The sky was blue. He breathed the fresh air deeply and vowed to never again take his freedom for granted.

His spirit had taken a terrible beating in less than three days. What would years of incarceration do to a person?

Henry's was between the jail and his apartment at 1114. As badly as Jesse wanted a drink, he wanted a shower even more.

CHAPTER ELEVEN

Weatherly ran the jail saga as a full-page op-ed piece opposite the editorial page. The story created quite a stir, both within the newsroom and in the community at large. Several older reporters were professionally appalled by the first-person gonzo journalism and personally offended by a cub reporter getting so much prestigious ink. Of course, all they said to Jesse was, "Nice story."

The story was a scoop in every sense of the word. First of all, the paper published it before the other newspaper in town, or any radio or television news sources. Secondly, the living conditions—no phones, clocks, newspapers, radio, or television, private toilets, and sleeping on the floor—genuinely surprised readers. All that, combined with the lack of jail staff, made people realize there was a dangerous and inhumane situation that needed changing.

The mayor's office issued a press release several days later, calling for the county commissioners to immediately hire an independent consulting firm to investigate the "old" jail. Weatherly waved the release triumphantly in Jesse's face. "Calling it the *old jail* means they want to build a new one."

Jesse frowned. "I'm pretty sure building a new jail isn't the only answer we need."

Weatherly handed the press release off to the city reporter who covered the mayor's office. Then he summoned Jesse to his desk and motioned for him to have a seat. "You know I can't have you doing the follow up to the jail story. Some people already feel like their toes are being stepped on. Melissa

Franken, in particular, doesn't think police reporters should be writing features. Obviously, I disagree, and I am her boss. She'll probably take it to the publisher, and I know that won't get her anywhere. He loves you."

Jesse didn't miss the moment. "He loves you more. You're the one who's turning me into a reporter in spite of the odds. I do owe it all to you and you know it."

Weatherly smiled warmly at Jesse for the first time. "Keep talking like that and you'll go far in this world."

Letters to the editor began pouring in about the jail expose. They all praised Jesse and the newspaper for bringing attention to what one writer called the "hidden injustice in our social fabric." This flurry of attention made feature writer Melissa Franken more furious than ever. She didn't speak to Jesse until August. Jesse knew she was biding her time to take him down.

Near the end of July, Weatherly summoned Jesse to his desk again. He thought it would be about Melissa, but her name never came up. Weatherly had other things on his mind. "I've got some good news for you. Your friend Chuck wants to go over to writing sports. God knows why. I'm gonna let him do it. He'll be good. He's a fine reporter, whatever he covers. So, what does that mean to you? It means Sylvia goes to the county government beat, and you take over her spot on the school beat."

Jesse was shocked. Schools were a big deal lately: busing for desegregation, teachers' unions fighting for higher pay and smaller class sizes, and the new "open classroom" approach to learning. Busing students out of their neighborhoods to create racial balance in centrally located schools had led to violent protests locally and across the nation.

"Oh man, do you think I'm ready for all that?" Jesse asked.

Weatherly pointed both index fingers at him. "Not only do I know you're ready, but I want you to get inside the schools like you got inside the jail."

Jesse was nervous about the promotion until he spent a few days with Sylvia, who introduced him around the Fort Wayne Community Schools administrative center. He even met Chester Miles, the bricks-and-mortar superintendent of schools who'd been telling the school board how to expand for years.

Soon after Jesse became the school beat reporter, Karl Stone, the state beat reporter who had befriended Jesse after the train derailment story, stopped by to talk. "You know, Jesse, this is 1974, the twentieth anniversary of *Brown v. Board of Education*. It might make a good story to see if our local schools are still segregated, no matter what the Supreme Court ruled."

Jesse was relieved that Karl had given him a clue that the Brown case was a Supreme Court ruling on segregation. Also, the notion of an anniversary story on anything had never occurred to him. He was flattered that Karl would pass along the concept, instead of keeping it for himself.

"You know what, Karl, that's a great idea. I'm going to do it. Any idea how to get started on a story like that?"

Karl smiled slyly like he was ready for the question and pleased to be asked. "Start with the elementary schools. I know for a fact there are three Black schools and the rest are white. Go to Norm Salinger, the public information officer for the schools. He's got records on that stuff and he'll tell you if you go at him the right way. Tell him you're doing a story on the problems with busing kids out of their neighborhoods to centrally located schools in order to achieve racial balance. Tell him you want to use the elementary schools as an example of how neighborhood schools are working out well."

Jesse marveled to himself that educated people could be manipulated so easily, but he knew it was true. "You want to work with me on this one, Karl?"

"No, I'd like to, but you know what they say. Stay on your beat. Besides, I loved what you did on the jail story. You blew everybody out of the water with that one. I never saw anybody coming up as fast as you. Be careful. There are those who can't wait to stab you in the back."

Once Karl left, Jesse basked in the glow of being accepted into the tight-knit club of veteran reporters. But could the segregation story backfire? He was beginning to realize that the best way to get stabbed in the back was to step out front. What Karl said about the elementary schools being segregated was true. Jesse already knew it. This was his hometown. The first time he'd ever come in contact with a Black person was in high school. His elementary and junior high education had been lily white. Playing sports against the Black schools in junior high had been intimidating. The Black kids were faster and tougher.

It took some time and persuading, but Jesse eventually got a one-on-one interview with the school public information officer. Norm Salinger was a tall, lanky man except for a noticeable potbelly that let the world know he hadn't done a sit-up in thirty years.

Salinger was quite helpful when Jesse approached him about the "neighborhood schools" story. He provided all the numbers for the elementary schools. The segregation was stark. One Black elementary school had only two white kids, four Mexicans, and one Chinese student. The other two schools had no white children.

"Go visit the schools," Salinger said. "You'll find the Black schools to be clean and orderly. Their reading and math skills are low, but that's to be expected."

Jesse started writing the quote into his notebook when Salinger said, "No, no, no. Don't quote me on that. I'd sound racist as hell."

Jesse put down his pen. "Why do you think that sounds racist?"

Salinger stood up from his desk and stared out the window through the blinds. "It sounds like they're dumb because they're Black, but that's not it at all. They don't do well because they come from single, working mothers who don't have time to help them learn. Mothers who never learned that well themselves."

Jesse put his pen back to the notepad. Before he could write anything, Salinger was waving both arms at him. "For Christ's sake, don't quote me on that either. Quote me on this: 'Teachers at the Black elementary schools are just as good as teachers at the white elementary schools.'"

That was all Jesse needed. The next morning, the story was on the front page with a big headline that read, "Fort Wayne Elementary Schools Still Segregated."

Norm Salinger was furious on the phone. His voice was contorted with barely controlled rage. "What are you trying to do, get me fired? The superintendent and every single member of the school board are so far up my ass I can't breathe."

"Wait a minute," Jesse said. "You said I could quote you on the teachers' thing. And, don't forget, I don't write the headlines. Copy editors do that. Reporters don't have any idea what the headline is going to say."

"You tricked me. I thought you were writing about neighborhood schools, not segregation. And, by the way, that photoshoot you've got scheduled is officially cancelled. You and your photographers are banned from school property until further notice."

The headline the next morning read, "*Journal Gazette* Banned from School Property." It ran with photos taken through chain-link fences that made the Black schools look like prison camps. In the accompanying story, Jesse had reactions from Black community leaders who expressed outrage at the illegal racial segregation. He also called the Federal District Attorney to ask if any legal or criminal action would be taken against the schools. The quote from the DA was a bombshell.

"There is nothing to stop any citizen or group of citizens from filing a federal lawsuit against the school system based on the 1954 Supreme Court case, *Brown v. Board of Education.*"

Weatherly loved that quote. "Unbelievable stuff, Jesse. Stay on it. See if any of the teachers at the Black schools will talk to you off the record. Knock on their doors when they're at home. Let them know right away you won't use their name."

Jesse took Weatherly's advice, but none of the teachers would talk. He could tell they were afraid to lose their jobs by the way they slammed doors in his face. That could have been a story on its own, but Jesse didn't write it. He decided to challenge his ban from school property by bringing a photographer along to the next school board meeting, a public meeting regularly attended by all media.

Nobody tried to keep him out. Every reporter in the city and surrounding area was there. When it came time for questions from the media, the other reporters deferred to Jesse to ask the first question. He felt strange to suddenly be the resident expert on schools, but he approached the podium and fired away. "What does the school board intend to do about desegregating the elementary schools?"

Superintendent Chester Miles stood up and glared at Jesse. "We could do a lot more about it if you weren't inviting the whole town to sue us."

The board president realized Miles was way out of line. "Superintendent, the question was directed to the board, not to you. Therefore, I invite members of the board to respond."

An audible gasp nearly sucked the air out of the room. Would the school board finally do something besides rubber stamp the superintendent's directives?

Three board members asked to be recognized. They were elected officials, after all, and they recognized the opportunity to make political hay. Each member spoke at length about the need to desegregate the elementary schools, although they disagreed completely on how to do it. After an hour of heated discussion, the board unanimously agreed to hire a consulting firm to look into the matter.

Jesse left the meeting with his television reporter friend, Jack Berry. Jack was sarcastic in his appraisal of the evening's events. "Boy, you're really turning this town upside down, Jesse. You got the school board to hire another consulting firm. They'll stall things out long enough for everybody to forget the headlines, and we'll all be right back where we started."

Jesse returned to the newsroom and wrote his story, quoting board members' comments on desegregation as well as the superintendent's angry outburst about potential lawsuits against the schools.

Weatherly cut the bit about the superintendent. "We don't want to highlight the lawsuit thing. Suing the schools looks about as bad as suing the Red Cross. And you don't want to make Chester Miles look like a fool. We'll be needing him as this story unfolds."

Jesse didn't argue with his city editor. He was still too new on the job to cross swords with the man who had reluctantly become his mentor and defender in the newsroom. *But it's censorship*, he thought. *And coming from my own editor*.

The censorship issue was deep. It started with what he decided to write, then continued with what sources said on and off the record. Then, it went through the filter of the editor and the publisher. Finally, it was left in the hands of the readers and their letters to the editor. Then there were the people who buy advertising. One story that hurt their business reputation and they'd withdraw thousands of dollars' worth of advertising. Add it all together, Jesse thought, and the "free press" isn't free at all.

Jesse's thought process depressed him to the point of wanting to change the topic in his own mind. So off he went with the Wayne Newton Fan Club to smoke a joint high above the presses and then float across the street to Henry's. Chuck, Glen, and Sherman were always ready to drink with him until closing time.

Jesse's girlfriend, Kelly, was already there and talking theater with Larry, who was thinking about casting her in his theater production of *Jacques Brel Is Alive and Well and Living in Paris*. Charles was listening to Jayne talk about how her French restaurant was actually born in Paris. Melissa from the paper was also at the table, quiet and moody. Empty glasses and bottles on the table indicated heavy drinking had been going on for hours. It was after eleven.

The Wayne Newton Fan Club walked into this drunken, intellectual fray like journalistic gunslingers fresh from a shootout with the bad guys of government. Kelly jumped up and threw herself into Jesse's arms. "Oh, honey, did you get the schools desegregated tonight?"

Larry stood up to make a toast. "Here's to Jesse Conover and all the reporters who are shaking this town up."

Everybody lifted a glass and cheered. Everybody but Melissa, who glared loudly at Jesse. Glen tried to bring her into the fold. "What's the matter, Melissa? You're part of this too. Come on. Lighten up."

Melissa stood up and pointed her finger at Jesse. "You haven't been around long enough to change anything. Back when I was the school reporter, we didn't try to make policy with our stories. We reported the news. We didn't try to *make* news. All you do is try to make waves so you can be the star of the show. I'll tell you what. I, for one, am sick of it."

A hush fell over the table until Kelly stood up and got in Melissa's face. "Why don't you shut your mouth? Jesse's doing something important. I'm one of the kids who went to those Black schools. They're not as good as the white schools and we all knew it, even as little girls. What do you think that does to a child? Don't try to tell me about standing on the sidelines and waiting for something to happen. Things need to change now. They were supposed to change twenty years ago."

Melissa made the mistake of pushing Kelly away. "Why don't you take a seat, girl? You're drunk."

Kelly pushed back hard with both hands and screamed, "Don't you call me girl, you white honkey bitch. I'll kick your ass right here and right now."

The two women pushed each other. Kelly was clearly the superior force. Melissa held her own quite well for an older gal until she slipped and dragged Kelly down to the floor with her. It happened so fast that everybody at the table, including Jesse, was paralyzed by the unexpected violence.

Kelly was on top of Melissa faster than a football player on a fumble. Melissa managed a couple of good kicks before Kelly got between her legs. She was drawing back to punch Melissa in the face when Henry jumped in to break up the fight. "Hey, hey, hey. Ladies, please. Get yourselves together. I can't have this in my bar."

Melissa got up from the floor, grabbed her purse, and issued a defiant parting shot as she headed out the door. "And another thing, Jesse. You can't write your way out of a paper bag."

"You better run away," Kelly shouted after her. "And don't come back."

Henry started clearing the table. "Donna, get over here and help me clear this table. I think what everybody needs is a fresh cocktail. Am I right?"

Nobody responded, not even Kelly, who was beginning to tremble from the booze and adrenaline.

Charles was the first to speak. "Melissa held her own pretty well, didn't she?"

Kelly was shaking and starting to cry in Jesse's arms. "I'm sorry. That was wrong. But that bitch pushed me and dragged me down. She's lucky I didn't kill her."

Larry put his hand on her shoulder. "I just want to say relax, my dear. You got the part. Best audition I've ever seen."

Kelly laughed a little as Jayne came over to hug her too. "I've been wanting to see that Melissa Franken get her ass kicked for a long time. She wrote a terrible review on my restaurant five years ago, and I'll never forgive her. So, thank you very much."

Jesse was surprised to see Kelly get so vicious in such short order. He'd never seen any woman get that violent so quickly, not even in the movies. He didn't like seeing that side of Kelly, even though she was defending him. Her stories about being beaten and sexually abused as a child suddenly made sense. She had learned to fight back, and fight back hard.

He turned to Glen. "What do you think about what Melissa said about my reporting?"

Glen took a swig of his beer. "I'm a little more old school than you, but I can see the role of journalism is changing. We're becoming more proactive. I loved your story on the jail. That took balls and it was a good read. The school story was good too. Don't listen to Melissa. You write well. She's just jealous. Unfortunately, I'm sure we haven't heard the last from her."

Chuck joined the conversation. "It's our job to stir the pot. If everybody sat around waiting for government to do the right thing, President Richard Nixon would be king. We've got Nixon on the ropes now for covering up the Watergate break-in. And why? Investigative journalism by the *Washington Post*, that's why. I'm on your side, Jesse. I love to see a reporter digging for the truth beneath all the lies and cover up."

"Woodward and Bernstein are leading the way, even if they're using an unnamed source called Deep Throat," Sherman said.

Charles could not resist. "Deep throat, I love that. It's got such a ring to it."

CHAPTER TWELVE

As Jesse became embroiled in social upheaval, he and Butch continued playing guitar and writing songs together almost every day at 1114 West Wayne Street. It was a musical escape from the news.

Their fingertips got good and calloused, and their vocal harmonies began to blend well. Butch mainly came up with the chord progressions and Jesse helped with melodies and wrote most of the lyrics. Writing for the paper left him at no loss for words.

Butch was beginning to teach Jesse how to play barre chords, a major step in the development of any guitarist. He also taught Jesse how to change the strings on his guitar. At first, Jesse tried to wiggle out of the task, but Butch wasn't having it.

"You've got to change your own strings. It's the best way to get in touch with your instrument and really understand how it makes music. Real guitar players change their own strings. You gotta become one with the wood and the wire."

In addition to writing songs, they learned hit songs by Hank Williams, Elvis, and the Beatles: songs like "Jambalaya," "Don't Be Cruel," and "I've Just Seen a Face." Once they got thirty-five tunes under their belt, Jesse began looking for paying gigs.

Amazingly, he found a one-night gig at a downtown bar called Mother's. He banged on Butch's apartment door one Sunday morning to break the news. Butch was still groggy, but Jesse was buzzing with the news. "Hey, man, we're playing this Friday at Mother's."

Butch wiped the sleep out of his eyes and opened them wide in wonderment. "Are they gonna pay us?"

Jesse walked in and sat down on Butch's beat-up sofa. "One hundred bucks a night for the whole band. We start at eight and play until midnight."

Butch went into the kitchen to make coffee. "What do you mean 'the whole band'? It's just you and me, right? Or did you hire a drummer in your spare time? What are we gonna do for microphones and a sound system? And are you really talking about five days from now? Who did you have to bribe to get this gig? I know you're a big-time reporter now, but nobody knows who we are as a musical act."

Jesse laughed as Butch peeked around the kitchen door, looking for answers. "That's a lot of questions, Butch. You want me to answer them all at once or one at a time?"

Butch stepped back into the living room. "Let's start with how did you get us booked?"

Jesse leaned back and put his hands behind his head. "I talked to Ed Caine at the club. You know Mother's. It's right on the west end of the Landing, that historic block downtown. It's a three-story brick building. I stop in there for a beer from time to time. The place is always dead, so I asked him if he'd like to have a big party there to fill his bar with heavy drinkers. He said he was ready to try something new and offered to try us out for Friday night. He wanted to pay us fifty bucks a night. I got him up to one hundred."

Butch sat down on the sofa. "That makes sense. We can pack that place with our friends. I can borrow some microphones and amps. We'll have to buy pick-ups for our acoustic guitars, but it's doable. That's a perfect spot, an empty bar right in the middle of downtown with plenty of parking. Let's do it."

"We can have players sit in on a few tunes," Jesse said, glad to see Butch getting excited. "What the hell, Kelly could bring in some of her stripper friends to liven up the place."

Butch jumped up from the couch, partly in excitement and partly to go get the coffee. "All we've got to do is invite everybody at 1114 to bring all their friends down and we'll have a good crowd right off the bat."

A good crowd right off the bat it was. Jesse and Butch sounded terrible at first. Actually, they didn't make any sound at all. They couldn't figure how to hook up the PA speaker or how to connect the microphones. Once they got everything hooked up, a screech of feedback made everyone cover their ears until Butch got the volume turned down. Fortunately, it was an indulgent crowd, willing to overlook any inexperience from their friends as long as the beer kept flowing.

Jesse was completely thrown off once his guitar was amplified. The sound wasn't coming from his instrument; it was coming from a speaker behind him. Butch was having trouble getting his microphone to quit sliding down on the stand. Instead of getting befuddled, Butch and Jesse laughed it off and drank beer, and tried to act like the sound difficulties were all part of the show. They kicked off the night with "Jambalaya" by Hank Williams, but had to restart the song three times to make adjustments to the sound mix.

They sounded better and better as the night progressed. The crowd sang along and drank themselves into a fine frenzy. The club owner was amazed to watch his bar accelerate from zero to sixty miles per hour in seconds flat. He kept pitchers of beer coming to the stage. Between sets, Jesse waded into the crowd with two full pitchers of beer, filling everybody's glass. He and Butch both thought the beer was part of their contracted payment.

They were set up in a bay window at the front of the long,

cavernous club. There was no stage and no stage lights except for one stained-glass lamp with a single light bulb that hung down from the high ceiling.

After a few drinks, most of the crowd wanted to get into the act. Several folk singers sat in for a couple of tunes. The crowd sang along whenever they knew the words, and hummed along and clapped and banged on the tables when they didn't.

At 11:30 p.m., as the party was reaching a frothy crescendo, Kelly paraded into the club with three strippers in revealing costumes, still oiled up from dancing at Poor John's. The crowd parted for them to shimmy through to the stage. Jesse and Butch played an extended version of "Hound Dog" as the ladies gyrated around them in sexual suggestion. Their skin shined under the hanging lamp while their reflections danced in the windows behind the band.

As the Elvis song ended, the painted ladies floated out the front door, blowing kisses and passing out feathers. A posse of aroused men followed them out the door and down the street to the strip club. Once the troupe was gone, people in the crowd looked at each other in wonderment, unsure of what they had just witnessed.

Mother's did not close at midnight that night. Ed Caine, the owner, was deliriously happy and every bit as intoxicated as most of the crowd. Caine was a wiry man in his fifties who was balding and thin and slightly hunched over when he walked. He looked like Ebenezer Scrooge come to life. He took the microphone at 1:00 a.m. and addressed the party. "I want to thank you all for coming out tonight." Cheers erupted. "We usually close at midnight, but we're going to let this party roll until the city makes us shut it down." More cheers. "How about a hand for my band?"

As the partisan crowd went wild, Caine had one more thing

to say before he left the microphone. "Hey, I've got an idea. How about if we bring these boys back tomorrow night?"

Back at 1114, Butch and Jesse collapsed on the couch at 3:30 a.m. in Butch's apartment after they had loaded in the guitars, amps, cords, microphone stands, PA speakers and monitors, and mixing board.

"You got any beer over in your refrigerator? I'm all out here," Butch hollered from the kitchen.

Jesse groaned as he got off the couch. "I've got something much better. I'll go get it. But I'll tell you what we really need."

A few moments later, Jesse returned with a bottle of Jack Daniel's. "What we really need are a couple roadies to help us haul all this gear we suddenly need."

Butch grabbed the whiskey bottle and went to get a couple glasses. "What we need are groupies who will double as roadies."

"Two different animals." Jesse held up his glass for a toast. "Here's to our first gig. May there be many more."

Butch gulped down his shot. "Tell me one more time why we couldn't leave our gear at the bar since we're playing tomorrow night."

Jesse plopped on the couch. "The club owner doesn't want the responsibility, and we don't even own our own system yet."

CHAPTER THIRTEEN

Living with Kelly proved to be a learning experience for them both. It was the shock of living with a woman that presented a huge challenge to Jesse. There was only one tiny bathroom and she was always in it. When he could get in, the sink and medicine cabinet and toilet top were completely covered with makeup accessories.

Kelly had stopped looking for her own apartment less than two weeks after moving in with Jesse. Even so, she was never happy with the living arrangement.

Kelly's problem with the apartment from day one was that it was too small. "There's no place to hang my clothes," she said. Jesse had no answer. He'd already given her most of the closet and three of the four dresser drawers.

"And where will my daughter sleep when she comes to spend the weekend? We're going to need a bigger place."

Jesse did not respond to that comment. He loved little Berta and he got along well with Kelly's mother, Alberta. He had developed a taste for southern fried chicken, black-eyed peas, and cabbage-collard greens with bacon bits. But he could feel himself being backed into a corner. A corner that included a six-year-old child.

Despite the pressure of living together in a small apartment, Jesse and Kelly loved being together and they weren't afraid to show it off in public, even when people stared in obvious disapproval and muttered discriminatory comments.

On the rare nights when neither of them had to work, Jesse

and Kelly loved going out to their favorite Italian restaurant, Figaro's, and then off to The Bombay Bicycle Club to dance the night away. Jesse was a good dancer, but he got a lot better once Kelly showed him her moves.

Life became interesting with Jesse's family as well. One afternoon, his mother invited him to join the family for dinner on Friday at the Fort Wayne Country Club, a place Jesse disliked for its snobby elitism and no-Blacks-allowed policy. Instead of turning down the invitation, Jesse had a new approach. "Mind if I bring a guest?"

"Of course not, honey," his mother said, sounding surprised that he would even consider accepting the invitation. "Bring whoever you want. We haven't seen much of you since you became a famous reporter."

"I'll be there with bells on," Jesse said, chuckling to himself. His mother had no idea Kelly had moved in with him, and she certainly had no idea he would be bringing a Black woman as his date to a place that was a throwback to an antebellum southern plantation.

Kelly jumped at the chance. "Little ol' me, a dinner guest at the slave owners' private club? I would be delighted, although it's not the ideal circumstance to meet your family. We'll be making quite a scene, I'm sure. And I know just what I'll wear."

Jesse hugged her. "My family will love you wherever they meet you. It's the rest of the dinner guests who will be quivering in their shiny little shoes."

Kelly backed out of the hug. "What if they throw me out?"

"Then we stage a sit down and make some news."

Kelly threw her arms back around him. "Jesse Conover, that's what I love about you. You're not afraid to make waves."

When the evening arrived, Jesse wore his new sport coat and a tie. Kelly wore black high-heels, a short purple skirt, and a floral flutter-top blouse that was see-through enough to suggest she might not be wearing a brassiere. Her black hair was styled in a top bun that tilted slightly to the left.

The dining room was packed and chattering when they walked in and headed for Jesse's family at a table in the rear. All conversation ceased as though someone had hit a pause button. The only sound was the clanking of a dinner fork dropping on the plate of an eighty-year-old female diner, who opened her mouth while it was still full of half-chewed Mediterranean chicken. Nobody moved a muscle. Even the Black waiters froze in place.

Jesse's father stood up to greet them as heads turned to follow Kelly's high-fashion runway walk. Jesse felt invisible as he followed behind for the grand entrance that seemed to unfold in slow motion. Jesse had to remind himself to breathe as he fought to maintain a straight face. It took forever to make it across the large dining room to his family's table.

A manager walked briskly toward Kelly and Jesse, but changed course abruptly as Kelly took the hand of Jesse's father. "Mr. Conover, it is so nice to meet you. And, Mrs. Conover, I'm so pleased to be included in the evening."

Jesse's mother flushed slightly as she stood up and gave Kelly a gentle hug. "Any friend of Jesse's is a friend of the family. Here, sit next to me."

"Mom, Dad, this is Kelly," Jesse said. "And Kelly, these are my parents, Max and Vaun, and my sisters, Amy and Laura."

Amy and Laura gave their big brother sideways glances as they smiled and stood up to shake Kelly's hand. Once the family sat down and began talking, the atmosphere in the room slowly returned to normal.

Kelly quickly demonstrated her poise and pedigree. "My mother is Dorothy Conway, Principal of Weisser Park Elementary School. You might have heard of her. She's on the City Planning Board."

His father recognized the name right away. "Oh yes, she's on the planning board and many others. She's quite a community leader. And what do you do, Kelly?"

Kelly didn't miss a beat. "I'm currently playing one of the lead roles in the university production of *Jacques Brel is Alive and Well and Living in Paris*."

His mother followed the campus theater. "Oh, that's going to be great. Anything Larry Borne does is wonderful. Didn't he win the national college competition for his production of *Dames at Sea*?"

"Why, yes he did," Kelly said. "And he might win again for *Jacques Brel*. The man runs a tight ship. He can be a prima donna, but he is the best. He could direct on Broadway, but he says he loves teaching too much."

And so, the dinner went smoothly following its unnerving beginning. Kelly brought a new level of fun and excitement to the gathering. She asked Jesse's mother lots of questions, and soon everyone at the table was talking at once. His father ordered two more bottles of wine. They arrived more quickly than usual, and Jesse noticed a bit more flourish in the pours of not one but two servers.

Waiters hovered around the table like worker bees serving the queen bee. Jesse never had his water glass filled so many times.

Kelly had asked the headwaiter his name and never failed to use it. "Thank you so much, Lawrence."

As the family was walking out after dinner, Jesse's mother grabbed him by the arm and jokingly whispered in his ear, "You love to see me squirm, don't you?"

He feigned surprise and innocence, but thought, *Why, yes I do, Mother. Yes I do.*

Jesse was feeling quite smug and proud of himself when he and Kelly arrived home for the night at their apartment. He was completely taken aback when she kicked off her shoes and sat down on the couch, then glared at him with an angry, furrowed brow. "You only like me because I'm Black. You show me off like I'm some kind of trophy you won at the civil rights march."

Jesse could tell by her ominous tone that this was no time to head to the refrigerator for a beer. He sat down and waited for her to continue. She said nothing, but her hard countenance looked sad. Tears welled up in her eyes. She stood up, loosened her hair, and stomped to the bathroom. He resisted the urge to follow her. She had never brought up the topic of race. Neither had he. Why the sudden change? Everything had gone so well with his family. He and Kelly had even laughed on the way home about the freaked-out diners at the country club.

Kelly finally emerged from the bathroom, barefoot and dressed in a long, purple robe. "I should have known I could never fit into your world."

Jesse stood up in protest. "The country club is not my world."

"I'm not talking about the country club. I'm talking about your parents. Don't get me wrong. They're wonderful people. But they were embarrassed to see you with a Black girl. They tried to hide it, but they were uncomfortable, especially at first."

Jesse motioned for Kelly to join him on the couch. She sat down but kept a space between them. "I'd like to see how you feel when you walk into a crowd of nothing but Black people."

Jesse took her hand and decided, for once, not to make a glib comment.

Kelly pulled her hand away. "Don't try to calm me down. The truth is, I'm really in love with you, and tonight I realized that our relationship is not going to be easy. And I wonder if you feel the same way about me. I mean, if you love me like I love you."

Jesse took back her hand and drew her closer. "I do love you, Kelly. You know I do. And I'm sorry if you got your feelings hurt tonight. I was thinking about showing those people how shallow and racist they are. I should have been more careful about your feelings. I guess I was showing off a little."

Kelly smiled as she got up and looked down on him. "Showing off a little? You always show off. Tonight, you were showing off a lot. And you loved putting your mother in the hot seat."

Jesse looked up at her and then down at the floor, realizing she had his number. "It's odd you would say that. I'm afraid it's true. But you know what? My mother loved you. My whole family loved you. What's not to love?"

Jesse wondered about his motives for being with Kelly. They had fallen for each other out of sheer sexual attraction and a shared rebellious nature. Race had nothing to do with it. But they both knew interracial dating would make big social waves, and that appealed to their inner rebels.

"What's your mother gonna do when she finds out I'm 'Brown Sugar' the exotic dancer?" Kelly asked.

"What did your mother do?"

Kelly pointed her finger not two inches from Jesse's nose. "You better leave my mother out of this if you know what's good for you. But, for your mother's information, I'm dancing to pay my way through college."

Jesse could see her beginning to lighten up. "Is that true?"

Kelly bit her lower lip. "It might be. I might need a little help. But it might be true."

CHAPTER FOURTEEN

By the summer of 1974, Jesse was becoming well known as the counterculture reporter at the *Journal Gazette*. So well known that he received an anonymous tip one afternoon that marijuana plants were growing in plain view near the sheriff's entrance to the Allen County Courthouse.

He was working on a story about the teachers' union getting ready to strike, but cannabis growing at the courthouse was too good to pass up. Once he told his city editor about the tip, Weatherly pointed him out the door of the newsroom. "Get on that right away while we've still got light. And take John with you. I want photos on this one."

John had a dry sense of humor, bordering on sarcastic. The thought of photographing marijuana made him chuckle as they drove to the courthouse, even though it was only five blocks away.

"Let me scout it out before you come walking down the sidewalk with your camera gear. I'll wave you in if I find any," Jesse said, and he got out of the car.

The caller said the marijuana was near the Main Street entrance, which was where most of the ranking county police walked into their headquarters. Jesse tried to be nonchalant as he strolled down the sidewalk and stopped to light a cigarette near the suspected grow site. A detective stopped to say hi. Like always, Jesse asked him if anybody on the force was making news. The detective shook his head and walked into the courthouse.

As soon as he left, Jesse walked off the sidewalk and into

the narrow, planted area beneath the eight-foot window of the sheriff's office. Sure enough, marijuana plants were growing taller than the shrubs and in full view of anybody walking by. A few plants were tall enough to be seen by anyone looking out the window.

Jesse signaled John to swoop in for the kill. The photographer was laughing so hard he could barely focus. The contraband was growing right under the nose of Sheriff John Meeks, an elected official known for his campaign promise to throw marijuana users in jail.

Sheriff Meeks must have seen them through the window because he came walking briskly out the front door as John was finishing the shoot. Meeks was a little taller than six feet and looked like he could model uniforms for a living. His tie was tight, uniform sharply pressed, and shoes brightly spit-shined. His dark brown hair was too perfectly wavy to wear a hat. He was wearing a full gun and equipment belt. His arms swung out from his sides like he was about to shoot it out at the O.K. Corral.

A photo idea clicked in Jesse's brain. He picked a tall marijuana plant and held it up for John. "Get a shot of the sheriff walking into this."

The sheriff clenched his jaw, but he didn't make a scene. He and Jesse were still on friendly terms from the jail story. "Maybe I should arrest you for possession. That's an illegal drug you're holding in your hand."

Jesse grinned and pointed at the more than thirty plants growing in the fertile soils of justice. "Maybe you should arrest yourself for growing it. What were you going to do? Sell it for campaign donations?"

Sheriff Meeks snorted as he walked into the shrubs to inspect the plants. "Yep, that's marijuana, all right. And we'll never catch the guy who planted it. These boys are getting tall. They're more than a couple of months old." He turned to one of the vice squad officers who had gathered at the scene. "Dig these plants up immediately and dispose of them."

Jesse got out his notebook and pen and waited for comment. By now, the sheriff was beginning to see the joke was on him. "I'll tell you what—and you can quote me on this—I don't think this is one bit funny. Drug use is no laughing matter."

Jesse and John went back to the newsroom. As Jesse was writing the story, he heard John yelping for joy from the darkroom. John was nearly running when he came out with the photo of the sheriff walking into what looked like a giant marijuana plant. "This might be the best photo I've ever taken of law enforcement."

Every reporter in the room, including Melissa, came over to marvel at the shot and have a good laugh. Weatherly put his hands on his hips and shook his head in amazement. "What did Meeks have to say about his crop?"

"He said he didn't think it was one bit funny. Drug use is no laughing matter," Jesse said with a smirk.

The reporters laughed harder at the quote than the photo.

"Lead with that," Weatherly said as the laughter turned to chuckles and then sighs of happiness.

The next morning, the sheriff's marijuana portrait was on the front page with the cutline: "Sheriff not amused by courthouse marijuana." Jesse's story was in the local section of the paper. His lead paragraph was the quote: "I'll tell you what—and you can quote me on this—I don't think this is one bit funny. Drug use is no laughing matter."

The last sentence of the quote became the motto for the Wayne Newton Fan Club.

The guys who planted the marijuana had to tell somebody

about it. They were thrilled to see their prank photographed in the newspaper. The young man who'd tipped Jesse off called the next day to congratulate him. "That was the best story I've ever seen in the paper, man. Way to go."

Jesse was beginning to realize why everyone wanted to tell his or her story. Getting named in the paper was only part of it. People needed to testify to reaffirm their existence. Life was so confusing that it could only be understood by telling tales, tall or small. Nothing really happened until you told somebody about it.

Meanwhile, the gigs at Mother's continued. Jesse managed to get Friday and Saturday nights off at the newspaper by agreeing to cover cops on Sundays. That meant he was busy seven days a week and drinking as hard as he worked.

Kelly was only working five nights a week, and she was beginning to complain that Jesse never seemed to have enough time for her. "Sometimes I wish I was your guitar. You pay more attention to that thing than you do to me."

Jesse tried to be conciliatory. "I know, baby, I know. Believe me, this pace is killing me. Something's got to give. I'm going to have to tell Butch we need a few weeks off. I know he's getting tired too."

Kelly rolled her eyes. "You do know I've heard all this before?"

Jesse was surprised that, as Kelly's enthusiasm for the band began to wane, Weatherly became more supportive. He even came to a couple of shows and loosened up considerably, drinking and carousing with his reporters. He took Jesse aside one night and said, "It makes me feel like the old days when I wasn't the boss. It was more fun back then, being one of the boys. Don't take these days for granted, Jesse. Someday, you'll look back on all this as the best time of your life."

CHAPTER FIFTEEN

The red light shone brightly over the front door of Caesar's Spa, a popular massage parlor in downtown Fort Wayne. It was the only light illuminating the dilapidated two-story building. All the windows were boarded up.

Jesse paused before entering. He wondered why a business that was trying to maintain a façade of legality would utilize a red light, the universal symbol for prostitution. He was amazed at how brazen the massage parlors had become in a town that billed itself as the "city of churches" and a great place to raise a family.

The parlors had suggestive storefronts, billboards, and ads in the newspapers. *Nightlife*, the widely circulated entertainment tabloid in town, advertised extensively for five different parlors. The ads were not subtle. They offered "full-body, Swedish massage" and "your own personal nude kitten." Accompanying one ad was a hand drawing of a nude man reclining with a smile on his face and a scantily clad woman massaging his stomach. The caption read, "We never rub you the wrong way."

Jesse had gotten the idea for the massage parlor story a week earlier, while a few reporters were in the newspaper cafeteria having lunch. Sylvia Johnson, the former school beat reporter, approached Jesse with a story idea.

"I've been wanting to tell you how much I liked the substitute teacher story," Sylvia said. "To tell the truth, I wished I'd written it when I was on schools."

"Coming from you, Sylvia, that is a real compliment. Thank

you for everything you've taught me. I couldn't have done it without you," Jesse said.

Sylvia smiled, revealing dimples in her cheek. "I hear Richard Williams of the *News Sentinel* is working on an expose of all the massage parlors in town. It might be a good story for you." She smiled again. "Enjoy your lunch."

After Sylvia left, Jesse sat there for a few moments longer and thought about what she had said. It would be a good story. He'd have to go straight to the publisher for this one, but it would still be a hard sell. The only way he'd go for it was if Jesse said the *New Sentinel* was about to break the story, and the only way to scoop them was to get into those places before they did. Only then could he expose the massage parlors for what they were.

Jesse thought a good lead for his story could be, "Prostitution is alive and well advertised in the city of churches."

Most amazing was the fact that no angry mob of church ladies was lighting torches and sharpening pitchforks in the name of Christian decency. No one was even blowing the whistle on the thinly veiled sex trafficking. The massage parlors had been around for more than a year and the community had yet to catch up with the changing times. The parlors had well-paid lawyers. Early police raids led to appellate court standoffs on free speech and probable cause issues.

Jesse could not believe his good fortune as a reporter. Why had no one blown the roof off this scandal before now? The story was ripe as a juicy, red tomato about to fall off the vine from its own weight. Then again, why had he not done his own exposé months earlier? The parlors were a running joke in the newsroom.

Weatherly agreed to the story in an instant. Publisher Longstreet followed suit and provided Jesse with an unlimited budget. "I can't believe I'm saying this, but make sure you only spend the money on sex. I'm not going to be paying for booze or hotel rooms or anything like that. We'll start off with five hundred dollars cash and see where we go from there. Bring me receipts if you can get them. And if you can't get receipts, keep a record of what you spent and where you spent it."

Jesse hesitated again before grabbing the brass door handle at Caesar's Spa. He was worrying about what might await him on the other side of the door. He'd never paid for sex before. What if the women were fat and ugly? What if they had no teeth? What if they thought he was a cop?

He had discussed with Kelly that the story would involve him having sex with prostitutes disguised as masseuses. She agreed it would shake the town up and make a powerful expose, but she hadn't considered how the whole thing would look in print. And what would his mother think?

He knew there were lots of customers inside. The "free chariot" parking lot behind the building was crowded with late-model luxury sedans. What if one of the johns recognized him and blew his cover as an investigative reporter? He closed his eyes and opened the door.

An attractive woman in her early twenties was smoking a cigarette behind a small desk. When she looked up, her movements were slow, as if her heavy makeup was weighing down her face. She was missing a canine tooth and chewing gum in a bored manner. Her evening gown was strapless. Jesse walked slowly over to her station and didn't know what to say or even how to introduce himself.

The woman shrugged her bare shoulders. Jesse would have to speak first. Parlor girls knew the police would not arrest unless a proposition was made. He put both hands in his pants pockets. "I'd like to make an order, I guess."

The woman looked at Jesse curiously and then giggled at his nervous reluctance. "You'd like to make an order, huh? Would you like fries with that?"

Jesse didn't know how to respond until he saw her grinning at her own joke. He smiled a little, and then coughed out a nervous laugh. "I'm sorry. I'm new at this. I don't really know what I'm doing."

The woman stood up, walked around the desk, and took Jesse by the arm. "Don't worry, we won't hold that against you. I can tell you're not a cop. You don't look dumb enough. Come with me. We'll go into this room over here to discuss what it is you want."

She was graceful as a jazz dancer and began humming softly as she led Jesse into a small room that looked like a doctor's office. A thin upholstered medical bed with a sheet draped over it nearly filled the space. The only other furniture was a wooden chair and a folding table with baby oil and rubbing alcohol on it. The place smelled like cheap perfume and baby lotion.

On the wall at the head of the bed was a list of items entitled, "Choices." A back rub was eight dollars, a full-body rub was twelve dollars, a French for fifteen dollars, and "the Works" for thirty dollars. Jesse decided to pay now and ask questions later. He pulled out his wallet and handed the woman thirty dollars. "I'll take the Works."

She took his money and turned around to walk out of the room. "Excellent choice, sir. I'm Misty. I'm your hostess. You just relax and I'll send one of the girls in as soon as she's ready."

The door shut, leaving Jesse alone in the tiny room to contemplate his fate. There was nothing sexy about the place. It looked more like a torture chamber than a pleasure nook. He felt perverted, waiting for sex like he should have taken a number. Sitting on the bed, he was attracted to rock music from a tiny speaker above. He looked up and noticed a row of multi-colored lights, set on dim, which barely illuminated the room. Several of the bulbs were burned out.

He was disappointed that Misty would not be his masseuse. She was long and lean and had some sense of humor and style. He had no idea who was going to come walking through the door. This was nothing like the movies where the character selected a woman from a lineup of gorgeous babes. He wondered if he should take off his clothes. He looked around the room for hidden cameras. The place was too shabby for auxiliary technology. Flocked wallpaper was peeling off the drywall.

"Love Train" by the O'Jays was playing on the radio. *Perfect*, he thought as he kicked off his boots and waited. *Looks like it's time to get on board.*

Sounds from adjoining rooms were creepy but entertaining. The walls were thin. A man, who sounded less than twenty feet away, groaned more loudly than Jesse thought would have been necessary under any circumstances. He heard a woman in another room cackling like a witch and calling out, "Good boy, Billy. Good boy."

The longer Jesse waited, the more noises he heard. There must have been a dozen small rooms nearby and they were all shaking. The two-story wood-frame structure sounded like it was creaking off its foundation. It was a house of whores.

He lay back down on the bed and realized he would definitely be making a hasty exit if he wasn't on assignment for the newspaper. He sat up with a start when the door swung open and banged against the wall. In walked a stocky woman in her early forties wearing a floppy blonde wig and a loose black negligee. She had a towel in her hand, drying off from a previous encounter.

"What you doing with your clothes on, man? I hear you got

the Works. Come on. Let's get naked. I'm about to blow your mind."

Jesse stood up and began taking off his shirt. "What's your name?"

The woman laughed in his face and began unbuckling his belt. "You don't have to worry about that. What? This your first time? Yeah, I can tell. So, here's how it goes. You get naked and lie on that bed, and then I get you all hot and bothered with this baby oil and then I turn you over and jump on top to finish you off. Any questions?"

Jesse complied as the woman began chattering away like she was making a batch of cookies. She talked about her two kids and her husband in prison, and how busy she had been lately.

"You come back and ask for me by name. Name's Tanya. I'll give you a discount."

Tanya was fluid with the baby oil and surprisingly good with her hands. By the time she turned Jesse over she had his full attention. She took him into her mouth without further comment or consent. He tried to ask how long her husband had been in prison, but her answer was more than garbled. At that point, Jesse realized an essential truth about being a reporter. Never interview anybody when she's giving you a blowjob.

As Jesse's animal instinct kicked in, Tonya jumped on top, slipped a condom on him, and tucked him into her folds in one surprisingly athletic motion. Before he knew what was happening, he was fully penetrating a chunky gymnast who was probably old enough to be his mother.

He was finished before he really got started. Tonya looked down and smiled at him like an army nurse in a field hospital. Then she slapped his face with her huge breasts a couple times and hopped off the bed. "I'd stay for the pillow talk, but I've got to keep moving. Don't forget to leave a tip. I might set a record tonight. Ta-ta."

Jesse raised his head to see her big butt walking out the door and then lay back down on the bed. He didn't feel used or cheap or dirty or unsatisfied. He felt relieved. One massage parlor down, six more to go. Paying for sex was not nearly as much trouble as he thought it was going to be.

He must have fallen asleep because the next thing he heard was Misty knocking on the door. "You okay in there? Tanya didn't hurt you, did she? Come on, now. Time to get up and go."

The *Journal Gazette* ran Jesse's two-part series on massage parlors in early August of 1974 under the heading, "Aye, There's the Rub!" Part I: "Reporter Buys, Gets Massage." Part II: "She Tells It Like It Is—Profitable." The stories went into scandalous first-person detail on the inner workings of places like Caesar's Spa, Aladdin's Harem, and Kitty's Studio of Massage.

Attorneys for the newspaper reviewed Jesse's copy and edited it heavily in a tense meeting before publication. A silver-haired lawyer in a nine-piece suit held up his hands like he was calling for a time-out. "You can't say prostitution is alive and well advertised."

Jesse looked at his publisher, Longstreet, and then at Weatherly before responding, "Why not? I thought the truth is a defense against any kind of libel allegation."

The attorney straightened up in his chair. "Who says it's true? You? That's one person's word against the fifty witnesses they'll have to say you're lying."

Jesse put his hands on his knees as if he was about to rise out of his seat. "If you're not going to believe me, then how can you run the story at all?"

Weatherly reached over and put his hand on Jesse's shoulder. "Nobody's saying we don't want to run the story. We're just talking about toning it down a notch or two. It's like this. You don't need to use the term *blowjob* to get across the oral sex concept."

Jesse looked around the room again. The stern looks on all faces showed him he didn't really have a vote in the matter. This was nothing new. He was getting used to Weatherly editing his copy with a heavy hand. Instead of getting angry and argumentative, Jesse relaxed in his chair and adopted a conciliatory tone. "Hey, I'm just the reporter. You gentlemen do what you gotta do. I'm glad you let me do the story in the first place."

Publisher Longstreet got up from behind his desk and walked over to shake Jesse's hand. He always wore a well-tailored suit. "I like your attitude, Jesse. You're a team player. Good show. And great stories. You're really shaking things up around here."

Jesse could see his cue to exit. He shook hands before leaving the room and did some politicking on his way out. "Let's not forget our city editor. Without Mr. George Weatherly, I wouldn't even be on the team."

By the middle of August, angry letters to the editor were calling Jesse everything from "a hedonistic show-off" to "an agent of the devil." This was Jesse's first encounter with public criticism. He didn't know what to make of it. The letter writers seemed to be confusing him with the parlor owners. He invited Chuck to Henry's for an early supper to talk about it.

"Why are they mad at me? I'm not running the parlors. Don't you think they should be angry with the people making money on prostitution?"

Chuck lit a cigarette as they waited for their hamburgers to arrive. "They're mad at you because you're the one glorifying prostitution. If it wasn't for you, they wouldn't have to hear about it."

Jesse leaned back in the booth. "I'm not glorifying anything. The stories showed the parlors for what they are, cheap and disgusting."

Chuck pointed his cigarette at Jesse. "Don't get me wrong, the stories were great, and everybody knows it. People keep asking what took us so long to expose them. And you know you're doing something right when you get that many letters on a story. I haven't seen that many, ever. But you've got to understand we are what we write about. If you write about schools, you're a teacher. If you write about city hall, you're a politician. If you write about massage parlors, you're a hooker."

"So, you're writing about sports now. Does that make you an athlete?"

Chuck laughed. "No, it makes me a coach. I get letters from people like I'm the one who lost the game with my poor play calling. And look at Hunter Thompson. He writes about drugs all the time, so he's a drug addict."

Jesse helped the waitress set down two beers. "He is a drug addict."

"See what I'm saying?" Chuck said before taking down half the mug in one guzzle. "You don't know he's an addict. You just think he is because of what you read."

They drank three beers with dinner and returned to the newsroom with a good buzz. Weatherly was waiting and invited them over to his desk. "So, did you two solve the problems of the world over dinner?"

Jesse folded his arms across his chest. "Chuck says we are what we write about. What do you think?"

Weatherly stroked his chin and thought about the question for a moment. He liked to look at the ceiling while formulating his thoughts. "We do get identified with our beats. I did a series on sewers about twenty years ago and people started calling me the 'rat reporter.' Anyway, don't be upset by the letters to the editor. We all knew you were an agent of the devil long ago."

Jesse and Chuck laughed.

"The important thing is don't let it go to your head,"

Weatherly continued. "You're getting a pretty big name now, and people are gonna be shooting at you. So, where do you go from here? How do you top the massage parlor exposé?"

Jesse unfolded his arms. "I'm not trying to top anything. I'm going back to schools and cops where it's safe."

But things took a turn a few days later. Jesse had to do some damage control with his mother and with Kelly and her mother. His mother called one Sunday after church. He was still half-asleep when he answered the phone.

His mother put on her stern voice. "Jesse, good morning. You sound like you're still asleep. Were you out all night visiting massage parlors?"

"Aw, Mom, come on. Not you too."

"Well, yes, me too. Do you know where I've been? I've just come from church where all anyone could talk about was how my son patronizes prostitutes and writes articles about it. How do you think I feel about that?"

"Like your son is doing a good job?"

His mother paused before letting him have it. "I know you think you're the Woodward and Bernstein of sex, but it's not coming off like that to my friends. They think you're promoting perversion. Your sisters are even getting teased. Now, I know you're going to do what you think you have to do, but if you need to keep writing these kinds of articles, why don't you move to another town to do it?"

Jesse got out of bed to try to organize his response. "Are you serious? Do you really want me to leave town?"

His mother softened her tone. "Well, I am mostly joking. But really, Jesse, can't you get back to reporting the news?"

Jesse breathed a sigh of relief. "I'll tell you what. For my mother, I'll get back to murders and plane crashes and bank robberies. The kind of stories that warm people's hearts."

"Now, Jesse, there's no need to get sarcastic. All I'm saying is what I've always tried to teach you. If you hang out with thieves, you're a thief. If you hang out with winners, you're a winner. It's the same with writing."

Kelly was awake by the time Jesse hung up the phone. "Who was that?"

"It was my mother complaining about all the comments in church."

Kelly rolled over in bed. "I'm the one who should be complaining. You're out getting laid all over town, and I'm supposed to be what? Okay with it all?"

Jesse knew she wasn't going back to sleep. He got back in bed and threw his arm around her. "You're the one who said I should do it. I wouldn't have done it without your okay."

Kelly gave him the cold shoulder and pretended to be going back to sleep. "No, I don't have a problem with sex for money. Hell, I do it every night. Well, I don't *do* it, but you know what I mean. What surprises me is everybody's reaction to the articles. Even the girls at work tease me about my man, the john. It's like you became a promoter for prostitution when you gave it all that publicity."

Jesse got up and put on some shorts. "Well, if it's any consolation, it's been a surprise to me too. I used to think actions spoke louder than words. Now I'm starting to think words speak louder than actions."

"They do when you print them in the newspaper under big, screaming headlines," Kelly snapped.

She got up and went into the bathroom to use the toilet and shower. Jesse knew he wouldn't see her for half an hour, so he went into the living room and played guitar while waiting for the coffee to brew. He was on his tenth song and second cup when Kelly came out.

She poured herself a cup of coffee, then sat down next to Jesse on the couch. "What you've really got to worry about is my mother. She says no woman should live with a man who hangs out in whorehouses."

CHAPTER SIXTEEN

Jesse didn't need to dream up feature stories to keep himself busy. News of the day was as relentless as waves on the beach. Sometimes, small stories turned into much larger ones. Jesse found that the deeper he dug into any story, the more interesting it became. One day he found himself investigating vandalism in a historic neighborhood that allegedly sent the property owner to the hospital with a heart attack.

Mrs. Beatrice Brand returned home at 9:30 p.m. from a church gathering on a summer night to find her yard and gardens completely ruined. Fences and planters were knocked over, birdbaths and yard gnomes shattered, small trees and shrubs cut down, vegetable gardens leveled, and lawns shoveled into ruin. She had to gasp for breath in the fading twilight. Beatrice was a heavyset woman. By the time she ran upstairs to wake up her sleeping husband, she was beginning to complain of what she thought was severe heartburn.

She and her husband, Ivan, hurried downstairs and had to sit down on the back-porch step when they saw what had happened to the landscaping they had worked so hard to create. Ivan was a short, barrel-chested man, had to fight back tears as he went into the house to get Beatrice something for her chest pain. When he returned, his wife of thirty-one years had fallen off the step and was lying in the dirt, clutching her heart. He called for an ambulance.

Jesse heard the call on the police radio and arrived at the scene with Dean Sorenson as paramedics were loading Beatrice into the emergency vehicle. Dean started shooting photos with a flash as Jesse began interviewing neighbors. They were eager to talk. A gang of teenage boys had been terrorizing the neighborhood for some time. The damage done kept getting worse. A garage had been burned down, and a beloved family dog had been left to die on a front porch with its stomach slashed. The dog recovered but the neighborhood's sense of peace and quiet did not.

Ordinarily, vandalism would not be much of a story, but it was potentially big news if it sent a woman to the hospital with a heart attack. Jesse was skeptical, thinking the woman's medical history must have had more to do with her hospitalization than the traumatic event. But a detective filling out his report at the scene told Jesse the woman was fifty-three and had no history of heart problems.

Jesse jumped in his car and drove to the hospital. The story was in the heart attack, not the ruined property. He knew the woman would tell him her life story if she could speak.

He gained access to Beatrice's bed in the emergency room with no problem. Two nurses recognized him and let him pass. He hurried down the hall and walked into the room without knocking. Beatrice was hooked up to intravenous lines, but she was able to speak. She burst into tears when Jesse introduced himself as a newspaper reporter. "Did you see what those terrible boys did to our garden?"

Ivan took her hand and turned to Jesse. "We've worked so hard on our property. We garden together. Somebody's got to stop those boys. They've ruined our lives and damn near killed my wife. Did you see what they did?"

Jesse stepped in to shake Ivan's hand. "Yes, I did. And it's absolutely terrible. I can't imagine how you two must feel. Especially you, Mrs. Brand. What are the doctors saying about your heart? Have you had trouble with it in the past?"

"Please call me Beatrice. I'm happy to meet you, Jesse Conover. Ivan and I read all your stories. We especially liked the one about the jail. But to answer your question, I've never had a heart problem. I'm fifty-three. I work full time as a manager in the meat department at Rogers Supermarket on Fairfield. Haven't missed a day of work in years. And now this. Thank God the doctors are telling me I'll be as good as new, but I don't think so. Those boys tore my heart apart when they ruined everything Ivan and I worked so hard to create. Now, it is true that things haven't been going all that well in our marriage. Ivan's been drinking too much, and he says I spend too much time at church. But we usually work things out in the garden . . ."

Ivan leaned over her bed. "Now, now, darling, we don't need to tell this nice young man everything there is to know. He's here about the vandalism, that's all."

Beatrice was not about to be quieted. "He's here about the heart attack. Those boys broke my heart, pure and simple. And please quote me on that."

Jesse was taking notes on his reporter pad. "Any idea who did it?"

Ivan and Beatrice answered in unison, "It's the Nahrwold boys."

The story ran under the headline, "Vandalism Shock Causes Coronary." The lead sentence was, "Those boys broke my heart."

Jesse tried to quote the Brands as accusing the Nahrwold boys, but Weatherly cut it out of the story. "We don't try to arrest people in the paper. If the cops think they're guilty, let them arrest the boys. Until then, we don't talk about it. And don't forget. They're juveniles. We wouldn't use their names in any event," he said.

The plight of Beatrice Brand struck a nerve within the community. Readers called the cops, but when that didn't work, they called the newspaper. Angry residents were fed up with kids getting away with what they called murder. The city desk was getting more than ten calls a day.

Weatherly walked Jesse down the hall outside the newsroom to teach him another lesson in journalism. "Stay on this story, Jesse. These people are fired up. There's going to be a neighborhood meeting soon where all hell will break loose. They'll be blaming the mayor and the police chief and anybody else they can think of. Find out when and where that meeting is going to be, and make sure you're the first one there and the last to leave. The best stories are the ones that hit closest to home. And this one is literally in everybody's backyard."

Weatherly's warning surprised Jesse. He thought the story had come and gone. But sure enough, one week later, more than fifty residents gathered for a heated two-hour meeting. Jesse was the only reporter there.

One homeowner after another told horror stories of the vandalism that had them living in fear in their own homes. A mob mentality had developed. The City Councilman for the district attempted to maintain order but lost control several times when tempers flared, and residents threatened vigilante justice.

One man shouted, "We know who these kids are. Their parents are never around to supervise, let alone discipline them. The police won't arrest them. Now they're threatening my kids. If one of my kids gets hurt, I'm gonna let somebody have it!"

He sat down to a round of wild applause from the crowd. Jesse had goose bumps from the anger in the room. Once the cheering died down, Beatrice Brand stood up to be heard. She was mostly recovered from her heart attack, but her voice was still weak. Ivan quieted the crowd so she could be heard.

"Good evening, neighbors. You all know who I am. I'm just plain old Beatrice, and I like to think of myself as a good Christian woman. That means I have to try to help these boys. And yes, we all know it's the Nahrwold kids. It's up to us to make them be civilized. So I want to share two things. Number one, Ivan and I have forgiven them. Number two, we've given the names of enough witnesses to the police so they can prosecute these kids like the juvenile delinquents they are. I'm told arrests will be made this week. So, let's not talk about taking the law into our own hands. It's already been done. They're going to jail or the youth center or wherever they put them."

Beatrice sat down to a standing ovation. Ivan held her hand. No one else felt the need to speak. The meeting ended shortly after her remarks. City Councilman Adam Johnson caught Jesse on his way out the door to try to get his name in the story. "Jesse, you can quote me on this. We're getting increased police protection in the area in case the vandals attempt to retaliate. There's strength in numbers like you've got here tonight."

The follow-up story ran under the headline, "Angry Citizens for Vigilante Justice." Jesse tracked the Nahrwold boys from their arrest through their convictions at trial and all the way to their incarceration at the Indiana Boys School. Weatherly made sure he stayed with it. "What you're learning is that stories don't really begin and end. They just evolve into new stories."

CHAPTER SEVENTEEN

The story of Jesse and Kelly was evolving. One Saturday morning at the farmers' market, Kelly had an idea that turned itself into a suggestion. "Why don't we have our mothers over for dinner?"

Jesse immediately recognized that Kelly was ready to take their relationship up a notch on the commitment scale. Part of him wanted to run out of the market, but another part thought it was a good idea. He had been to Kelly's mother's house many times for dinner and found her to be warm, welcoming, and a wonderful cook. It was time to return the favor. Besides, he needed to convince her he wasn't a whoremonger. Kelly had been to his parents' home. So, why not get the parents together?

He started adding six more ears of corn to the basket. "Sounds good to me. We can have corn on the cob and greens and salad, and you can make your famous pork roast."

Kelly threw her arms around him. "Oh, thank you so much, Jesse. We'll make it a night to remember."

It turned out to be a night nobody could forget. Jesse borrowed enough silverware from his 1114 mates to set a mix-and-match table in the living room. Kelly made the greens and pork roast, and Jesse made a giant tossed salad in a wooden bowl he'd borrowed from Butch.

Jesse's parents were first to arrive. His mother gave Kelly a big hug. "This place smells fabulous. And look at the table. You two have gone all out. I love it."

Jesse's father presented two bottles of wine. "I brought a white and a red, just in case."

Kelly was still wearing her cooking apron. "Thank you so much. We'll have those with dinner. And Jesse and I have two whites and two reds, just in case." His father laughed and gave her a hug that might have lasted a few seconds too long.

"I know you both like Manhattans," Kelly said. "And so does my mother. She'll be coming with Robby Wyman. He's a great piano player. You might have heard of him. He plays all over town and even in Chicago. Anyway, I made up a batch. Can I get us all a Manhattan?"

The cocktails were excellent, and the small apartment seemed more spacious by the time they were ready for a second round. Jesse's mother was beginning to catch enough of a buzz to ask Kelly an inappropriate question. "What happened to your father?"

Kelly was in the kitchen making drinks when she heard the question. She walked back into the living room and said, "I never knew my father. I understand he was a musician, but Mom never talks about him. He's never sent one dime of child support. Never came to visit."

Jesse glared at his mother, and she seemed to realize she'd been too forward with her question. Thankfully, his father changed the topic. "So, where's your mother? It's getting close to eight o'clock."

Five minutes later, they heard two people talking loudly as they walked up the stairs toward Jesse's apartment. By the time they arrived, the terrible truth was obvious to everyone in the room. Kelly's mother, Alberta, was highly intoxicated. Her date for the evening was trying to settle her down about something.

When Alberta entered the room, she tried but failed to keep her words from slurring. "Do you know where your daughter has been all day?" she addressed Kelly.

Kelly tried to avoid the question and her mother's state of

mind as she made introductions. "Mom and Robby, this is Max and Vaun Conover. They're Jesse's parents. And you know Jesse."

Max and Vaun were not surprised to hear that Kelly had a daughter. Jesse had discussed little Berta with his parents on several occasions and, while they were concerned about their son taking on the additional responsibility of a child, they were doing their best to remain open-minded and closed-mouthed on the subject.

Alberta regained her poise to shake hands all around. She was tall, thin, and elegant. It was easy to see where Kelly got her style. It looked for a minute like Alberta might be able to sober up, but then she whirled on Kelly and repeated the question about Kelly's daughter.

Kelly led her mother back into the kitchen. "I thought Berta was with you, Mom."

"You thought your daughter was with me?" Alberta said in a loud voice that everyone heard from the living room. "You thinking about something does not cut it. You got to know some things. For your information, she wandered over to the neighbors. I've been trying to call you all afternoon, thinking she might be with you. And what about that whore-dog boyfriend of yours? Doesn't he care about your daughter?"

Jesse made the mistake of going into the kitchen to get Robby a drink, and Alberta let him have it. "There he is now, Mr. Irresponsible. Don't you even give a damn about Kelly's daughter? I thought little Berta was with you today, but I guess I should have known better."

Jesse realized that Alberta wanted him to be more involved with Berta, even though he had never volunteered for the responsibility. The only time Jesse spent with Berta had been at Alberta's house for Sunday dinners.

"Did you find her?" Jesse asked.

"Yes, I did," Alberta said with such vehemence that Jesse felt her spit on his face. "And no thanks to you. She came wandering in about seven thirty. That's why we're late."

Jesse quickly made a drink, then went back into the living room to hand it to Robby. "How long has she been like this?" he asked.

Robby shook his head. "She was loaded when I picked her up. You know she's not like this. She must have been drinking over Berta going missing."

Kelly and her mother were shouting at each other in the kitchen. It wasn't a conversation anyone in the living room could understand. That's when Jesse's mother made her big mistake. She set down her second Manhattan and went back to the kitchen to make peace.

The shouting stopped and the three women seemed to be getting it together. Jesse couldn't hear what was being said until he heard his mother raise her voice. "It's not my son's job to take care of your granddaughter."

There was a brief lull in the conversation. Kelly and Alberta were clearly taken aback by his mother's comment. Alberta was the first to recover. Her tone started off stern and then rose to a high-volume shriek. "Oh, so you're going to come in here and tell me how to raise my children? Don't you dare even think about it. You better shut your mouth, or I'll shut it for you—you white, honkey bitch."

That was all Jesse needed to hear. He'd heard that same phrase come out of Kelly's mouth right before she became suddenly violent at Henry's. He leaped into the kitchen and got himself between his mother and Alberta. "Now, now, ladies, there's no need for that kind of talk. Robby, can you come in here, right now, please? I think it's time to take Alberta home. She's had a trying day."

Alberta was still combative and cursing everyone in the kitchen, which was not big enough to accommodate the five-person scrum. Jesse and Robby each grabbed Alberta by an arm and gave her the bum's rush out of the kitchen and through the front door of the apartment. Butch, in the apartment next door, watched in amazement as Robby forcibly escorted a still screaming Alberta out the main door of 1114.

Jesse followed Alberta and Robby, trying to be diplomatic. "We still love you, Alberta. I'm sorry about Berta. Thank you, Robby, for taking her home. We'll get together another time."

Jesse closed the door behind them and watched through the window as Robby struggled to get Alberta into his car. He knew she would be deeply embarrassed by this uncharacteristic moment, if she even remembered it. He walked back up the stairs and answered Butch's wide-eyed, unspoken question. "Kelly's mom got drunk and called my mom a white, honkey bitch. No big deal."

Butch nodded and smiled.

Jesse went back to his apartment. Everyone was sitting in the living room with a look of shock on their faces. He held out his arm wide. "Well, that went . . . great."

Jesse's mom started crying. "Oh, this is all my fault. I should never stick my big, nosey nose into somebody else's business."

Jesse held her in his arms. "No, Mom, you were only trying to help."

Kelly was crying too and joined in the hug. "I am so sorry about my mother. I've never seen her like that. I'm sorry she called you what she called you."

His mother took a step back, then folded in her husband's arm. "I guess that's what I am. I'm just a white, honkey bitch."

Jesse's father couldn't help but laugh. "No, that's not what you are. Good work, Jesse, breaking the mothers up. I think it's a good thing Alberta went home. We won't hold it against her, Kelly. These things happen. But I do think it's time for us to go home as well. It wouldn't be right for us to stay after Alberta and her friend had to leave."

Kelly started to protest, but Jesse convinced her that his father was right. His parents left after hugging both of them goodnight.

Kelly sat down on the couch and stared at Jesse. "I can't believe that just happened. I am so sorry. I haven't seen my mother like that in a long time. She's having trouble raising Berta for me. I don't know. Sometimes I think we should just have Berta come live with us."

CHAPTER EIGHTEEN

J esse worked a year and a half at the newspaper before taking his first weeklong vacation. He'd been too busy becoming a reporter and a musician and being in a demanding romantic relationship to think about taking time off. Once he thought about where he'd like to go, an idea took shape in his mind. It was something he could only do on his own.

He would hitchhike to Los Angeles the last week in August with only seven dollars in his pocket and do a series of travel articles titled, "A Dollar a Day to LA." The concept was a conscious effort to escape the pressure-cooker existence he had created for himself. The adventure was designed to be just what he needed: a way to get out of Fort Wayne on his own and take an overdue personal inventory.

Jesse decided to pitch the idea to Publisher Longstreet, to see if the paper would fly him back once he got to southern California. He made an appointment after he cleared the idea with Weatherly.

Longstreet leaned back in his chair and clasped his hands behind his head when he heard the proposal. "That's an idea I would buy into. You know I love your enthusiasm, Jesse. And I love the way you get into a story and write it from the inside out. But what makes you think you can do it in a week on only seven dollars? What happens if you run out of rides and money and die of thirst in the desert?"

"Then you get a refund on the plane ticket," Jesse said with a big grin. He was pretty sure he could do it. He'd hitchhiked thousands of miles in high school and college when he couldn't afford any kind of transportation. He knew the secret to hitch-hiking. It was the same lesson he was learning on a new level as a reporter. It was all about being a good listener.

He also understood the first rule of the road was to travel light. The backpack should weigh no more than thirty pounds so you could swing it into the back of a pickup truck or carry it on your lap. Jesse packed a good sleeping bag, a ground tarp, two changes of clothes, a canteen, a toothbrush, a stick of Old Spice deodorant, and a harmonica, key of C.

Not for publication, he added a daily ration of dried fruit and nuts, vitamins, and seven packs of cigarettes. He wore jeans and an army shirt, no underwear, and his black leather jacket to use as a pillow at night. He kept his wallet in the pack. He couldn't afford to lose it. It contained his driver's license, seven one-dollar bills, and an airline ticket. He wore sturdy hiking boots and packed two extra pair of socks. Jesse would be prepared for the *hiking* in hitchhiking.

It was beginning to rain when his first ride squealed to a halt on Interstate 69 to Indianapolis. Jesse piled into the front seat of a 1962 Chevrolet Impala and smelled alcohol on the driver's breath right away. "Rain's a good thing," the driver said. "It'll wash away your tracks." Jesse grunted in agreement as he wedged the pack between his legs.

The driver's name was Ralph. He introduced himself as an alcoholic who'd been up most of the previous night on a vodka binge. "Yeah, my wife put me in the nuthouse three times for the booze, but she left me for good about a month ago."

Ralph had a big belly that rubbed against the bottom half of the steering wheel when he got excited, explaining how his wife didn't understand him. His driving speed accelerated with his emotions up to ninety-five miles an hour. Jesse made no comment as a ranting Ralph passed cars like he was trying to win the Indy 500.

Jesse didn't mind. Ralph's driving wasn't erratic. And he was headed all the way to Indianapolis. He handed Jesse a bottle of vodka from under the driver's seat. "I got a disease. They call it 'organic brain syndrome.' Doc says I got less than a year. Wouldn't you keep drinking?"

Jesse took a pull and handed the bottle back. "I don't know how long I've got. Might be less than you. Who knows?"

Ralph took a big swig and began talking to himself. "You know, he's right. Maybe we ought to stop drinking. Maybe the wife had a point. Maybe I should get back to driving truck." He turned to Jesse. "What do you think? Should I back off the bottle?"

Jesse recognized a trick question when he heard one. "You'll quit drinking when you're ready. And if you're never ready, well, then you'll just keep drinking."

Ralph howled as he slapped the top of the dashboard. "Now that's the exact right answer."

Jesse laughed with him and took another big swig of vodka. Ralph chattered all the way to Indianapolis and ended up driving five miles out of his way to drop Jesse off at the exit to Highway 36. "Good luck, my friend. Don't take any wooden nickels."

Jesse got out of the car and started walking west, wondering if, deep down, every single person in the world was as self-centered and wounded as Ralph.

Choosing Route 36 from Indianapolis to Denver was a calculated risk. Jesse knew the rides would be short on the two-lane, blacktop highway. But at least the roadway would rise and fall with the countryside instead of knifing through the terrain with all the interstate highway charm of an invading army. The road would be a time machine back into the agricultural America of the 1950s when small towns were the rule rather than the exception. Besides that, state police across the country were beginning to arrest hitchhikers on the interstate.

The old highway did not let Jesse down. He didn't have to wait long between rides. People were friendly through the peaceful green hills of Indiana, where trees arched over the road and fishermen waited for action on their lines over brown rivers on painted iron bridges.

By 10:00 p.m., Jesse was stuck under the lights of an intersection in Springfield, Illinois. After two hours of watching headlights flash by, even playing harmonica couldn't ease the frustration. He dug into his pack and ate his first packet of dried fruit and nuts. So far, he hadn't spent a cent.

Jesse was walking down the road and away from the lights, looking for a place to unroll his tarp and sleeping bag, when a tired old man picked him up and offered him a warm beer. Once again, the driver wanted to talk about his failed marriage. Jesse listened politely until the man dropped him off in front of an abandoned mobile home court in Pittsfield. Was every marriage a disaster? Jesse wondered as he walked back into the darkness until he found a flat spot near a rundown garage with broken windows.

Before he put his pack down, he heard the deep, menacing growl of a big dog. It was close. Jesse couldn't tell if it was coming from inside or outside of the garage. Either way, he wasn't hanging around to find out. He ran back toward the road, unable to see where he was going. He didn't make it very far before bashing his leg into the fender of a junk car. The impact sent him sprawling, face first, into tall grass. The snarling and barking dog was getting closer. Jesse jumped back up and ran toward the road with his pack bouncing up and down on his back. He could almost feel the dog sinking its long teeth into his backside.

He made it to the road and turned around to face the beast. His heart was pounding. He picked up a rock and drew back his arm in a David-and-Goliath move. But there was no giant to smite. No snarling beast to slay. The dog had not followed him out of the darkness. Its barking didn't sound so dangerous in the distance.

He bent down to catch his breath and check out his leg. His jeans were torn. He had a five-inch gash, not too deep, on his right shin. It was starting to hurt, but Jesse hardly noticed. He was shaking from the escape. He pulled out a pair of socks and cleaned the wound as best he could with a little water from his canteen. Realizing he would need to seek better treatment in the morning, Jesse crept off to sleep in the backyard of the nearest home.

Jesse woke up to find a middle-aged woman in a baby-blue bathrobe staring at him as he was lying in her backyard behind the tomato plants. She looked at him with cautious curiosity, like she thought someone may have dropped a dead body off during the night. She hurried back inside the house. Jesse was still half-asleep when he saw her following her husband into the backyard to investigate. They stopped dead in their tracks when Jesse sat up to stretch. He looked at the surprised couple and realized he had some fast-talking to do.

"I'm sorry to be here. I'm a newspaper reporter from Fort Wayne, Indiana, doing a dollar a day to LA story. I'm a writer and I'm hitchhiking, and I'll get out of here right away."

The man approached cautiously. Once he realized Jesse was not a threat, he introduced himself. "No need to be in such a rush. I'm Jonas Johnson and this is my wife, Mildred. And you might be staying for breakfast. I've got a good friend who's an editor in Fort Wayne. Name's Kenny Allen. You know him?"

Jesse stood up in a hurry to shake the man's hand. "Do I know him? He's the Sunday editor. He's the one who'll be running my series on hitchhiking to Los Angeles."

"We'll give him a call while my wife makes breakfast," he said as he looked over Jesse for reaction.

Jesse was excited. "Yes, that would be great fun. I can't believe the coincidence. Kenny will love it. And to think, the only reason I ended up here was that guard dog over at the motor home."

Jonas looked down at Jesse's leg. "Let me go in and get my first aid kit." He looked more closely at the cut. "Yeah, I can handle this. We won't need a doctor. Did the dog bite you? We can't stand that animal. He barks all the time."

Jesse looked at the wound. "No, I ran into a car trying to get away from it."

Jonas straightened up and scowled. "You must have been pretty fast. That dog's on a thirty-foot chain. He's a mean one. And, like I said, he barks all day and half the night. He drives us crazy. They ought to tear down that old mobile home dump."

Jonas treated Jesse with soap and water and iodine that stung and a good bandage. The two talked about newspapers and the news of the day until coffee and food were served at the picnic table in the backyard. Breakfast was ham and eggs with toast and potatoes. Jesse had never tasted anything quite so good. It was salty and savory and satisfyingly homemade.

Mildred was pleased by Jesse's appetite. "You eat like you haven't had food in a week."

Jesse nodded with his mouth full until he could speak. "I've only been on the road for one day, but it feels like a week."

Jonas interjected. "You know, Pittsfield is the world's hog capital."

Jesse smiled. *Every place is the capital of something*, he thought. "That explains the ham. This might be the best ham I've ever had. And it's sliced nice and thick."

Mildred poured fresh coffee in their cups. "That's Pittsfield ham, best in the world."

After breakfast, they got Kenny Allen on the phone. Jonas talked to him for quite a while, and then handed the phone to Jesse. Kenny did all the talking. "What are you doing at the house of my old friends, Jonas and Mildred? They're great people, aren't they? Glad to see you made it safely to Pittsfield. Heard you hurt your leg. Weatherly's right. You are a con man. Trespass on somebody's lawn and scare them half to death and then get them to cook breakfast for you and doctor you up."

"I was nobody until I dropped your name," Jesse said.

"Keep it up, kid," Kenny said. "You better get a move on if you're going to make it to L.A. You've only got six days left and about two thousand miles to go."

Jesse left the Johnsons' warm hospitality shortly after breakfast with a promise to be careful. Arm in arm, they waved goodbye from the back porch of their white ranch-style home. Jesse felt something very reassuring about their kindness. It was nice to see at least one couple living happily ever after.

Two hours and five rides later, Jesse plopped down to play harmonica outside the Rocket, a truck stop west of Hannibal, Missouri. The notes were flowing freely and bending just right. He had just crossed the mighty Mississippi River and passed through Mark Twain's hometown. He was feeling pretty Tom Sawyer, full of mischief and ready for adventure.

Out of the corner of his eye, he noticed a young woman shuffling out of the restaurant. She looked like a cross between a hippie chick and a skid row Raggedy Ann doll. She had no shoes, just oversized socks. Her only piece of luggage was a lunchbox. Jesse called out to her, "You must be rich to afford restaurant food."

She came over and sat down next to him. She hung her head so low her dirty blonde hair touched the gravel driveway. "I've only got thirty-seven cents. They won't even let me use the restroom. I'm trying to get back home to Los Angeles. Everything got stolen at a truck stop in Ohio. The drivers treat me like I'm a hooker. And I'm not. I'm starving is what I am. You got anything to eat?"

Jesse gave her one of his daily rations of dried fruit and nuts. She took it from his hand with a look of profound gratitude. "This is the nicest thing anybody's done for me in a long, long time." She ate slowly from the bag, one nut at a time. "You mind if I save the rest of this for later?"

Jesse did not tell her he was headed for Los Angeles. He stood up and went into the truck stop to get change for a dollar. The woman was still eating one nut at a time when he came out and gave her fifty cents. "You can get a piece of cherry pie in there for fifty cents. Eat that and get an ice water and they'll let you use the restroom. Once you clean up, hang out near the gas pumps. Somebody will give you a ride."

She smiled, and Jesse realized that she was quite attractive beneath her road grime. She looked about eighteen years old.

She shifted into flirtation with a slight shrug of her right shoulder. "Can I come with you?"

Jesse shouldered his pack. "The problem with that is I don't have a car. I'm hitchhiking. That's a solo gig. What you need is somebody with a vehicle."

He walked to the road and turned around to watch her pulling her hair into a ponytail as she walked back into the restaurant. *Best fifty cents I ever spent*, he thought.

Rides were scarce until two teenaged boys picked him up around 4:00 p.m. They were from a private high school in Illinois, touring colleges in a 1973 Chevy Caprice station wagon owned by their parents. They immediately offered beer from the cooler between them in the front seat and passed a smoking joint to the back seat. As Jesse took a hit, the driver tried to pass a slow-moving farm truck. The passenger screamed at the oncoming traffic and the driver ducked back behind the truck just in time.

Both boys laughed hysterically at the near-death experience. Jesse took another hit to sooth his nerves. The ride was turning into something out of Jack Kerouac's *On the Road* with Neal Cassady driving and taking too many driving risks.

The rich kids dropped Jesse off outside Hiawatha, Kansas. He walked back into an isolated patch of forest, gathered wood, and built a fire in the middle of a circle of tall hackberry trees. Home was already becoming a pleasant memory. The tension of being on news alert began to fade from his body. He wondered how Kelly's night was going at the club. And how 1114 was faring in his absence. And what mayhem was making news in Fort Wayne.

The fire died down and the stars shined brightly through the trees. The heavenly light show covered the Kansas plains like a fluffy comforter. The night chill was crisp and clean. Jesse fell into a deep sleep.

He got many rides the next day and into the night until he was finally dropped off about one mile west of Bird City, Kansas, twenty-five miles from the Colorado line.

Hungry and ready for a hamburger instead of dried fruit and nuts, Jesse walked toward a red neon sign in the distance. It was going on 9:00 p.m. The light was the only sign of life in Bird City. He felt like an alien, casting no shadow in the empty world between the vast, rolling landscape of the Great Plains and the surreal infinity of the stars above.

When Jesse arrived after a long hike, the neon light turned out to be an all-night bar, restaurant, and gas station. He walked in, put his pack next to a bar stool, and talked the bartender into a beer and a burger for a buck. The beer was cold and frothy, and the burger arrived in short order. It was juicy and delicious and piled high with lettuce, tomato, onion, and pickles. He was beginning to feel human again when a farmer sat down and offered to buy him another beer.

Jesse was glad for the company. He knew the man needed to talk, and he was ready to listen to whatever story he had to tell. Turns out the farmer had been a tank commander in World War II, one of seven survivors out of a platoon of men. He talked about the German Tiger tanks and how they blew three Sherman tanks out from under him. He whispered when he recalled the brutal, Nazi S.S. troops. "Don't believe everything you see in the John Wayne movies. The war was a nightmare for me. Still is."

The farmer bought Jesse beer until the bar closed at midnight. The two men shook hands in a silent goodbye. Jesse stumbled out into the darkness and spread his tarp out in a nearby field.

His three days on the road had been filled with compelling tales told by total strangers. Since none of these people knew he was a reporter, Jesse realized that his ability to get people talking had nothing to do with being in the news business. It was all about listening. Or more importantly, about asking the right questions.

Rides were scarce the next day in western Kansas. It was so hot Jesse made footprints in the asphalt for entertainment. Worse than the heat, the flies had apparently mistaken him for a pile of manure.

A big-rig trucker squealed to an airbrake halt to give him a lift. Jesse had to light up a cigarette in self-defense in the smoke-filled cab. The driver chain-smoked his way across the barren flatlands of eastern Colorado until the Rocky Mountains appeared in the distance through the bug-spotted windshield. They looked more like clouds than giant rock formations.

The driver kept up his running commentary. "They look good from here, but they're no fun when you're driving this big ol' gal through them in the snow."

As they bounced into the outskirts of Denver on the truck-worn road, a jet plane screamed across the highway, taking off from the nearby airport. After days on a rural highway, the city seemed frantic to Jesse. The mountains that had looked so dignified from a distance had their majesty tarnished through the industrial haze. From close range, they looked more patient than proud.

The trucker dropped Jesse off on the west side of Denver. Traffic was heavy but nobody was stopping. Jesse knew he was in trouble. He'd heard the Denver police were hard on hitchhikers. Sure enough, a squad car with a flashing red light pulled over and slowed to a near stop, forcing Jesse off the road and stopping on the spot where he had been standing. The cop got out of his car, all spit and polish, reflector sunglasses, and shiny badge. He rested his hand on the butt of his pistol and laid down the law.

"Don't you know hitchhiking is completely illegal in Colorado?"

Jesse had his hands up in surrender. "I'm from Indiana, and I've only got four dollars and fifty cents left to get to California."

The cop folded his arms across his big belly. "Maybe you need to get a job like everybody else so you can afford transportation. Tell you what, you get off this highway right now and, if I catch you back up here, I'm hauling you in."

Jesse was relieved to hear he wasn't being arrested. "You mean I have to walk all the way out of Colorado?"

The cop took off his sunglasses like he thought Jesse was sassing him. "That's about the size of it. The only way you can get a ride is if somebody stops to offer it. But you can't be on the highway, and you can't be sticking your thumb out."

As the officer was raising his voice, a longhaired young man pulled his Volkswagen bus behind the squad car and yelled out the window, "Excuse me officer, but does this gentleman need a lift?"

The cop did a double take and then turned on Jesse with a hateful stare. When Jesse responded with an innocent shrug, the officer turned his wrath on what he saw as the interfering driver. "Well since you're so kind, and now that you're here, let's see your driver's license, inspection sticker, and vehicle registration."

The Good Samaritan passed the officer's tests. Jesse jumped

in the bus and they drove off without waving goodbye. The driver explained to Jesse that he had been a police officer himself for a short time. "The laws are such bullshit I just couldn't enforce them. You're lucky I came along. They're throwing people in jail for hitchhiking. How bad is that?"

They talked about how the police were getting too powerful until the Volkswagen bus driver took Jesse up into the mountains on I-70 west and dropped him off. "You'll be good up here. The cops are only bad down in the city."

Within minutes of sticking out his thumb, a beautiful twenty-six-year-old woman named Marilyn picked Jesse up. She wanted to talk about the bad marriage she was leaving. Hearing about a breakup from a woman's point of view was pretty much the same as listening to a man. The story was always about how crazy the other person had been.

Marilyn was looking for someone to take her camping. "I'm not even sure I can get a fire going." She said it like she was talking about something more than a campfire.

Near Glenwood Springs, Marilyn pulled into a scenic stop along a river that had a perfect swimming hole behind a rock formation. She looked around and saw no other people. "Let's go skinny dipping."

Jesse hadn't had an offer like that in . . . maybe never. Instead of thinking things through, he stripped down and waded into the cold water without hesitation. He needed to wash away four days of road grime. Marilyn got naked and waded in right behind him. She was pert and perfect without clothes. She threw her arms around his neck and kissed him on the lips. A pleasure jolt ran down the length of his spine.

She backed off and they played in the water like they'd known each other since childhood. She had a bar of soap she was only too willing to share. Washing each other's backs was turning into a full-blown sexual event until several other bathers arrived. Jesse and Marilyn splashed the soap off each other and got out of the water. They were laughing together as the newcomers stared at them in amazement.

By the time they were getting dressed, Marilyn was already planning their trip to Aspen. "We can rent a cabin by a stream outside of town and stay for the rest of the summer." She was getting ahead of herself and way too far out for Jesse.

Tempted though he was, he had to pull his pack out of her car and set the record straight. "I can't stay with you. Much as I'd like to. I've got to get to LA. It's a thousand miles away. I've got to get going. Unless, of course, you'd like to take me there."

Marilyn considered the California proposition longer than Jesse thought she would, but she eventually decided on heading to Aspen by herself. She gave Jesse a quick hug, got in her car and drove off, leaving him on the highway faster than he could even think about how to say goodbye. As he watched her car disappear down the road, Jesse wondered if the dizzying experience had even been real.

The hitchhike from western Colorado to California became a complete blur. He had to walk five miles through Grand Junction, sleep under his tarp in the rain in Utah, and ride all night through the desert to Las Vegas. Near the end of the journey, Jesse was running out of emotional and physical endurance when he found himself in an impossible situation.

He was stuck on Highway 1, near Palo Alto, California. It was late at night. The road was winding tightly, and the ocean fog was thick. There was a cliff on one side and a rock wall on the other. There was no place for a car to pull over and give him a ride. Vehicles swerved at the last second to miss him by inches as they passed. Drivers honked their horns like it was his fault conditions were so dangerous.

He thought about how sad it would be to have come so far and gotten so close to LA only to be wiped out on the last leg of his trip by a skidding sports car. But this wasn't his first hitchhike. He knew his luck would change. It had to change in a hurry if he was going to make his flight back to Indiana the next day.

That night, he rolled up in his tarp as best he could and slept behind a road sign for some protection from oncoming traffic. By morning, he was soaking wet and shivering uncontrollably from the Pacific chill. He knew it would take a miracle or two to make it to the airport on time. Even so, he had the distinct feeling he was going to get lucky.

Sure enough, a yoga teacher with a heart of gold risked her life to stop and pick him up. She chatted about meditation on the way to Big Sur. A counselor from the Esalen Institute picked him up next and took him all the way to Santa Barbara. Then a wine salesman from Laguna Beach went way out of his way to drop him off at the airport terminal.

Jesse made it to the Los Angeles International Airport one hour before his on-time flight was scheduled for departure. He was out of cigarettes and dried fruit, but he still had a dollar in his wallet.

CHAPTER NINETEEN

By the time Jesse made it back to 1114, he needed a vacation from his vacation. The action-packed week on the road boggled his mind. Every person he met had a story to tell and a strong need to tell it.

Kelly was waiting for him in nothing but a teddy when he dragged his backpack into the apartment. She threw her arms around him and they kissed deeply. She danced away as his hands slid down her backside. "Let's get you in the shower. You smell like Nevada and half of California."

Jesse was all soaped up when Kelly joined him in the shower that was too small for two and pressed her naked warmth against him. "Let me show you how much I missed you," she said as she helped him rinse off and escorted him into the bedroom. She kissed her way down his chest and stomach. Jesse entered a swirling world of sensuality as she took him into her mouth and gently caressed the rest of his body with hands of silk. It was almost too much for him. He had to back away and hold her at arm's length. "Let *me* show *you*," he said.

They rolled into bed and took their tender time with each other until their emotions kicked into hot and heavy. They were slick with sweat. Kelly's moans turned into deep groans as Jesse plunged into her deeply and felt himself slipping past the point of no return.

They shuddered and gasped into each other as the Earth ceased rotating on its axis. Jesse understood the meaning of life as he became one with the universe. Kelly kissed him on the lips. He wanted to stay inside her forever. She smiled as he opened his eyes and fell into hers.

No words were spoken. They were out of breath. Jesse finally lay down beside her. They fell into a sweet slumber of satisfaction.

The sun was streaming through the window and lighting up Kelly's face like an angel. Jesse rolled over and looked at his watch. It was a little after ten. He got out of bed, careful not to disturb her, and went straight to the front room for his guitar. It surprised him to realize that he had missed playing music as much as he had missed Kelly.

Playing harmonica on the road had been musical enough, but it was tough to sing along when you were sucking and blowing on a C harp. He couldn't wait to get his hands back on the six strings. The case creaked open and emitted its musty aroma of wire and wood and sweat and marijuana. He picked up the guitar like a mother picks up a baby from its crib.

It fit perfectly on his right leg as he sat on the couch. He removed the pick from the strings and played an open E string. It resonated beautifully even though he could tell it was flat. He tuned up the instrument, using the harmonica as a pitch pipe. His fingers quickly found their way on the fretboard. In about an hour, he was playing and singing like he'd never missed a beat.

After Kelly had showered and spent her considerable time getting ready for the day, she came into the living room, looking beautiful. "You get back on that guitar like a junkie on dope. You're making me feel like a rock-and-roll widow," she said, sounding jealous.

"Don't be silly, baby." Jesse set the guitar on the couch and stood up to give her a hug. "Come on, now. Look how gorgeous you are."

Jesse felt triumphant to be back in the newsroom. He was comfortable in the writing arena that had once been so intimidating. It was good to see the reporters who had become his friends. Everybody gathered around and peppered him with questions about the cross-country hitchhike. Even Weatherly got up from his desk to join in the fun.

"So, you conned your way across the country and made it back in time for work. I'm impressed. Good to see you made it in one piece. And by the way, you're on cops today," Weatherly said.

"So much for being a big-time feature writer," Chuck laughed. "Welcome back to reality."

Sherman put his arm around Jesse. "Glen's off this week so you got cops Monday and Tuesday and I got it the rest of the week. Should be a slow news day today. It's Monday. Maybe we'll do a little Wayne Newton Fan Club meeting later."

Melissa walked by Jesse's desk and ignored him in the most obvious way possible. She looked away as she called out, "Oh, Mr. Weatherly, can I speak with you for a moment about the zoo story?"

Sherman and Chuck rolled their eyes at Melissa's cold-shoulder routine. Chuck called her on it. "Melissa, aren't you going to welcome Jesse back to the newsroom?"

She turned and acted surprised to see the three of them staring at her. "Oh, you boys know I don't do that kind of thing."

"What, you're too busy getting into bar fights with women?" Sherman scoffed.

A groan of disapproval went up from the ten reporters

within earshot. It was clearly a low blow even though the fight between Melissa and Kelly at Henry's had reached legendary status in the newsroom.

"Oh please, people," Chuck said. "What? Too soon to talk about it? Or don't we all know that Melissa can dish it out, but she can't take it?"

Melissa stomped over to Weatherly's desk, whispered in his ear, and pointed her finger at Jesse and his pals.

Jesse got up quickly and went over to Weatherly's desk. "Listen, Melissa, I don't want any hard feelings here. Why don't we—"

"Why don't you shut your mouth and go back to your desk? We're having a private conversation here." Melissa spit out her words like she was aiming for his face.

Weatherly intervened. "Hey, hey, you two. Why don't you both get back to work. We don't have time for this petty bullshit. We've got a paper to put out."

Jesse went back to his desk and sat down to read the morning and afternoon papers. He needed to catch up on what had been going on around town. Melissa's imperious attitude was hard to believe. She was biding her time to exact her revenge. *Good luck with that*, he thought. *Wait until you read the hitchhike series. That's really going to drive you crazy.*

The rest of his shift was uneventful. Nothing much was happening on the police beat as Jesse made his rounds from the jail to the detective bureau to the sheriff's office. A few arrests for drunken antics and drug possession, the usual.

By 8:30 p.m., he was wondering what he could turn into a story when news came over the police scanner that a private plane had crashed near the airport. Weatherly heard about it and had one word for Jesse. "Go."

Jesse grabbed a notebook and pen and ran out the door to

jump in his car, too excited to coordinate with a photographer. He knew the way to the airport, but he would have to follow the lights of emergency vehicles to locate the crash scene. He didn't know how big the plane was or how many people were on board. It was a private plane so there couldn't be that many.

His heart was beating hard as he clenched the steering wheel and felt the familiar rush of big-news adrenalin. He was high on the real thing, chasing down a story. But this wasn't just any story; it was a plane crash. He'd never covered one. This would be front-page news for sure.

Then it hit him as he caught sight of two ambulances and a firetruck speeding down the highway. He was getting excited and having a good time while people—real human beings— were dying in a farmer's field. Or maybe the crash hadn't been fatal? Either way, it didn't matter. Other people's tragedy had become his idea of a good time.

A fleeting notion caught up with him. The world was all about him. Nothing mattered except *his* story. No matter how many bodies they found, *his* byline would still be on the front page. Being a reporter had twisted his mind and numbed him to any kind of human suffering. The world was now nothing but one big story to Jesse.

He didn't have time to search his soul or make any resolutions about helping others instead of feeding off their misery. The closer he got to the accident scene, the more he became entangled in a traffic jam of emergency vehicles. There were so many flashing lights and screaming sirens it felt like the world was coming to an end.

He parked his car on the side of the road and started walking as he saw a bright white spotlight fifty yards into a soybean field. He stumbled on the uneven and muddy ground as it occurred to him what he was about to witness. This wasn't going to be pretty. It was going to be blood and guts, human meat and dismemberment messy.

"Hey, buddy, where do you think you're going?" a fire captain shouted at him.

"Hey, Chief Dafforn, it's me, Jesse Conover from the *Journal Gazette*."

"Didn't know it was you, Jesse. Brace yourself. They haven't covered the bodies."

Jesse stepped into the brightly lit accident scene and sucked in his breath. A decapitated human head, bloody beyond recognition, was resting on the crushed and flattened landing gear. What looked to have been the body was mangled into hamburger meat on the broken left wing of the single engine plane. What was left of the cockpit had the stench of death and disemboweled human organs. It smelled like diarrhea, vomit, and badly spoiled meat. He had to back away to keep from puking.

There was a stillness in the air that felt like spirits departing this world. Jesse slipped out of reporter mode and regained his humanity momentarily. He was floating, happy and sad at the same time, making some kind of connection with the victims. The grief their loved ones were certainly going to feel made him look up to the sky. The moon was half full and shining sadly.

The silence was broken by shouts from a member of the search team. "We've got another one over here!"

Jesse didn't walk over. He didn't want to see another pile of carnage.

Medics began covering the bodies with plastic tarps. It was too soon for body bags. Remains would have to be scooped up as they were tentatively identified.

The plane was ripped apart. It no longer looked like an aircraft. The tail was sticking straight up in the mud, twenty yards from the rest of the twisted wreckage. Camping gear was scattered far and wide. There was no fire at the scene. A Civil Air Patrol member speculated the plane ran out of gas. He said he couldn't smell fuel in the plane's wing tanks.

As Jesse was taking notes, a heavyset man with a bald head and bushy gray sideburns wearing bib overalls and carrying a huge flashlight grabbed him by the arm. "I saw the whole thing. I saw it all." He looked at the wreckage rubble and had to turn away as the last bloody body was being covered. "Oh my God, I saw it all. Those poor people."

Jesse walked him out of the light, stunned to have an eyewitness find him instead of the other way around. "It's okay. Don't look at it. There's nothing we can do now."

The man cried as he told his story. "I was in the den watching television. It was about 8:30 p.m. I know because there was a commercial on, and I looked at the clock when I heard a plane coming in way too low. We're not that far from the airport, but this thing was . . . I thought it was going to blast right into the house. And then it sounded like it was circling away. It was loud until it made a funny sound like it was sputtering.

"I got up and ran outside, yelling at my wife and son to get in the bathroom and hide in the tub. I looked up and the plane was circling back so low I could see it from the little light on the back porch. And then it just fell out of the air like somebody dropped it. It went down, nose first. Made a thud you could hear half a mile away. It shook the ground under my feet. It didn't explode. There was just a very small flash. I saw it all. It wasn't fifty yards from my house."

The man sat down on his haunches to keep from falling over. "Oh my God! Those poor people! How many died? Nobody could have survived. That plane fell straight down. It didn't glide. It wasn't anything like I thought an airplane would look.

"I ran back in the house and called the police. Then my son and I walked back into the bean field with a flashlight. I been farming that land my whole life. We were afraid of what we were going to find. Once we saw the plane totally disintegrated and what was left of the bodies, we headed back to the house in a hurry. It was scary in a weird way. I guess what was so spooky was how quiet everything was."

"What did you tell your wife once you got back to the house?" Jesse asked.

The man stood up straight. "Well, my son did most of the talking. He told his mother nobody was alive out there in the field. She hugged me and we both started crying and hugging. Then my son joined in. We're not the crying kind. It just hit us hard and all of a sudden. Like it could be us dead if that plane hit the house."

"How are you feeling now?"

"I don't know. Lucky to be alive, I guess. Sorry it happened. Wondering who those people are . . . or were. Oh, God, I saw it happen right in front of me with my own two eyes. I wish I could unsee that plane falling out of the sky. I'll probably be seeing it for the rest of my life. It went into slow motion there for a second. It was terrible, like it wasn't really happening. I guess I'm just going to have to accept it. There's nothing I can do about it now. There never was anything I could do about it."

Jesse wrote down his name and address. The man grabbed his arm again. "You're with the *Journal Gazette*, aren't you?" Jesse nodded. The man let go of his arm. "You can quote me on all that. And tell the police they can come to the house if they want to talk. I've got to sit down and have a beer, or maybe two or three."

Jesse looked back into the blinding light of the rescue operation, which had turned into a recovery effort. Somehow, he had to find out who died. Dean Sorenson arrived on the scene and managed to snap a few photos of the wreckage and the plastic-covered bodies before officials began clearing the scene. A crowd had gathered along the roadway and in the field.

Jesse and Dean walked back through the muddy fields to the road and returned to the newspaper, Dean to develop film and Jesse to question aviation sources by telephone. The chief controller at the airport tower said he had two-way contact with the plane before it crashed. He heard no sounds of panic in the plane or from the pilot. The plane was a six-seater Cherokee, and the pilot was a local businessman on the way home from a camping trip in Colorado with his three daughters and a neighboring girl.

Jesse was surprised when the controller identified the victims and their ages. The pilot was forty-one-year-old Robert Daniels, a Chevrolet dealership owner, well known by way of his ubiquitous television commercials. The celebrity of the victim made the plane crash a much bigger story. Passengers were his daughters, Susan, fifteen, Jackie, twelve, and Jennifer, six. The other victim was a neighbor, also named Jennifer, twelve.

Weatherly made him call the widow for comment. Mercifully, she didn't answer the phone.

The city editor was uncharacteristically impressed with Jesse's story. "Boy, you're home one day and you track down an eyewitness account of a local celebrity in a fatal plane crash. That's getting back in the saddle with style. I can't believe you got the names of the victims. And how on God's green earth did you find the one guy who saw the whole thing?"

"He came up to me in the bean field next to the wrecked plane and started crying," Jesse said.

Weatherly tilted his head in surprise.

Jesse continued. "I wasn't feeling the story until I saw that farmer crying. I was too busy chasing the facts. He was a big, burly guy wearing work boots and overalls. He was embarrassed to be overcome by emotion. I could tell by the way he kept trying to wipe away his tears."

"How about you?" Weatherly asked. "Did you shed a tear for those people in the field?"

Jesse shook his head. "I felt sad, but I didn't cry." He hung his head a little and lowered his voice. "Do you ever feel like we make a living on other people's misery?"

Weatherly looked at him like a concerned coach. "You can't get emotionally involved in a story. That's the subjective part you get so caught up in. But that's not what being a reporter is all about. Journalism is about being objective. It doesn't matter if what you see makes you happy or sad. If it's news, we write about it. If a dog bites a man, that's not news. Happens every day. But when a man bites a dog—now that's news, and we don't worry about how much he hurt the dog."

Jesse nodded and began thinking out loud. "Hard to believe Robert Daniels is gone. I wonder if they'll still run all his crazy commercials on television. Should I do a separate story on him?"

Weatherly smiled. "Way ahead of you. Melissa Franken's doing a sidebar on him that'll probably run longer than the plane crash story if I can make room for it."

CHAPTER TWENTY

Jesse was busier than ever after his hitchhiking story and working through the trauma of the plane crash. The news stories were getting so weird it felt like the world was turning upside down.

The school beat was heating up as racial imbalance collided with federal quotas. School bus drivers were being attacked by unruly students. The Ku Klux Klan was rearing its ugly head. Rattlesnakes were biting preachers, and heroin addicts were turning to methadone.

To complicate matters further, his weekly musical gigs with Butch at Mother's were getting more popular. The two of them were rehearsing more than ever and writing new songs. Dreams of rock-and-roll stardom were beginning to feel possible. They talked about adding a third member to sing high harmony and wondered if they should book time in a studio to record their songs.

None of this went over very well with Kelly. "Do you even care how I feel anymore, Jesse?"

He tried to hug her, but she backed away and put her hands on her hips. He knew he needed to respond. "Of course, I care, but I can't talk about it right now. I'm late for work."

She let go a parting shot as he walked out the door and down the stairs. "I'll tell you how I feel. I feel like a third wheel. That's how I feel."

Jesse knew better than to turn around and argue with her. It was Saturday, and he was headed for the newsroom to write the second article of what would be at least a ten-part series on the cross-country trip. The article wouldn't be published until weeks later when the Sunday features section had room to run it.

He was already writing in his head as he got in the car. The sad truth was he couldn't write at home. Something about the apartment was beginning to feel quite crowded.

Meanwhile, the national news was earthshaking. On September 8, 1974, President Gerald Ford granted a full pardon to former president Richard Nixon, the only United States president to resign from office.

Weatherly had previously assigned Jesse to get the local reaction story to Nixon's resignation on August 8. The "pardon" story turned out to be pretty much the same as the "resignation" story. Nixon supporters thought the resignation was bad and the pardon was good. Nixon haters, predictably, felt exactly the opposite.

The interesting thing to Jesse was that people from all points on the political spectrum now viewed the media as *making* news instead of simply reporting it. Nixon people hated Woodward and Bernstein and the *Washington Post,* and blamed them for bringing down their beloved president by using an unnamed source known only as Deep Throat.

Nixon haters, on the other hand, turned Woodward and Bernstein into national heroes. Reporters were becoming as popular as their stories. The rising ranks of the counterculture loved the mysterious anonymity of Deep Throat and its roguish reference to the pioneering pornographic movie of the same name. Jesse had quickly learned the importance of anonymous sources. Very few people from any profession were willing to talk "on the record" anymore.

He went door to door in all kinds of neighborhoods and reported on how deeply the country was divided, politically and personally. But the real news was how bifurcated society was becoming in its opinion of the media. At one house, Jesse was welcomed in as a champion of the people. At the next home, the door was slammed in his face.

Weatherly had a swift rebuke when Jesse tried to write about the emerging and polarizing influence of the news media. "Let's not make us more of the story than we already are."

The world seemed to be falling apart at the seams in the fall of 1974, as far as Jesse could tell. Nowhere was this more evident than in student attacks on school bus drivers. Jesse had heard rumblings from the teachers' union that students were becoming progressively more disruptive on the buses. Teachers had long been complaining of an overall decline in student behavior. They blamed school administrators and parental lawsuits for taking away teachers' rights to discipline students in the classroom.

Jesse hadn't been able to pinpoint an incident of school bus violence until he got a call one afternoon from a young girl, who refused to identify herself. She said a school bus driver had been attacked by students and injured in front of Elmhurst High School on the school district's southwest side.

Jesse jumped in his car and ran red lights as fast as he could all the way to the scene. He arrived at the school office in time to interview the bus driver, an angry and still crying Stella Miller. "What happened to your face?"

Stella sniffled and looked around to make sure no one else was listening. "There was a Black boy wanting to sit next to a white girl. She wouldn't move over and he wouldn't sit down, so I stopped the bus and tried to get him to sit down. He wouldn't take a seat, and a bunch of students started calling me names. I decided to take them back to school and turn them over to the principal."

"What happened to your face?"

Stella's face was badly scratched and bruised. Her nose looked broken. She was short and heavyset. Her entire body jiggled when she cried. "I sent one student in to get the principal and held the door shut so no one could leave. That's when a big white girl jumped me and clawed my face with her long fingernails, and two boys—I don't know what race they are—gave me a bloody nose and beat me on the head."

Jesse grabbed a phone on the nearby desk and called for a photographer.

Stella continued, "They pushed me back into the driver's seat. It turned into a mob attack. I'm pretty strong, though, and I was able to fight my way out of the corner."

"Shouldn't you get some ice on that face?" Jesse asked.

"I was told to wait here," she said. "I don't know what's going on. All the kids have run off by now, I'm sure."

Just then, the principal walked into the room and demanded Jesse identify himself. He was wearing a rumpled brown suit-coat and a shirt with no tie. When he found out Jesse was a reporter, he exploded in an immediate rage. "We don't talk to the press about this kind of thing," he shouted at Stella. "You know better than this."

Then the little tyrant turned his wrath on Jesse. "And you! You get the hell out of here right now. You're trespassing. I will call the police. This is a private matter."

Jesse held his ground. "This is a public school. There has been an attack on one of your bus drivers. Why don't you go ahead and call the police? This is a criminal matter. I'll wait right here. The public has a right—"

The principal wasn't about to have an argument with an intruder from the press. He quickly lowered his head and tried to push Jesse out of the small room. It didn't work. Jesse outgunned him by thirty pounds and twenty-five years. The man's leather-soled penny loafers with no pennies began to lose traction on the linoleum floor as Jesse pushed back.

This wasn't the first time Jesse had been shoved around by principals. He flashed back to Miss Lancaster slamming him into the lockers for no good reason when he was eight. Or maybe she had several good reasons. Once she retired, Mr. Johnson took over the child abuse chores. By junior high school, a smart-mouthed Jesse Conover was being sent to a new principal's office every year for all kinds of paddling and verbal abuse.

Jesse had to wonder at the judicious turn of events as he held the furious principal at bay by pushing back on his reddening bald head. He scolded the principal. "Now, *you're* breaking the law and *I'm* calling the police."

The principal realized he couldn't overpower the reporter. He took his hands off Jesse and stormed out of the room.

Stella's eyes were wide. She couldn't believe anybody was standing up to the principal, her ultimate authority. "He's going to call the police, you know."

Jesse shrugged his shoulders like he didn't care.

Stella looked over her shoulder. She was having second thoughts. "Maybe I shouldn't be in here talking to you."

"Or maybe you should," Jesse said. "How else is this going to stop?"

Stella nodded and let her story out in a confessional torrent.

"One of the drivers on the junior high route got punched so hard she lost three false teeth. It's going on all over. Ask any driver. Oh no, that won't work. They won't talk to you for fear of getting fired."

Jesse sat down in a chair next to her. "So, tell me about yourself. How long have you been with the schools?"

"Fifteen years I been driving. Students have been getting more unruly for the last ten years. I'm forty-nine years old and I've got six children. None of them would ever behave like those evil kids on my bus. I'll tell you what. My husband's going to have a fit when he sees what those brats did to my face. And I'll tell you another thing. The next time something like this happens, someone's going to look as bad as I do now. I don't care if they are underage. I'm going to protect myself."

Stella was still talking when the principal returned with a police officer in tow. "There he is, Officer. That's the trespasser who tried to push me out of my own school."

Jesse shook his head and pointed at the principal. The officer turned to Stella, the only neutral witness. "What did you see?"

Stella looked like she was under hot lights in an interrogation cell. She breathed deeply and gulped audibly. "Well, now, Officer, I've got to tell the truth. I don't want to lose my job, but I've got to tell the truth." She pointed to the principal. "He's the one who started pushing. The reporter might have pushed back, but it was the principal who started it."

The principal glared at Stella. "How dare you lie to the police, Stella. You go on and tell him how this man who doesn't belong in our school tried to push me out of my own building."

Stella shook her head sadly. "But that's not what happened, and you know it."

The principal slapped his open hand on a student desk. "You don't give me much choice here, Stella. I don't like doing this, but I have to. You're fired. Not for what happened on the bus. For lying to the police."

Jesse put his hand on Stella's shoulder to comfort her. "She's telling the truth, Officer. He attacked me." Then he spoke to the principal. "You firing her for telling the truth is going to look pretty bad in the morning paper. I can see the headline now." Jesse held out his hands as if the words might appear out of thin air. "'Principal Attacks Reporter. Fires Bus Driver for Telling the Truth.'"

Jesse took a threatening step toward the principal. "I'll bet you won't be able to push people around to get out of that unprofessional can of worms."

The principal's face was getting so red it looked like he might be having a stroke.

Jesse broke the medically induced silence. "But I'll make you a deal. I won't press charges on you, and I won't write about your little temper tantrum if you let Stella keep her job."

The principal sputtered something that sounded like an agreement and marched out of the room without saying another word. The police officer looked at Jesse and smiled. "Sounds like a good deal to me."

Jesse wrote the story like the incident with the principal never happened. But he did call at least a dozen bus drivers who told him how bad the problem of student attacks on drivers had become. The fact that they all requested to remain anonymous made good copy and told another story altogether.

It felt good not backing down to that bastard, Jesse thought. *But I threatened him with the power of the press. Yes, I did it to save Stella's job. But I changed my story to keep a deal with a bully. The power of the pen is going to my head. No doubt about it. I've got to be more careful in the future not to abuse my position with the newspaper. It's already starting to make me feel invincible.*

Two days after the school bus driver story, Jesse found himself writing the lead sentence to another story that proved the truth was stranger than fiction. "A rattlesnake worship service ended in tragedy last night, leaving a thirty-two-year-old man in serious condition from a poisonous snakebite at Parkview Memorial Hospital."

Jesse made it to the Hiway Holiness Church of God on Orange Drive while most of the twenty-five persons who participated in the service were still milling about after the ambulance transported the snakebite victim.

The head pastor was a man in his thirties with slicked-back hair, suspenders, and a white shirt with a clip-on bow tie dangling off the left collar. "This has hurt my heart," he said, fighting back tears. "Elmer is very close to me. Maybe God didn't want him to handle the snake tonight. God never makes mistakes."

As hospital officials were scurrying around the city to locate a special serum for intravenous therapy, Jesse asked the obvious question. "Why are you using rattlesnakes in church?"

The pastor raised his right hand with his index finger pointing to the sky like he'd been waiting his entire life to answer that question. "Pick up your Bible and read it. Mark 16:18, King James Version, 'They shall take up serpents; and if they drink any deadly thing, it shall not hurt them; they shall lay hands on the sick, and they shall recover.'"

Members of the congregation gathered around Jesse as their pastor spoke. Jesse was feeling surrounded as he asked another obvious question. "So, what went wrong tonight?"

The pastor held up his hands to quiet a murmur of disapproval from his followers. "The Lord works in mysterious ways. In that sense, nothing went wrong tonight. Elmer's been handling snakes for two years and never got bit. I don't know. We've got eight rattlers for this church. Maybe the one that bit him didn't get his share of the food tonight."

The thought of eight rattlesnakes for one little church made Jesse look nervously around the floor. "Or maybe if you play with fire, you're going to get burned."

A short, elderly woman wearing a shawl stepped up to Jesse and shook her finger in his face. "The only people who will certainly burn are the non-believers. And you sound like one of them."

The pastor quickly escorted Jesse out of the church as the congregation began to boil with self-righteous indignation. "We'll pray for you," several parishioners shouted after them.

The pastor was trying to explain how he'd been involved with snake services since he was a child as Jesse jumped in his car and left the scene. It was way past time to flee the snake pit. He shivered as he stepped on the gas. He'd always had an unnatural fear of snakes. He looked in the back seat to make sure they hadn't put one in his vehicle.

Back at the newsroom, Weatherly jumped out of his chair as he read the copy. "Oh, come on, now. Eight rattlesnakes for one little church. You're making this stuff up as you go."

Several reporters turned to watch Jesse's reaction. He stood up at his desk and held up his hand like he was being sworn in to testify in a court of law. "Swear to God" was all he said.

Weatherly waved him off. "All right. All right. I believe you. Just make sure you follow up tomorrow. I want to know if the rattlesnake bite killed the preacher, or whatever you want to call him."

"He's going to live. I already checked."

Weatherly raised his voice to completely fill the newsroom.

"Don't you think you ought to put that in the story? It's kind of like the most important part. Oh, never mind, I'll put it in myself."

"It's already in there, after the intravenous treatment thing. See, it says he's expected to survive," Jesse said.

"Oh, right," Weatherly said. "Well, you've got to make it more obvious. I'll say it again for the last sentence. Here's how you do it. 'By 11:00 p.m. last night, hospital sources listed the patient in serious but stable condition.'"

CHAPTER TWENTY-ONE

Butch and Jesse's gigs at Mother's on Friday and Saturday nights were always well attended. Media reporters, Larry Borne's theater people, Jayne Milson's restaurant workers, Charles Allen's dancers, and the creative crowd from 1114 and the West Central neighborhood showed up regularly.

People didn't come just to hear the music. They crowded in to be part of the action. It was a swinging singles scene with no cover charge and pitchers of beer for three dollars. The parking lot out back made a great hangout for smoking pot. The owner encouraged it and hired Fort Wayne Police Officer Donald Jackson to provide outdoor security. Officer Jackson not only looked the other way; he was known to partake in the smoke and flirt with the women.

By September of 1974, the flamboyantly gay Dale Smith joined Butch and Jesse's musical group to sing the high line on three-part harmonies. The crowd started paying a lot more attention to the music. Dale added a new level of showmanship, playing tambourine and percussion instruments with a dancer's flare. He was six feet tall, athletic, with shoulder-length curly hair and a face destined for the silver screen. His chin was strong, and his eyes had a Paul Newman sparkle when he smiled.

Jesse bought a nice little PA on time payments from the eclectic Music Man store on Fairfield Avenue. The system had two main speakers that pointed toward the crowd, and two monitor speakers that pointed back at the band. For the first time ever, the band could hear itself well.

Butch came up with the band name: Wyler.

"What kind of name is that?" Jesse asked. "It doesn't sound like anything I've ever heard."

"That's the point," Butch said. "It's unique. People will love it. I used to be in a band called 'Mother Wyler,' and I always thought it would be so much cooler if it was just 'Wyler.'"

Dale wasn't shy about offering his opinion. "I love it. It sounds kind of witchy. We obviously can't keep calling ourselves, 'Butch and Jesse.' And by the way, this is my second weekend at Mother's. Are we ever going to get paid?"

Jesse and Butch looked at each other like they were amazed they hadn't thought about the money much sooner. They weren't accustomed to hitting up bar owners for money. Truth be told, they were having too much fun to worry about finances.

But Dale was right, and Butch and Jesse were embarrassed about letting things slide for so long. That very Saturday night, Jesse asked owner Ed Caine about paying up.

"I think that's an excellent idea," Caine said. "Why don't you come in tomorrow at noon so we can settle up? We're all much too loaded to talk numbers tonight."

It sounded like Caine had been expecting the accounting session for some time. Jesse wondered what numbers needed discussion.

All three members of Wyler showed up to meet with Caine at the appointed hour. "Welcome, my fine young men." Caine grinned like the Cheshire Cat. "How are my future rock stars feeling this fine Sunday? Not too hung over, I trust."

"Here's a list of times we've played here. It shows sixteen nights as a duo and four nights as a trio," Jesse said.

"Let me stop you right there," Caine said. "We never agreed on more money for the trio."

Butch leaned on the bar. "It's one hundred dollars a night

for the duo, and one hundred and fifty dollars a night for the trio."

Caine threw his hands in the air like he was being robbed. "Okay, okay. I didn't agree to it, but I must admit, it does sound fair. So, I'll pay one fifty a night for the trio. What would that total?"

Jesse laid his bill on the bar. "It's sixteen hundred dollars for the duo, and six hundred for the trio, for a grand total of twenty-two hundred dollars."

Caine reached under the bar and produced a piece of paper of his own. He laid it on the bar. "That's a lot of money I owe you guys, but you are more than worth it. Now, let's calculate your bar tab and see where we end up."

"Bar tab?" Jesse was surprised. "You never mentioned anything about us paying for booze. It was always in the contract. Part of our deal."

"No, no, no," Caine said. "We never discussed who would pay for the beer you were passing out every night to the crowd like it was free beer. Let me assure you, there is no such thing as free beer. Somebody has to pay for it. Why should that somebody be me when it was you guys sloshing it around all night?"

Jesse sat down on a bar stool and growled at Caine. "You never once charged us for the beer. Or the shots for that matter. You led us on into thinking the booze was on you. And that makes sense. Us giving it away is like a loss-leader for you so you can sell more at the bar."

Caine smiled. "I tell you what. Let's just see how this bar tab adds up." He brought out a hand-crank adding machine and began the tally.

Jesse and Butch were in shock, realizing they never had clarified the drink arrangements.

Caine finished his calculations and said triumphantly, "It all adds up to $2,754.75 without tax. So, how much did you say I owe you?"

Butch clenched his fists. "We're not going to do it like that. Here's how it's going to be. You pay us what we're owed, or we're walking out of here right now and telling all of our friends to never come back."

Jesse pointed his finger at Caine. "This place will be just as dead as it was before we came along."

Caine chuckled nervously. "Now, now, gentlemen, there's no call for anger. We can work this out. In fact, I've been thinking of a plan where we can all make a lot more money."

Jesse and Butch, moments ago ready to walk out the door, let the man speak.

"Here's what we do. We start charging two dollars a head at the door, and you guys keep it all. The more people you bring in, the more money you make," Caine said.

Dale did the math out loud. "If we bring in two hundred people, which is about what this place will hold, we make four hundred in one night. I like where this is going."

"What if we charge three dollars at the door?" Butch asked.

"Too much," Caine responded quickly. "Don't get greedy. You're not big stars yet. Lots of folks won't pay any cover at all."

Jesse was developing a new respect for Caine. Who would have thought he'd be keeping track of all that booze they'd been throwing around? "It does sound like it could work. But what about the current bar tab?"

"We call it even for now and, from here on out, you play for the door and pay for your drinks unless I specifically offer a round on the house, which I will do frequently in the case of a good crowd."

Butch wasn't quite ready to admit he'd been completely

outmaneuvered. "Or we could sue you for the twenty-two hundred dollars you owe us and never play here again."

Caine knew Butch was grasping at straws. "You're not foolish enough to throw away what you've built up here. You can pack this place every night with the right promotion."

"And who pays for that?" Dale asked, showing a much keener eye for business than Jesse and Butch had demonstrated to date.

"Tell you what," Caine said as he set up four tall glasses on the bar and began to make Bloody Marys. "These are on the house, by the way. And, I'll pay for flyers and posters and a few radio spots just to see what we can do."

The trio looked at each other and nodded as Caine handed each one a drink. "What do you say, boys? Here's to turning Mother's into the hottest club in the area."

They drank one drink, then one more and, finally, one last one for the road.

"Let's not go overboard," Caine said. "I never could afford the way you guys drink. And it is Sunday afternoon, for heaven's sake."

Jesse barely made it to his Sunday shift by 2:00 p.m. with a vodka buzz that quickly developed into a pounding headache. The newsroom on Sunday afternoon was deserted except for a few editors at the copy desks. He took four aspirin and drank glass after glass of cold water. One Bloody Mary would have been enough to ease the pain of Saturday night's overindulgence. Three Bloody Marys doubled the hangover.

Jesse was amazed to find himself thinking, for the first time ever, that he might be developing an alcohol problem. *I won't have any more today, that's for sure,* he thought. *And I won't drink during the week until after work at eleven.* Even as he conjured up the new drinking discipline, he knew he wouldn't be able to keep it.

Nothing was happening on the Sunday police beat. The halls of city and county buildings were eerily empty as he made his rounds. Even the lockup was quiet.

Working as a reporter could be like being a commercial airline pilot. You had the thrill of takeoff, followed by thousands of miles of boredom, climaxed by the sheer terror of landing in a violent crosswind with three hundred human lives in your hands.

Once Jesse's head stopped pounding enough to hear himself think, he got to work on the tenth and final article of his hitchhike series. He would finish the article today. The series had been appearing on Sundays and copy for the last article was overdue.

Only in writing the stories did the impact of the journey come into focus. The trip didn't turn out anything like he thought it would. Everywhere he went, people were struggling with each other and with the world in general. Married people seemed to be suffering the most.

As a child, Jesse thought the grown-ups understood everything, and that one day he would have it all figured out. Now he knew people only pretended to know what was going on. Nobody got a break from life's pain and loss.

He wanted to write about happy and successful people. What he found on the road was mostly disillusioned and miserable souls. Thinking about them was letting the air out of his tires. But that wasn't how he really felt. That was the hangover talking. What he needed to restore in himself was the attitude of gratitude.

Remembering the Great Plains and the Rocky Mountains

and the Pacific Ocean was enough to make him feel more positive. And all those people with their unsolvable problems were actually kind-hearted enough to offer a free ride to a total stranger.

After his shift, he went straight home to Kelly. She didn't dance on Sundays. They were making spaghetti when she started to open a bottle of wine. Jesse took a gentle hold of her hand. "Let's not drink tonight. I need to back off the bottle for a while."

CHAPTER TWENTY-TWO

One snowy Friday in mid-October 1974, Publisher Stephen Longstreet summoned Jesse to his office for a private meeting. Things had been going well for Jesse. His hitchhike series had been extremely well received. He was sure the publisher wanted to congratulate him on a job well done.

One step inside the office told Jesse this was not the case. Longstreet rose from his desk and motioned for Jesse to have a seat in the oak armchair across from his desk. Jesse realized the man was upset. His hair was graying around the temples, and his mouth and jaw were set in a tight grimace. He didn't say a word. Instead, he turned his back on Jesse and stared at the wall as if he was looking out a window that wasn't there. A deep chill ran the length of Jesse's spine.

Longstreet had never been anything but supportive and friendly to Jesse. The silent treatment was a complete shock. Jesse waited it out.

The publisher finally turned to look at Jesse with sadness in his eyes. "Jesse, you've confronted me with a problem that has had me troubled the past two nights. Frankly, I don't know what to do about it. I'm hoping you can help me out."

Several possibilities flashed through Jesse's mind, but he decided to let his employer make the first move. Instead of continuing, Longstreet waited for Jesse to speak. Jesse had a sinking feeling the topic was going to be drugs and alcohol, but he kept his response neutral.

"What can I do to help?" Jesse said.

Longstreet sat down slowly into his burgundy leather wingback swivel chair. The older man closed his eyes and took a deep breath through his nose as if dealing with a difficult child, then opened them with a sternness Jesse had not seen.

"Jesse, you are a marijuana user and dealer, and you've got half my staff hooked on pot."

Jesse let the words sink in and slowly began to come around to his own defense. "First of all, most of that is completely untrue."

Longstreet raised his eyebrows as though he felt a confession beginning to unfold. Jesse waved his hands in denial. "You know I won't lie to you. We are in the business of telling the truth. You taught me that. So, I'll tell you the truth."

Jesse paused. Longstreet looked him in the eyes.

"It is true that I smoke pot. I think you already know that. I've been smoking since college, and I don't think there's anything wrong with it. I'm in favor of legalizing it, and one day I'm sure it'll be as legal as whiskey. What is *not* true is this: I'm not a dealer. I don't sell drugs unless you call splitting an ounce of pot with a friend *dealing*. What's really not true is that business about half your staff being hooked on pot. I don't know where you're hearing this, but any scientist will tell you that marijuana is not an addictive drug like heroin or cocaine. You don't get hooked on it."

Longstreet nodded, then played what he must have thought was his trump card. "What about this Wayne Newton Fan Club?"

Jesse flashed back to the last club meeting at Glen's house the previous week. It went late night and well into the next morning. Chuck had invited a new reporter from the Women's page named Sandy. He acted like it was a get-acquainted gesture, but it was obviously his way of asking her out on a date.

Things had gotten pretty rowdy at Glen's house, smoking pot and drinking heavily. Yes, there had been some bouncing around and group hugs and singing to Rolling Stones records, but it was all fun and games. Nobody got molested or harassed.

"Wait a minute," Jesse said. "I'll bet all your information is coming from Melissa Franken. She talked to Sandy, that new reporter on the Women's page, and came running to you with all the dirt she thought she had."

The look of surprise on Longstreet's face told Jesse he had guessed correctly. "I know Melissa's been here a long time, and she's a good reporter and a friend of yours," Jesse said. "But let me tell you, she's so jealous of me she'd blow anything out of proportion if she thought it would hurt me."

Longstreet remained silent for a short time, then said, "Who's this Sandy? How would she have anything to tell Melissa? And what about this Wayne Newton Fan Club thing? Is she blowing that out of proportion?"

"Absolutely," Jesse said. "Yes, a few of us get together, mostly at Henry's, and we do call ourselves that. But it's got nothing to do with dealing drugs. It's mainly a joke. Our motto is that thing the sheriff said when we found the pot under his window, 'Drug use is no laughing matter.'"

"The sheriff is right about that," Longstreet said with a deep frown.

Jesse lowered his voice to let the publisher know he was taking the issue seriously. "Yes, I suppose some drug use is no laughing matter. But smoking marijuana is no different than drinking alcohol at cocktail parties. It's just people getting together and having fun. That's all Wayne Newton is. And we invited Sandy one night. We smoked a little pot and drank some beer. So, Sandy tells Melissa, and Melissa runs to you like we're drug dealers. It's ridiculous. Ask Sandy. She'll back me up."

Longstreet sighed. "Well, all right. I'm glad to hear you say you're not dealing drugs. But what you do reflects on this newspaper, and we don't want people thinking we're a bunch of potheads. So, I don't know what I'm going to do about this. I'm going to talk to everybody before I make a decision."

Jesse frowned, confused. "Does that mean I'm still working today?"

"Yes, go on, get back to work. And send in Glen. He's next. I can't believe this is going to take up my whole afternoon."

Jesse left the office relieved and pissed. It looked like he might be keeping his job, but he could not believe the backstabbing. He quickly grabbed Glen and gave him the lowdown in a fierce whisper. "Melissa ratted out the Wayne Newton Fan Club. I told him we smoke pot, but we don't deal drugs."

Glen's eyes narrowed. "That's a good thing to tell him because that's the truth. Who told Melissa? Oh, no, it was that Sandy girl, wasn't it?"

Jesse nodded for him to get in the office. "We'll talk later."

One by one, the members of the Wayne Newton Fan Club got called on the carpet. And, one by one, they told the publisher that Melissa Franken was stretching the truth beyond recognition and that she didn't know what she was talking about.

Nobody spoke to Melissa or Sandy for the rest of the day, which came to be known as "Black Friday." The Wayne Newtons didn't know if they were going to lose their jobs or not. When eleven o'clock rolled around, they convened at Henry's to plot their revenge. There were only four of them: Jesse, Chuck, Glen, and Sherman.

"I say we slash Melissa's tires and break out her windshield. Tonight, right now," Sherman said.

Everybody laughed as the beer arrived. They knew he wasn't serious.

"What we do is a big fat nothing," Glen said, always the voice of reason. "Any retaliation will only give her more ammunition."

"We've definitely got to cool it on getting high over the presses," Chuck said.

"Did we tell Sandy about that?" Jesse wondered.

Glen set down his beer mug. "Come on, Jesse, nobody knows what all we said that night. It probably got mentioned. She probably even knows I'm gay. Good God, I wonder what Melissa will do with that."

"Probably nothing," Jesse said. "Don't look now, but she has never had a boyfriend."

"What do you mean by that?" Glen asked.

"No, no," Jesse backpedaled, sensing he may have offended Glen. "All I'm saying is that if Melissa is gay, she might not think being gay is particularly gossip worthy."

"What are we going to do about Sandy?" Chuck asked. "She might be totally innocent. She needs to know Melissa can't be trusted."

"What if she tells Melissa?" Sherman asked.

"It won't matter if she does," Jesse said. "Melissa knows we know she ratted us out to the publisher. I say we get revenge on her by not playing her game. We start being super nice to her. That'll drive her crazy."

"If we keep our jobs," Glen said. "And by the way, let this be a lesson to us all. Let's be a lot more careful about who we invite to our meetings."

It took a couple weeks for the Black Friday scandal to resolve itself in a letter to all employees of the *Journal Gazette*. The letter reminded employees that smoking marijuana was illegal and said that anyone caught smoking would be terminated.

Everybody was amazed that all the thunder and lightning blew over without raining enough to even leave puddles in the streets. Jesse had been worried about his job. So had the rest of the staff, even those not called on the publisher's carpet. Nobody was entirely innocent, and everybody knew it.

Tension did not let up in the newsroom. It only got worse in November. Melissa had a few supporters, but most of the staff treated her like a traitor. Several reporters who had been her friends now kept their distance. Weatherly called a newsroom meeting to tell everybody to get over it, but nobody did.

Sandy was mortified that her comments to Melissa had caused so much trouble for her fellow reporters. She apologized to Jesse as they were about to pass each other in the hall outside the newsroom. She had truth in her eyes and an urgent smile. "I'm so, so sorry about talking to Melissa. I was only telling her how much fun we all had. I had no idea she would blow it all out of proportion and run straight to the publisher."

Jesse gave her a hug. "Nobody's blaming you, Sandy. You could not have known how evil Melissa can be."

Sandy fought back tears. "She was so nice to me in the beginning. And so helpful. She was more than a mentor. It was almost a mother-daughter thing. Now, she won't even talk to me. Or anybody else for that matter. She knows everybody hates her for what she did."

Her tears made Jesse realize how hard-hearted he had been. He was surprised he was beginning to feel sorry for Melissa. "We don't hate her. At least I don't. She's old school, and she doesn't want to change with the times. I'm sure the drug culture scares the hell out of her. She hates first-person news stories, and she doesn't even know what gonzo journalism means. She loves to accuse me of wanting to be the star of the show."

"She's jealous," Sandy said as she changed her direction and walked with Jesse down the hall to the cafeteria. "She wants to be the only one writing feature stories. Way too late for that. She thinks you're stealing her thunder, but you aren't. She's still a damn good reporter."

Jesse stopped and looked at Sandy with a new appreciation. "You know, you're right. She's always been good. She's been good for decades. Her story last week on the three rivers of this city was downright brilliant. It's disgusting how polluted they've become."

They walked into the cafeteria and were surprised to find Melissa sitting at a table by herself, looking hopelessly forlorn. She had a bowl of soup in front of her, but she wasn't eating. Her hands were folded on the table in front of the bowl and her head was bowed. She wasn't praying. She was staring at the soup.

Jesse grabbed Sandy's arm and steered them both to Melissa's table. Melissa pretended not to notice them standing there until Jesse addressed her in a friendly tone. "Hey, Melissa, nice story on the rivers. Who knew they became one with the sewer system every time it rains?"

Melissa looked up. Her eyes were glossy, and it looked like she'd been crying. "Thank you, Jesse. I needed to hear that today."

Sandy extended her hand. "Can we be friends again?"

Melissa shook her hand, nodded, and smiled weakly. She didn't say anything. Jesse and Sandy did not join her at the table. They moved on to get a cup of coffee.

Jesse sensed a lightness in his step. A weight lifted off his shoulders. Being mad at Melissa was a burden he didn't know he was carrying until it was gone.

Sandy looked at him and asked, "Do you think she means it? That we can be friends again?"

Jesse took a careful sip on his hot coffee as they walked out of the cafeteria. "I don't know how Melissa feels, but I'm getting tired of wasting so much energy being angry."

Tensions in the newsroom gradually eased back into the frantic pace of gathering and writing the daily news.

CHAPTER TWENTY-THREE

Jesse had no idea what he was getting himself into when he decided to do a story about a man winning custody of his ten-year-old son. The lead paragraph was simple enough: "It cost Peter Garrison $1,200 to have his son returned. He didn't have to pay ransom; the money was spent on legal fees."

The public outcry on a father taking a child away from his mother was so intense that Jesse had to stop answering his phone. Letters to the editor began pouring in, quoting everything from the Bible to the *Saturday Evening Post* on why men shouldn't be raising children alone.

One night, three grandmotherly women wearing long suffragette dresses burst into the newsroom, carrying signs and shouting about how the divorce epidemic was destroying the American family and ruining the country. The loudest of the three was wearing an all-white dress with an American flag sash. Once she found out Jesse's location in the room, she and her two friends marched over to his desk.

The woman wearing the flag screamed at Jesse, "You write stories like that and you destroy the American family. We mothers have it tough enough without men like you talking about things you don't understand. Things you are genetically incapable of understanding!"

Jesse remained calm in the face of the harangue. He had seen Weatherly pick up the phone to call security. None of the other reporters made a move. This wasn't the first protest group to make a scene in the newsroom.

Within a few moments of the suffragette outburst, Harold

Johnson came limping into the room in his gray security-officer uniform with no hat and nothing on his utility belt but a flashlight. He was well past seventy years old, too thin, and of pasty complexion. Even so, he barked out an order in a surprisingly authoritarian tone, "Ladies, you must leave the newsroom immediately."

The women turned to look at him and paused, momentarily, to consider his command. It looked like they might comply until the shortest of the three women raised her walking cane and cried, "Let's get him, girls!"

Poor Harold disappeared in a sea of skirts. He and the woman with the cane pushed each other off balance and ended up on the floor. Harold wrestled his way on top of her as she swung her cane wildly.

Jesse and Sherman grabbed the heavyset woman who was trying to pry Harold off the cane lady. She was still swinging her balancing stick like a crazed ninja, and Sherman howled in pain as she banged him on the shin. Jesse tried to step on the cane but missed and got wacked on the ankle.

Weatherly leaped up from his desk with surprising agility and grabbed the woman with the flag while staying out of range of the swinging cane. Chuck arrived with two sports reporters and jumped into the fray. "Come on, boys. Let's get the flag lady out of here."

Once Harold got to his feet, the cane lady stopped swinging long enough to haul herself up and into a standing position. The reporters hustled the leader outside. The heavy woman and the cane lady followed, realizing they were outnumbered by a determined news team. They continued to rant and rave as the police arrived in great numbers.

The cane lady raised her walking stick once more and shouted, "Equal rights does not mean men can be mothers!"

The cops snatched the cane out of her hand. They knew a deadly weapon when they saw one, and they weren't about to listen to the three women's maternal sloganeering. They asked Weatherly if he wanted to press charges.

Weatherly was so completely out of breath it took him a moment to take his hands off his knees and stand up. "Just get them out of here and tell them not to come back. Thank you very much. We don't want to be the ones throwing little old ladies in jail," he responded in a coughing voice.

The women were firmly escorted away by at least ten police officers and placed in the flag lady's Ford Country Squire station wagon.

The reporters eventually got back to work and finished writing the morning paper. After deadline at 11:00 p.m., half the newsroom adjourned to Henry's to celebrate the defeat of the throwback suffragettes.

Even Weatherly joined in the fun. "They came, they saw, we conquered."

Weatherly took Jesse aside the day after the scuffle and walked him down to the cafeteria for a cup of coffee. "I don't know how you do it, but everything you touch blows up in our face. That's not a bad thing. I used to call you a con man, but now I'd just say you've got a nose for news. How did you know this custody thing would be so big? I didn't see it coming. When you asked to do the story, I thought it was pretty boring as far as human interest goes."

Jesse thought about pretending he had his pulse on social trends of the times, but he ended up being honest. "I had no clue. I didn't realize I was on to something until I started researching the story. The county clerk told me that four million dollars was paid in child support last year, and only two of the payers were women."

"See what I've been talking about?" Weatherly said. "You got a man-bites-dog story going here. When a woman gets custody, it's not news. When a man does, you got a riot in the newsroom."

Weatherly's analysis was ringing in his ears the day after the cafeteria chat when Jesse interviewed the judge to see how much trouble the ruling had caused him. The judge would only speak off the record. "You can't quote me on this, but I've never seen such a shit storm in all my thirty years on the bench. You'd think I was King Solomon threatening to cut a baby in half so each woman claiming to be the mother could get half a baby. No, the women in town are up in arms about this case. My wife and I can't go to church anymore."

Jesse wanted to write a story on the public outcry over the decision. Weatherly wasn't having it. "You want to pour gasoline on the fire? No way. We've got plenty of 'public outcry,' as you like to say, in our letters to the editor. Besides, the editorial writers are working on it."

Jesse was amazed by Weatherly's attitude. "What do you mean the editorial writers are working on it?"

Weatherly put down the news copy he was editing and rolled his eyes. "You know, they've got an opinion about everything. And that's what this whole child custody thing is. It's one person's opinion against another's. You wrote the news story and it was good work. Now, you've got to step aside and let the editorial page beat it to death."

"Maybe Dan Lynch will do a cartoon about it," Jesse said sarcastically.

Weatherly laughed. "He's already on it."

Jesse couldn't believe it, so he went over to talk to Lynch, the recently hired cartoonist and newly initiated member of the Wayne Newton Fan Club. "What's this I hear about you doing a child custody cartoon?"

"Oh, yeah." Lynch put on a snarky grin. "It's already done. Here, take a look. You know you wrote a good story when I do a cartoon on it."

He held up his drawing on cardboard. It was Lady Justice, blindfolded, holding scales in one hand and a hugely oversized sword in the other. At her feet was a baby with a mother on one side and father on the other. The caption read, "Can somebody give me a hand with this sword?"

As the days went on, Jesse couldn't go anywhere without being confronted about the story. Neither side of the case planned to appeal the court's decision, but the case would definitely be heard in the court of public opinion. His mother, Kelly, and Kelly's mother all thought the court ruling was very nearly a criminal act. They were not hesitant to let Jesse know he was an accomplice for writing about it.

Kelly was his harshest critic. Child custody was a touchy topic for her. Her daughter's father had threatened her with a custody suit, trying to get out of paying support. As it turned out, he left town and never saw his daughter, nor did he pay child support. "You know, Jesse, you choose what you write. You glorify every case you write about. So, I don't know why you've got to pick the one custody case out of a million where the man wins."

"That's what news is," Jesse said. "It's not news if the sun comes up in the morning. News is what happens out of the ordinary."

Kelly's face contorted into full pout. "So that's why all the news is bad?"

"It depends on the way you look at it," Jesse argued. "The

custody case could be good news to fathers wanting to get custody of their children."

Jesse stood by his story to all critics until he received a fateful call from Barbara, the woman who described herself as custody-winner Peter Garrison's ex-wife. "Did that lying bastard ever tell you about his girlfriend? That's right, her name is Bonnie Tucker, and you can quote me on that. You've made him into some kind of a heroic single parent. Let me tell you something, mister. He wasn't thinking about his wife and son when he was out whoring around."

Even as Barbara berated him, Jesse realized he had committed the ultimate journalistic sin. He had written a completely one-sided story. He never thought to interview the woman who lost her son in the court fight.

After a half hour of listening to Barbara's blues and taking furious notes, Jesse consulted with Weatherly.

"I just got a call from Garrison's ex-wife," he said as he plopped in the chair.

"Hold it right there," Weatherly interrupted. "You can't listen to an ex-wife or an ex-husband. The other side is always cruel and crazy. It's just so much 'he said, she said.' That's why we don't cover divorce court."

Jesse's shoulders sagged. "But I never got both sides of the story. It never crossed my mind to interview the mother."

Weatherly thought about that comment for a full ten seconds before responding slowly and carefully. "Your story wasn't about why the marriage failed or why the judge did what he did. It was about the unusual case of a man winning a child custody case."

Jesse's face lit up with an idea. "We could do a follow up from the woman's point of view."

"Let the mother write a letter to the editor like everybody

else," Weatherly said. "There'll be plenty more child custody cases to write about. They'll be making a child custody movie before you know it."

"I was talking to a divorce attorney the other day," Jesse said as he stood up to leave. "He told me the courts are getting backed up with child custody cases and a lot of them are being filed by men."

Weatherly nodded and smiled. "That *is* a great story idea. Make sure you pass that on to the court reporter. Jerry will have a field day with that one. That's all the follow up we need."

CHAPTER TWENTY-FOUR

Jesse and Kelly were having serious relationship issues as the 1974 Christmas season began to take its social toll. Jesse was spending too much time with his band and with his coworkers in the bar after work. His resolution to cut down on drinking had faded as life became more contentious on the home front. Kelly was coming home from work drunk more often than not.

To add even more stress, Kelly wanted her daughter, Berta, to move in for the holidays. "It'll just be for a week or two," she yelled from the kitchen at Jesse in the living room. "Come on, Jesse, she loves you. Wouldn't it be wonderful to do Christmas morning right here with our baby girl?"

Jesse did not like the "our" part of the baby girl reference. But Kelly and Berta had always been and always would be a package deal. Deep down, Jesse had known this all along. His friends and even his parents had warned him. Cheri, his teacher friend from 1114, had told him months ago that this would happen. He had been too smitten to listen.

Now, he responded carefully to Kelly. "This place isn't big enough for the two of us, let alone adding a six or—what is she now—a seven-year-old child to the mix. Who would watch her at night when we're both working?"

Kelly crossed her arms and stared at him. "You could pick her up from my mother's after work."

Jesse sat up straight on the edge of the couch. "I don't get off until 11p.m. and then we go to Henry's."

"Maybe you could spend a little less time at the bar," she said with a raised voice.

Jesse stood up like a third grader taking on a fifth-grade bully at the playground. "That's quite a suggestion coming from a girl who dances naked for strangers all night long *in a bar.*"

Kelly got an evil look in her eye.

"No, wait," Jesse said, "That's not really fair. I know you work hard at your job. All I'm saying is we both work too late to take care of a child. And what about the nights the band plays at Mother's?" He backpedaled to keep things from getting out-of-control ugly.

Kelly glared at him like thoughts of violence were still on her mind.

"How about this?" Jesse quickly said. "Let's get a bigger place and then we can talk about moving Berta in. You know I love taking her to the park and to the zoo. This isn't something we need to decide right now. We can do Christmas morning at your mother's and everybody's happy."

This seemed to make some kind of sense to Kelly. She relaxed her combative stance. "You better never try to come between me and my little girl," she said in a stern voice.

Jesse resisted the urge to point out that her wild lifestyle had already estranged her from Berta. The accusation would only drive the wedge further. Jesse had seen Kelly get violent with Melissa in their bar fight. And he had seen her mother go ballistic at the dinner party with his parents. He didn't want to be on the receiving end of that type of wrath.

Days later, things had cooled down with Kelly. Jesse had tried his best to consider her wishes. He had put the band on hold for a few days, and she was respecting that. So Jesse wasn't expecting trouble when he got home after work on a Sunday.

Kelly sprang off the couch and pummeled him about the

head and shoulders with her fists. "Don't you dare walk in here like you did nothing wrong. My mother had to call me so I could read the Sunday paper about you having sex with some floozy in Colorado."

Jesse ducked out of her flurry of punches like a boxer bouncing off the ropes from a corner of the ring. "What are you talking about? I never touched her. She wanted me to go to Aspen with her and I said no. That's all that happened."

Kelly ran around the coffee table and came at him again. She landed a roundhouse right on Jesse's left temple that rang his bell. When she tried to follow with a left cross, he grabbed her arm and threw her on the couch, hard. Every time she tried to get up, Jesse pushed her back down.

"Don't even think about hitting me again. And what makes you think you can just punch me in the head?"

He did not want to hurt her, and he would never lay a hand on a woman. He also didn't want to get arrested for domestic battery even though he was acting in self-defense. He quickly backed away.

"You shamed me in the newspaper," Kelly screamed. "Talking about getting naked with that girl and sharing her bar of soap. How stupid do you think I am?"

"Why are you so mad about this? I got laid at every massage parlor in town and you didn't get upset."

Kelly was out of breath. "That was different. That was for money. And we talked about it before you did it."

"Oh, so it's okay if money's involved? Is that how you handle your business at the club?"

Kelly's eyes widened and then she pretended to be emotionally wounded as she buried her head in a pillow. Jesse felt bad about his cheap shot. He placed his hand on her shoulder, and she swung her legs around his and leaped off the couch in a surprisingly gymnastic move. She swung on him with both arms flailing like a windmill.

Jesse tried to block her attack. "Kelly, come on, you're out of control. Stop this craziness. We can sit down and talk about it. I didn't do anything wrong. If I did, I wouldn't write about it, now would I?"

Kelly stopped hitting him. "That's your problem, Jesse. You think writing about things makes them okay. Makes the world a better place. Well, guess what? It doesn't. It only makes you feel good about yourself. You're just a spoiled white boy who got it all on a silver platter. You don't know shit about the real world."

Jesse lowered his head, but he didn't drop his guarded stance. "Here's what I know, Kelly. Your conduct is way out of line. I'm not going to put up with it. So, here's what you're going to do. You're going to leave right now." He started pushing her back toward the door to the apartment. "I'm kicking you out."

They yelled at each other for half an hour. It became obvious to Jesse that she had been feeling unwanted for some time. The more he thought about it, the more he realized she was right. He didn't want her living with him. It had nothing to do with her not paying rent. Nothing to do with her coming home drunk way too often. Nothing to do with their sex life beginning to cool off.

Jesse finally admitted something to her that he hadn't admitted to himself. "Look, Kelly, it's obvious we can't live together. All we do is fight. You moved in so quick I didn't realize what I was giving up. I was having fun living alone. I want my life back."

"I'm not going anywhere, you cheating bastard. I'm calling the cops, that's what I'm going to do."

"Go ahead and call them," Jesse yelled. "Your name's not even on the lease. They'll put you on the street faster than I will."

Kelly grabbed a lamp and yanked the cord out of its socket. She held it over her head like she was going to use it on Jesse. "Don't even think about it," he said, lowering his tone to a growl. "One more move and I'm going to put you down."

An eerie calmness overcame Kelly quite suddenly and relaxed the contorted muscles of her raging face. The anger left her like the light went out when she disabled the lamp. She put the lamp down and took a seat on the couch as though none of the violence had transpired. Jesse was puzzled until he saw her pull out a bottle of whiskey from behind the seat cushion and take a huge swig.

"So, that's what this is all about?" Jesse realized he was out of breath. "This is about you being drunk? What? You're hiding bottles of booze around the house?"

Kelly smiled like a patient teacher trying to make a point. "Don't try to make this about me, Jesse. It's about you and how you always get your way and how everything is so easy for you. Don't you think we're all getting sick of reading about how wonderful you are?"

Jesse didn't respond. He was spooked by her Jekyll and Hyde. He knew that a couple more pulls on the whiskey would put her back in attack mode.

"All you think about is yourself, Jesse. It's not enough to be everybody's front-page darling. No, not the great Jesse Conover. He's got to be a rock star too. Your head's getting so big I'm amazed you can still fit through the door. It's no wonder there's no room for me in your life, let alone my daughter."

Yes, she knew how to push his buttons. He tried not to get angry, but it was too late.

"You're the one with the big head full of whiskey. Why don't you put the bottle down and take a good look in the mirror? You're the one who's left no room in her life for Berta."

That was the number one on the list of things not to say to Kelly. She leapt off the couch in a fury, tripped on the throw rug, and landed in a heap at Jesse's feet. He held her down as best he could, but she rolled over and kicked furiously.

Two courses of action became apparent. One, he could knock her out. That wouldn't do. He'd end up in jail. Two, he could flee the premises even though it was his apartment.

As he was considering his options, Kelly managed to get to her feet and scramble into the kitchen. He knew right away it was time to run; too many potential weapons in the kitchen.

He ran out the door and down the stairs. She was in hot pursuit behind him. He stepped left as he hit the bottom landing, just in time to avoid a flying waste basket filled with garbage that exploded into coffee grinds, eggshells, and banana peels when it hit the wall.

As he opened the main door to leave 1114, he looked back and saw the two women who lived in the downstairs apartments looking at him with horrified expressions on their faces. He didn't need to explain the situation. They'd heard most of it through the ceiling.

Jesse ran out the door, down the steps, and jumped into his car. He started the engine and pulled away from the curb in one fluid motion. He could see that Kelly did not follow him to the street.

He was shaking with adrenaline as he drove to Chuck's apartment. A wave of emotions came over him: anger, sadness, frustration. Suddenly, the strangest memory of his time with Kelly popped into his head. As mad and as shaken up as he was, the flashback was a good one. It was the time he and Kelly got caught nude sunbathing at his parents' cottage on Lake Michigan.

He couldn't believe the "nudist scene," as it came to be known, would come to mind as he was being forced to flee his own apartment. Jesse chuckled at the bizarre memory as he banged on the door of his friend's apartment. He and Kelly had great times together. Hard to believe they could be coming to an end.

It was almost 2:00 a.m., but Chuck was still up. "What happened to you?" he asked. "It looks like you've been in a fight. Are those scratch marks on your neck?"

Jesse came in and collapsed into Chuck's well-worn, brown vinyl couch. "Kelly got drunk and attacked me. I had to flee for my life."

Chuck got two beers out of his refrigerator and handed one to Jesse. He smiled impishly, showing the slight gap between his two front teeth. "It was the hitchhike article on the naked babe in Colorado, wasn't it?"

Jesse almost choked on his beer. "What? You too? What's the big deal about a skinny-dip?"

Chuck pulled up a chair and sat down across from Jesse. He put his beer on the glass coffee table between them. "Jesse, Jesse, Jesse. It was that bit about sharing the bar of soap and how beautiful she looked in the sun and water. I couldn't believe they kept that stuff in. It was pretty racy for the Fort Wayne Sunday paper."

"Yeah, I kind of knew that when I wrote it. To tell the truth, I thought they'd cut it." Jesse took a long chug of beer and laughed.

"You love making waves, don't you?" Chuck laughed with him. "So, what did Kelly do?"

"She jumped me and started punching me as soon as I walked in the door."

"No shit? She was actually hitting you?"

"Like a street fighter." Jesse finished his beer with another long pull. "You got another one? I'm still shaking."

"Yeah, yeah." Chucked jumped up to grab another beer. "Tell me more. Did you hit her back?"

Jesse told him the whole story as they smoked cigarettes and drank two more beers apiece. Chuck listened carefully, like a good reporter, and then concluded, "You're right. She's got to go. Next thing you know, she'll have you in jail. You better hope she hasn't called the cops already."

That hadn't occurred to Jesse. "Oh, shit. Maybe I should call the police myself."

Chuck was ever the level-headed one. He'd spent a couple years on the Kokomo police force before turning to journalism. "You got weed in the apartment?"

Jesse's paranoia grew deeper with every question. "Yes, I do. And she knows where it's at."

"You better hope she doesn't cut herself and say you did it."

Jesse jumped off the couch and paced back and forth in front of the sliding glass door to Chuck's small balcony. "Shit, shit, shit! This whole thing's gonna blow up in my face."

"It already has, my friend. The shit has already hit the fan," Chuck said. "We've just got to figure out how to clean it up. So, number one, don't call the cops. From what you say, she's too drunk to get them involved. Number two, chill out here. You can sleep on the couch. Call your father first thing in the morning. He's a lawyer. He'll know what to do."

Jesse met his father at the apartment the next day at noon.

Kelly wasn't there. His father was firm and direct with his advice. "She's not on the lease. Let's pack up her stuff—all of it—and leave it on the front porch. Don't let her back in under any circumstances. Don't even talk to her. She can ruin your life in a hurry."

As they packed up Kelly's belongings and stacked them on the porch, Jesse began having second thoughts. She didn't have much, but what she did have looked pathetic in piles on the porch.

"This feels pretty mean and cold. Don't you think it's a little harsh? She's got no place to go. I thought you liked Kelly."

His father sat him down on the porch steps. "Let me tell you something, Jesse. Once a person shows her true colors, you better pay attention. Yes, I know she's a lovely person. She's bright and beautiful and charming. But not when she's drunk. And if she keeps on drinking, it will only get worse. From a legal standpoint, you've got no choice. If you've got a drunk woman threatening to have you arrested, she's got to go. Either that or you've got to go. I've had lots of clients end up in jail for something they didn't do."

"I know you're right, Dad, but this is more than a strictly legal situation."

His father spoke sternly. "No, it's not. You told me yourself things weren't working out that well between the two of you. Besides, you're too young to get tied down to a woman with a child. No, Jesse, the only good break is a clean break."

"I just hate breaking her heart."

His father laughed. "Don't give yourself so much credit. She'll get over you in a hurry. She's young and beautiful. She'll find another fool in no time."

Kelly's possessions remained on the front porch for two days. Jesse felt worse and worse every time he walked by her stuff. Finally, Cheri helped her move into Apartment Six on the bottom floor of the carriage house behind the main house at 1114. Jesse was not pleased that Kelly rented a place in the house.

"How was she?" Jesse asked.

"She was sad," said Cheri. "She said you two had a fight, but she couldn't remember about what. I told her what I heard from downstairs, and she acted shocked."

Kelly knocked on Jesse's door a few times after the breakup, but he never responded. She called and he hung up on her. She had mutual friends try to talk to him, but Jesse told them it was really over, and he wasn't going back.

Even as he maintained a firm resolve, Jesse did not believe he and Kelly would never get back together.

CHAPTER TWENTY-FIVE

Five days before Christmas, Jesse was feeling sad and lonely over his breakup with Kelly. He wanted to go see her in the worst way, but he knew he couldn't. Sending mixed signals would only make everything more difficult.

Rather than sitting around and feeling sorry for himself, he got himself a one-day gig as a mall Santa. Maybe that would cheer him up.

Weatherly was all for it. He needed a feature story for the slow-news holidays. The mall owners recognized the opportunity for free publicity and promptly gave one of their Santas the day off.

Jesse managed to fit into the Santa suit, stomach padding and all. By the time he put on the white wig and beard, he looked pretty convincing. The pants were too short, and the high black boots were too small. That was no problem for his sponsors at the mall. They dashed down to the shoe store and borrowed a pair of brand-new size twelve boots that shined like the elves themselves had spit-polished them. The short pants tucked into the high boots and no one was the wiser.

For the next four hours, one child after another sat on his lap or wiggled to get off. He got puked on by not one but two infants, wetted down by several over-excited preschoolers, and kicked in the shin by a nasty third grader whose mother thought he was just being cute. And, yes, a couple older kids wanted to pull off his beard to prove he wasn't real.

Even so, most of the children were delightfully awestruck, happy, and hopeful. Jesse's "ho, ho, ho's" got bigger and friendlier as he got the hang of the deep belly laugh. The line of children and their mothers stretched all the way past the shoe store and down to the fast food court.

Jesse got into performance mode. He sang "Rudolph the Red Nose Reindeer" and "All I Want for Christmas Is My Two Front Teeth" on several occasions. He almost forgot that the kids were coming to see Santa Claus, not Jesse Conover.

Two high school girls dressed as Santa's helpers urged him to spend less time per child. So did the photographer, who was making money by the portrait. The mothers were grimly determined to have their child in a photo with Santa, even if it meant waiting half the afternoon.

The important moment for Jesse came when he was looking into the wide, hazel eyes of a five-year-old girl with big blonde curls and a snowflake jacket. One look in those eyes and he fell into the Christmas spirit like a coin into a wishing well.

She was frightened and hanging on to her mother's hand, hesitating when it was her turn to sit on Santa's lap. Jesse knew a big laugh wouldn't help so he offered gentle encouragement. "Well, hello there, Santa's been waiting to see *you*. Come on over and tell me what you want for Christmas."

Her mother let go and gave her a little push. That was all the child needed. She trotted over to Santa with her arms stretched out to be picked up. She sailed into Jesse's lap and looked him square in the eyes.

Jesse was dazzled. Her eyes were wide and trusting and dancing in anticipation. He wanted to give her the world.

"And what's your name, little girl?"

No answer. Just that amazingly open stare of pure love and joy.

"Do you remember Santa from last year?"

She nodded her head and spoke clearly. "My name is Linda."

"Linda. That's a pretty name. And what would you like Santa to bring you for Christmas?"

No answer again. Her thumb snuck into her mouth. Her mother laughed and a lightbulb flashed. Jesse asked her again what she wanted for Christmas.

She looked down at her lap as if pondering the question. Then she raised her head quickly. Her eyes twinkled with delight. "Supwises!"

Jesse gave her a big hug. "Ho, ho, ho, Santa's got plenty of those in his bag."

She giggled and slipped off his lap to take her mother's hand again. As she was walking away, with a little prompting from mom, she turned and waved. "Bye, bye, Santa. May-we Cwistmas."

From that moment on, the rest of the day floated by like colorful clouds at sunset. Jesse started seeing the truth in the eyes of every child who sat on his lap. It wasn't complicated. It wasn't expensive. It was joyous and free.

It was love. Their eyes connected him to something much bigger than himself. They gave him love and expected nothing in return.

All that truth and love turned out to be pretty hot and sweaty. After four hours of lifting children into his lap, Jesse's Santa suit was soaked. His back and arms were sore, and the boots were killing his feet.

The photographer was exhausted by the effort but excited by the money he made. "Best Santa ever. I never took so many photos so fast in my life." He offered a twenty-dollar tip, but Jesse declined. Santa's helpers were only too happy to accept the money on his behalf.

Jesse had one request for the photographer. "Can I get one photo of myself as Santa?" The photographer nodded. "And can you make it one of me and that little girl named Linda?"

"What's her last name?"

Jesse looked at him and smiled as he took off the fake beard. "I have no idea. But she was sucking her thumb when you took the picture."

The photographer promised to do the best he could as Jesse went back to a small dressing room to get out of the wet Santa suit. He hoped the mall people would wash it before the next Santa had to wear it.

Jesse was so inspired by his experience that he wrote the story in first person, as Santa Claus himself:

> It was awful. It was only two days away from Christmas and I just couldn't get with it. Me, Santa Claus, the guy everybody counts on to be merry-merry and spearhead the gift exchange with a super sleigh ride.
>
> I was going through the motions. Somehow, it seemed nobody cared about Christmas anymore. Were they all too depressed by the world mess to take time out for each other?
>
> In Fort Wayne, I parked the sleigh on top of a huge shopping center and went downstairs to see if anybody would recognize me.
>
> Sure enough, everybody was too busy looking at shelves and shelves of consumer items to notice my entrance. It was so crowded, and people were more worried about getting around each other than exchanging Christmas greetings. Nobody seemed to know anybody anyway.
>
> Feeling worse than ever, I walked to the center of the

mall. I knew they would have a chair set up for me there to talk to the youngsters. If anything could cheer me this Christmas, it would be the children.

Lo and behold, there were hundreds of tiny people waiting for me. Short folk with freckles and toothy grins looking up innocently at the adult world. Happy little ones hanging onto grown-up hands.

They saw me coming about forty feet away. A collective squeal of delight went up. "Santa's here, Mommy, look over there; there he is." And, "Is that really Santa Claus? Do I get to talk to him and sit on his lap, Dad? Can I pleeease? Can I?"

There it was right in front of me. The spirit of Christmas. The kids had it. But how did they ever get it if the adults seemed to have forgotten it? Suddenly, I understood.

Almost magically, a booming "Ho, ho, ho, Merry Christmas, kids," came from deep down inside of me. The children's delight was contagious. I felt like a kid again myself. Their parents got caught up in the spirit.

I settled into my chair, ready to put heart and soul into my work for the first time in days. *Bring on the kids*, I thought. *They've got the secret. And bring on any adult who has the good sense to act like a kid once in a while.*

Jesse's heart was singing carols again.

The story went on for another twelve paragraphs. Weatherly liked it so much he ran it on Christmas day under a big headline: "City Youngsters Restore Santa's Christmas Spirit."

The night before Christmas, Weatherly came over to Jesse's desk and sat down across the typewriter for a professional chat. "It's about time you wrote a feel-good piece. Enough with the plane crashes and child custody and sexy hitchhike stories. This is exactly what I needed to read for Christmas. Our readers will love it."

Jesse grinned like a kid who just got what he wanted for Christmas. "Why, Mr. Weatherly. You old softy."

Weatherly chuckled as he lit up a cigarette. "It's okay. You can call me George. Makes me feel old when people call me mister."

Jesse spent Christmas day with his parents and his sisters. It was a relief to be with his family and without so many newsworthy distractions.

Jesse's mother had an announcement to make once the gifts had been opened. "This morning I read an absolutely uplifting article in the paper. And it was written by my son, our very own Jesse. We are all so proud of you." Then she read the Santa Claus article, pausing for mini rounds of applause and uplifting commentary between paragraphs.

Jesse was surprised by the effect his own words had on him when being read with pride by his mother. The article sounded comforting. It was soothing and kind, a blessed respite from the harshness of hard news.

He resolved in that moment to be gentler with readers in the future. He'd been banging people on the head like drums in his personal parade. *Yes, all the world is a stage,* he thought, *but I don't always have to have the lead role.*

Thoughts of Kelly came to him throughout the day. He hoped she was doing well with her mother and Berta. His mother must have known what he was thinking when she sat down next to him on the living room sofa. "Jesse, I know you're missing Kelly today. Have you seen her or called her?"

Jesse was not surprised his mother could read his mind.

"No, I'm not going to contact her for a while. Dad says the only good break is a clean break."

His mother stiffened and looked across the room at his father, who was watching their conversation. "Clean breaks are only good when we're talking about breaking bones, Jesse. From what I hear, you and your father moved her things out on the porch and left her to fend for herself."

Jesse leaned into his mother and whispered so his sisters would not hear, "She was going to get me thrown in jail. She hit me in the head with a closed fist."

His mother put her hand on his shoulder. "I'm sure your father gave you good legal advice. But listen to your mother. You call Kelly today and wish her a Merry Christmas. You can't throw a woman away like she was an old shoe."

Jesse knew she was right. He'd been feeling guilty about not contacting Kelly. "You know she's living in the carriage house at 1114."

His mother held up her right index finger. "I'm not saying go see her. And I'm not saying invite her over. I'm just saying be kind and let her know that you still care about her. Otherwise, she'll feel like you were using her all along. And I know that's not true. I know you still have feelings for her."

Jesse's father joined the conversation. "I'm afraid I have to agree with your mother. We're all feeling bad about you and Kelly. She's a good girl until she drinks too much. Give her a call. Let her know you're sorry that things didn't work out."

His mother leaned in to straighten his hair. "And don't say, 'Let's be friends.'"

At four o'clock, Jesse returned to 1114 to meet up with Butch and Dale for a Christmas jam in Butch's living room. The three-part harmonies sounded especially good that evening.

Dale was in the holiday spirit. "Nothing beats the gift of music."

"What we need to do," Butch said, "is take our songs into the studio and make a record."

Jesse agreed. "I know just the guy to do it. He won't charge us much. He's got a little place on Hanna Street."

Dale was surprised. "Hanna Street. That's down in the inner city. We'll all get mugged. Or worse."

"No, no," Jesse said. "It's right next to the Southside Gardens restaurant. We'll be fine."

Dale put down his tambourine so he could get down to business. "How are we going to pay for all this?"

Butch got up and leaned his guitar against the wall. The rehearsal was morphing into a meeting. "How about we take all the money from the Mother's gigs and save it until we have enough to make a record?"

Jesse was strumming chords on the guitar. "We don't have to wait that long. How about we each put up two hundred dollars and see how far that gets us?" he said.

The three members of Wyler agreed on that plan and spent what was left of Christmas making a set list for the recording session.

The band called it a night after midnight, and Jesse went home to his adjoining apartment. He walked in and turned on the lamp next to the couch. It was eerily quiet. He felt empty.

He wanted to call Kelly, but she probably didn't have a telephone yet. He walked back to the bedroom and looked down on the carriage house where she was living. The lights were still on. It didn't look like she had company. There was no movement in the apartment.

Jesse wanted to go to her but realized his motives were not entirely pure. Kelly suddenly appeared in her window and looked up toward his apartment. He ducked away from his window, hoping she hadn't seen him.

CHAPTER TWENTY-SIX

January of 1975 was big news. President Ford signed the fifty-five-mile-per-hour speed limit into law. *The Wiz* opened on Broadway with an all-Black cast. The North Vietnamese "liberated" Phuoc Binh Province, and the Weather Underground bombed headquarters for the State Department in Washington, DC.

Lots of news, but none of it was happening in Fort Wayne. Jesse covered boring school board meetings and teachers' union gatherings and tried to write them into interesting stories, but it was impossible.

Maybe it's time to relocate, he thought. He could probably land a job in Chicago or Detroit, but that would mean leaving the band and 1114 and all his friends at the paper. It didn't feel like the time to leave. Weatherly still had a lot to teach him. But something way outside of his hometown was beginning to call his name.

Jesse wasn't one to pray for guidance. He was learning to put his faith in the power of events to show him the way.

Sure enough, he got the phone call around 9:00 p.m. on February 3. A male voice screamed into the phone. "The Landing is going up in flames!"

Jesse didn't take time to ask the caller his name. He hung up the phone, jumped out of his chair, and yelled at Weatherly, "The Landing's on fire. I'm on my way."

Glen was on vacation, so Jesse was covering cops that night. The city editor waved him out the door and began organizing a coverage team as the newsroom sprang into action. The

Landing was the most historic part of the city. The name came from Fort Wayne's days as a major boat landing on the Wabash and Erie Canal. It was a one-block stretch of four-story hotels, restaurants, and businesses.

Jesse could see smoke rising two hundred feet in the sky as he stormed out the newspaper. He ran the three blocks down Pearl Street to the fire scene. He passed Henry's and kept sprinting past the Perfection Bakery building with the rotating sign on top that looked like never-ending bread slices coming out of a loaf.

He passed Poor John's where Kelly danced and turned the corner to come face-to-face with the largest wall of flame he had ever seen. The towering inferno made the train derailment fire last year look small by comparison.

The first fire trucks screamed in and began deploying crews and hoses to battle multiple blazes. It was already too late for many of the buildings. The 141-year-old Rosemarie Hotel in the middle of the block was completely engulfed in smoke and fire, as was the five-story Old Fort Draperies Office at the west end of the street. It looked like the whole block might go up in flames.

Police and fire vehicles kept arriving. Safety teams secured both ends of the street. Jesse was already inside the combat area when it was cordoned off limits to the public and press.

Hotel guests were evacuated in their nightclothes and not allowed back in to retrieve valuables. Tipsy patrons of the Hotel's Bar None speakeasy stumbled down the sidewalk in search of another tavern. Attorneys and businessmen talked their way through the police barrier to rush into offices and salvage files and records.

Jesse got names and quotes from panicky participants as the scene became progressively more dangerous. Fireballs of debris floated to the ground, and a hail of sparks sizzled on contact with waterlogged streets. Firefighters were hosing tons of water on the blazes and all points in between. Strong wind gusts blew water spray blocks away, causing icy streets in the below-freezing temperatures.

Firemen were using water pressure from hoses to break top-story windows to get at the flames. Aerial ladders lifted firefighters to break out the most stubborn upper windows with poles. A fire chief Jesse knew grabbed him by the arm. "See that wall in front of you? It's about to collapse. We've got to get out of here now."

It was too hot to stay where they were anyway. With blazes on both sides of the street, temperatures rose to 150 degrees and higher at street level. The fire chief grabbed Jesse again and dragged him twenty yards down the sidewalk. "Move, move, move! She's coming down."

Jesse could hear the roar of the building collapsing behind him as he ran. It sounded like the sky was falling. Brick and mortar debris fell hard enough to bruise his forearms and shoulders as he tried to protect his head.

He and the chief barely escaped being crushed and buried. They were both covered in ash and brick dust as they brushed themselves off and stared at the thirty-foot pile of rubble in the middle of the street that had been a four-story building only moments earlier. Steam from the water and heat rose off the mound of destruction. All was eerily quiet for a few moments as everyone on the scene witnessed the mini apocalypse in stunned silence.

Jesse hugged the chief and thanked him. The firefighter was out of breath. "I'm not sure if I saved you or you saved me. If I hadn't been getting you out, I'd be buried under those bricks right now."

The chief took off his broad-brimmed combat helmet. His hair was matted down with sweat, and his rugged face was caked with ghostly plaster dust. "One thing I've got to tell you, people should know. That hotel owner had a slew of fire code violations. He's been going broke long as I remember. I wouldn't be surprised if this is arson. I count three separate fires in three buildings, and they all spread too quick."

Jesse tried to ask the hotel owner's name, but the fire chief was yelling into his bullhorn, "All right, everybody, report in. Anybody hurt? Anybody missing?"

Jesse ran into a vacated restaurant in a building that had not yet caught fire and located a telephone. Amazingly, it was operational. He called Weatherly. "This whole place is going up in flames. It's a disaster. We need photographers and reporters down here now."

Weatherly was calm and commanding. "Stay with the chief. I've got John and Dean on the way for photos, and Sherry and Chuck coming for backup. Where are you? Can we get our people into the scene?"

Jesse was excited by Weatherly's use of the word *backup*. That meant he would be writing the lead story, not Chuck or Sherry. "Have them come in the east side. I'll get them in at the corner of the Keystone Building."

An idea came to Jesse as he stared up at the hotel blaze. "And get Melissa down here too. There's a great sidebar story about the people who got evacuated from the hotel and its bar. Some of them are down at Mother's Bar. It's still open and they're serving drinks and popcorn."

Minutes later, Sherry, Chuck, and Melissa met Jesse at the appointed spot. They looked like a combat team on night patrol. There was no fear in their eyes, only excitement at the monster news story unfolding before them.

"What happened to you?" Chuck asked. "You look like you've been buried alive."

"I almost was." Jesse pointed to the pile of rubble in the middle of the street. "I was running away when that collapsed building missed me by about ten yards. Be careful. The sky *is* falling."

Melissa and Sherry listened to Jesse's briefing, then went off on their own into the burning block. Jesse grabbed Chuck and told him the building on the west end of the street was probably going to collapse. "Where are John and Dean? They've got to get those shots."

Chuck and Jesse started wading through the fire hoses coiled like a massive pile of giant snakes covering the entire street.

"I think John and Dean are already on the west side," Chuck said. "I'm sure they'll split up and find their own way into the scene. It's not their first rodeo, but I bet they never saw anything like this. Feels like we're in the middle of World War Three."

At that moment, a fireman lost control of his hose and soaked Chuck and Jesse hard enough to knock them down.

"Shit," Chuck yelled. "I'm all wet and it's going to freeze on me."

"Sorry about that," the firefighter yelled as he regained control of his hose and continued dousing the towering blaze.

Jesse laughed as the two got to their feet. "Talk about getting swept off your feet. Stay close to the fire. Nothing's going to freeze in this heat. Look, we're already steaming."

Chuck shook himself off and squeezed the water out of his thinning hair. "I ought to get that guy's name and put him in the story as a careless asshole."

On their way to the other side of the block, Chuck and Jesse caught up with Sherry. She had run ahead into the fire scene and was passionately kissing a firefighter who was trying to adjust his gear before entering a smoke-filled building.

"Be safe in there. I can't lose you. Be careful," she said.

"Jesus, Sherry," Chuck said. "Now is not the time to make out with your boyfriend. Why don't you go interview the fire chief and the public safety director? They're right over there."

Sherry was a damn good swing reporter, meaning she bounced from beat to beat. It just so happened her boyfriend was a firefighter. She regained her composure. "Right. Sorry. I'll go talk to the chief."

Once Sherry left for her assignment, Dean came rushing over. He was excited and out of breath. "You boys having a little marshmallow roast tonight? Why are you all wet?" He took a photo of the wet reporters and chuckled.

"We got hosed," Chuck said as he gave Dean a handshake. "Is this the biggest fire you ever saw? No telling how many buildings are going down."

"Look." Jesse pointed to the last building on the west end of the block. "That's going to be the next one to fall. The chief said so, and it looks like he's right. Come on, Dean, let's get a shot of that flaming brick wall before it comes down."

"We'll have to be quick," Dean said as the three men ran over to the blast furnace blaze, holding their hands in front of their faces to block the heat. "Right here. This is as close as I'm getting." He snapped a couple of quick shots.

"Good enough," Chuck said. "We're out of here right now. This thing is ready to fall."

No sooner did the three journalists dash across the street than the second building of the night collapsed in a thunder of brick and building debris.

The fire chief ran up to Jesse. "I thought I told you to stay away from falling buildings. Pull any more close-up bullshit like that and I'm going to throw you out of the party! That goes for all three of you!"

"How are you keeping it from spreading to all the buildings?" Chuck asked.

The chief took off his helmet again. He was covered in black grime. His voice was hoarse from smoke inhalation and exhaustion. "To tell the truth, we're not containing it worth a damn. It got too big a head start on us. It spread too quickly. We've already lost, what, three out of fourteen buildings? What we're doing is sending scuba teams in to save the ones that haven't caught fire yet. It seems to be working down the street, but it obviously didn't work here on the corner."

"Any chance of spreading to other blocks?" Jesse asked.

"Always a chance," the chief said. "But, fortunately, this old block is pretty isolated from the rest of town. The damn wind is a problem. We've got crews on the backside to keep it from jumping the alley. Look at this mess. I've got every firefighter in the city on this thing, and all we're really doing is watering the ruins. This is terrible. It's the worst thing I've ever seen. These buildings have been here hundreds of years and now, tonight, on my watch, they're going to be gone forever. It hurts me to look at it. It really does, it hurts me to look at it."

With that, he staggered over and sat down on the bottom step of a fire truck to get a drink of water from a five-gallon cooler. Jesse started to follow him, but Chuck held him back. "Let him go. He already gave you the quote of the night."

"What's that?" Jesse asked.

"'It hurts me to look at it. It really does, it hurts me to look at it.' That's the quote. That's exactly what he said. Use the whole thing. Use the repetition. It adds emphasis. And don't forget, this is a community tragedy, a historic, bad thing. This town will never forget tonight. It will never be the same. Neither will we."

Jesse looked at Chuck in profound appreciation. Up until that moment, the entire event had been a big adventure for Jesse. But the gravity of the disaster hit him. This fire would change the cityscape forever. Jesse kicked himself for being too self-centered.

There was no time to contemplate historic impact. A crew chief came by and told the reporters about a fire team trapped on the third floor of a building in the middle of the block that was catching fire.

"I'm on it," Chuck said. "Come with me, Dean. Jesse, you stay here with the chief. Make sure Sherry doesn't get hurt. Don't let her know about the team that's trapped."

Jesse looked down the block as flames continued to rise from several buildings. The fire was bigger than ever. Suddenly, he was more tired than he had ever been. He went over to the fire truck and sat down next to the chief. "Man, I'm not sure I can walk anymore. I can't even breathe."

The chief handed him a cup of water. "You better get out of here and get a shower. You inhaled too much dust. It can put you in the hospital."

Jesse took a long drink and looked at the chief. "How do you handle all this?"

The chief stared up at the blaze like he could find his answer in the flames. "You do it for your brothers. Your fellow firefighters. It's the working together that makes it doable. That, and protecting the public from nights like this."

Jesse couldn't help but look up at the flames. "Look at that fire. It's beautiful. It's got a mind of its own."

"And it will kill you," the chief said. "Now listen, when you write your story tonight make sure you let everybody know what it's like to feel the heat and choke on the smoke."

Jesse promised he would do just that. He felt the notepad in his hip pocket. He hadn't taken it out all night. He hadn't taken a single note. He knew he wouldn't need it. Events of the night were permanently seared onto his brain.

He took one long last look at the hundreds of people fighting and watching the blaze. *Each one is a story worth writing*, he thought.

Jesse tried to brush the soot out of his hair with his hands. Gray ash fell over the bathroom counter and into the restroom sink at the newspaper. He wiped it away, but it smeared over the wet counter. He grabbed a few paper towels from the dispenser and wet them, then wiped up his mess, but it only made it worse. He was in a bit of a daze. His face burned. His eyes burned. His lungs hurt. His throat was dry.

He returned to the newsroom and was surprised at how excited Weatherly was acting toward him, like a football coach encouraging his quarterback. "Start with a description of the devastation, and then hit them with the chief's quote to start the second graph. Make sure you put the chief's name in a couple of times. Show the reader how it feels to fight the biggest fire this city has ever seen."

Soot was falling all over his typewriter. He brushed it away. As he cranked a roll of paper into the typewriter, the lead sentence came to him. "The Landing on Columbia Street became a snake pit of fire hoses by 10:00 p.m. Monday night as towering flames destroyed three of the city's most historic buildings."

Melissa was at her desk, hunched over her typewriter like

nothing else mattered. Her square jaw was set, hair as full of soot as Jesse's. She was pounding out her story about the bar manager of the hotel who cried all night as she watched the ornamental palace of a hotel burn into a total loss. The manager had lived and worked there for more than twenty years.

Sherry was at her desk, writing the story from the fire fighters' point of view. Her boyfriend had not been injured. She was on the phone as she typed, probably with him. Mascara ran down her cheeks. Her forehead was so smudged with soot it looked like she was on a combat mission.

Chuck was writing up his interviews with the mayor and other public safety officials. He looked ecstatic to be back writing hard news after his stint as a sports reporter.

Jesse looked at Melissa. She was enthralled in the fever pitch of writing on deadline. The newsroom was humming. She looked up and caught him staring. She smiled and gave him her first collegial nod.

Jesse smiled back.

Half the newsroom crowded into Henry's after deadline on the night of the fire.

Jesse saw Melissa walking in the back door. He worked his way over. She was still dirty from the fire, but she let Jesse give her a hug.

Melissa remembered her manners and backed up to scold him. "Don't think you're going to sweep me off my feet just because you helped me get one of the best stories of my life."

"What a night," Jesse said. "This place is a mad house. We got cops and firefighters and survivors and onlookers in here. Let's see if I can get us a drink."

"That you can do." Melissa followed in his wake and yelled

her order in his ear as he eased through the packed crowd to get to the bar. "I'll have a scotch on the rocks, Johnny Walker Red, and make it a double."

Melissa raised her scotch in a toast to Jesse. "I want to say thank you. Thank you for throwing me back into the fire. I knew I wasn't done yet."

Jesse laughed and clinked her glass as she kept toasting. "And one more thing. Working with you tonight made me realize I've been just a little bit of a bitch."

Jesse took a long drink of his beer and smiled at her. "Did you say 'bitch' or 'witch'?"

Melissa gave him a tight smirk. "Very funny. Guess I had that coming. Listen, I want to talk about this arson business. The gal who runs the bar at the Rosemarie Hotel gave me the best interview I think I've ever had. She told enough stories about what people do in that hotel to make you think the good Lord burned it down in vengeance. But that's not all. She said that Pete Simmons, the guy who owns the hotel, torched the place. He was clearing everybody out way before anybody smelled smoke."

"Everybody knows it was arson," Jesse said. "And if Simmons set the hotel fire, he set the other two fires to confuse the issue. If he only burned down his own building, it would look too much like an insurance claim."

"How could anyone do that?" Melissa asked as she finished her drink and held up her glass for another. "The Rosemarie was one of the most beautiful old buildings I've ever seen. He could have sold it if he needed the money."

"Maybe we should give old Pete a call," Jesse said.

Melissa shook her head as she waved her empty glass at the bartender. Dust floated off her short brown hair. "No, that's not how we do it. Pete would just deny it. What we do is talk to his insurance company. Their investigators will do all the work for us, and they'll leak the results to keep the heat on the police and prosecutor."

Jesse nodded as Melissa got him another beer. She made an athletic reach and he saw for the first time how sensual she could be once she relaxed. He loved the way she was using *we* when she talked about reporting. And he couldn't believe the forty-five-year-old reporter was finally giving him some highly usable investigative tips.

Chuck walked into the choking bar with a stack of newspapers, hot off the press. He passed them out and the crowd broke into reading groups.

The photographs were stunning, especially the flaming wall that looked like it was already falling. Jesse's lead story was next to Melissa's feature story. Their bylines were practically touching.

Chuck sidled up to Jesse, squinted his eyes, and scrunched up his nose. "Did I just see you making nice with Melissa?"

Jesse gave him a bear hug. "You say that like it's a bad thing, Chuck. She's really not as horrible as we all think. She's actually a lot of fun."

As Jesse spoke, Kelly and a couple of her dancing pals entered the bar. As usual, the crowd parted for the foxy ladies to make a grand entrance. Kelly walked by Jesse like he wasn't even standing at the bar.

Chuck pretended to shiver. "Now that's the coldest shoulder I ever saw. She blew by you like February."

CHAPTER TWENTY-SEVEN

It was March before Jesse saw it coming. He was busy in the newsroom and, in his spare time, getting to know the beautiful art teacher who moved into the apartment below him at 1114.

No arrests had been made in the Landing fire. It looked like police and insurance investigators were coming up empty handed. They found plenty of evidence indicating arson but nothing except suspicion to link the hotel owner to the crime.

Spring was still a month away in northern Indiana, but the hopefuls and groundhog believers thought it was right around the corner. Jesse, Butch, and Dale could see their breath as they hauled instruments into Rob Ashe's recording studio on Hanna Street. It was Saturday morning, and they were hungover from the Friday show but too excited to notice.

Stepping into the concrete block building, the three members of Wyler realized they were safe inside even though the neighborhood was becoming a high-crime area. There were no windows. The walls were painted black and covered with gray Styrofoam insulation boards and acoustic panels that looked like upside-down egg cartons. The heavy steel door was insulated on the inside and fortified outside with metal plating.

Rob had long blond hair and a bodybuilder's swagger, handsome as a cross between Robert Redford and Kirk Douglas. He welcomed the musicians to his studio. "Don't believe all that bullshit you read in the paper about this being a high-crime neighborhood. No offense, Jesse. I know you're a good reporter, but as you can see, I've got a fortress here. Your cars are safe in the back lot. Oh, that reminds me. Wait a second while I go out and lock the gate." Then he left.

Dale asked the obvious question. "If it's so safe why does he need to lock the gate?"

Rob came back as the question hung in the air. He took one look at the musicians and smiled. "Just a precaution. Never had a car broken into. The fence is ten feet tall with three strands of barbed wire on top. And I pay a couple guys a few bucks a month to keep an eye on the place."

Jesse didn't care about the neighborhood. He was in musical heaven. He'd never seen so many lights and levers and dials and gauges. The floor was covered in an all-weather carpet with bouncy rubber backing. "Look at us, boys. We're finally in the studio. I smell a hit record in the works."

"Not so fast, Jesse." Rob was plugging in guitar amps and running microphone cables. "Let me get you set up. Do you want to face each other when you sing?"

Butch was tuning his guitar. "That'd be great. Three mics, right in the center of the room. Would that work?"

"Let's put you each in a separate room so we don't record on each other's mics," Rob said. "We'll do it live. You'll each get the same mix in your headphones. How many songs you got?"

"At least thirty." Dale banged his tambourine for emphasis.

Rob did a double take. "Thirty songs? How many originals?"

Butch stood up to adjust the height on his mic. "They're all originals."

Rob shook his head and laughed. "I've never tried to record even one third that many songs at once. I know you're well-rehearsed. I heard you at Mother's. Liked what I heard. That's why you're getting the six-hundred-dollar special. We'll do a demo track and see how many we can get down in two days. Then we'll listen and see which ones we want to work on more."

It didn't take long to get a mix on three voices and two guitars. Dale's percussion instruments would come through his vocal mic. The studio magic began when the headphones went on. The trio looked at each other like they'd boarded a spaceship. Everything sounded larger than life.

"I'll take a little more of whatever you've got on my voice," Dale said.

Rob talked to them through the headphones by his microphone at the mixing board. "No can do, Dale. Everybody's going to want more of this and that, but too much of a good thing muddies the mix."

Butch chuckled. "We wouldn't want to muddy the mix, now would we, boys?"

"No thank you, sir." Dale shook his Maracas. "No Muddy Waters for me, please."

They were giddy with excitement. They'd never heard themselves sound so good. The three of them got distracted in self-congratulation. Rob got their attention. "Let's roll. Whenever you're ready. Start when you see the red light on the wall behind me."

The light went on and they played near-perfect takes of five songs in a row, leaving five-second gaps between songs. Rob let them go. The song titles were "Cherry Cola," "Rebekah," "Freedom Train," "Honey Darlin' Baby," and "Secret Sail."

They stopped to catch their breath, drink water, and retune the guitars.

Rob stepped out from behind the board as they removed their headphones. "Unbelievable, guys. Absolutely crazy. I never had anybody put down five songs without stopping. You even left gaps between the songs."

Butch nodded like it was no big deal. "How are we sounding?"

Rob grabbed Butch by both shoulders and tried to shake him into the significance of the moment. "The singing is right on. The songs are great. I would have stopped recording if you weren't just killing it. Come on, put your headphones back on. I'll play back thirty seconds of each song. See what you think."

Jesse was pleased to see Rob getting so excited. The grins on Dale and Butch's faces got broader as they listened to the playback. The harmonies sounded big-time good.

Jesse felt himself falling in love with the process of recording music in a studio with a sound engineer at the mixing board. It was a life-changing moment. His world tilted on its axis. He would never be the same. All of a sudden, it felt like he was born to write and record songs.

Rob suggested they continue by doing one song at a time. "Record and listen, record and listen. If we make it one song at a time, great. If we make mistakes in the middle, I'll stop, and we'll do over. Sound good?"

The band agreed to proceed and charged ahead like the training wheels had been taken off their bicycles. By eight o'clock, they had recorded fourteen songs. They only had do-overs on three tunes. They were completely caught up in the energy of the session.

Jesse looked at the clock on the wall and had to become the voice of reason. "I hate to say this, but we've got to get our gear out of here and set up at Mother's to start playing by nine thirty."

Rob waved his arms like he could change the schedule. "You can't play tonight. You're coming back here tomorrow at noon, right? You can't record all day, play all night, and come back the next day to record more songs. Your voices will be blown. I know you guys. You'll be drinking and smoking all night long. You can't do it. It can't be done."

All three members of Wyler listened to him, looked at each other, and shrugged their shoulders as if to say, "Why not?"

The gig at Mother's turned into a free for all once Jesse announced they'd been in the studio all day making a record. People bought them beers and shots all night long. Wyler was no longer just another local band; they were recording artists.

The club got more crowded as the night continued. Excitement levels were high on the stage and off. The band sounded tight, but the vocals didn't sound as good live without the studio effects.

Butch had a partial solution. He pointed at Jesse and Dale. "When in doubt, turn it up."

By midnight, the booze was taking its toll on the band. They were getting sloppy enough to slur their words. The crowd was too drunk to notice. Dale took Butch and Jesse aside. "All right, I'm drunk and my voice is shot. I think Rob was right. We're going to be a mess tomorrow unless we shut it down early."

Jesse looked over at the front door. "Don't look now but people are still lining up to pay the cover charge."

"Let's just stop drinking for the night." Dale said. "That way we can keep playing and still be okay to record."

Jesse and Butch looked at him like he'd lost his mind. They'd never played a single note of music without drinking alcohol and smoking marijuana. Dale held his ground. "I'll show you how." He went up to the bar and got a pitcher of water with ice and three glasses.

The band made it through an entire set drinking nothing but water. People kept buying them drinks. Trays of beer and shots were piling up on the table to the left of the stage. Jesse appealed to the crowd. "All right, everybody. We've got free beer and shots up here for anybody who wants them. We can't drink anymore because we've got to be in the studio again tomorrow."

People came up and grabbed the free booze, mysteriously leaving only three shots of tequila behind. The band couldn't help themselves. They couldn't let the shots go to waste. Jesse made a toast. "Here's to the last shot of the night. We can't waste good booze. There are sober people in Japan."

The three mostly drunk musicians managed to shut down a little early and not stay up the rest of the night, drinking and smoking with their friends to celebrate the successful performance.

By noon the next day, they were upright and ready to record. They fueled themselves with nothing but coffee and water. Rob was playing their tape from the day before at full volume through the main speakers when they arrived and loaded in their amps and guitars. He blasted through snippets of five songs before turning it down to address the band.

"You guys did some phenomenal work yesterday. It doesn't look like you were too hard on yourselves last night. How you feel?"

Butch pulled his guitar out of the case. "Aces. We're good to go."

Dale handed Rob the cup of coffee he brought for him. "Here's a cup to get you going. Hey, we sound great on the big speakers. Nice work."

"Thanks, man," Rob said as he took the lid off his coffee. "We ready to get ready?"

Dale held up his plastic coffee cup like he was making a toast. "We were born ready."

It was only the second day of recording and the band already felt right at home in the studio. The set-up was quicker, and the headphone mix sounded as good as it had the day before. Unfortunately, the vocals were rough.

Rob was undaunted. "Run through a few songs, get warmed up. We'll start recording when your voices come around."

It only took two and a half songs before Butch stopped playing and addressed Rob. "We're good to go."

The band ran through twelve more songs, one at a time. They sounded better than the day before. The red recording light gave them a new sense of urgency. They were beginning to realize that what went down on tape was what they would be listening to for a long time.

They finally quit at 9:30 p.m. Nine and a half hours never passed so quickly. They drank water between songs and stopped for a couple bathroom breaks, but they never thought about eating lunch. They did smoke cigarettes and a couple of joints, but that was it. No booze.

The studio experience vaulted them up a couple rungs on the ladder of musical professionalism. Butch listened to the playback with great concentration. "Man, imagine how good these songs are going to sound with bass and drums and keyboard."

Jesse and Dale agreed. The stars in their eyes were shining more brightly than ever. Jesse was wrapping up mic cords when he surprised himself with what came out of his mouth. "You know, I think I could do this for a living."

CHAPTER TWENTY-EIGHT

Jesse's songwriting dreams were put on hold one week after his two-day recording session. Weatherly summoned him to the city desk. Jerry Shackleford, the forty-two-year-old reporter who covered courts, was already seated across the desk from Weatherly. He sat up ramrod straight, although he slouched when he walked. "Shack" was just under six feet tall and always wore a perfectly knotted bow tie and Buddy Holly eyeglasses. He had a hawk nose and a stubborn chin, not a ladies' man by any means. He was married with two rowdy teenaged boys.

"Ah, Jesse," Weatherly said with telltale grandiosity. Something big was up. "Shack here is taking a two-week vacation in April and you're going to cover courts while he's gone."

Weatherly and Shack watched for his reaction. Jesse tried to stay cool, but he couldn't. Courts was a big deal. It was murder trials, lawsuits about money, and more legal language than he would ever understand. "I . . . I wouldn't know where to begin."

Weatherly motioned for him to take a seat. "Of course, you wouldn't. Karl Stone usually fills in when Shack is out, but Karl's on the state government beat down in Indianapolis. Besides, I want to see what you can do with it. Courts is the toughest beat there is. About a third of our stories, both local and national, come out of the legal system. Shack's been covering it for fifteen years now."

"And I still don't know what I'm doing." Shack joked with Jesse for the first time, ever. The older reporter always kept to himself, didn't say much, but he wrote some of the most dynamic copy in the newsroom.

"Shack's going to take you on his court rounds and teach you the ropes. You already know how to do it. You just don't realize it yet," Weatherly reassured him.

"Think of it this way," Shack began. "You've covered lots of crime on the police beat. Courts is about those same stories, but a little farther down the timeline of justice. You've been writing about the criminal when he gets arrested. I write about him when the court decides if he's guilty."

Weatherly leaned back in his chair and looked at the ceiling. "I love it when you talk about the timeline of justice, Shack."

Shack acknowledged the backhanded compliment with a quick nod. "It's simple. We start at the clerk's office for the divorce filings. Then we go through the criminal court dockets to see who got what sentence. After that, we hit the civil courts to ask the court reporters if any big cases are coming down."

"Wait." Jesse held up both hands. "What's this about criminal and civil courts? Are there different kinds of courts?"

Shack lowered his head and got a stern, tutorial tone to his voice. "Most people don't know this, and we don't always do a good job explaining it, but there are two very different systems of law in this country. One is criminal law where the government tries to throw people in jail. The second is civil law, which is anything but civil. Don't let the name fool you. Civil courts are where people fight about money and civil rights issues like busing students for racial quotas."

Shack's brilliant breakdown of the court beat continued as he took Jesse on his rounds of the Allen County Courthouse. "Now listen. This is going to be like drinking water from a firehose. Don't wrap your lips around the nozzle or you'll explode. Step back a good long way, let the water pool up, and dip your cup in to sip a little at a time."

Jesse stopped in his tracks, realizing he had just heard an

analogy he would steal for the rest of his life. Shack didn't stop walking or talking. Jesse ran to catch up as the veteran reporter led him into the courthouse. They walked to the center of the rotunda on the intricate patterns of colored-tile floors. Looking up three stories, they could see the historic murals and spectacular stained-glass dome.

Shack extended both arms above his head in a rare gesture of enthusiasm. "Behold. The rule of law. It's bigger than us all. It stands for civilization itself. Without it, we would all be at the mercy of street gangs and rogue armies."

Jesse was speechless. He was truly and thoroughly intimidated. This was a huge place, filled with many courts and hundreds of employees. How could one reporter possibly cover it all?

Attorneys were walking in every direction, each one looking well dressed and completely confident in where he was going and what he was doing. All the attorneys were men. There were only two female attorneys in the entire county. Women were mostly court reporters or secretaries.

I'll never be that sure of myself, he thought. *All these guys with briefcases went to school for years to understand how to navigate these high-ceiling halls. I'm going to make enough mistakes to get myself thrown in jail, or at least thrown off the courts beat. No, don't think like that. You can do this. Remember how intimidated you were by the police beat at first. What is now terrifying will soon become commonplace.*

Shack brought him back to reality. "Come on, we'll start with the easy stuff. The Clerk's on the second floor. Let's walk up there and get the divorce notices."

Jesse followed him up the well-worn stone steps with a nauseating feeling of foreboding. The entire courthouse smelled like an old law book after you pulled it off the shelf, blew off the dust, and cracked open the leather book spine to get a whiff of yellowing pages.

Shack took him to a room behind a criminal court and sat him down in front of a stack of criminal court dockets at least two feet tall. "Some kind of action has been taken on each one of these cases," Shack explained as he opened the first file. "Look, here's the order, right on top, if you can read the judge's handwriting. Yeah, this case just got continued today. That means they put it off for another day. That happens a lot. Not news unless it's an important trial that got delayed for some reason."

Jesse wondered how he would know what was important and what wasn't.

Shack continued, "Read this order. A man got sentenced to twenty years in jail for shooting somebody. See, it's all there in black and white. Nothing that complicated." He shifted through the file. "Here's the affidavit for probable cause. Tells you everything about the case."

"What's an affidavit?"

Shack lowered his head and looked over his glasses at Jesse like he was realizing how much his younger colleague had to learn. "An affidavit is just a signed written statement. Don't let the fancy words fool you. Lawyers use them to scare the rest of us, but they're all pretty simple once you know what they mean. Now, if you want a good story, you get the names and addresses from these files and get out there and talk to the people involved. That's what separates the men from the boys."

Jesse knew what he was talking about. "It's like don't write your story from a police report."

"Exactly." Shack slapped him encouragingly on the shoulder. "And remember, there are two lawyers in every criminal case. The prosecutor represents the state—he has the burden to prove his case beyond a reasonable doubt. The defendant also has a lawyer. If he's too poor to afford his own attorney, a public defender gets appointed. Interview the lawyers. They're your best sources. They'll usually talk to you. They all want their name in the paper."

Shack's one-week crash course on courts was the best training Jesse had ever received. Even so, he felt abandoned when his mentor left for vacation. Worse than that, his third day on courts, Jesse found himself covering a murder trial. Shack had warned him about the trial but thought it would be continued by either the prosecution or the defense. He explained that lawyers often continued cases for reasons like witnesses weren't available or newly discovered evidence needed to be exchanged and examined.

Jesse marveled as sixty citizens marched into court for jury duty, single file. It was amazing how much of the community would be involved. Shack had explained that jury selection was an important part of any trial. It was open to the public, as were almost all court proceedings.

The jurors mostly looked down at their own feet as they filed in, but when they did look up, they saw the intimidating splendor of the massive courtroom. At one end, the judge's desk was raised two feet above the floor and flanked by a witness stand on the left and a seat for the bailiff, a deputy Sheriff, on the right. State and national flags draped behind the judge's desk. The court reporter, who took down every word spoken in court to keep a record of all proceedings, had a smaller desk in front of the judge's bench.

The room had twenty-five-foot ceilings and was ornately decorated with fresco paintings of settlers and Native Americans and bas-relief sculpture of mythological and Biblical characters and ancient Greek and Roman judges.

Jesse's favorite relief sculpture showed a settler being burned at the stake by Native Americans. He knew that was how each and every prospective juror was feeling. He was feeling a little burned-at-the-stake himself as he took a seat and settled in to learn what he could about criminal jury trials.

It didn't take long to realize this was going to be nothing like *Perry Mason* on television. It was boring. Picking the jury took all morning. The prosecutor and defense attorney asked prospective jurors questions to determine if they could be fair in this particular case. From their questions and the judge's opening remarks, Jesse gathered the defendant was charged with murder and that he was claiming self-defense.

Once jury selection was completed, The Honorable Herman Busse, Judge of the Allen County Circuit Court, called for a lunch break before beginning the actual trial.

During the break, Jesse asked the prosecutor how he thought the trial was going. The prosecutor, Adam Godfrey, was a short man in his late twenties with blond hair. His collar was as tight as his smile. "It's a little soon to ask that question, but I'll say this for the record: We've got twelve jurors seated with one alternate in case anyone gets sick—four women and eight men, and the alternate is a woman. They all seem capable and ready to listen to the evidence and reach a fair verdict. And remember, the verdict has to be unanimous in Indiana."

"So, if only one juror thinks the defendant is innocent, you lose?"

The prosecutor snapped his briefcase shut. "That's what 'unanimous' means. But I don't lose. The people of Indiana lose."

Jesse kicked himself mentally as the prosecutor hurried off. His questions had been stupid, and he'd given himself away as knowing nothing about trial work. *Come on, man*, he thought. *You can do better than that. Don't come at them with questions. Let them come to you with comments.*

No sooner had the thought crossed his mind than the defense attorney came over to talk. He had graying hair around his temples and was dressed in an expensive blue pin-striped suit with a bright red tie. "Good morning, I'm Patrick Middleton, attorney for the defense. Are you getting the drift of our defense?" he asked. "The victim—excuse me, the alleged victim—beat my client half to death. Then my client gets in his car, grabs his gun, and shoots his attacker, who was standing at the driver's window threatening more violence."

Jesse was able to spot the flaw in the self-defense theory. "So why didn't your client just drive away?"

Middleton narrowed his gaze. "Because he was afraid for his life," he snapped. "That's all I've got to prove, and he walks out of here. And you watch, he'll do it. I'll have him take the stand, and he'll convince at least one member of that jury he thought he was going to die. He's only five-feet-seven, one hundred thirty-five pounds. The guy who beat him up was six-two, and over two hundred pounds."

The defendant, Harold Rutledge, was a twenty-nine-year-old African American man. He had shot and killed Jay Wilson, a white man. The racial deck of playing cards was stacked in favor of the prosecution. "Forty years earlier," Middleton said, "There wouldn't have been a trial in Indiana. The Black man would have been lynched in the public square the day after the shooting."

Jesse noticed the defendant was dressed in street clothes for the trial. But once it was time for lunch and the jury had been excused, the sheriff's deputy-bailiff handcuffed the defendant and took him away through the door that led to a holding cell.

The man had not been able to post a bond while he waited nearly a year to get to trial. The judge allowed the man to wear street clothes for his trial since having the jury see the defendant in prison garb would be highly prejudicial.

Jesse didn't have time to eat. He had to cover all the other court cases of the day. There were fifteen stops on his rounds. He was baffled that the paper expected one reporter to cover all of this. *How can Weatherly send me off to my first murder trial and not provide any back up? One thing for sure, if I miss something the afternoon paper will blow it up like some kind of big scoop.*

Jesse was back in the courtroom after lunch and taking copious notes as the trial began with each side delivering opening statements. Prosecutor Godfrey attempted to portray the defendant as a drug dealer bent on revenge for losing a fight over illegal profit.

Middleton portrayed his client as the victim of an unprovoked and life-threatening attack by a drug-crazed addict. While both sides suggested cocaine was somehow involved in the case, it sounded to Jesse like each attorney was talking about an entirely different set of facts.

Jesse searched the faces of the jurors and wondered what was going on in their minds as they listened to the opposing versions of the facts. His maturation process as a reporter had developed from becoming a better listener, to asking good questions, to asking follow-up questions, to wondering what people were thinking so he would know which questions to ask.

Godfrey presented its case first. The chief detective took the witness stand in a rumpled suit and a wide tie and told the jury the basic facts of his investigation. The victim had been unarmed, and the "murder weapon" was found in the defendant's car, which had never left the scene of the shooting.

Middleton's cross-examination of the detective focused on the significant head injuries the defendant sustained as a result of the attack. He also asked questions to reveal that only one round had been fired from the .45 caliber handgun, and that the defendant's vehicle never left the scene.

"What significance, Detective, do you attach to the fact that the defendant's vehicle never left the scene?"

"It means he did not attempt to flee," the detective said.

"And does not attempting to flee indicate to you the defendant thought he had done nothing wrong?"

"Objection, Your Honor." Godfrey leaped to his feet. "The detective cannot possibly know what was in the mind of the defendant."

"Objection sustained," the judge ruled instantly. "Defense counsel, you may proceed, but do not to make closing arguments in your questions."

When court adjourned for the day, Jesse dashed around the courthouse to make sure he wasn't missing anything from other judges. He was back in the newsroom by 5:30 p.m., which was plenty of time to write his first murder trial story. He led off with a flair: "The question of reasonable doubt hung over the jury today in the murder trial of David Rutledge."

Weatherly looked over Jesse's shoulder and read the first sentence. "No, no, no. Spare me the purple prose. Start off with the fact that a jury was selected today in the murder trial of Rutledge. Then talk about opening statements. Don't take sides. You're making it sound like reasonable doubt has already been established. That means you're for the defendant. You might think he's innocent, but you must maintain journalistic integrity. And, in case you don't know what that means, it means neutrality. Every story is like a pancake. It has two sides, and you can't eat one without the other."

Jesse was grateful for the advice. It was Weatherly's favorite saying. Not a day went by that he didn't yell it across the newsroom at some reporter who wasn't writing both sides of her story.

Before court began the second day of the murder trial, Godfrey approached Jesse with considerably more respect than he had shown the day before. "Nice job on the coverage. I liked the mention of the judge sustaining my objection on why the defendant didn't leave the scene."

Jesse remembered his resolution to not ask stupid questions, but he couldn't help himself. "So why do you think the defendant stayed at the scene?"

"It doesn't matter. It's irrelevant," the prosecutor said. "What matters is the defendant shot an unarmed man when he, the defendant, was already safe in his car."

The second day of trial was all prosecution witnesses, including the coroner, a ballistics expert, and even the mother of the victim, Jay Wilson, who testified tearfully about what a "good boy" her son had been.

On the third day, the prosecution called one last witness, a bystander, who testified that Wilson was at least ten feet away from the car when the defendant fired his weapon.

Middleton turned the evidence around with one question. "Was the man who got shot chasing the man who shot him?"

"Yes."

"No further questions."

Godfrey tried to save his witness with redirect examination. "Was Mr. Wilson carrying a gun or any other kind of weapon?"

"Objection, Your Honor," Middleton raised his voice and stood up. "That question has been asked and answered. And we also object to the characterization of the deceased as a 'victim.' The only victim in this case is my client, the defendant."

Judge Busse held up his hand to stop the defense counsel from continuing. "Hold it right there. I'm going to grant the objection on the asked and answered, but counsel has been warned not to incorporate his closing argument in the questioning of witnesses. That includes making objections. You are admonished, sir, to refrain from making argument in your objections."

Jesse was impressed with the defense counsel. *The guy's good*, he thought. *He made his point, and nothing could erase it. The judge might as well have said, "Ladies and gentlemen of the jury, please un-ring that bell."*

Once the prosecution rested its case, Middleton took most of the third day bringing in character witnesses on behalf of his client. The best witness for the defense was Mr. Rutledge's boss at the aluminum foundry, who testified Rutledge was an excellent worker who almost never missed a day of work and who had, in fact, worked a ten-hour shift on the day of the shooting.

"To the best of your knowledge, was Mr. Rutledge a drug dealer?" defense counsel asked.

Godfrey stood up, raised his voice, and threw his arms in the air. "Objection, Your Honor. This man's employer has no idea what happens once he leaves work!"

"Objection overruled," Judge Busse ruled. "You've introduced evidence calling Mr. Rutledge a drug dealer. We'll let the jury decide that question after they hear from his employer." He turned to the witness. "You may answer the question."

"What was the question again?"

Middleton was only too happy to repeat. "Was Mr. Rutledge a drug dealer?"

The witness glanced quickly at the jury and shifted in his seat. "Oh, yeah. Sorry, I forgot the question. But I can say no,

Harold Rutledge is not a drug dealer. He is an honest, hard-working man."

Middleton turned to the jury and raised his voice slightly as he held out his hand to the witness. "Thank you. No further questions."

By the morning of the fourth day of trial, Jesse's three front-page stories had attracted so much attention that he was no longer the only newsman in the room. Reporters from the rival afternoon paper and all the surrounding small-town papers were in attendance. Television and radio had to wait outside the courtroom in the hall since electronic recording devices and cameras were not permitted in the courtroom.

Middleton presented the defendant as his last witness. Harold Rutledge broke into tears as he told the jury that the man who'd beat him and chased him had been his friend in high school. "But that night he came after me for money. When I told him I didn't have any, he started beating me. He said I had a job, so I had to have money. He's so big. And he was crazy. Like he was on drugs or something. It wasn't the same guy I knew in school.

"He hit me in the head so hard and so many times I couldn't even see. Then he chased me, and I ran to the car to get away. I was so scared I grabbed my gun before I started the car. Once I fired the shot, I was afraid to look out the window. I was hoping it just scared him."

The jury did not react one way or the other to his testimony. Godfrey did his best to cross-examine Rutledge on the fact that he knew Jay Wilson was unarmed.

"He was not unarmed," Rutledge blurted out in frustration. "He had two big arms and he was killing me with them."

Middleton rested his case following Rutledge's testimony.

Closing arguments from the prosecutor and defense counsel

were spirited. After arguments, the jury was directed to a private room across the hall from the courtroom to begin its deliberations.

Once the judge retired to his chambers, everybody left the courtroom except a sheriff's deputy, Middleton, Harold Rutledge, and Jesse. There was no telling how long it would take the jury to reach a verdict, if they could reach a unanimous verdict at all.

Jesse took his chance and opened the gate between the court and spectator sections. Seeing no objection from Middleton, he sat down next to Rutledge and asked the only question he could think of under the incredibly stressful conditions. "How are you doing?"

Tears rolled down Rutledge's face as they had when he was on the witness stand. "I'm sorry he died, man. I truly wish none of this had happened. That prosecutor wants me to spend the rest of my life in jail. The pictures the coroner showed of Jay Wilson dead were terrible. Did you see the jury look at me like they didn't care what I was saying? I didn't do anything you wouldn't do. Man, he was beating me to death. What would you do?"

Middleton interrupted to ask Jesse a question. "So, you've been here for the whole trial. You be the jury. Guilty or not guilty?"

Jesse didn't have to think about his response. He grabbed Harold Rutledge by the shoulder. "Not guilty. He's not a drug dealer, and he didn't flee the scene, and he was being beaten within an inch of his life. He was afraid for his life."

Rutledge sniffled and looked up at Jesse. "You really think so?"

"Yes, he really thinks you're innocent and so will the jury," Middleton said.

Jesse left to make his rounds and check his sources in other courts. He returned an hour later, and then again, an hour after that, and for a third time an hour later. The defendant and his attorney were still sitting alone in the trial courtroom with a sheriff's deputy, who was trying not to fall asleep outside the judge's door.

"Did you hear anything yet?" Rutledge asked.

"Nothing yet." Jesse sat down next to the defendant. "The bailiff won't even tell me if they've selected a foreman."

The defendant let out his breath like he was deflating and lowered his head to his arms on the table. "I should have taken the plea deal for twenty years. They're going to send me to jail for the rest of my life."

Middleton advised Rutledge to lower his voice. "Take a deep breath. This might take hours. That's it. Sit down. Breathe. It's going to be all right."

Jesse realized the fact that Rutledge had a gun in the first place did not help his case. He did not mention this fly in the ointment to the defendant.

Just then, he heard the bailiff knocking on the judge's door. "We've got a verdict, Your Honor."

The bailiff led the jury into the courtroom. None of them showed any signs of what the verdict might be. Then Judge Busse returned. When the judge asked the jury if they had selected a foreman, it was not someone Jesse would have predicted. It was juror number five, a male insurance salesman.

At that point, all action in the courtroom began to take place in super slow motion. It took the foreman forever to hand the verdict to the judge, and the judge took more than his time unfolding and reading it to himself before announcing it to the courtroom.

"We, the jury, find the defendant not guilty of the charge of murder."

The defendant jumped up and hugged his attorney as the jury filed out of the courtroom. Then he came to the rail and hugged Jesse. "I'm free. I'm free. I been in jail almost a year for something I didn't do, and now I'm free."

Jesse was nearly as relieved as Rutledge, whose elation was contagious. No doubt about it, Jesse had gotten personally involved in the trial. Weatherly had saved him from himself. His stories had not taken sides, even though he wanted to argue the defendant's innocence every single day.

Now, he could finally write the words he had been wanting to write: "Defendant Harold Rutledge was found innocent of murder yesterday by an Allen County jury."

CHAPTER TWENTY-NINE

The thrill of writing a colorful murder trial story took nearly a month to wear off as Jesse became buried once again in the black-and-white slog of daily news.

The school beat was still about teachers threatening to strike but never actually going on strike. The police beat was cops and robbers as usual, no big fires or natural disasters. Planes weren't crashing in farmers' fields, vandals weren't giving old ladies heart attacks, and all the massage parlors had been busted and closed.

The most exciting news of the month was the end of a story, not the beginning. On April 30, 1975, North Vietnam renamed Saigon, Ho Chi Minh City. The war in Vietnam was over. Jesse never thought he'd see the day.

The day before, an iconic photograph appeared in newspapers around the world of a lone American helicopter precariously perched on top of a tiny rooftop in Saigon. Ladders leading to the helicopter bent under the weight of too many people who were trying to board the flight.

Jesse was thrilled the hated war was ending, but a small part of him was embarrassed for his country slinking away from defeat like a dog with its tail between its legs. And what would newspapers look like without daily horror stories from Vietnam on the front pages?

Jesse could feel his world turning. The next chapter in his life had been creeping up on him for some time. He felt it tapping him on the back, trying to get his attention. He was too busy to turn around. Now, it was whispering in his ear. He was listening, but he couldn't make out what it was trying to tell him.

His band, Wyler, was still playing at Mother's and selling twelve-song cassette tapes of their recordings. It was becoming increasingly obvious they would have to leave northeastern Indiana to make anything happen in their musical careers. As Dale liked to say, "Once you get to the top in Fort Wayne, you're still at the bottom."

Kelly moved out of the back apartment at 1114 and into an apartment down the street with a couple of her dancing friends. She made it a point to avoid Jesse at all costs, or to ignore him completely when their paths accidentally crossed.

The thrill seeker in Jesse realized it was time to shake things up. And what better way to do that than continue his quest to write a first-person account of every job in the city? Weatherly laughed until he choked when Jesse said he wanted to be a garbageman for a day.

"I'd pay good money to see that," Weatherly said as he regained his breath.

The National Serv-All Garbage Company was only too happy to accommodate. The next Monday morning, as the tomato-red sun was rising, Jesse found himself riding the back of a garbage truck with Lee, a thirty-three-year-old father of three, who wore an orange hat that said, "Garbage is Beautiful."

The route for the day included 350 homes in a suburban district on the north side of town. It was biting cold, so Jesse rode with Lee in back with the garbage. Garbagemen usually rode on step platforms on the side of the truck behind the rear wheels. But now, to get out of the wind, Lee had them riding in the garbage collecting bin of the truck with the compacting blade that could crunch a sofa like a toothpick. "Careful now," Lee warned. "Get caught in that thing and it's all over. The main thing is don't let the rear door close on you."

Lee was just under six-feet tall and 190 pounds of solid muscle. He wore tan, quilt-lined coveralls with a hood that rested on the back of his head. His bright blue eyes were quick and intelligent. He looked more like a Nordic ski instructor than a garbageman.

He had all the athletic moves necessary for efficient garbage collection. He could jump off the truck, grab a can of garbage with each hand, and bang the contents into the compacting bin before the truck came to a complete stop. Then he'd slam the cans back on the pavement and hop back on the truck in one fluid motion. Lee liked to make a lot of noise along the route. "Time for people to be up anyway."

Jesse was twenty-five and thought he was in good shape, but he had a hard time keeping up with Lee as the garbage truck driver swept through the first section of expensive homes in a flash. At least the workout warmed him up. He'd worn jeans and a black leather jacket but no long underwear and no hat.

The collection process came to an abrupt halt at a narrow spot in the road with garbage piled high on either side. The road was down to one lane because cars were parked two feet off the curb on each side. Jesse and Lee had just stepped off the truck in opposite directions when a man in a suit and tie driving a Mercedes laid on his horn. The truck was blocking his way.

The man rolled down his window and shouted, "God damnit, you're going to make me late for work!"

Lee set down two garbage cans and walked slowly toward the driver, who blasted his horn again in frustration as he rolled his window back up. Lee remained calm as he arrived at the driver's door and motioned for him to roll the window back down.

Once the driver locked his doors and reluctantly rolled down the window a crack, Lee had a couple suggestions for him. "Why don't you get out of that fancy car and help us with this three-weeks of garbage your neighbors have left on their lawns? Or maybe you could knock on their doors and have them do a better parking job?"

"Why don't you just move the truck?" The man sounded more exasperated than angry.

Lee looked up at the sky and stretched his arms over his head. "You know, we might have done that if you hadn't been honking your horn like you were the only guy in the world who had to work today."

The Mercedes driver looked Lee up and down and then dropped his head down onto the steering wheel. It looked like he might start blowing his horn again. Then he raised his head and shook it like a dog shaking water off its coat. He opened the door and slowly got out of his car.

Jesse walked toward the two of them, thinking a fight was brewing. But the man in the fancy car surprised them as he loosened his tie. "All right, all right. I'll load some garbage. I can see it's the only way I'll get out of here."

"My man," Lee shouted in delight as he walked back to the garbage heap and handed the man a can.

The garbage driver was so surprised to see a man in a suit hauling garbage that he got out of the truck and lent a hand as well. With four men working, they had the garbage pile loaded in record time. The man in the loose tie rubbed coffee grinds and grit of unknown origin off his hands and headed back for his car. "Sorry about the horn, gentlemen. It's been a pleasure doing a little *real* work with you guys this morning."

The garbage truck moved out of the way. The man said to Lee as he drove by, "In case you couldn't tell, I grew up baling hay on my daddy's farm."

The garbage driver leaned out of the truck window and scratched his head in wonder as he watched the fancy car pull away. "How does a horn-blowing jerk become a good guy in such a short time?"

"He took one look at Lee and figured he didn't want to get his ass kicked," Jesse said.

Lee smiled big and showed off a healthy set of teeth. "It's all about the garbage. Hauling garbage brings out the best in people. Just look at me."

The three men got back to business and started having fun seeing how fast they could pick up the refuse. The driver wasn't even bringing the truck to a complete stop at most pick-up sites. Lee was chattering away about how he and his wife were going to put their kids through college.

"Yeah, I'm done with the garbage route about noon each day. Then I go to my junkyard business. That's where I really clean up, if you'll pardon the pun. You'd be surprised what I find for the junkyard from the pick-ups. Anything really good, I call the wife and she comes to get it. I carpeted the inside of my van with a big piece of shag somebody threw out."

They were rolling by a house with no cans out front when a woman came running outside in her bare feet and bathrobe. "Wait for me. Wait a minute please. I've got two cans in the garage. My son forgot. Please wait. I'll pay extra."

Lee banged on the side of the truck for a stop. Without saying a word to each other, he and Jesse jumped off and ran to the woman's garage to grab her overflowing cans. The woman ran back into her house and returned with a five-dollar bill for each of them. She was bouncing on her feet in excitement.

Lee took both bills with a wide grin and said, "We'll put this in the college fund for the kids." Jesse nodded his agreement.

They dumped the garbage in the truck, and Jesse set his can down on her front lawn. "Come on, now," Lee said. "We'll put them back where we found them."

The woman thanked them profusely as they returned the empty cans to her garage. Jesse looked back from the truck as they rolled away. She was waving goodbye with her mouth agape like she'd just seen the Lone Ranger of garbage rearing up on his steel horse and calling out, "Hi-Ho, Aluminum!"

Jesse laughed and marveled to himself. *Who would have thought I'd learn lessons in civility and chivalry from a garbageman? This Lee guy is something special. So is the driver. Then again, most people will surprise you if you give them half a chance.*

The warm and fuzzy feelings didn't last long. The truck stopped in front of a large pile of stone. The homeowner came storming out when it became apparent his stones were not getting picked up.

"Hey, what about all that stone? It's garbage. You've got to take it away."

Lee waited until the man stomped up to the truck before speaking in a civil tone. "We can't pick this up, sir. The stone would ruin our compactor."

The older man wasn't wearing a coat. He hugged himself, shivering as he became belligerent. "You can take the damn stone. I've seen you haul away bricks. And you take worse stuff than bricks."

Lee remained firm. "Can't take the stones. Our compactor won't take them. They're bigger than bricks."

"What's it going to take?" The man held out his arms as if begging for mercy. "Money? What is this? Some kind of shakedown?"

Lee taped the side of the truck twice for a takeoff. The man chased the truck down the road to the next stop, shouting obscenities all the way and giving them the finger. "I'm calling the police! I'm going to get the police out here to make you do your job!"

Lee shrugged his shoulders and shook his head as he said to Jesse, "Some people just won't listen."

Jesse and Lee laughed in the indignant man's face as the truck pulled away. Jesse yelled at Lee over the noise of the accelerating truck. "I never thought there'd be so much public relations in the garbage business."

Lee just shook his head and shouted, "You have no idea."

By the end of the route, Jesse was exhausted. They'd been lifting garbage cans up to eighty pounds each for nearly six hours. "You got to get used to it," Lee said as he saw Jesse trying to stretch out the stiffness.

Photographer Dean Sorenson arrived shortly after the garbage truck pulled into the National Serv-All lot. Jesse had called for photos from a pay phone along the route as he realized what a great story he had on his hands. Dean obliged with some action shots of Lee and Jesse and the driver hoisting trash cans into the truck.

They retired to the break room for a cup of coffee. "Just be thankful it's not summer," Lee said. "All those bags of grass can break your back. And it's hot, and it stinks, and the bags break. And then there's the flies." He sipped his coffee. "You know, we only make four dollars and twenty-five cents an hour, helpers start at three dollars and eighty cents. But we're negotiating for a raise. We've only got thirty trucks and more than sixty thousand customers."

"Tell him about the lady and her purse," the driver said.

"Oh, yeah." Lee chuckled. "Every so often we get somebody who thinks she lost her purse in the garbage. We tell them we can't look for it after the compactor presses it. They don't want to hear that. What they do understand is they've got to go out to the landfill once the truck dumps the garbage."

"And lots of them do just that," the driver said. "You should see them out there, even after dark, rooting through mountains of garbage trying to find something like a wedding ring or a wallet."

Jesse found that image intriguing. "Do any of them ever find what they're looking for?"

"Oh yeah," Lee said. "One gal dug her diamond engagement ring out of the landfill. We should have given her an award. But I guess the ring was reward enough."

The driver took a sip on his coffee and smiled slyly. "Yeah, life's like a garbage dump. You got to dig through big piles of bullshit before you find the good stuff."

Jesse laughed in delight as he noted the quote.

Lee slapped the driver playfully on the shoulder. "Come on, you know that's my line."

CHAPTER THIRTY

A leather-skinned woman stood mesmerized in front of a larger-than-life sculpture of her Lord and savior. Her dark shawl and long, gray skirt were well-worn from years of raising children and grandchildren in poverty. Deep brown eyes still shone from her wrinkled face as she whispered prayers in front of the ornate golden altar at the massive Santa Domingo Church in Oaxaca, Mexico.

She raised her face to bask in the baroque splendor of the towering altar before putting two arthritic fingers to her lips to blow a soft kiss. Her trance looked to be a grateful plea for spiritual comfort and material mercy in her final years of life.

The old woman made the sign of a cross with the grace of ten thousand previous prayers and left a peso on a wood-carved pedestal in front of the wide marble steps. She looked up at the thirty-foot sculpture of the bleeding Jesus Christ hung from the cross.

The crucifixion was the centerpiece of the altar. It was gruesome. Bright red blood of the Christ ran from every wound on his body. The crown of thorns looked particularly painful, deeply embedded into the skin. The woman crossed herself again and shook her silver-haired head in suffering shared. She turned away to gather two young girls into her skirt, taking each one by the hand. Her head remained bowed as she ushered the girls quietly and briskly from the church.

Jesse watched her from the shadows until the tall doors shut behind her with a gentle thump. *Such a faith,* he thought. *What a comfort it must be to believe the son of God died for our sins. But so*

*strange to see a dying peasant savior surrounded by such aristocratic
splendor.*

The altar was five stories tall and practically filled with
twenty-four-karat gold. Gilded stucco reliefs, fresco paintings,
and larger-than-life sculptures of angels and apostles formed a
giant wall of religious symbolism. Light entered the cavernous
worship arena through sky-high stained-glass windows. The
light show was brilliant and soothing and achingly prismatic.

Once the grandmother and her girls left the sanctuary,
Jesse turned his attention to the curving staircase leading to
the golden pulpit that was to the left of the altar. A one-armed
custodian had been silently polishing the hand-carved wood
since Jesse arrived an hour earlier. *Now that guy's got job security*,
Jesse thought. *He could never finish polishing all the wood in this
church, even with two arms and an altar-boy assistant.*

Jesse was on day three of a two-week hitchhike through
Mexico for the *Journal Gazette*. Publisher Stephen Longstreet
had paid for a round-trip plane ticket to Mexico City. Jesse
would fly in, hitchhike around Mexico for two weeks, and fly
back.

It had been nearly a year since Jesse's "Dollar a Day to
LA" series of articles had been so well received by readers,
his ex-girlfriend Kelly's violent reaction notwithstanding. He
had traveler's checks for the Mexico trip, although he was
determined not to spend any money. He knew the only way to
truly experience a country was to throw himself at its mercy.

The Mexico trip had become a spiritual pilgrimage for Jesse
long before he ended up in the Oaxacan sanctuary. He wanted
the faith the old woman had, but the more he chased it, the
further away it got. He kept trying to fill the hole in his soul
with one thrill-seeking adventure after the other. Smoking
and drinking to excess only made the hole larger. He felt an

emptiness inside, and he was looking to find a cure on this journey.

A nagging voice inside his head told him he needed to find a faith like the old woman had in order to take himself out of the center of the universe. He knew that the more he tried to impose his will on the rest of the world, the less the universe would open up to him. But he was caught in the throes of trying to figure out what he was going to do with the rest of his life.

So, he wasn't taken completely by surprise when the question of whether to be a reporter or a musician was asked and answered, as if by magic, on the first night of the journey.

Jesse made it a point not to bring a map. He surrendered itinerary control. The road would lead him where he needed to go. He walked south from the airport through the horrifying slums of Mexico City. There were no rides to catch, only mind-numbing poverty and starvation. People were dying in the street. Beggars surrounded him. The stench of open sewers, rotten meat, and smoking kerosene gagged him.

The weight of his forty-pound backpack, combined with the burden of human suffering, nearly brought him to his knees. He stumbled through miles and miles of decrepit shanties and hopeless eyes before the air became breathable.

Outside the city, the sun scorched long, dry valleys. Only dusty, green cactus plants seemed oblivious to its one-hundred-degree heat. Truck rides were few and far between. Jesse was parched by the time the sun began going down. The warm 7 Up in his canteen was gone.

A battered truck stopped with a growl and a hiss. Three T-shirted men in the cab looked Jesse over carefully as he tried to tell them he was headed for Oaxaca. One of them directed him to the back of the truck, which was piled high with cases of something. Jesse thanked them in Hoosier Spanish and climbed aboard to find a teenage boy riding on top.

The lad peppered him with questions as the truck picked up speed and the wind blew through their hair. Jesse's lack of Spanish turned the conversation into a language lesson as the boy pointed out objects of interest and identified them in Spanish.

Jesse couldn't believe his good fortune when his young traveling companion opened up one of the cases on the truck and handed him a beer. It took a moment for the glorious truth to sink in. He'd gotten a ride on a beer truck.

The beer exploded as Jesse popped the can and sucked foam to keep from getting soaked. It was light but had good taste. It was warm, but it was wet and free. And Jesse was more than thirsty. The kid kept the beer coming as they rolled through one adobe town after another, about thirty kilometers apart. After five beers, the truck jolted to a stop for the night on a back road of another little town.

Jesse grabbed his pack and clambered off the truck with a good beer buzz. He waved goodbye and began walking aimlessly, lost in a foreign town with nowhere to go. He was exactly where he wanted to be. He stopped walking to contemplate his situation and concluded that nothing beats a complete change of scenery to get a better look at who you are.

Unfortunately, he couldn't see anything. The town was completely dark. There were no streetlights. He wondered if they even had electricity. He couldn't remember if he'd seen lights on the way into town.

He walked slowly, careful not to fall into a hole or bump into anything. He needed to find some kind of park or vacant lot to spend the night. As his eyes began adjusting to the darkness, he heard the faint sounds of a rock and roll band. Rock and roll in this town?

He followed his ear, thinking it might lead to a jukebox, which could be connected to food and drink. But the closer he got, the more he realized it was a live band. The music was primitive and unpolished. He turned a corner, coming out of an alley, and heard the sound coming from a low-slung adobe building across the street. No doubt about it. This town had power.

He knocked on the door, but the music inside was too loud for anyone to hear. Slowly, he pushed open the door to find four young men with electric instruments and amplifiers playing under a hanging lightbulb in a room with a dirt floor.

Now here's a sign, he thought. Out here, in the middle-of-nowhere Mexico, he'd stumbled upon a rock band. If all roads, even dirt roads, led to rock and roll, the road was definitely telling him something about his future.

The band got over its shock at having a stranger walk into their late-night jam session. They could tell from his backpack and wild hair and the peace sign he flashed that he was a hippie vagabond just passing through. The drummer nodded to a microphone lying on the keyboard, suggesting Jesse put it to use.

Jesse reached into the shoulder bag that contained his passport and traveler's checks and pulled out a harmonica. The guitar player gave him a look of wide-eyed approval. Jesse blew a few riffs and realized he was amazingly in tune with the band. He wailed like his life depended on it.

The young musicians played their three-chord progression with a new fever. It could have been any one of a hundred rock songs, so Jesse started singing "Johnny B. Goode" by Chuck

Berry. The band sang along on the chorus, but the really freaky thing was how well the guitar player rocked the lead licks. He had it down, note for note. The band was rockin' and rollin'. Even the lightbulb was swinging.

It didn't take long for an audience of at least twenty children and passersby to gather and start singing and clapping along. After the first extended song, the cheering was pure jubilation. Each member of the band high-fived Jesse as the crowd tried to get as close to the action as it could.

Jesse kicked off the second song with the only Spanish he knew. *"Uno, dos, tres, cuatro!"*

Nobody knew what the song was going to be, but they all started playing "Gloria" by Van Morrison. Jesse sang lead and the whole crowd shouted out "G-L-O-R-I-A" on the chorus. They all knew the song and how to spell the name via the miracle of radio in rural Mexico.

Near the end of the song, the light went out and all the instruments went silent. Nobody seemed surprised or disappointed. Someone lit a candle and the drummer rocked on with the drum solo from Iron Butterfly's "In-A-Gadda-Da-Vida," note for note. The flickering candlelight turned the ceiling as surreal as the relentless pounding of the floor toms and kick drum. Jesse thought he'd died and gone to heaven. The light came back on just before the drum solo ended, and the band finished off the classic song like they'd written it themselves.

Once the musicians finally got too tired to play anymore, crowd members showered them with a beggars' banquet of meats and cheeses and fruit, along with wine and water and tequila. Once the feast and the festivities gradually ended, Jesse slept well on the dirt floor.

Jesse spent his second night in Mexico in the town of Oaxaca, sleeping on the roof of a hotel in the shadow of the Santa Domingo Church. A traveling couple from California told him about the roof as soon as he walked into the city after an eight-hour hitchhike. "It's only ten pesos a night," the young woman said. "That's less than eighty cents. And there's lots of cool people, playing music and partying."

He arrived at the hotel after a long walking search around seven in the evening. A sign at the top of the stairway to the roof said, "Please don't urinate in bottles." Jesse climbed the creaking wooden stairs, wondering what kind of establishment needed to post a sign about bottle urination.

The rooftop was bathing in the evening sun. He knew right away he had found a crash pad of legendary proportion. It was rimmed with a five-foot brick wall, crowned with broken glass to keep birds from roosting, forming a wide balcony surrounding an open-air courtyard below. Laundry flapped at one end, and rows of potted plants and flowers decorated the other side.

Packs and sleeping bags of at least twenty low-budget travelers leaned against the wall. A friendly fellow with a blond beard and an English accent greeted him. "Welcome to Paradise. You sleeping on the roof or getting a room?"

"What do you do about going to the bathroom up here?" Jesse asked.

The Englishman laughed. "Don't worry. There's a common toilet downstairs. The wait's never that long. And it's beautiful up here, if it doesn't rain."

Jesse shook his hand. "What do you do when it rains?"

The Englishman looked up at the sky. "I've been here for a week and it's been dry. But if it does rain, I suppose we'll all be getting wet."

Jesse claimed a vacant spot on the roof by setting down his pack. The Santo Domingo Church next door looked like a friendly giant staring over the rooftop wall. Before long, Jesse was jamming with several musicians and drinking cold beer as the April moon rose over leafy trees from a small park next door. By the time stars filled the sky, the huge domes and towers of the church loomed heavenly and surreal in their spotlights.

The jam continued until the church lights went out and the owner yelled up from the courtyard that it was time to be quiet. Food and water and a bottle of mezcal circled around until the unusual assortment of international vagabonds unrolled sleeping bags and went to sleep.

Jesse spent much of the next day exploring the busy markets. Bright vegetables and fruit under white canvas awnings stretched for blocks around the city's square. He was careful not to drink the water or eat anything fresh until he'd washed it with bottled water.

Craftsmen of leather and clay had their wares on display for the curious tourist crowd. Jesse walked up and down roads and alleys, but he always ended up at the front entrance to Santa Domingo Church. The church was calling his name.

Once he finally walked inside, he understood immediately what the church needed to teach him. It was eerily quiet in the sanctuary—a far cry from the hectic bustle of the square and its markets. He marveled as he walked toward the altar and took a seat on a pew outside the glow of the altar. *This is what I need*, he thought. *Peace of mind. I've got to stop my mind from racing and worrying.*

He was taking deep breaths and exhaling slowly when he saw the old woman enter the church with her two granddaughters in tow. He watched carefully as she became serene in her exercise of faith. By the time she left the church he knew what he had to do. He had to find his faith. And something told him he couldn't do that in a crowded tourist town. He resolved to head south to the Pacific Ocean.

CHAPTER THIRTY-ONE

A bus piled high with luggage on top and people hanging out the windows made a comedic, lopsided approach as Jesse waited on the dusty edge of a two-lane blacktop road. The destination sign on the bus said "Puerto Angel."

The driver stopped and let Jesse know the only place he could possibly ride was on top. The bus was completely packed with a crush of sweating passengers.

Jesse shouldered his backpack and climbed the metal ladder on back to get to the top of the bus. The driver took off so quickly that Jesse had to throw himself onto the cargo to keep from falling off the back. He and his pack became hopelessly entangled in taut tie-down ropes. It took some struggling, but he eventually wiggled out of the pack and managed to lift his head above the jumbled pile of baskets, furniture, tires, and luggage.

At last, the wind was in his hair again. Little did he know it would take seven harrowing hours over a treacherous mountain road to reach the coast, less than 240 kilometers away.

The primitive nature of rural Mexico unfolded before his eyes as the bus began its slow ascent into the mountains. Riverbeds were three-quarters dry with scores of women bathing and rubbing clothing clean in the shallow water. Small adobe dwellings were mostly clustered together along the road, but some families were on their own, carving out a small-farm existence from tiny thatched shanties on rocky hillsides.

Just when Jesse thought the ride couldn't get rougher, the road turned to dirt and the bus became a bucking bronco.

He bounced on the roof, clinging to tie-downs on the shape-shifting load. Around sharp turns, the road shrunk to one lane. The top-heavy bus leaned over cliffs that fell hundreds of feet straight down to rocks in the valley. Jesse hung on to his pack and shoulder bag for dear life. By the time they neared the top of the Sierra Madre Mountains, the bus was actually in the clouds.

As if by a series of miracles, the bus arrived in Puerto Angel at 9:00 p.m. The first person Jesse spoke to in the village was a woman named Anna from Denver. She was just leaving the only bar in town and came over to say hello to the newcomer. Jesse was pleased to meet someone who spoke English.

Anna directed him to a thatched-roof, pole-barn of a hotel high on a hill overlooking the scenic port. "Trust me. It's the only place to stay. We call it the Tiltin' Hilton. My friend Sara and I have been crashing there for two weeks. The view is to die for."

Jesse wondered why people came up to give him directions before he had to ask. Maybe I'm being guided by a strange force I don't understand, or maybe I just look lost.

Anna walked up the steep path with him as they got acquainted. She loved the fact he was a reporter. "I've been trying to get on at the *Denver Post* for almost a year now."

At the top of the hill, she showed him how to check in. "Basically, you just claim your little room with its rope bed and pay for it tomorrow. The old man who runs the place is sleeping now. He watches the place all day to keep thieves away. Don't worry about leaving your stuff here. It'll be safe. Now, come on. Let's hit the waves. You look like you could use a bath."

They walked down to the beach and stripped down to skinny-dip. Jesse made a mental note to not write about this part for the newspaper. The last skinny-dip he wrote about cost him his relationship with Kelly and shocked his mother and all of her friends at church.

The saltwater soothed his sore feet and ankles. It foamed like beer and sounded like an eternal lullaby. He waded in up to his waist and rinsed road grime off himself.

"Look out," Anna called. "Here comes a—"

Before she could finish her warning, a five-foot wave had him in its clutches. It spun him upside down and whirled him like he was inside a clothes dryer until it slammed him to the sand. The awesome power of the ocean shocked him and knocked the wind out of him. He held his breath and tried to roll with the aquatic punch. Then he had to dig in to fight the undertow.

Anna laughed herself silly as he staggered back onto the beach. "You really do need to take up body surfing."

Anna got dressed quickly. "Come on, put your clothes on. We can still get water and wine and maybe a sandwich at the bar. They stay open late for us wino beach bums."

The hypnotic beauty of Puerto Angel was in full view the next morning when Jesse looked down on it from the Tiltin' Hilton. A panoramic horseshoe of rugged cliffs created a pristine harbor with clear waters of green and blue. From a distance, it looked like you could reach out and hold it in your hand.

Small hotel-restaurants with thatched roofs under palm trees were protected from the relentless waves of the Pacific Ocean by a wide beach. The narrow dirt road looked like a footpath. Wooden fishing boats lounged on the sand. It was one of the last unspoiled villages on the southern coast of Mexico.

The Mexican owner of the Tiltin' Hilton introduced himself to Jesse. He was short and bald, in his fifties, with a high-pitched voice, and a kind smile. He wore a loose-fitting white peasant shirt with white baggy beach pants that showed off his deeply tanned bare feet. "Welcome to my humble house. You will be happy here, I am sure. I heard you come in last night with Anna. She is a wonderful young woman. So, relax and enjoy. You can pay me whenever you want, and you can stay as long as you like. The rate is only two dollars a day."

Jesse felt completely at ease in the man's presence. It was as if he had entered the mystic realm of a shaman. His host emanated a calm peace as he showed him around the place. It was a two-story bundle of fitted tree branches held together by baling wire. There were ten tiny sleeping rooms separated by thin walls of plywood. The sturdiest part of the makeshift building was the wood plank floors. The structure leaned into the steep hill like a drunk against a wall, hence the Tiltin' half of its nickname.

Anna and her friend Sara were the only other guests. Over breakfast at a beachfront café, they insisted on taking Jesse to Zipolite, a deserted beach only miles away that they swore was even nicer than Puerto Angel.

Walking was the only way to get there. Small children picked fruit and herded goats as Jesse and the women from Denver trudged to the beach down a wide, dirt path, sweating in the blistering morning sun. As they arrived, Jesse could see it had been worth the hike. The beach stretched nearly a mile along frothing surf, inhabited by nothing but shady palm trees and fallen coconuts.

"They call it the 'Beach of Death,'" Anna shouted as she got naked and ran into the water. "Watch out for the undertow and the riptide."

Jesse and Sara stripped and followed her into the thunder of the crashing water. They stayed close to shore, but the water was wild as a carnival ride. Anna and Sara were more than enticing as their saltwater skin reflected golden in the late morning light. Jesse was mesmerized by the naked and nubile young women frolicking in pounding, frothing surf. He felt like Odysseus strapped to the ship mast of his own restraint while being serenaded and enchanted by the Sirens of Titan.

He was trying hard not to stare at his exotic female companions when he caught something out of the corner of his eye that frightened him at first. It was a leaping fish. Or some kind of a board. Yes, it was a surfboard. A man was riding that board in most expert fashion, and as he came out of shooting a monster curl, Jesse could see the man was naked.

Jesse, Anna, and Sara had put on shorts and shirts by the time the naked surfer beached his board and came over to talk. He had no tan lines, and his body was as finely muscled as a comic-book superhero. His hair was blond, but his long beard had a touch of gray. His forehead was broad, and he had blue oval-shaped eyes. He had a glint in his gaze like a lifeguard who just spotted a struggling swimmer.

"Hey, guys, I'm Daniel. Welcome to the best beach in the world."

The women were speechless at the site of such a specimen of masculinity. Jesse made conversation. "Where'd you learn to surf like that?"

"LA in the sixties. Huntington Beach. Before everything got too crowded." Daniel could see the women were a little uncomfortable, so he made them an offer. "Hey, wanna learn how to surf?"

Anna and Sara were eager to try. So was Jesse. Once everybody stripped down again, the naked surfer didn't seem so naked.

Daniel took them out on the board, one by one. The women couldn't get beyond the breakers, but they had a blast trying. Daniel was quite the teacher. "We have much to learn from the ocean. But you must remember, surfing is one of many paths to spiritual harmony. As you learn to move on the ocean, you learn to move inside yourself."

As his new students took a break from getting slammed to the sand, Daniel showed them the magic of surfing as only a master could. He twirled on the board until he got to the tip where he hung all ten toes with the dainty precision of a ballet king. From the beach it looked like he was walking on water.

Hopping back to the middle of the board, he leaned hard to turn the board into the curl of the wave. He disappeared into the tunnel of water, came out the other end, reversed direction, and slid down the backside of the wave so it could slam the beach without him. All the while looking like a bronzed Greek god with rippling abdominal muscles.

Jesse and his new friends were awed by the demonstration, but Daniel only laughed good naturedly at their screaming and shouting enthusiasm. He handed the board to Jesse. "Don't fight the ocean. Underneath each wave is a power you can use to your advantage."

Jesse recognized the lesson but still had a hard time getting beyond the breakers. On the fourth try, he dove under a huge wave, hanging tight to Daniel's board, and found himself speeding out to sea under the power of a reverse current. The ocean had welcomed him into her playground. It felt like he had escaped gravity itself. He was floating more freely than ever. He paddled out into the briny bliss over mountains of rolling water.

Forty yards from shore, he turned the board around and waved. Daniel waved back but pointed frantically at something behind Jesse. A huge wave was about to swallow him alive.

Jesse had never stared a twelve-foot wave in the face. It looked like a sea dragon about to swallow him whole. He paddled in a panic to get away from it. The ocean rose beneath him. Before he knew what was happening, he caught the wave and was riding it much faster than he wanted to go.

His arms were tired from all the paddling, but he managed to push himself up to a squatting position. He couldn't believe it. He was surfing. He stood up to a low crouch and held both arms out wide to keep his balance as the wave roared toward shore.

Just as he finally understood what it meant to be sitting on top of the world, he realized he had no idea how to turn or stop.

Daniel was waving directions, but Jesse had no idea what they meant. All he knew was he didn't want to be on the board when the wave crashed onto the beach. He leaned left and started to turn, but his feet came out from under him and he flew off the board backward and upside down with his legs fully spread.

Like the night before when the wave caught him by surprise, the churning ocean whirled him around like a tennis shoe in a dryer. He didn't know which way was up until he felt a hand grab his wrist. Daniel was excited. "You caught a wave, man. And you rode it. Great wipeout. You meant to do that, didn't you?"

Jesse had a hard time leaving the Tiltin' Hilton and the warm company of Anna and Sara. The three of them had become much more than close. But Jesse knew he had to keep moving.

After several days of beach living, he exchanged addresses with Anna and Sara and promised to send them copies of his articles. He walked to the road and turned around to see them standing arm in arm and waving goodbye.

Man, he thought, *what kind of fool are you? Why leave heaven on earth? You're going back to Indiana? You could at least stay for a few more days. No, no, get ahold of yourself. You've got a plane to catch. And a job you love.*

He hitchhiked up the coast toward Acapulco. The winding road was straight out of *National Geographic*, miles of deep blue Pacific Ocean crashing into rocky cliffs dotted with palm trees that looked like festive umbrellas on parade.

But it was hot and dusty, and the truck rides were always short.

Near the end of the day, Jesse decided to walk into the hills to watch the sunset. He ended up hiking nearly a mile inland to the top of what had looked to be a nearby hill. As he took off his pack, he noticed a young Mexican man in a floppy work hat taking slingshot practice on a cactus at thirty paces.

Thwack! The slingshot stone hit the cactus dead center.

Jesse applauded the shot and walked over to shake the man's hand. He was short and wiry with a thin mustache and a crooked grin. He offered Jesse the slingshot and gave him a stone to try his luck on the cactus.

As the two men took turns on the slingshot, they talked steadily. When Jesse couldn't say something in Spanish, he simply said it in English. It didn't matter what language was used. They were about the same age. Voice inflection, sign language, and visual cues from facial expressions got the message across.

As the two talked, a woman came up the hill. The man introduced her as his wife and sent her home to get something.

When she returned with a moist and meaty mango, Jesse pulled out a health food candy bar. The Mexican man's eyes lit up with the taste of chocolate, honey, and peanut butter. The woman politely giggled her refusal.

After the snack, the couple invited Jesse to their home near the top of a neighboring hill. It was an adobe hut with a side kitchen made of tree branches and scrap wood. A sturdy-looking woman in her fifties was in the kitchen making dough. A huge pig grunted at her feet, begging for scraps from the meal preparation.

Jesse was introduced to all seven of the other adults and children who lived in the three-room hut. It did have a concrete foundation and a tile roof that extended over a wide front porch. Poor as they were, the house had a fabulous view of the ocean in the distance.

Dinner was excellent, rice and beans with some ham bits in corn tortillas. Afterwards, the family gathered around a kerosene-filled Coke bottle for light. Jesse played a couple songs on the harmonica to the delight of the children. The adults sang melodic folk songs until it was time for bed. One of the women unrolled a mat for Jesse on the porch.

He watched the moon as he listened to dogs and donkeys barking and braying. *Amazing*, he thought. *These people don't even have doors to lock at night. The closest thing they had to a door was the curtain between the kitchen and the main room.*

Jesse slept soundly through the night. In the morning, the older woman fixed him a small cake and a cup of coffee with cream. He packed up and waved goodbye as the sun was rising. Workers with machetes were already congregating along a dirt road, waiting for trucks to take them to the fields.

Once Jesse finally truck surfed into Acapulco, he was hardly ready to immerse himself in the decadence of high-rolling tourists. Even so, he decided to splurge on a twenty-dollar room at the Marriot Hotel. He hadn't bathed in anything but saltwater for more than a week. The room had not one but two double beds, shag carpet, three tables, one full-size couch, two chairs, a wall-sized mirror, telephone, walk-in closet, and a balcony overlooking the ocean.

As Jesse looked at himself in the mirror, he realized why the desk clerk had hesitated to rent him a room. His clothes were filthy, and his hair was frizzy as a freak show. He guessed he smelled like a wild boar, but he was nose blind to his own stench.

What would that family of nine do with a room like this? he wondered. They'd think they were dreaming. The grandmother would look out the window at the chaos below and wonder what happened to the peaceful fishing village she knew as a girl.

Jesse showered, using the hotel soap, shampoo, and body lotion. He had to admit it felt wonderful to be clean again. He took a deep breath through his nose. He smelled like bananas and eucalyptus and Crème de Coco.

The beach scene at the hotel was claustrophobically crowded so he took a walk to the outskirts of town. He was not surprised to find thousands of locals living like animals in squalid huts just outside the tourist bubble.

It won't be long until these poor people start causing real problems for the rich ones, he thought. *But a poor family in a loving home will be happier any day than a bunch of rich people in a fancy hotel who don't have time to get to know each other.*

Jesse caught an express bus to Mexico City the next day and flew back to Indiana. His head was filled with tales of the beer truck, the village rock band, the church lady, the hippie rooftop, the mountain bus ride, the Tiltin' Hilton, the naked surfer, and the slingshot man. He had a great series of stories to write for the newspaper.

More importantly, the trip had slowed down his mind. It showed him that racing thoughts only kept him running away from who he was and what he wanted to accomplish.

CHAPTER THIRTY-TWO

Donald Jackson was a good cop. He walked the downtown beat for years and kept the peace in an unorthodox manner. He wasn't arrest happy. He broke up fights and sent the combatants their separate ways. He arranged for drunks to get rides home. He didn't yank kids out of cars and shake them down for dope. Bar and restaurant owners loved him because he protected their businesses without calling in backup and shutting down the entire street. He wasn't a big man—five-ten, one hundred and seventy-five pounds. But everybody knew he could slam a perpetrator up against a wall or take him down and cuff him if need be.

Jesse knew Officer Jackson well because he worked security at Mother's. They talked every night when the band stepped out back to take a joint break. Don (as everybody called him) didn't give a damn about marijuana. "It makes people peaceful, not crazy like booze."

There was no better news source than Don Jackson. He gave Jesse the inside scoop, off the record, on everything from murder investigations to police department politics. He knew everybody, and they all trusted him with everything they knew.

Jesse had been home from his Mexico hitchhike a couple months when the call came over the police radio that a police officer had been shot in the head in front of After Dark Bar. He knew right away it was Don, but he desperately hoped he was wrong. The officer had not been named, but the bar was a hotspot on the downtown beat.

After Dark Bar was only a few blocks from the newspaper.

It was the roughest bar in town. The patrons loved a good fight, and better yet, a brawl. Don was good friends with the owner. His policing was the only thing that kept the place open.

Jesse dropped everything when he heard the news and ran down Pearl Street even faster than he had the night of the Landing fire. Red lights were flashing everywhere as he made the scene. The first police officer he questioned delivered the bad news. "It's Don, for sure. He kicked some Black guy out of the bar, and the guy came back with a gun and shot him in the face. It doesn't look good."

Medics lifted the critically wounded officer onto a gurney. Jesse barely recognized his friend as they threw a sheet over his bloody and distorted head. Jesse's stomach churned and his heart raced. It looked like someone had pronounced his friend dead at the scene.

"No, the sheet is just to protect him from infection," the officer explained as he lowered his head in sadness. "It's a gaping wound. Terrible, terrible thing. He might not make it."

Glen, the police reporter on duty, came up to Jesse out of breath. "Jesus, Jesse, I should know better than to try to keep up with you, What the hell happened?"

Jesse told him what he knew as they loaded Officer Jackson into the ambulance. The medics were in a hurry. The hospital was only two blocks away, but their patient was losing too much blood to survive for long.

Glen started interviewing anybody who would talk. Jesse stared in horror at the ambulance leaving until he saw its red lights flashing and reflecting on the giant cross in front of St. Joseph's Hospital. *This can't be happening*, he thought. *Don is the one guy we all thought was invincible. He never had to use his gun. Nobody ever came after him. He was too tough. How could this be happening? I was just joking around with him last Saturday night.*

Jesse spotted the bar owner, Roger Replogle, standing by his Cadillac in the parking lot. Roger was short and heavy. He looked like a mobster with his slicked-back hair and nose that had been broken many times. He wore a black shirt with a red tie, but he wasn't even Italian, much less a Mafioso.

Roger was in tears as Jesse came up to stand next to him. He hugged Jesse hard even though he didn't know him that well. "It was that goddamned Sammy Paige," he sobbed. "Don told me a hundred times not to let him in. It wasn't that he was Black. I've got Black customers and we all try to get along. No, it was just Sammy. He'd get drunk and out of hand right away. I never should have let him in. I should have listened to Don. But I didn't want to look prejudiced or anything. I never knew he had a gun. He didn't have a gun in the bar. I know that much. He went out to his car and got the gun."

Roger blew his nose in a tissue. "Don grabbed him by the arm and marched him out the door. That's all. Sammy was putting his hands all over some white girl and her boyfriend was about to kick his ass when Don walked in. He didn't even get mad at Sammy. He just hustled him out the door. It was Sammy as usual, being a drunk asshole."

"Do you know the name of the girl or the boyfriend's name?" Jesse asked.

Roger took a full step back as if he suddenly remembered he was talking to a reporter. Then he went on talking, more slowly than before. "Officer Jackson made sure everybody was settled down after he got Sammy out. I even shook his hand and thanked him. Oh my God. We shook hands just before it happened. We shook hands and he opened up the door and started stepping out and . . . oh God, I can't believe it happened."

"What happened, Roger?"

"The bastard shot him point-blank in the face. I was right

behind Don, walking him out the door when it happened. I'm amazed I don't have blood all over me. I saw the flash from the gun barrel. Don jerked backward and fell to the floor before I could grab him. It happened so fast I couldn't believe it was happening. And then I thought he was going to shoot me. But I looked in Sammy's face. And then into his eyes. They got really big. The gunshot was so loud. I never heard anything so loud. I think it shocked some sense into Sammy."

"What happened next?"

"I looked at Sammy and he looked at me with those big eyes, and then he dropped the gun and just stood there. His arms went limp and he hung his head. He didn't try to run or anything. He just stood right there, like he was frozen in his tracks. He was pretty drunk. He might not even have known what he was doing.

"I ran back inside and called the cops. It only took a couple minutes for them to make the scene. Sammy was still standing there. He hadn't moved an inch since he shot Don. Two policemen put his hands behind his back and cuffed him and took him away in the car, no fuss, no muss."

A woman in a short skirt that was too tight for her chubby thighs came running up, screaming, "Oh, Roger! My Rog! There you are. I've been looking all over for you. I thought you got shot." She threw her arms around him and almost knocked him down. "I'm so glad you're okay. I don't know what I'd do if I lost you."

She kissed him on his lips and cheeks and forehead, and then the two of them cried in each other's arms. Jesse felt like crying, too, but he couldn't. He was completely stunned that his best friend on the police force had been shot and was probably dying in the hospital at that very moment.

The Wayne Newton fan club gathered in mourning on the railroad tracks behind the building to smoke cigarettes and collect their thoughts. They all knew and loved Officer Jackson from covering cops. His information was always reliable.

"You realize what's going to happen, don't you?" Chuck said.

"Yeah, it's gonna start a race riot," Dan, the cartoonist, said.

"Oh, yeah." Sherman slapped his forehead. "Black guy shoots white cop. Wow, I didn't even think about that."

Chuck exhaled carefully and lowered his voice. "All the racists on the police force are gonna come out in white robes and hoods. I don't know about the Klan, but I wouldn't want to be Black in this town for a good, long while. But you know the really strange part? In a couple of days, the Black community leaders will start saying this is all the cop's fault, and the Black man only acted in self-defense."

Jesse could not accept that comment. "They can't do that. I was there. The club owner told me. Don settled a bad scene and saved Sammy from getting his ass kicked for being drunk and obnoxious. There's a whole bar full of witnesses."

The group fell silent and wandered across the street to Henry's. They sat down at a table near the jukebox without saying a word. The bar was uncharacteristically quiet.

Larry and Jayne came over to the table. Larry was distraught. "What's this I hear about a police officer getting shot? It's not our Donald is it?"

The reporters nodded their heads sadly. "Yes," Jesse said. "It's Don. He's still alive over at St. Joseph's, but we don't know if he's going to make it. He got shot in the face at close range."

"Oh, no." Jayne leaned onto the back of Dan's chair for

support. "I love Don. He took me home one night when he could see I was in no shape to drive. This is terrible. He'll be paralyzed for life if he survives."

Larry put his arm around her. "Don't talk like that. It's bad enough as it is. We don't know what's going to happen."

"How old is he?" Jayne asked.

"He's thirty-seven," Jesse said, thinking that sounded pretty darn old.

"So young." Jayne put her hands over her face and cried as she sat down.

Charles, the dance instructor, came rushing in the front door of the bar without making his usual sweeping, grand entrance. He carried his hat and cape in his right hand as he hurried over to the table. "He's still alive. I just talked to a nurse at the hospital. He's alive and he might make it."

The table was all ears as he sat down, eager to share his news with the reporters. "It was a .32 caliber bullet and it went right through his jaw, but that bone probably absorbed a lot of the impact. The bullet ripped through muscles and nerves before it entered his brain. He's got serious damage, but they think he can still see. The bullet is lodged in his brain. They can't get it out for some reason."

"Who did you talk to?" Sherman asked.

"A nurse who helped with the initial operation. I can't tell you her name. She doesn't want to lose her job."

The table was speechless as another round of drinks arrived. Glen walked in. He had just finished the story, and he was still high on the rush of deadline writing.

"We're front page on this one, boys and girls," he said too triumphantly for the mournful situation. Looking around the table at the sad faces, Glen immediately toned it down. "John Musser got a great shot of the medics loading Officer Jackson into the ambulance with the bar logo in the background. It's a terrible thing, but Officer Jackson's alive as of now. He might make it. I couldn't get much out of the hospital."

"Did you get that it was a .32 caliber that entered through the jaw and lodged in the brain and they can't take it out yet?" Chuck asked.

"No. Where did you hear that?" Glen asked.

Charles was so pleased to be part of a scoop he grabbed Glen by both shoulders. "I talked to a nurse who helped in the surgery."

Glen started putting his coat back on. "Bullet through the jaw, still lodged in the brain, .32 caliber?"

The entire table nodded as Glen ran out the back door of the bar and across the street to the newspaper with critical information to add to his story.

"Man, news travels fast at Henry's," Dan said.

Two weeks after the shooting, the Reverend Joshua Rosemount came to Fort Wayne to speak at a rally in support of the shooter, Samuel Lee Paige. Turnout among the Black community was heavy. Rosemount was a nationally known civil rights leader. The huge Methodist Episcopal Church in Fort Wayne was overflowing. People who had to stand outside were listening to the proceedings through two small speakers on the front steps. The parking lot was packed.

Once he talked his way into the church as a member of the press, Jesse was one of the few white faces in the crowd. People stared at him. He was trying not to feel uncomfortable when he felt a gentle tap on his shoulder from behind.

He turned around to see Kelly, smiling slyly in his face. "How do you feel now, white boy?"

Jesse thought she was going to make a scene, but she dropped the "I told you so" attitude and led him to a better viewing spot near the pulpit. She didn't say another word to him. When he turned around to thank her, she had disappeared into the crowd.

The oratorical skills of the civil rights leader were impressive. He began speaking in low tones. He spoke of his days with Martin Luther King Jr. and of recent racial problems in Chicago and all over America. He spoke of Samuel Paige and recognized members of his family on the stage. His voice became more powerful as he admonished local officials not to rush to justice in a case with "obvious racial overtones." He was careful not to argue Paige's innocence. His diplomacy was that of a man who was running for political office. Yet, his message was undeniably righteous as he spoke in general terms about the need for racial equality.

Jesse wanted to interview the reverend after the speech, but he couldn't make it through the crowd. He wanted to ask him if he knew that Officer Jackson had been shot in the face for no good reason. He wanted to tell him that his friend had been nearly killed trying to help a drunken Black man out of a racially charged situation.

Walking away from the church, Jesse realized it was just as well he couldn't get close enough to interview the civil rights preacher.

Nearly five weeks after the shooting, Jesse finally got to interview Officer Jackson in his hospital room. He looked surprisingly like his old, mischievous self, still handsome in a Tony Curtis way with ringlets of curly black hair falling on his forehead. The hole on his jaw where the bullet entered was mostly healed, but the six-inch scar on the side of his neck still bore testimony to the operation that saved his life. He also had an indented scar on the front of his neck from the tracheotomy.

His smile was as big as ever, and he was able to weakly shake Jesse's hand. He had to fight back tears as he attempted to speak. The man who had such an easy way with words now had a terrible stutter.

Jesse's eyes filled with tears as Officer Jackson finally managed to speak the words he'd been waiting to tell the press. "I will . . . go back . . . to my . . . beat."

His wife, Janice, was by his side as Dean Sorenson snapped photos for the newspaper. She was trim and attractive and trying to put on a brave face even though she looked too tired for tears.

"Yes, you will, honey. You'll get back on the beat. We all have no doubt about that." She turned to Jesse. "He's making incredible progress. Much better than the doctors thought he would. Today is the first day since the shooting he's been able to button his pajamas."

Jesse pointed at his crippled friend. "He knew I was coming."

Officer Jackson laughed out loud and raised his right arm almost to his shoulder. Then he slouched in pain from the effort and lost his smile.

"Sorry," he said, trying to regain his good humor.

Jesse asked about the fundraiser held for him by downtown merchants. He smiled again, and Janice answered for him. "I think they've raised more than six thousand dollars. That'll be a welcome relief if we can get to it before the hospital does. Thank heavens the health insurance plan for the police force is pretty good."

Jesse decided it was time to ask the tough question.

"So, what was it like getting shot in the face at point-blank range?"

Officer Jackson smiled at Jesse's direct manner while Janice recoiled at his bluntness.

"I saw . . . flash . . . next thing . . . face up . . . going to die . . . saw people . . . crying . . . fight to . . . survive."

Janice stepped in for her husband as Jesse scribbled down the quote, word for word, pauses and all. "The thing is, Don knew Sammy. They weren't friends by any means, but they knew each other well. Don gave him lots of breaks and even loaned him a little money once. That's why he's so confused about why Sammy would shoot him. Don was trying to help when Sammy shot him for no reason at all."

She lowered her head and her body shook in silent sobs as she ran her fingers through her husband's hair.

Officer Jackson interrupted her to change the topic. "Sammy will . . . get out . . . on parole . . . before . . . I get . . . better."

His halting words had the ring of truth. They stopped all conversation. Jesse was at a complete loss for follow-up questions.

Janice got back to talking about her family. "Our three teenagers have taken it the hardest. Their dad was always this larger-than-life hero. They can't adjust to him not being able to walk or even talk."

Jesse sat and talked with Officer Jackson and Janice long after everyone else had gone. They tried to catch each other up on the latest police and newsroom gossip, but there was no way to lighten the somber mood. Janice eventually gave Jesse a nod that said her husband needed to rest. Jesse bent down and gave his favorite cop a long but gentle hug. Both men fought back tears.

He left Officer Jackson's room in a state of emotional shock.

His friend was never going to get better, no matter what the doctors tried to do. Tears flowed down his cheeks. They tasted salty. It did not feel good to cry. Jesse realized he had never tasted his own tears.

CHAPTER THIRTY-THREE

Public school teachers finally went on strike for better pay and formed picket lines at entrances to Fort Wayne schools in September 1975.

Carrying homemade signs and huddled beneath umbrellas in a chilling rain, small bands of teachers hardly looked like they had the power to close schools attended by nearly forty thousand children. But by midmorning, more than sixty picketing groups merged into a foot-stomping force of two thousand defiant strikers at a rally inside the huge sanctuary of St. Mary's Catholic Church.

Jesse was amazed by the contrast. He'd been interviewing teachers on the lines all morning. They'd been mostly grim and determined. Now, they were screaming their lungs out and raising their hands over their heads. Teachers who looked vulnerable on the picket lines had turned into an angry mob in the church.

Many were standing on their chairs as the chant began. "Fair pay for teachers. Fair pay for teachers." The power of their combined voices rose to the top of the fifty-foot ceiling and shook the rafters. The excitement in the place of worship was electric. Years of pent-up frustration gave way to the jubilation of finally taking action.

Since Jesse was in charge of the school beat, Weatherly had allowed him to organize his strike-story team. He chose Chuck to help him interview teachers on the picket line, and Melissa to go inside the schools to talk to administrators and teachers who had crossed the line and gone to work in spite of the strike.

Chuck found a married couple who were both teachers. The wife chose to strike, and the husband chose to work. The wife was not at all happy about her husband's decision. "He won't strike, but I'll bet he'll take the money."

"Do you know why he wouldn't strike?" Chuck asked.

"Oh, he still thinks he's going to be a principal when he grows up," the woman replied curtly.

As he was interviewing the wife, another female teacher drove up to the picket line and asked if anyone had seen her husband, a junior high teacher. The woman was aghast when told her husband had crossed the picket line and gone in to work. "I can't believe it. He told me he was going to strike."

Melissa got inside North Side High School on her own where she found a teacher grading papers in an empty classroom. "I would have struck if it had been on anything but money. I don't think money is an issue you should shut down a school for."

A group of teachers sitting in an elementary school teachers' lounge reluctantly agreed to discuss with Melissa their motives for coming to work. "I'm here because it's illegal to strike," one older woman said with her hands on her hips. "What they're doing out there is teaching students to break the law."

A younger man in a white shirt and tie confessed, "It does make you feel kind of silly to be here without the kids."

The woman sitting next to him scowled like she wanted to douse him with her coffee. "We've got an obligation to be here," she said, "whether the students are here or not."

Once the strikers assembled into an educated and agitated mob at the rally, their union president called out to them on the microphone. "We said we could do it and we've done it." The teachers gave him a resounding, standing ovation as newspaper, radio, and television reporters from all over the region recorded every word and the decibel level of every cheer.

The rally did serve as a publicity stunt for the benefit of the media. "But it's more than that," Chuck said. "It's the strength in numbers thing. The group gives each member more confidence and determination."

Melissa agreed. "I'll bet there's some school board members shaking in their shoes at the size and strength of this teacher rally."

Jesse stepped outside for a smoke. He was surprised to find the church completely surrounded by an intimidating number of police officers, some of them in riot gear. He walked up to a sergeant he knew. "What are you guys going to do? Arrest all the teachers?"

The sergeant smirked. "No, we're not going to arrest any teachers even though it is against the law for them to strike. We're here to protect them and make sure no trouble breaks out."

"Like what kind of trouble?" Jesse took out his note pad.

The sergeant did not like the idea of being quoted. He made a quick about-face and returned to supervise his men.

Jesse ran back into the church and grabbed his friend Jack Berry from the television station. "Jack, get a camera out here quick. The cops have the place surrounded. It looks like trouble."

Jack stepped out with Jesse and started shooting video right away. "Here, hold the camera," he directed Jesse. "It's running. Point it at me and make sure you get all those cops in the background. I'll do the talking."

With that he began speaking into a microphone. "Fort Wayne police in riot gear have surrounded St. Mary's Catholic Church on Lafayette Street. At this time, two thousand teachers are inside the church at a rally for the city-wide strike that began this morning."

Jesse panned the camera to show the long line of police

officers and to get a good shot of the church. Jack slapped him on the arm to get himself back on camera. "Some would call this an unnecessary show of force. There have been no signs of trouble at the church. Fifty police officers surrounding a church could be seen by some as intimidation, pure and simple, designed to challenge the teachers' constitutional right to freedom of assembly."

Jack stayed outside with his camera while Jesse went in to tell the chief negotiator for the teachers that the police had the place surrounded. "Tell everybody not to worry. They're not going to arrest anybody. The school superintendent and his buddy, the mayor, are only trying to intimidate you."

The negotiator took the microphone and addressed the rally. "I am informed that the police have the church surrounded." She was interrupted by a loud chorus of boos. "I am also told they are not here to arrest anyone. They're simply making a show of force." The booing got much louder. She waited until she could speak again. "I'd say the only show of force on this day is happening right here in this church." The teachers' cheering was tumultuous.

The rally didn't last much longer after that. Teachers left the church in high spirits and walked by the police officers in defiant silence, as they had been instructed by their leaders. A few saluted the police sarcastically, but no one engaged them verbally. Except for one older junior high mathematics teacher who yelled instructions loud enough for the entire area to hear.

"Keep moving people. There's nothing to see here. Just keep moving."

One day after the strike began, Allen Circuit Court Judge Hermann Busse ordered the teachers back to work, noting the strike was against state law. The strike continued despite the court order. Forty percent of elementary teachers went to work, thirteen percent in junior highs, and thirty percent in high schools. Teachers refused to budge on their demand for a ten percent raise, even though the schools indicated they might raise pay by 7.5 percent.

Weatherly called the strike-story team to his desk. "I don't care about all this percentage bullshit. Neither do our readers. This is about teachers and parents and kids. You've done a pretty good job on the teachers. Now, get out there and talk to the kids and their parents about this strike."

Melissa, Chuck, and Jesse looked at each other as if to say, "Why didn't we think of that?"

Chuck went out with Dean Sorenson and got great photos and quotes from kids playing in the parks. Mostly, they were glad to be out of school, but more than one youngster suggested the adults were acting like children.

Jesse went to the central YMCA with photographer John Musser. The place was packed with kids. Jesse and John fought their way through crowds of unruly children until they finally cornered a program director.

The man had a whistle in his mouth, but he wasn't blowing it. He was doing his best to remain calm in the storm. "We've never had so many kids here, even on Christmas break. We've got too many, as you can see. We're going to have to send some of them home."

Melissa got an earful from every mother she called or interviewed in person. They all wanted the strike to end. "Get these kids back in school." "They're driving me crazy." "I've got no one to take care of them when I should be going to work."

No doubt, it was the mothers of the city who gradually brought the teacher strike to an end by complaining to both sides of the negotiation. It only lasted four days, but it was the longest four days Jesse could remember. He had managed to anger the school superintendent by quoting him as saying, "The only two things a union ever wants is more money and less work."

The superintendent confronted Jesse about the quote on the sidewalk outside the administration building. "All you did was throw gasoline on the fire while negotiations were still in progress."

Jesse tried to remain respectful. "Excuse me, but you're the one who said it. And you said it in a roomful of people. Did you think no one was listening?"

Once the storm of the teachers' strike passed, Wyler got back to a regular rehearsal schedule at 1114. The sessions usually turned into a party as friends and people from the house dropped by to hang out and catch a buzz. The vocal trio was sounding better than ever. New songs were being written at a steady rate, polished up and arranged, and put on the set list. Wyler was in a state of prolific creativity.

Dale had returned from a vacation in New Orleans with a new plan for the band. "We've got to move to New Orleans. They've got so many places to play. There must be a hundred bars on Bourbon Street alone, and we could play them all. And here's the good thing. The crowd does the traveling, not the musicians. The tourists come and go, the musicians stay put."

CHAPTER THIRTY-FOUR

Jesse's next investigation began, as they always did, with Weatherly calling him to the city editor's desk in November of 1975. After nearly three years working together, Jesse and his boss had become quite fond of each other. Weatherly saw his young, hustling-reporter self in Jesse. And Jesse was amazed by how many tricks Weatherly still had up his sleeve.

They'd pretty much closed the generation gap, except for the hair-length issue. Weatherly lost the battle, inch by inch, but he still wouldn't let Jesse grow a beard.

The city editor smiled warmly as his protégé approached. Jesse knew that smile. He was about to be thrown into a brave new world of confusing fact patterns he would have to write about and explain to the public.

Jesse decided to air a grievance before Weatherly handed him the new assignment. "I do have to complain about that robbery last Friday in front of the French restaurant on Calhoun Street."

Weatherly pretended to not know why Jesse was concerned. "What's the problem? You're the one who's so buddy-buddy with the owner, Jayne Milson, your pal from Henry's."

"You know what I'm talking about. I wrote it up with the address and name of the restaurant. When I read the paper the next morning, there was no address and no restaurant name. Like it happened in mid-air. There was literally no scene of the crime. All I want to know is, did you take that stuff out or did somebody else axe it?"

Weatherly pursed his lips and lowered his eyes in the closest thing to sheepish Jesse had ever seen from him. "All right. I cut it. I was ordered by the publisher himself. That restaurant is a big advertiser and they don't want their business hurt by being the site of criminal activity."

"Unbelievable," Jesse said. "So much for journalistic ethics."

Weatherly leaned back in his chair. "They call it the newspaper business for a reason. That reason is that it is a business. The owners are trying to make money here."

Jesse knew only too well where the conversation was heading. This wasn't the first time something like this had happened. He shook his head, shrugged his shoulders, and let Weatherly know he was ready to hear about the next assignment.

Weatherly put his elbows on the desk and rubbed his hands together like a hungry man sitting down to dinner. "Jesse, I've got something big for you. Really big. So, hear me out. It's not going to sound good at first, but it's important." Jesse cocked his head to the right like a dog trying to understand its owner and waited for Weatherly to continue.

"You've pretty much seen it all. And you've done well. But now I'm going to ask you to turn everything upside down. That's right. Instead of looking at the blue sky, I want you to look underground at the deep, dark underbelly of the city."

Jesse thought he might be talking about some organized criminal operation or drug-dealing distribution system.

Weatherly made him wait for it. "I'm talking about the sewers and the septic systems, and all the human waste dumping into the three rivers of this city and county."

Jesse was relieved and disappointed at the same time. "I thought Melissa did a story on that a while back."

"No, her story was good as far as it went, but it barely scratched the surface. If you flipped the city upside down, there's another whole city to be found. A system of pipes and tubes and tunnels and ditch tiles that tries to deal with all the waste of two hundred thousand people. The worst thing about this underworld is that it's more than one hundred years old in too many places."

Jesse was puzzled. "So, doesn't everybody already know that?"

"They don't know it like you're going to tell them. I want you to turn this town upside down, literally. I never told you this, but when I was a young reporter myself, one of my best series ever was on the underground mechanics of a city. But that's not where I want you to start. I'm getting rumblings from the health department that they're about to crack down on all the septic systems in the county. There are thousands of them, and they're not connected to any city sewer. Lots of them leak into ditches that flow directly into the river."

Jesse had a sudden rush of realization. Environmental stories were hot. The 1960's counterculture had focused attention on the need to clean up the world's polluted water and air. Greenpeace was founded in 1971. Even Richard Nixon had been swayed to start the Environmental Protection Agency in late 1970.

"Okay, I get it. Sounds good. How should I get started?"

Weatherly was pleased to see that Jesse was ready to take the ball and run with it. "Start with Jon Bonar. He's an engineer with the city, and he's very opposed to septic systems. He'll get you going."

Jesse called Bonar for an appointment. The engineer was willing to talk, but he suggested meeting at Henry's. "I can't be seen talking to the press at the City-County Building. This thing's going to blow sky high. The state wants to start regulating septic systems, but builders and developers don't want to see that happen. We're talking about the mink and manure set, rich people who want to build McMansions in the countryside. Funny thing is, wealthy as they are, nobody wants to pay for sewers that far from the city. It would cost a fortune."

Bonar had a full head of wavy blond hair and a stubborn Scottish chin. He laid it all out for Jesse, off the record, in a half-hour conversation in a booth at the bar. "Septic systems are just shit tanks that drain into filter beds of sand and gravel. They're not connected to any sewer. There are probably twenty thousand of them in the county. When they get clogged, homeowners don't pay to repair them. They bypass them and let them discharge into ditches or drainage tiles that eventually dump into the rivers."

Jesse was writing furiously in his notebook. "I'd think the Board of Health would put a stop to all that."

Bonar leaned closer to Jesse. "It's the Board of Health who hands out septic approvals, but the board has no inspection system whatsoever. If you ask me, somebody's getting paid under the table." He straightened the lapels on his blue polyester suit as he got up to leave. "Or they don't have the budget to keep an eye on things. Either way, they've created an environmental disaster."

After his conversation with Bonar, Jesse contacted the State Board of Health. He was told the local health board was breaking the law by approving septic systems. In fact, a ranking official from the state board put it in a letter. "The only agency permitted by the Stream Pollution Control Law to approve filter beds, or septic systems, is the Stream Pollution Control Board."

Jesse realized he had a story that could shake up most of the expensive housing additions and developments in the county. It was a story that did not pass the smell test in more ways than one. It smelled like corruption and incompetence and human waste at the same time.

Weatherly rolled up his sleeves after hearing Jesse's story, clearly relishing the task at hand. "We'll never find out what's really going on with the local Board of Health until we run the story. So, go ahead. Give it your best shot. Stories like this have a way of smoking out the truth."

Jesse wrote a dramatic lead and Weatherly approved it: "Allen County is drowning in its own sewage."

He gave the story as much of a human touch as he could by visiting homes serviced by septic tanks. Homeowners most upset by the lack of sewers were those who lived along ditches that transported the slimy sewage of their neighbors.

One woman said the ditch near her house had a "wicked" smell and attracted rats. "We went downtown to complain, and we were told the ditch does not exist. I told them there must be a ditch around city hall because of all the rats who work there."

Jesse took his investigation to city and county officials. Most of them were well aware of the long-standing septic problem, but nobody had any plans for a solution. Bonar continued to feed Jesse valuable engineering information off the record. "More than ninety percent of the land in Allen County does not filter."

In another booth-in-the-bar meeting, Jesse asked Bonar the big question. "So, now that the fur is beginning to fly, can you tell if the housing developers are paying off the Board of Health?"

The engineer shook his head slowly. "You know, I suspected that for a long time, but the more I get to know the people involved, the more it looks like good old-fashioned bureaucratic incompetence. The Board of Health doesn't have the staff to handle the septic mess, so when people want permits, the health director just rubber stamps them. Nobody wants to do the work."

Jesse's story dropped a smoke bomb into the proverbial sewer of city and county government, causing widespread finger-pointing. The Board of Health vowed to begin an inspection program, the county commissioners said they would review the septic application process, and planners said they'd been trying to sound the alarm for years on the septic system problem.

It's always amazing, Jesse thought, *how quickly things are going to get cleaned up after an exposé in the newspaper. Everybody gets busy covering his own ass. And then it's even more amazing how long it takes to get so little done about the actual problem.*

Five days after the first article, Jesse did a follow-up on how the web of polluted drainage ditches provided breeding grounds for mosquitoes that carried the encephalitis disease. The article noted the county was spending great sums of money spraying dangerous chemicals to kill mosquitoes while unwittingly multiplying their numbers in the ditches with septic runoff.

One week later, he wrote a story on how much of the recent $3.5 million sewer expansion was lying idle while the city continued experiencing an "ecological catastrophe." A newly constructed underground main sewer remained virtually unused because no money had been allocated for the lateral "ribs" of the system to reach out to malfunctioning private sewers.

Jesse labeled the bureaucratic incompetence an "underground bridge to nowhere," and his words became front-page headlines. Embarrassed county commissioners tried to explain that the next phases of construction would connect all elements of the new sewer. Unfortunately, they had no plans in the works, or funds budgeted, for the promised solution.

While the story evolved, Jesse was beginning to feel disconnected himself, like he had his own bridge to nowhere buried deep in his soul. How would sewer stories advance his career? And how would journalism connect to his future? Would he keep reporting the news or take a more musical path?

Every time he thought about it, he saw those Mexican kids playing rock and roll in their dirt-road village.

Jesse took a terrible teasing from his friends at Henry's over the sewage stories. Charles swooped into the bar one night after deadline and paraded over to the Wayne Newton Fan Club table. "Oh, my, my. What's that odor? Oh, it's just Jesse and his sewer stories."

The reporters howled as they made room for the dance instructor to take a seat.

Chuck was quick to comment. "That's our boy, Jesse. He's making the world safe for shit to float downhill."

Dan joined in. "I know it's a big bunch of stories, environmentally significant and all that, but I can't come up with a cartoon about it for the life of me."

"How about one of Jesse pushing a giant turd up a hill, like that guy in Greek mythology, what was his name?" Glen offered.

"Sissypus," Sherman shouted with glee.

Larry walked up to the table amidst gales of laughter and corrected Sherman. "That's Sisyphus, and he was rolling a rock up a hill in hell because he was such an asshole in life."

"That's it!" Dan stood up and shouted. "A guy rolling a toilet up a hill."

"What's the caption?" Chuck asked. "What is he saying?"

Jayne came up and put both hands on Jesse's shoulders. "He's saying sewage is an uphill battle. Right, Jesse?"

Dan sat down and asked for a pen. "That's not bad at all, Jayne. Not bad at all."

"Just be sure to give me a byline," Jayne said as she sat down and took her drink from the waitress.

CHAPTER THIRTY-FIVE

The winter of 1975-76 was a rough one for Jesse. It was cold. The snow was deep. He was buried by boring school board meetings and small-town council sessions. Worst of all, there seemed to be no end to tales from the sewer.

The fun went out of the sewage stories for Jesse once he had thoroughly exposed the problems of bypassed septic systems and hodgepodge sewers. The web of civil corruption he suspected had revealed itself to be nothing more than decades of bureaucratic incompetence. Weatherly summed it up succinctly, "No one's to blame when everyone's at fault."

One bright spot in Jesse's world was his developing relationship with Jody, the art teacher downstairs in apartment two at 1114. She was thin, but shapely, a cross between Audrey and Katherine Hepburn. Jesse loved hanging out in her apartment. She was a great cook, the bay window in her bedroom was filled with flowering plants and vines, and she had a kick-ass stereo system.

He fell in love with her right away, although he had not admitted it, even to himself. He wasn't ready to dive into love. It had been more than a year since his breakup with Kelly, but the memories were still painful.

Jody was smart. She didn't come on too strong or too fast. And she didn't let Jesse tell her what to do.

Wyler was beginning to play private parties and public venues in addition to playing at Mother's. They were booked for concerts in the park in May and June. Music was getting to be a second full-time job. Butch and Dale were ready to head down to New Orleans and take the musical world by storm.

Jesse could feel himself coming to a fork in the road. Sooner than later, he would have to choose between journalism and music. But he knew decisions had a way of making themselves. One minute, you don't know which way to go; the next, you're already on your way.

So he didn't worry about it much. What he did worry about was coming up with a story that would beat the winter blues. The idea for just such a feature nearly ran him down one snowy night as he walked across the street from the newspaper offices to Henry's.

Jesse heard the danger coming before he saw it through the storm. The scraping noise of a double-wide snowplow was even louder than the thundering diesel engine of the towering truck that was skidding out of control and coming right at him. He leaped backward to narrowly avoid the plow blade. He was still backpedaling furiously as he was slammed hard, knocked down, and buried by an avalanche of hurtling snow.

The driver honked his air horn like he was laughing and apologizing at the same time. Jesse wiped the snow out of his eyes and hair and struggled to his feet. He was uninjured except for a bruised ego. He looked around to see if anyone had witnessed the comically embarrassing moment. The street was empty.

He was a human snowman. Snow was trapped in the armpits and sleeves of the coat he hadn't bothered to button on the way out the door. Melting snow was already beginning to run down his neck and chest. He shook himself like a wet dog as he climbed the three steps up to the side door of the bar. He took off his coat as he stepped inside and shook it out to leave a pile of snow on the floor.

Henry gave Jesse a warm welcome. "You want a shovel with all that snow you just dragged into my bar, thank you very much?"

"I almost got run over by a snowplow," he said to Henry. "But I got a great idea for my next story."

Henry was laughing at how covered with snow Jesse still was. "Get this man a draft beer and a shot of whiskey, on the house," he yelled to the bartender. "This is what you get for writing all those massage parlor stories. God's trying to clean you up. Next thing, he'll be washing your mouth out with soap."

"Don't you want to hear my story idea?"

Henry handed him the beer from the bartender and drank the shot himself. "Oh, yeah. What is it?"

"I'm going to write about winter from the snowplow driver's point of view."

The winter-wonder world of a massive snowstorm looked ominous and surreal from ten feet above the road as Jesse rode shotgun on a city snowplow. Twenty-four-year-old Rod Dawson was driving the plow truck like a cowboy rides a rodeo bull. "Hang on tight. It bucks hard when the blade catches the pavement. There's a seatbelt somewhere on the floor if you can find it."

It was 8:30 p.m., and the three-year veteran of the street department was ready to go all night. His voice was low pitched and hoarse from chain smoking as he yelled to be heard over the diesel-engine rumble. "There's only twenty trucks for the whole city. We been round the clock since the middle of January. We just got the major streets cleared, and we were starting into the residential areas when all this shit started coming down."

As he spoke, the snowplow hit a crack in the pavement. The impact was so hard it lifted the rear wheels of the truck off the ground for a moment until the blade kicked back off the crack. Jesse slammed into the windshield and lost his notepad and pen.

Rod kept both hands on the wheel. Once the truck had all four wheels on the ground, he had to steer hard to avoid a parked car. He cursed colorfully if not poetically. "People want their roads plowed, but they don't have enough sense to park somewhere not in the way. Here's a flashlight. Okay. It's on. Find your stuff. And get that seatbelt on up here and buckle down."

Jesse found his pen and note pad, and both ends of the seatbelt. He buckled up and cinched down hard. "Man, I'm lucky I didn't go through the windshield."

"You okay? We can't be banging up reporters on my watch."

"No, I'm good. How fast do you usually drive?"

Rod downshifted and came to a near stop at a traffic light. "I'll get her up to forty on an open road I know is good. But, here in the city, I'm lucky to get twenty. They say ten is safest. Believe me, that's plenty fast if you hit a pothole wrong or run into a manhole cover that's out of whack."

Jesse hung on tighter as Rod shifted through the gears and sped up to thirty-five on a main east-west road. He had to yell at Rod over the noise of the engine and the blade scraping on the pavement. "So, what's it like running a snowplow? Are people always happy to see you?"

Rod threw his head back and laughed. "Oh, hell no. Not at all. One guy this morning, a middle-aged guy, just finished digging out his driveway when I came by and buried his entry in three feet of snow."

"Oh, man," Jesse related. "I got buried about a week ago."

"Yeah, well this guy was not happy at all." Rod was still

chortling. "He got so mad he was jumping up and down. I tried to wave that I was sorry, but you know what that old bastard did?"

"What?"

"He threw his shovel at the truck. I was long gone. Fifty feet away. And he threw that thing like he thought he could hit me. I almost backed up and gave him another layer of snow. Can you believe that? He threw his shovel at me. Like I'm not out here doing my best to help assholes like him."

Jesse shook his head and laughed as he took notes.

"And another guy—just to show how different people are— another guy on Paulding Road sees me coming. I'm moving fast and snow is shooting out all over the sidewalk. He doesn't run or get mad. He just turns around and takes it on the backside. And, I'm telling you, I really creamed him good. Not that I meant to. But I almost knocked him down. I look in my mirror and he just shook it off like nothing and kept walking. He didn't even wave. Goes to show how different people are. One guy throws his shovel, another guy brushes it off."

As Jesse was, once again, marveling at the common-sense philosophies of the working man, he noticed the flashing lights of a police car pulling up behind the snowplow. Rod immediately slowed down and plowed off to the side of the road.

"Not this bullshit again. These cops think they're God's gift. One of them actually gave me a warning ticket for speeding last week at three thirty in the morning. I shouldn't have to tell them we work for the same city."

The officer turned off his emergency lights, got out of his car, and climbed up the two ladder steps on the driver's side of the truck. Rod rolled down his window and the officer stuck his head in.

"You got any idea how fast you were going?"

Rod instantly recognized the cop as a good friend from high school. "Good Lord, Tommy. You gotta stop. I got work to do."

"You know I'm just messing with you, Rod. I heard you had a newspaper reporter on board, and I wanted to see if he was misquoting you and shit."

"Is that Tommy Coulardot, son of Charlie?" Jesse leaned over and looked at the officer sideways. "I'm so glad you stopped us. This man has taken me hostage."

The three young men on the snowplow had a good laugh, giving each other a hard time. Rod jerked the truck forward a couple times, trying to throw Tommy off balance. Tommy reached in and tried to grab Rod's bomber cap with the earflaps. Jesse leaned over and honked the air horn. The unrelenting snowstorm had turned them into playful boys.

Rod eventually turned the conversation back toward the business at hand. "What's going on, traffic wise?"

"Pretty big pileup on West Jefferson, near the shopping center. I'd steer clear." Tommy jumped off the truck and yelled at Jesse. "Make sure you spell his name right."

Rod got the truck back up to speed. The snow came down so fast and flaky, he could barely see the road. "You know, this snowstorm is as much of a crisis for us as a big fire is for the fire department. I know, people die in fires, but people also die when the ambulance can't get down the road. Matter of fact, firetrucks go nowhere without us."

Jesse kept taking notes as he watched the deep snow spreading high and wide off the speeding snowplow. "So, how long can you go tonight?"

Rod turned toward Jesse like the question took him by surprise. He crinkled up his big nose and grinned a mouthful of uneven teeth. "How long can I go? I got to go all night. Long as it's snowing, I'm going. I started at noon today and it looks like I'll be plowing until at least noon tomorrow. Around four in the morning is the hardest time to stay awake. But once the sun comes up, I can go all day, no problem."

Jesse added a couple quotes to his notebook. Rod watched him out of the corner of his eye and kept driving. "What are you writing down?"

"Some of your better quotes. 'Firetrucks go nowhere without us,' and 'Long as it's snowing, I'm going.'"

Rod was pleased to hear his own words coming back at him. "I said all that?"

Jesse flipped back through his notebook. "You said all that and more." He read him several more quotes. Rod raised his head proudly and turned slightly toward Jesse. He wanted to hear more of himself.

Jesse steered back into the interview. "How long before this truck runs out of gas?"

"We'll run out of gas long before she does. We've still got more than half a tank. She's got one hundred gallons to her, gets about three gallons to the hour. We don't go by miles per gallon. Every mile's different. But if I need to get gas, the guys back at the shop can fill her up fast. And they can change plow blades and tires like a pit crew at the Indy 500. All the trucks are old. It's lucky our guys know how to keep them on the road. What we need are twice as many trucks. Be sure to put that in your story, will you?"

Jesse nodded and put pen to paper again. He found himself intrigued by Rod. The man was intelligent. "How long you gonna be with the street department?"

"Not that much longer," Rod said as he downshifted and

braked hard for a car that pulled right out in front of him. "Now, see there. It's assholes like that guy who make this job tough. People drive their absolute worst in a snowstorm. It's like the snow flips on the stupid switch in their brains."

Jesse waited to see if he would have to repeat the question.

Rod didn't take long to get back on track. "No, I'll probably be here a couple more years. My dad has an auto body shop in Seattle. He wants me to come out and help him expand the operation."

"Sounds like a great opportunity," Jesse said. "What's keeping you here?"

Rod hesitated before answering. "Well, my mom lives here. She and Dad split up when I was fifteen, almost ten years now, I guess. Doesn't seem that long. Then again, sometimes it feels like forever. Anyway, she still needs help. I'm living with her and paying the bills. She's doing great, about to graduate from nursing school. Once she gets on her feet, I'll be gone."

Two thoughts came to Jesse's mind. First, Rod was proving the point that if you listened and asked the right questions, everybody wanted to tell you their life story. And, second, there was a news story and probably a book in every single soul walking the planet.

He asked another, less personal, question. "What's the worst part about driving a snowplow?"

Rod thought about the question while lighting a cigarette. He took a deep drag and filled the cab with his exhale. "I suppose the worst part is the people who own the parking lots. They get their snow shoveled out onto the streets and they always get mad as hell when we push it back. Which is ridiculous when you think about it. They can't just block the road with their snow. Who do they think they are?"

Jesse rode around town with Rod until 3:00 a.m. The snow-plow feature story wasn't due any time soon. He could have stayed on the truck all night. But after nearly six hours on the road, Jesse was exhausted and getting sick of the smell of oily rags and diesel fumes and cigarettes and working-man body odor. He was also hungry. They had only stopped twice for coffee.

Rod pulled the big truck to a squeaking halt in front of the newspaper building. "Here's the end of the line for you. Go get a double cheeseburger and a couple beers for me."

Jesse held out his hand for a handshake. "It's too late for Henry's. We should have stopped sooner."

"Not me," Rod said. "Once I get going, I can't stop. It's too hard to get going again."

"You are a machine behind that wheel, man. I can't thank you enough for tonight."

"No problem," Rod said as he finally let go of Jesse's hand. "You can ride with me anytime. And, hey . . . make sure you put in the part about us needing more trucks."

"Don't worry, I will," Jesse said. "And I won't just quote you. I'll get the head of the street department to say it too."

Jesse started to get out when Rod grabbed his arm. "And, hey. Don't put in any of that stuff about my mom and dad, okay?"

Jesse looked Rod in the eye. "Not to worry, my friend. That's between you and me."

Funny, he thought, *how every news source, from the mayor to the snowplow driver, thinks he can tell a reporter what to write. And, in some ways, he can. A good reporter will always respect the difference between on the record and off the record.*

Jesse jumped off the truck and headed for his car as Rod

rumbled the plow truck back onto Main Street. At this point in his career, Jesse had graduated to driving a four-speed, red Volkswagen Beetle. There was no mistaking its rounded shape, even buried in nearly a foot of snow.

The little car would get him home, for sure. After all, the 1964 television commercial advertised it as the car the snow-plow driver used to get to work. The weight of the engine over the rear wheels gave it serious traction. Jesse had a new appreciation for the commercial.

The car wasn't locked, but Jesse had a little trouble opening the frozen driver's side door. Snow fell onto the driver's seat. He brushed most of it off, got in, and put the key in the ignition. The trusty Beetle started right up. He revved the engine for a little bit and got out to wipe off the snow. It was deep and cold, and he had nothing to use but his gloved hands and a broad stroke of his arm in its winter coat.

Something about his time on the snowplow made Jesse want to clean every bit of snow off his car. He got the windshield and the hood and the headlights and even the front bumper. Then, he did the same for the rear and both sides of the vehicle.

It was still snowing, but not as hard as it had been all night. Jesse got in and turned on the headlights. They reflected brightly on the gray brick wall of the newspaper building. Snowflakes shined in the light like tiny angels, dancing happily as they floated to the ground. All was right with the world.

The Beetle felt a little cramped after his time in the giant snowplow. His line of sight was down to snow level as the little car did some plowing of its own to get out of the parking lot. The main streets were cleared, but Jesse had to barrel into a snowdrift to park in front of 1114.

He forced the driver's side door open through the snow and got out to breathe deeply in the stillness of the wintry night. He was standing where he thought the sidewalk might be when his reverie was interrupted by a snowplow scraping down West Wayne Street. It was Rod, waving out the window and blasting his horn with his crazy earflaps blowing in the wind-stream, burying Jesse's car in another foot of snow.

CHAPTER THIRTY-SIX

Jesse was lost and alone in a mob of pedestrian traffic along West Lafayette Boulevard in downtown Detroit. It was 8:20 a.m., and everybody was rushing to get to work on time. Jesse had a two-day job tryout at the *Detroit Free Press*, beginning at 9:00 a.m. That gave him some time to find the building.

A low-flying bird made him look up. What he saw took his breath away. Two imposing statues of the goddesses of Commerce and Communication were guarding the massive front doors of a fourteen-story Art Deco limestone building. Above the statues was a stone-carved arch of owls, snakes, pelicans, and seahorses.

The building's façade was adorned with bas-relief sculptures of famous men, including Ben Franklin, Horace Greeley, and General George Armstrong Custer. Sculptures of a plane, a ship, a train, and a truck paid tribute to the evolution of modern transportation.

One neck-craning look up the intimidating tower of power told Jesse he had reached his destination. It took a few seconds for his eyes to finally focus on the huge, carved lettering above the arch: *The Free Press*.

He froze in apprehension and awe until people from both directions began bumping into him. He shook off his nervousness and walked through the doors. The entrance was lined with Italian stone carvings. The arched lobby ceiling was ornamentally decorated with hexagonal tile patterns. He headed straight for the row of elevators. He didn't want to look like some gawking tourist.

The next forty-eight hours would determine the new direction of his life. It was May 11, 1976. If he got the job, he would continue his career in journalism. If he didn't get the job, he would take a break from reporting and head down to New Orleans to play Bourbon Street with his bandmates.

He'd been waiting for months to arrive at the crossroads, that place or challenge that would decide his future. Now, he knew this was it. The job tryout was his fork in the road.

Truth be known, getting a job at the prestigious *Detroit Free Press* was a long shot. Besides, after more than three years of chasing down the daily news, he was ready for a break. But he was keeping an open mind and determined to cast his fate to the wind. This interview was the chance he gave himself to rise in the ranks of journalism.

Jesse had decided to leave the *Fort Wayne Journal Gazette* on March 8, his twenty-sixth birthday. Reporting in his hometown had become like watching television reruns. He was beginning to feel trapped. The birthday bells in his mind echoed from churches on far away hills, calling him to explore new worlds.

Sometime in that drunken birthday night, the decision to leave town was finalized. It wasn't the booze that did it. What made Jesse finally decide to leave the paper was realizing that his self-destructive behavior was an escape attempt. Getting too comfortable made him do crazy things to simulate the high road to adventure.

Becoming a reporter had given Jesse the keys to the city. But it was the same city he'd been in his entire life. Kevin Wilson, his friend from the editorial page, had moved on to the *Detroit Free Press*. It was Kevin who helped arrange for Jesse's job tryout. "It's time for you to move up, Jesse. The *Free Press* is one of the best papers in the country."

Jesse finally sat down with Weatherly to give his two-week

notice during the first week of April 1976. The city editor was not surprised. He'd seen Jesse getting restless and beginning to lose interest.

"The only thing I'd say to you is this," Weatherly spoke carefully. "Don't make a lateral move. I know you want to hit the road with your band. That might not even be a lateral move. In fact, odds are you'll go down in flames. This thing at the *Detroit Free Press* is a definite step up. Oh, I wish I were your age with that kind of opportunity. Don't pass this up, Jesse."

Weatherly's words were ringing in Jesse's ears as he walked into the doors of the *Detroit Free Press*. He reminded himself not to come on too strong.

The newsroom was similar to the *Journal Gazette*, except this one had a long row of massive windows that allowed natural light to shine on the paper clutter of nearly forty desks. It wasn't until this moment that Jesse realized he'd been working in a newsroom with no windows for years.

He squinted as the sun came pouring through tall panes of historic wavy glass. He felt enlightened.

The clatter of typewriters and teletype machines was music to his ears. The place felt like home. He looked around and spotted a tall, thin man with brown curly hair down to his collar. Jesse knew he was the city editor by the way he was yelling orders across the newsroom to a reporter.

The man's name was Andrew Boyer. Jesse knew that from the letters he'd received. He had not expected the man to be so young. Andrew was barely in his thirties, but he looked like he could be leading a protest march. His face was predatory, hawk nose and deep-set eyes. He wore faded jeans and an untucked flannel shirt. Up to that point, Jesse thought all editors were chain-smoking curmudgeons in their late fifties.

He walked cautiously to the city desk and extended his

hand. "Good morning, Mr. Boyer. I'm Jesse Conover from the *Fort Wayne Journal Gazette*."

"Call me Andy, if you please. I'm still a reporter at heart. None of that 'mister' stuff." He smiled vaguely until he re-åmembered Jesse Conover was on schedule for a job tryout this morning. He recovered quickly. "So, you're Jesse Conover. Kevin Wilson's told me a lot of good things about you. Nice to meet you. As you can see, I'm busy right now with morning assignments. Have a seat at that desk right there and I'll get with you soon as I can."

I'm nothing but a pain in the ass to this guy, Jesse thought as he grabbed a copy of the paper and sat down to read it. *I'm just one more person he doesn't want to hire. He's probably got friends who would kill for the job. He could have at least showed me where the coffee is or how to find Kevin Wilson's office.*

Jesse listened to Andy without watching him as the young editor directed his staff. No doubt about it, the city editor knew his stuff. More importantly, he treated his people like coworkers, not underlings. Jesse knew right away he could get along with Andy. But after an hour, he was wondering if the editor had forgotten about the job tryout. Finally, he heard his name called.

"Conover, come on down and sign in please. I've got something for you."

The city editor briefed him on the assignment. A middle-aged woman had found a wounded bird on her backyard birdbath and was nursing it back to health. "I know, it sounds like bullshit, but here's the deal. She always wanted to be a veterinarian and now she's getting her chance. Let's see what you can do with it. You'll be riding with one of our photographers, Justin Jordan, so you won't get lost. He's got the address. Be back by one or let me know where you are."

Justin was a tall Black man wearing John Lennon eyeglasses

and a waist-length tan leather jacket with at least thirty pounds of camera gear slung over his shoulders. He was friendly as he led Jesse to the garage and packed the equipment into the trunk of his 1974 Mercury Comet. "Looks like we're off on one of Andy's wild goose chases."

"What do you mean?" Jesse asked as he slid into the passenger seat.

Justin grimaced and looked like he'd said too much, too soon. "Oh, nothing. I probably shouldn't say that. Andy's a good city editor. But he's new to the job. Let's just say he has some folksy ideas on what makes news."

Jesse took a deep breath and blew his lips in a huge sigh of disappointment. "I didn't come to the big city to write the dreaded wounded-bird story."

Justin laughed and slapped the steering wheel with both hands as he pulled out of the parking garage. "Wounded-bird story. I love it. Sounds like you've been doing this for a while. Don't worry. Maybe I can get an award-winning shot of a canary limping around on one crutch. Put us both on the front page."

Jesse chuckled politely as he looked out the window at the intense freeway traffic. "Is it always this busy?"

"Oh, yeah," Justin sounded like a disc jockey as he dialed up CKLW Radio. "This is the Motor City, baby. You have arrived in the automotive capital of the world, not to mention the epicenter of soul music and Motown Records."

Jesse couldn't help but be impressed. "So, what's it like, working for the *Free Press*?"

The seriousness of the question reflected on Justin's face. He turned the radio off. Jesse could tell from the photographer's silence that he was about to become painfully candid.

"To be truthful, man, it sucks. The pay's no good, and they work you to death. We tried to get a union in, and they fired half the staff. That's how Andy got his job. I'm not saying it won't look good on your résumé. But as for me, I'm heading to Los Angeles. That's where it's at these days. They got lots of beautiful women there, waiting for me to make 'em look like stars."

Justin's confession made immediate sense to Jesse. *Why stay in the Midwest,* he thought, *when all the glitter and glamour are on the West Coast?*

Mrs. Beatrice Gooding was dressed in her Sunday best and waiting eagerly for the *Free Press* to arrive. Someone must have told her there would be a photographer. Her makeup and jewelry were way too much for the elderly, gray-haired woman.

"Come in, come in. I'm so excited to have you in my humble home," she bubbled. "It's just me since my husband died. Well, me and Missy now. She's in the bedroom. I've got a big cage for her back there by the window. She's a robin. That's the state bird for Michigan, you know. She was lying in the bird bath under my silver maple tree, so still I thought she was dead."

Jesse took out his notebook and held up his hand to let her know she was talking too fast.

Beatrice covered her mouth with her hand. Her eyes were wide. She looked mortified. She took off her bifocals to clean them nervously. Her face was puffy and kind with a sweet smile that made her red lipstick look almost clown-like. "Oh my goodness. I'm so sorry. I talk too much when I get excited. And where are my manners? Would you two gentlemen like a cup of coffee or maybe even a glass of milk? I made my special chocolate chip cookies. They're great for dunking."

Justin was friendly and tried to put her at ease. "I would

love a cup of coffee. But can I see Missy's room first? I'd like to check the light."

Beatrice clapped her hands in excitement as she forgot about the refreshments and led the reporters down a short hall. She adopted a nurse's demeanor as she opened the bedroom door and introduced her patient. "Missy, you have visitors. These two men are going to take your picture for the paper. Can you say hello?"

Justin and Jesse saw the photo opportunity right away. Light was brilliantly streaming into the cage from the window. Missy was standing by her birdseed and water. Her left wing was strapped around her body with white bandaging tape. The bird cheeped and chucked like it was glad to have company.

"She doesn't really need the wrap anymore," Beatrice said. "I put it back on so you could see how I fixed her."

"Good thinking," Jesse said. "How do you know she's a female?"

"Look how fat she is," Beatrice said. "She needs to get out soon so she can build a nest. That, and she's not as brightly colored as the males."

"Are you going to let her go?" Jesse asked.

Beatrice didn't answer the question as the bird sang and danced and tried to get out of its bandage. Justin took photos and talked to the bird as if she was his most favorite Robin ever.

After a few minutes, Beatrice led her guests back into the kitchen for coffee and cookies. She looked suddenly sad. "Yes, to answer your question, I'm going to release her back to nature. As a matter of fact, I thought maybe we'd do that today. She needs to nest. She's about to pop out her eggs. I could set her on the bird feeder, and you could get a picture of us. Who knows? Maybe she won't want to leave."

   Jesse and Beatrice talked for a half hour about her love for animals and how she had to drop out of veterinary school after one year when her twins were born. "I tried to finish, but there was no way. After the kids were grown, I thought about going back, but then my husband got sick."

   Once the interview was completed, Beatrice walked Jesse back to the birdcage. Making chirping noises, she took Missy out of her cage and gently removed the wing strap. The bird sang happily as Beatrice carried her in two cupped hands to the birdbath in the backyard with Justin shooting photos all the way. Jesse was impressed by the photographer's enthusiasm and effort.

   Beatrice placed the robin on the feeder. "There you go, Missy. This is right where I found you four days ago."

   The free bird sat on the feeder and sang for much longer than Jesse expected. Beatrice was beaming. "She's saying thank you. Isn't that the sweetest thing you ever saw?"

   Justin kept taking photos as the bird finally spread its wings and flapped them to make sure it could fly again. Moments later, he got what Jesse thought would be a great shot of the bird rising from the outdoor feeder as Beatrice held out her hand in goodbye.

   Missy flew to the top of a Maple Tree in the backyard and made a long, slow circle above as if to say thank you to Beatrice. She then flew away at an impressive speed and disappeared beyond the roof of the neighbor's garage.

   Beatrice was still crying tears of joy and sadness as Justin and Jesse thanked her for her hospitality and bid her a fond farewell. They made their way to the car, loaded up, and took off.

   "Nice lady," Justin said as he maneuvered through heavy

traffic on the way back to the office. "Hated to see her cry when that bird flew away."

Jesse nodded and turned to Justin. "Isn't it funny how you can get such high drama out of everyday events? The best part of the story is her letting the bird go back to nature. It broke her lonely heart, but she did what she knew was right."

"You've got good interview skills," Justin said.

"Thank you, Justin. That means a lot coming from you. Photographers are hard to impress. And, not to stroke you right back, but I was amazed by your energy and attention to detail, even on a story that's probably going nowhere."

They passed a car being driven by a young Black man with a Krishna haircut. His head was shaved except for a long, thin *shikha*, or ponytail, sprouting out the top. Jesse's reporter instincts began sounding bells and whistles. The hair stood up on the back of his neck.

"Pull that guy over," Jesse raised his voice as he rolled down the passenger window and began waving at the driver. "That guy is a story."

Justin steered the car close enough for Jesse to yell out the window, "*Detroit Free Press*. Can we talk?"

The Krishna driver and his passenger in the front seat were both young Black men. They were startled and wary of Jesse's antics at first. They stared back at him with stern faces.

Jesse realized it was a good thing his driver was Black. Justin gave them a big grin and a peace sign. The Krishna driver gave a head nod for Jesse to follow as he got off at the next exit. "I hope you know what you're doing," Justin said as he pulled up beside the two strangers in a shopping center parking lot.

Jesse got out of the car and kept a non-threatening distance as he called out an introduction. "Hey, man, thanks for stopping.

We're with the *Detroit Free Press*. I noticed your Krishna haircut. It's far out. You look like a news story to me."

"I am a news story, my friend," the man said as he got out of the car and came over to shake Jesse's hand. "I'm a Hare Krishna. This haircut and my religion just cost me a good-paying job as a bus driver for the city of Detroit. I call that discrimination. What do you think?"

Justin started fumbling with camera gear like he was being charged by a rhinoceros. "You guys mind if I take photos? This *is* one hell of a story."

"Take all the pictures you want," the Hare Krishna said. "Just make sure you spell my name right." He turned to his friend. "Is this too weird? Were we not just talking about calling the *Free Press*?" His friend nodded and grinned as the Hare Krishna continued. "I just lost my job this morning. Never gave me no warning or nothing."

Jesse knew he had the rare, man-bites-dog news story. Young people all over the country were being fired for having too much hair. Now, here was a guy being fired for not having enough hair. And he was Black. And young. And he had that strange little ponytail.

The only thing he didn't have was the orange Sari worn at the airport demonstrations by people playing tambourines and chanting "Hare Krishna." He was still wearing his bus driver uniform, which was a great thing for Justin and the photographs.

"Are you a Buddhist?" Jesse asked.

"No, sir. Buddhists shave their heads. Hare Krishnas have the tail. What we call the Shikha. Hare Krishna is actually a branch of Hinduism. But we believe in Krishna as supreme god. We chant 'Hare Krishna' because the mantra has good vibrations for the soul."

After an extended conversation on Buddhism, versus Hinduism, versus Hare Krishna, Jesse was convinced the man was serious about his religion. He turned the questioning to the employment issue. "Why would that little ponytail and Hare Krishna cost you your job?"

The Hare Krishna was blunt. "White people are racist to begin with. Being Black is bad enough, but when you go threatening their Christianity, white folk get mean in a hurry. This discrimination they got on me is racial. It's religious. And it's wrong."

"The three *R*'s," Justin joked.

Once they got back to the newspaper, Justin went to bat right away for Jesse. "Andy, no shit, he pulled this guy off the freeway. We were going seventy miles an hour. He saw the Krishna haircut on a Black guy, and he knew it was a big news story. I thought he was crazy. But he saw it, and he felt it, and it's a big story."

The city editor agreed. "All right, then. Great work. Now get me the follow-up. Flesh it out. Talk to the bus company. Hell, get me Mayor Coleman Young on the phone. He won't put up with this bullshit for one minute."

Jesse spent the afternoon working on the story. He got a no comment from the bus company, but the mayor's office agreed to launch an investigation into the matter.

After reading Jesse's copy, Andy Boyer taught him an important lesson. He held up Justin's photo of the two Black men. "What's wrong with this photo?"

Jesse shook his head and shrugged his shoulders. The photo looked great.

"What's wrong is there are two people in the picture. The story is about one bus driver who got fired. You don't need to put his friend in the photo just because he was there. It's all about narrowing the focus. So, take out the paragraphs about the friend and I'll crop him out of the photo." Andy smiled. "What you've got here is a great story. The best I've ever seen or even heard about on a job tryout. But tryout or not, it's a strong, compelling story. Good show."

Jesse bowed slightly in appreciation of the compliment. The editor continued with a collegial smile. "Oh, and by the way, I still need the bird story. You can do it tomorrow. Justin tells me you've got a good way with people. That's important in this business, as you know."

Andy was treating Jesse like he already had the job. What unbelievable good fortune! Certainly, the fates had blown the Hare Krishna story his way to ensure he would continue on the path of journalism.

Jesse spent the night in a hotel and slept well. In the lobby the next morning, he saw his Hare Krishna story on the front page of the Detroit Free Press. The photo was big and bold. More importantly, and most surprisingly, his byline was on the story. There it was. Big as day. *By Jesse Conover*.

Jesse rode a pink cloud into work at the paper. The first thing Andy said to him was an even bigger surprise than finding his story on the front page. "The *Associated Press* wire service picked up the story. You're in seventy-nine papers across the country so far. That's seventy-nine and counting. Unbelievable. Congratulations. I never got picked up like that."

Several reporters came up to introduce themselves and congratulate him on the story. Jesse appreciated the camaraderie and basked in the warm glow of congratulations, but he couldn't linger long. He had a two-hour psychological test to take. He wondered to himself why they would bother with a test when he was already hired.

The test was a breeze. Jesse answered the questions like the hustling reporter he was. When they asked if he walked up stairs one at a time, two at a time, or at a run, he knew the obvious answer was at a run. When they asked how he responded to yellow traffic lights he answered, of course, that he drove on through.

He spent the rest of the afternoon writing the bird story. It turned out better than he thought. He led with Beatrice in tears as she released Missy back into the wild. Andy read the story and nodded his approval. Justin's photographs were emotional masterpieces. The paper ran two of them with the story the following day. One showed the bandaged robin sunbathing in her cage. The second photo featured Missy taking off from the birdfeeder with Beatrice's hand in the shot, letting go and waving goodbye at the same time.

Jesse looked out over the newsroom. The late afternoon sun poured through the windows, casting film noir shadows. He was in a daze. The two days at the *Free Press* had been a dream come true. Everything about the place felt so right, so inevitable. He had been foolish to think he could ever leave journalism. The reporter in him had clearly won the job-tryout test.

He still had conflicting thoughts and emotions. How will I tell Butch and Dale I'm not going to New Orleans? *That's going to be hard*, he thought. *I pretty much promised I'd be there with them. But that was back when getting a job at the Free Press seemed like an impossibility.*

He heard his name being called out. It was the managing editor, calling from the door of his wood-paneled office at the far end of the newsroom. Jesse knew this would be his moment of triumph. He wondered if he had any bargaining power in terms of salary and benefits. Maybe he could get a little time off before he started working.

The managing editor was a heavyset man in his early sixties with bushy eyebrows and a walrus mustache that covered most of his mouth. Jesse was thrilled to take a seat across the desk from one of the most powerful men in the newspaper business.

He knew right away something was terribly wrong. The man in charge looked at Jesse with sadness and sympathy in his eyes. Between the eyebrows and the mustache, it was hard to tell if he was trying to smile or simply wincing in pain. He didn't beat around the bush.

"Jesse, I'm sorry to have to tell you this, but I can't offer you the job."

Jesse was so surprised by the statement he thought he must have misunderstood the man. His mouth dropped open in disbelief.

"I know, I can't believe I have to tell you this," the editor said. "Your story on the front page is excellent and it's on the wire all over the country. Not to mention you pulled it off the freeway on a job tryout. I've never seen or heard anything like it."

Jesse was still in shock. He was speechless.

The editor opened up a folder on his desk and held up a piece of paper. "See this memo? It's from our testing department. You flunked your psychological exam. Worst results in the five years we've been giving the test. By far."

Jesse was gathering his thoughts. He spoke slowly and deliberately, barely above a whisper. "You're telling me you can't give me a job because of what some shrink says?"

The managing editor had to smirk at that remark. "You tested out beyond reckless. I have no doubt you slanted your answers to show what a hustling reporter you are. That's a problem in and of itself. What we're looking for is the opposite of somebody in a hurry. We're looking for careful and cautious.

We want our reporters to be extra careful with the facts and take the steps one at a time. No running in the halls, if you will. We want our reporters to stop at yellow lights.

It's caution we're looking for, not hustle. We started using the test in the first place because two of our reporters—you might have read about it—got caught making up stories."

"Hold it right there," Jesse interrupted. "Are you saying I'm not honest? That's just not true. Never has been and never will be."

The editor held up his hands. "No, no, no. I'm not saying that at all. Nobody is questioning your integrity. What I'm saying is our board of directors won't let me hire anybody who doesn't get a certain score on the test. I, personally, think it's complete bullshit."

"How about if I retake the test and focus on being cautious and careful and taking the proverbial steps one at a time?"

The older man shook his head so slowly that Jesse knew further argument, or even discussion, would be a waste of time. His surprise began turning into anger. The *Free Press* had revealed itself to be the bureaucratic press, shackled by psychiatric censors. He wanted to trash the old man's desk and start a fire in his wastebasket. Instead, he stood up, shook the editor's hand, and managed a smile as he spoke in clipped cadence.

"Well then, that's that. Thank you for your consideration. I did have a wonderful time writing for your fine newspaper."

The man hung his head as Jesse walked out slowly and opened the door carefully. He was determined not to burn any bridges. He heard the editor's solemn goodbye. "I'm sorry it turned out like this. I truly am. I know you would have been a great addition."

Jesse walked out of the *Free Press* building in a daze. He

turned around to look back up at the limestone edifice. It did not seem like the tower of truth it had once appeared to be. He wanted to throw rocks through the windows. He looked around. There was nothing to throw. Everything was solid concrete.

He walked the streets of Detroit faster and faster, back to his car in the parking garage. The sun was beginning to set on the metropolitan skyline. The buildings no longer looked majestic once they were cast in shadow. Silhouettes of sadness contemplating evil made him feel claustrophobic.

Choked by resentment at the total absurdity and unfairness of the *Free Press* experience, Jesse's knees went weak and wobbly. He bent over to grab them and steady himself. It all felt like a big mistake, something he could correct with a letter or a phone call. His mind raced into the dead end he knew it would reach.

He had been to the top of the mountain and the mountain said no.

Anger filled the first half of his drive back to Fort Wayne. How dare they turn down a reporter who pulled a front-page story off the freeway on a job tryout? All ten knuckles were white as he clutched the steering wheel in self-righteous indignation. His first instinct was to write a story about the arbitrary and capricious nature of the *Detroit Free Press* hiring policies. But no, that would not work. He would only expose himself as the fool who flunked the psychological examination.

The Beetle began to shudder. Jesse looked down at the speedometer. He was going ninety-five miles an hour. The little car was never designed to go that fast. He took his foot off the gas and slowed down to get into the right-hand lane on the interstate highway behind a semi-tractor-trailer truck. He needed time to think. Frustration at not getting what he thought he wanted was making him feel like a prisoner in his own skin.

Then something strangely liberating happened as he drove past the "Welcome to Indiana" sign and turned on the radio. A scratchy signal tuned in from Detroit. The Temptations were singing "Ain't Too Proud to Beg." The music began to soothe him. The beat got him nodding his head until, gradually, he relaxed his grip and began tapping his thumbs on the wheel.

I don't know what you're so upset about, he said to himself. You never thought you'd get that job, and you only really wanted it when you knew you couldn't have it. You ought to be relieved you didn't get the job.

"I'm not relieved, I'm pissed off," Jesse shouted as he pounded the wheel with both hands. "I showed them what I could do, and they didn't care." He lowered his voice, as if trying to reason with his yelling self. "Maybe I am better off not working for those people."

Jesse tried to talk himself down for thirty miles as the Detroit radio signal gradually faded out. He turned the radio off. He had to admit that the thought of becoming a full-time musician had been creeping up on him for some time. He was more than ready to take a break from the daily news grind. Maybe he never wanted the *Free Press* job in the first place. Maybe he subconsciously botched the psychological exam.

No, that wasn't it at all. He'd done his best to skew the test results in his favor as a hustling reporter. And he'd made his own luck on the job tryout.

He turned the radio back on as he got within range of the Fort Wayne stations. The music helped him think. He wasn't about to apply at newspapers in Chicago or New York. He could have looked at Detroit as a bump in the road instead of a dead end. But, deep down, he wanted to try something new.

He smiled as he passed the truck he'd been following. If anything, Detroit taught him he'd become the reporter he set out to be. He had climbed the mountain to its peak. It didn't really tell him no. It simply asked, "What now?"

Jesse looked over the breathtaking view from his emotional summit. There were mountains to climb as far as he could see. He didn't have to climb the same one forever.

The reporter in him began asking questions and listening to the answers. It was time to examine his own story. Why was he leaving his hometown and successful career? What could he hope to accomplish as a musician? Was he on a mission or simply running away?

The answers were somewhere between following the path with heart and the selfish pursuit of musical fame and fortune. But the answers were just words trying to make sense of what was really going on. He couldn't explain it, but he could feel it. The road was beckoning.

He thought about Weatherly saying every story is like a pancake; it has two sides and you can't eat one without the other. He laughed and had to look at himself in the rear-view mirror when he realized that music and journalism were the two sides of his story, his personal pancake. It was impossible to choose one or the other. He'd have to eat them both.

He turned the radio up as he exited the highway and headed for 1114. His mind raced with the thrill of new directions and challenges. There was no doubt about where he was heading or what he was going to do. It was time to make a living as a musician in New Orleans or die trying.

ABOUT THE AUTHOR

Mark Paul Smith has been a trial attorney for nearly forty years. After returning from the Hitchhike in 1972, he became a newspaper reporter for four years and then played in a rock band on Bourbon Street in New Orleans for several years. He's still playing in bands as his legal career morphs into writing novels.

He and the artist Jody Hemphill Smith own Castle Gallery Fine Art in Fort Wayne, Indiana.

OTHER BOOKS BY
MARK PAUL SMITH

A JESSE CONOVER ADVENTURE

During the 1970s on a magic mushroom harvesting adventure in the Bayou, a young, aspiring rock and roll musician discovers the voice of Voodoo, which not only alters his life, but the life of his band, the Divebomberz.

When the band is on the verge of making it big, tragedy strikes and Jesse Conover is confronted with the hard truth that life is often a spiritual obstacle course designed to see if you can get over yourself.

A book for rock and rollers of all ages and for restless souls who have chased a dream only to discover that what they really needed was with them all along.

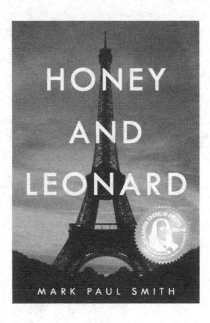

Honey and Leonard are in their seventies when they fall in love. Leonard is in the early stages of Alzheimer's and Honey thinks her love will cure him.

When their heirs try to keep them apart, they flee to France in violation of court orders. Pursued by police, press, and private investigators, they become an international media sensation. In a time just before cell phones and the internet, they become the Bonnie and Clyde of love.

Their whirlwind romance encompasses arsenic poisoning, elder law, Alzheimer's, an Eiffel Tower arrest, and a Paris jail break.

And through it all Honey is in the middle of the difficult process of discovering that love does not conquer all. Or does it?

Mark Paul Smith graduated college on an Air Force scholarship with dreams of becoming a pilot. He had some downtime after graduation, so before reporting for duty so he decided to hitchhike the world. A decision that would change his life forever.

As he traveled, his approach to life and his future decisions changed. Being an American was not popular in those days, but the people of the world showed Smith kindness and kept him alive when he ran out of money. The long road to decision showed him that people everywhere want peace, not war.

Mark Paul Smith's hitchhike from Indiana to India in 1972 changed him from being an Air Force Officer into a conscientious objector. His faith in the United States of America was restored when he sued the government and won his case in federal court. His journey is one of faith, contemplation, and awakening, mixed with the freedom and abandonment of the seventies.